HIS WICKED CHARM

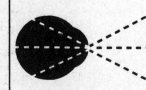

HIS WICKED CHARM

CANDACE CAMP

THORNDIKE PRESS

A part of Gale, a Cengage Company

GALE
A Cengage Company

Farmington Hills, Mich • San Francisco • New York • Waterville, Maine
Meriden, Conn • Mason, Ohio • Chicago

Copyright © 2018 by Candace Camp.
The Mad Morelands.
Thorndike Press, a part of Gale, a Cengage Company.

Thorndike Press® Large Print Basic.
The text of this Large Print edition is unabridged.
Other aspects of the book may vary from the original edition.
Set in 16 pt. Plantin.

LIBRARY OF CONGRESS CIP DATA ON FILE.
CATALOGUING IN PUBLICATION FOR THIS BOOK
IS AVAILABLE FROM THE LIBRARY OF CONGRESS

ISBN-13: 978-1-4328-5135-4 (hardcover)

Published in 2018 by arrangement with Harlequin Books S.A.

Printed in the United States of America
1 2 3 4 5 6 7 22 21 20 19 18

HIS WICKED CHARM

PROLOGUE

1892

The door opened. The room beyond lay in darkness, broken only by a swath of moonlight. There was no reason to be frightened, yet some nameless, faceless terror iced Con's veins. Still, he stepped inside. The fear in him was worse.

The walls of the room were curved, disorienting, and everywhere he looked were clocks — standing, hanging, scattered over tables and stands, lined up in cabinets. Brass hands winked, catching the dim light. Con moved farther in, his heart pounding, and stopped at a narrow table. The tiered rows were padded with dark velvet, and they were lined with not clocks, but compasses, their needles pointing in unison toward the windows. Turning now, he saw that compasses stood in the cabinets and hung on the walls amid the clocks.

He was too late. He knew it with a certainty that closed his throat: he would fail. Con ran toward the window, but he didn't move. The needles on the compasses began to whirl. Running, gasping, he reached out, knowing he'd never reach it in time. Someone screamed.

Con's eyes flew open, and he jerked upright in the bed. His lungs labored in his chest, his heart thundering, and he clenched his muscles, fists curled so tightly his fingernails bit into his palms. Sweat dried cold on his skin.

It was a dream.

He glanced around him. He was in his own bed, in his own room. It was only a dream.

Through the open doorway to the adjoining sitting room, he could see Wellie perched in his cage, regarding Con with bright black eyes. That scream must have been the parrot's screech.

The bird moved from foot to foot and rasped out, "Wellie. Good bird."

"Yes. Good bird." Con's voice came out almost as hoarse as Wellington's. He sank back onto his pillow, closing his eyes. It had been nothing but a bad dream and easily explained — today was Alex's wedding day. He was worried about oversleeping and failing in his duties. The problem was he'd been having the exact same nightmare for weeks.

CHAPTER ONE

When Con awoke again, sunlight was shooting through a crack in the drapes straight into his eyes. For the second time, he bolted upright. Heaven help him. After all that, he'd overslept. He jumped out of bed and began to shave.

Wellington called Con's name and flew into the room, taking up his favorite position atop a bedpost. "You wretched bird — screeching like a banshee in the middle of the night, yet not a word when it's time to get up."

Wellie let out a noise that sounded disturbingly like human laughter. Con grinned and patted his shoulder for Wellie to perch on it. Con stroked a finger down the parrot's back.

"It's just you and me now, boy," he said softly. "Alex is going on to better things."

There was an odd pang in his chest; Con had felt it more than once lately. He couldn't be happier for his twin — Sabrina was perfect for Alex and loved him madly. Alex was over the moon about marrying her. There was nothing in the world Con wanted more than his brother's happiness. And yet . . . he could not help but feel as if a piece of him was leaving.

With a sigh at his own selfishness, Con set Wellie aside and headed downstairs. He found Alex in the dining room, gazing out the window — shaved, dressed and ready to go eight hours before the ceremony. Casting an eye over his twin, Con said, "Eager or terrified?"

"A little of both." Alex let out his breath in a whoosh. "Thank God you're finally up."

"Why didn't you wake me?" Con asked, going to the sideboard to fill his plate.

"Because it was four o'clock in the morning. Wellie woke me up screeching, and I couldn't go back to sleep. I didn't think you'd care to be awakened."

"Where is everyone?"

"The women have gone to Kyria's to help with the last-minute preparations. Though what any of them could do to set up a party, I cannot imagine."

"Mmm. Maybe Thisbe has a formula for it."

Alex grinned. "Or Megan and Olivia have

investigated the subject."

"I'm sure Mother will enjoy trying to persuade the servants to go on strike." Con returned to the table.

Alex took a seat across from Con. "Not like Wellie to sound off in the middle of the night like that. One has to wonder what set him off."

"Does one?"

"Con . . . did you have that dream again?"

"Yes. It's not important."

Alex grunted softly. "It certainly doesn't seem to have affected your appetite."

"Little does." Con gestured toward the pristine expanse of table in front of Alex. "What about you? Have you eaten any-thing?"

"I had a cup of coffee."

"No doubt *that* will calm you down."

Alex rolled his eyes and went over to pull a piece of toast from the rack. "You're not going to distract me from your dream."

"I know. But there's nothing new to tell. It's the same dream I've had five times now. I'm in a bizarre round room. There are clocks and compasses everywhere, and I have this feeling of absolute dread." He paused. "Maybe it's panic rather than dread. I feel as if I'm late. I'm sure it's just because of the wedding. I'm worried about not getting to the jeweler's in time for the ring. Keeping this family in line. Being late to the church. All that."

"I have never in my life known you to be so concerned about being late," Alex said flatly.

"You've never gotten married before." Con shrugged it off. "Speaking of being late, why the devil are you all turned out in your wedding coat this early? You'll be creased and stained by the time the ceremony rolls around."

"I know. I'll change. It was just . . . I couldn't think what else to do." Alex sighed. "This is going to be the longest day of my life."

"Why so nervous? You've been champing at the bit for weeks. I can't imagine you're having second thoughts."

"Lord, no, nothing like that. But I can't rid myself of the fear that something will keep it from taking place. That Sabrina will decide to call it off at the last minute."

"The woman's mad for you. Anyone can see that."

"I woke up this morning thinking, what if the Dearborns grab her again?"

"Idiot. She's at Kyria's, with all that brood to protect her."

"I know. Not to mention her friend Miss

14

Holcutt."

"Indeed. I'd warrant Miss Holcutt could scare off any chap with wicked intentions."

Alex smiled. "You're inordinately hard on Lilah."

"It's inordinately easy to be hard on Lilah," Con tossed back.

"I think the reason is you're also rather sweet on Lilah." Con's contemptuous snort only made Alex grin. "Not to mention the fact that she's the only woman to turn down your advances."

"That's not true."

"Oh, really? What other girl has told you no when you asked her to take a stroll in the garden? For that matter, what woman has turned you down about anything — excluding our sisters, of course?"

"Dozens, I'm sure." Con paused. "Well, a few. I'm not universally approved of, you know. You're the one who's the perfect model of a marital prize."

"I'm not the one who's a charming rogue."

"I beg your pardon. I *am* charming, of course, but hardly a rogue."

Alex laughed and reached over to steal a sausage from Con's plate. "Actually, I'm surprised you aren't pursuing Lilah. I would think she would be a challenge to you."

"Maybe I would." Con's lips curved in a

faint smile. "If she weren't your future wife's bosom friend. That makes things awkward."

"Not necessarily. Not if the two of you suited."

Con snorted. "What is it that makes a reformed bachelor want to take all the rest of us down with him?"

Alex ignored his plaintive question. "Miss Holcutt is rather attractive."

Con thought of that bright hair, an indescribable color somewhere between gold and red, that dewy skin, the long slim body beneath her conservative gowns. "Rather attractive" didn't begin to describe Lilah.

"That's the problem. Lilah Holcutt is the sort of woman who leads you on a merry chase, and once you manage to catch her, you can't imagine why you wanted to. She's priggish, self-righteous, humorless and critical. She'd make any man's life a misery. Besides, she's made it quite clear that she detests me."

Alex crossed his arms, regarding Con thoughtfully. Con was grateful that before Alex could speak again, their mother swept into the room. "Alex. Dearest."

Both men rose. "Mother. I thought you'd gone to Kyria's."

"No, dear. I'm of little use there. Neither are the others of course. Kyria and Miss

16

Holcutt could easily handle it all themselves, but it's a nice bit of sisterly time. But I'm not going to pass your wedding day away from you." She took Alex's face in her hands. Tears glittered in her eyes. "I can scarcely believe you're getting married. It seems only yesterday you were in leading strings."

"I'm not the first of your children to marry," Alex protested.

"I know. But those times, I knew I still had my babies. Now it's my baby getting married."

"You have Con."

The duchess smiled at her other son. "Yes, but it won't be long before you are married, too, Con."

"Nonsense. You'll have me around to bother you for years," Con told her lightly. "I doubt I'm marriage material."

Emmeline Moreland chuckled. "Now, where have I heard that before?" She patted Con's cheek. "And you were never a bother. Either of you."

"Mother, how could I marry?" Con laughed. "I'll never find a woman who compares to you."

Hours later, Con stood beside his brother as Alex's bride made her way slowly down the aisle on the arm of Uncle Bellard. Con was unsure whether Bellard was supporting her or Sabrina was holding up their small and shy great-uncle. Bellard had been thrilled when Sabrina, having no male relatives of her own, had asked him to escort her, but this afternoon the old man had been dithering about, several shades paler than even the groom.

Alex, oddly enough, lost his nervousness the moment Sabrina came into view. Black-haired and blue-eyed, with a strawberries-and-cream complexion and a bewitching smile, she was a vision, and Alex could not take his eyes off her.

Con looked across at Sabrina's maid of honor. Lilah Holcutt was tall and willowy, and when she smiled, her lips curved in a faintly lopsided way that never failed to send a sizzle through Con. It was fortunate for him, he supposed, that Lilah was not prone to smile often . . . at least not around him. She was more apt to send him *that look.* The one that said she found him irredeemably foolish. Strangely enough, that one, too, set off a little tickle in him.

She was especially attractive today. Her face was too well formed, her form too alluring, her hair too fascinating a color for her to ever be anything but lovely. But today there was something different about her.

18

Con suspected that his sister Kyria had something to do with that. Lilah's red-gold hair was not pulled back into its usual neat twist that stopped just short of severe. Nor was her blue dress the plain pastel frock she normally wore.

Her gown was a rich vivid blue that accentuated the color of her eyes, with a scoop neckline and a fall of soft lace at the sleeves, leaving much of her arms bare. She had beautiful arms. And her hair, that bright blend of red and gold that Con had never seen on anyone else, was swept up into a soft roll, with a small strand on either side curling down beside her ears in a way that made a man's fingers itch to touch it.

Lilah's gaze had been on the bride and groom, but now she glanced over at Con. He sent her a friendly wink, and she frowned. Obviously he had again earned her disapproval. With Lilah, that was easily done. It was one of the many reasons it was wise to avoid her.

But then, wisdom had never been Con's guiding principle.

CHAPTER TWO

The celebration after the wedding was held at Kyria's house, and it was easy to see Kyria's touch. Great swaths of white satin and silver netting were draped artistically about the ballroom, glowing in the warm light of the wall sconces, and the air was perfumed with the scent of hundreds of white roses, creating a richly romantic backdrop. In the garden, tiny lanterns lined the pathways and dotted the branches.

A small orchestra was playing at one end of the room, the dance floor empty as Alex took Sabrina out for their first dance as a married couple. Lilah stood with the others, watching them.

Sabrina gazed up at her groom with such love that it almost made Lilah's chest hurt. Lilah tried to imagine what it must be like to feel so much for another person that one's face simply shone with it. Lilah had some difficulty with the notion. She herself did not lack for suitors, many of them quite eligible men, but she had never felt even a tingle of such feeling.

Alex clearly was just as much in love as Sabrina. Lilah had watched him earlier as Sabrina came down the aisle, his face alight with love. She had glanced at Con then, wondering what he felt on this occasion. It must be strange to lose one's twin to marriage. Irritating as Con was, Lilah had felt a little pang of sympathy for him.

But then Con had flashed that cocky grin at her and winked. In the middle of a wedding. It was typical of the man. She didn't know why she bothered to feel sympathy for him. Constantine Moreland never took anything seriously. Well, almost never — Lilah had seen his face two months ago when Alex was kidnapped, and Con's face then had been downright frightening.

When the stately first waltz ended, other couples joined the newlyweds on the dance floor. Lilah glanced around, certain she would see Con among the dancers. She wondered who he would choose as his partner. He had never seemed to favor any particular girl with his attentions. He had even danced with her one time.

Though he would never do so again, no doubt. Lilah blushed at that memory. Con thought her prudish for the way she had reacted when he asked her to walk in the garden with him after their dance. Lilah knew now that she had been impulsive and silly; she had only recently come out, and her greenness had showed. Not that she had been wrong — a man didn't ask a young girl to walk in the garden at a party unless his intentions were less than virtuous. But she had learned since then how to turn aside such a man without resorting to anything so overwrought as a slap.

Lilah scowled down at her glove, needlessly fussing with the button. Out of the corner of her eye she saw one of Alex's cousins making his way toward her. Albert had apparently taken a liking to Lilah; he had dogged her footsteps all day. She'd managed to slip away each time, but she had the gloomy suspicion she wouldn't be able to dodge him this time. She could hardly be impolite to one of the Moreland family, but, having danced with Cousin Albert at the engagement party, Lilah knew that taking to the floor with him would not only be a dreadful bore but also a very real danger to her toes.

Hoping he had not realized she'd spotted him, Lilah started to turn away. Just at that moment, a man behind her said, "Miss Holcutt. Would you care to dance?"

"Con!" She whirled. "Oh, thank God."

His green eyes twinkled. "What an un-expectedly enthusiastic response. I daresay you must have seen Cousin Albert setting his course."

"Yes." There was no need to pretend politeness where Con was concerned.

She took his arm and Con whisked her away to the dance floor, pulling her to him and seamlessly joining the other dancers. Lilah had forgotten what it was like to dance with Con — so quick and light, his hand firm on her waist, holding her a trifle closer than was appropriate. It was easy to match his steps, to follow the guide of his hand. He was an expert dancer, and one had only to let go and trust him.

She could not keep from smiling up at him. It was better not to encourage Con — he was already too full of himself — and she was always careful not to do anything that would draw attention, but right now she was enjoying herself too much to care.

When the music ended, Lilah was flushed and breathless, surging with energy. She would have liked to dance again, but of course, that would never do; even Con would know better than that. Whipping open her delicate ivory-and-lace fan, she tried to cool her overheated face. Con led her toward the open windows, snagging two glasses of champagne from a passing waiter and handing her one.

Lilah rarely drank wine of any sort, but she was too thirsty not to take a great gulp of it. It fizzed in her mouth, tingling and cool, yet with its own delicious sting as well, and she drank the rest of it. Con's eyebrows shot up.

"Careful. I can't have you getting foxed on me." He plucked the empty glass from her hand and set it aside.

"I won't. It's just so hot in here."

Con glanced toward the French doors, standing open to the terrace, then back to her. "Dare I suggest we step outside? I assure you I won't try to lure you into the garden this time."

Lilah cast him a speaking glance and took his arm, turning toward the open doors. "One can only wonder why you did so the first time, considering that you think I'm such a prig."

He chuckled and took a sip from his glass. "I am, as you have pointed out, entirely too impulsive."

"That's no answer." But Lilah was feeling too companionable at the moment to pursue the subject. Her customary annoyance with

Con had vanished with the waltz.

They strolled the length of the terrace, now and then passing another couple doing the same. Lilah lifted her flushed face to the cool night air. She began to hum the waltz beneath her breath, wishing she could dance along the terrace. She smiled to herself at the idea of causing such a commotion. Con's jaw would drop. She had to press her lips together tightly to hold back a giggle.

Perhaps she shouldn't have gulped down that glass of champagne. It wasn't like her. Or perhaps it had been the dance, whirling around the room in Con Moreland's arms. That, too, had been unlike her. Mostly likely it was because she was with Con; there was something about him that encouraged misbehavior.

He said inappropriate things that made her laugh. His smile, his wink, that twinkle in his eye just before he did or said something outrageous, enticed one to go along with him. If he had been a woman, people would have termed him a temptress. She wasn't sure what one called such a man. *Dangerous* came to mind.

She glanced up at Con, so close beside her she could feel the warmth of his body. As if sensing her gaze, he turned his head. With only the mellow light streaming from the windows of the ballroom behind them, Con's face was half-shadowed, his eyes dark. But the dimness could not hide how handsome he was — the firm chin and square jaw, the way his mouth curved up slightly, as if he was about to break into a grin.

It was odd how much he looked like his twin, yet she had never felt a twinge of attraction to Alex. When she first met Con's brother, she had realized almost immediately that he was not Con. There had been no spark running along her nerves, no tightening of her stomach. Alex was easy to talk to; with Con, Lilah always felt as if she needed to be on her guard.

If she wasn't careful, she might stumble. And Lilah was a person who liked her feet firmly planted on the ground. It was disconcerting to have this uncertainty. It was even more alarming that it also excited her. Surely that was not how it ought to be.

They reached the end of the walkway and turned to look out over the garden below. Delicate paper lanterns lit the garden paths, but up here on the terrace, they were deep in shadow. Con set his glass on the wide stone balustrade and leaned casually against a column, his eyes on Lilah rather than the view.

Lilah's pulse picked up. It was dim and secluded here, the occasional sound of a voice a distant background. She remembered the other time she had stood on a terrace with Con, almost breathless with a volatile combination of excitement, anxiety and a guilty certainty that her aunt would not approve.

"Tell me, truly," Lilah said impulsively, "that night . . . Why did you ask me to dance, much less stroll in the garden with you? I understand your doing so tonight — I'm your new sister-in-law's friend, and you must be polite. But why did you ask me to dance back then?"

"Have you looked in a mirror?" Con countered.

"You were swept away by my beauty?" Lilah cocked a skeptical eyebrow. "There were dozens of pretty young girls there, and I would wager I am not the sort you normally dance with. Much less take out on the terrace with ulterior motives."

"My motives weren't ulterior. I thought they were quite straightforward."

Lilah was reminded why she found him irritating. She turned away, fixing her eyes on the flowers and shrubs below. "Was it — did you do it because I was newly out? Because you thought I would be so naive I

27

wouldn't realize I was risking my reputation?"

"No!" Con's voice was filled with affront and astonishment. "It wasn't like that. I didn't ask you to dance because I thought I could trick you into anything. Do you really think that badly of me?"

Lilah relaxed, surprised at how relieved she was by his indignant response. "No. Well, perhaps I did wonder a bit. Afterward." When he never approached her again.

"I asked you to dance because I wanted to waltz with you. I asked you out on the terrace to spend more time with you without the noise of the party. And I asked you to take a stroll through the garden because . . . very well, I did hope I might get a chance to kiss you. But I didn't want to kiss you because you were the low-hanging fruit on a tree."

"Or to add another girl to your collection?"

"My collection!" Con goggled at her. "What the devil do you take me for? I don't have a collection. I'm not some rogue out seducing young ladies. Good Lord, Lilah, but you are a suspicious woman."

"It's not absurd to suspect that," she retorted. "You find me rigid, prim and proper."

"You forgot judgmental."

"Oh, yes, sorry — and judgmental." She crossed her arms, glaring at him. "So why would you want to dance with such a woman?"

"If you must know, it was because you were wearing lilac stockings."

"What?" Lilah stared at him.

He shrugged and turned away, now the one to keep his eyes on the view. "You asked."

"But why . . . How . . ."

"It's nice to know I can render you speechless."

"That's absurd. How could you know what color stockings I had on? *I* don't even remember what color they were."

"Clearly the sight of them made more of an impression on me than it did on you." Con glanced back at her. "I was standing at the foot of the stairs when you came in. You were so terribly prim and proper, all in maidenly white, modestly covered to your neck, your face blankly polite, your hair braided and curled into a knot like a governess, your chaperone glued to your side. I thought, there's a beauty, but she looks an utter bore."

"How kind of you," Lilah said drily.

"Then you climbed the stairs, lifting your

skirt to keep from stepping on it, and I saw your ankles. You were wearing bright lilac stockings. And I thought, there's more to her than meets the eye." He paused, considering. "Besides, you have lovely ankles."

Lilah gaped at him, then began to laugh. His reasoning was so strange, so very Con-like — flattering, insulting and preposterous all at once — that she couldn't work up either affront or anger, only a baffled amusement.

"You should do that more often," Con told her.

"What?"

"Laugh. You look beautiful."

"Oh." She hoped the darkness concealed her blush. Otherwise, Con would doubtless tease her about it every time they met.

Except, of course, she would not see him now that the wedding was over. Constantine Moreland didn't frequent the sort of parties Lilah attended with her aunt. He preferred more exciting entertainment. Even when they did attend the same function, Con did his best to avoid her. Her life now would return to its usual pattern. Lilah sighed as she thought of the weeks ahead, paying calls and receiving visitors in her aunt's parlor.

"What is it?" Con asked. When she glanced at him questioningly, he explained,

"You sighed just now. Is something wrong?"

"What? Oh. I didn't realize I had." Her cheeks, already pink, flamed. "I was, um, just thinking that things would settle back to normal now that the wedding is done."

"Yes, it will likely be more boring."

"I didn't mean that," she protested. "I meant, it will be quieter. Calmer. But that's a good thing. One can rest and relax and, um . . ."

"Embroider handkerchiefs?" Con suggested, raising an eyebrow.

She glowered. "I'm sure there will be nothing so mundane for you. You'll be off chasing ghosts or seeking the meaning of Stonehenge."

"Hopefully I'll find an adventure or two to pass the time." He grinned down at her. "Here, now, don't look so grim." He smoothed his finger over the lines of her frown, then moved to her cheek, lightly skimming a strand of hair that had escaped its pins.

Self-consciously Lilah moved to pin the stray curl back in place, but Con reached out to stop her. "No, don't. It's lovely like that."

"Like what . . . A mess?" She forced a bit of tartness into her voice to combat the sudden heat his touch stirred in her.

31

"I doubt that anything about you is ever a mess." Con stroked his thumb lazily along her cheekbone. His smile was still there, but different now, no longer amused but warm and inviting. There was a look in his eyes very like the one she'd seen in Alex when he gazed at Sabrina. Dark and a little hazy.

Lilah's breath caught in her throat, and her thoughts went tumbling madly. She definitely should not have drunk that glass of champagne. Con leaned in. Lilah tilted her face up.

Masculine laughter burst from the ballroom as three men stepped out onto the terrace, chatting among themselves. Lilah froze. What was she doing? Con had been about to kiss her. And she had been about to let him. Worse yet, she had been about to kiss him back. "I — I'm sorry — I shouldn't — goodbye."

Lilah slipped around him and hurried back into the ballroom.

CHAPTER THREE

Lilah was bored. She had spent the morning in the drawing room with her aunt, answering correspondence. There was little of that, as her father, to whom she had once written faithfully, had passed on two years ago, and it had been many years since she'd exchanged letters with his sister, Vesta. Sabrina, with whom she had maintained the longest, largest correspondence, was away on her honeymoon.

She missed Sabrina. Her friend had lived in London for only a couple of months, but for that time it had been as if they were together in Miss Angerman's Academy for Young Ladies again. Sabrina was not the only one she missed. In the process of preparing for Sabrina's wedding, Lilah had become friends with the Morelands, as well. All the Morelands had returned for the wedding, along with their spouses and broods of children. It made for an occasionally chaotic environment, but one that was always entertaining and congenial.

There had been any number of lively conversations with the duchess, ranging over a host of topics, and though Lilah and the very forward-thinking Duchess of Broughton had disagreed from time to time, their discussions were invigorating and even enlightening. Megan told entertaining stories about her years of reporting and traveling the world with her husband, Theo Moreland. Kyria, vibrant and warm, was almost impossible not to like — as were the duke and his diminutive uncle Bellard, a veritable treasure trove of knowledge once one got him started.

Thisbe, Theo's twin, was a scientist who spent much of her time in her laboratory working on things Lilah neither understood nor, really, cared to understand. But Thisbe was also possessed of a dry wit and an easy, outgoing nature much like her twin's, and Anna, Reed Moreland's wife, was a quiet spot of serenity amid the noisy bustle of activity at Broughton House.

Lilah had especially come to like Olivia, the youngest of the Moreland daughters. Olivia, though she shared with Constantine an odd interest in the occult, was as devoted a reader as Lilah, and once they discovered their mutual interest in books of mystery and danger, they had spent many a pleasant afternoon chatting.

The days since the wedding had seemed quite empty. Lilah hadn't any reason to visit Broughton House. Without her friend Sabrina there, it seemed a bit presumptuous to make a social call at the house of a duke, at least until they had called on her. Lilah would hate to be thought a social climber.

Worse . . . what if Con were at home? What if he thought Lilah was there in the hopes of seeing him? Given the way she had behaved the other night — it made her blush even to think of it — he would be justified in assuming she was setting her cap for him. Nothing could be further from the truth of course. Lilah would never pursue any man, much less someone like Con. He would be the last person she would want to marry — not that he would ever ask someone like her.

Con probably thought it was funny that such a prim and proper woman as Lilah had acted so unlike herself. He knew she had been about to kiss him. No doubt he would tease her about it. He would laugh, that rich, warm laughter that made one want to join him, his lips curving up and his eyes lighting with mischief. It was most unfair that his teasing made him even more attractive.

That was the root of the whole problem with Constantine Moreland — he was so utterly appealing. Lilah liked the straight black slashes of his eyebrows — the way they lifted when he was amused or drew together fiercely when he frowned. She had more than once felt a strange desire to reach out and smooth a finger along one of them. His eyes were such a sharp green, darkened by that thick row of black lashes. Those cheekbones, that jaw, that chin. That mouth. Thank goodness she had always had firm control of herself and had kept such thoughts hidden.

But then she had destroyed all her efforts by going out onto the terrace with him. Standing there in that dark secluded corner with him, a situation so intimate, so warm, so ripe for seduction. Turning her face up for his kiss. If only she hadn't drunk that champagne. If only he hadn't asked her to dance.

No. She must not call at Broughton House, even if she could come up with a good reason to do so. She should settle back into her normal life. It might take a bit of time, but she would become accustomed to it. Being around the Morelands had been exciting. Entertaining. But that wasn't how Lilah lived. She was not flamboyant; she didn't crave adventure and excitement; she wasn't driven by wild uncontrollable passion. All she had ever wanted was a quiet, pleasant, rational life. The sort of life she had.

Lilah gave a little nod of her head, feeling a bit as if she had won an argument. She glanced over at Aunt Helena, whose head was bent over her embroidery. Lilah was forcibly reminded of Con's comment about spending her days on embroidery.

"Do you need anything done?" Lilah asked. "Is there an errand I might run for you?"

Aunt Helena looked up and smiled. She was a small, neat woman, her blond hair now touched with gray at the temples. Lilah felt an upwelling of affection. Aunt Helena had welcomed her and raised her, and Lilah could never repay her for that. It was no easy task to take on a girl of twelve and guide her into womanhood, to train her in proper behavior and the ins and outs of society. Con might sneer about mundane things like needlework — and, frankly, Lilah was not fond of embroidering either — but there was nothing wrong with spending one's time that way. And her aunt's work was excellent.

"Oh, no, dear, no need for that. Cuddington has gone to the apothecary to pick up my tonic, and Mrs. Humphrey has the house in order as always. Why don't we discuss our calls this afternoon?"

Calls weren't what Lilah had in mind to relieve tedium. They *were* tedious, more often than not. But Lilah held back her sigh. Making and receiving calls was a fact of life.

"I thought we would go early in the afternoon," Aunt Helena said. "That way we'll be back by the time Sir Jasper comes."

"Sir Jasper is visiting us this afternoon?" Lilah asked in some dismay. "He was here just two days ago."

"Well, of course, I don't *know* he'll call on you." Aunt Helena gave her a small, conspiratorial smile. "But given his recent behavior . . ."

Her aunt had hopes that Sir Jasper had matrimony in mind. Unfortunately, Lilah suspected she was right. She wished Aunt Helena would not encourage the man. But she had no desire to get into a discussion of that, so she said only, "Who were you thinking of visiting?"

"Mrs. Blythe, of course, to thank her for that lovely little dinner party last night. And it's been some time since we've called on

Mrs. Pierce." Lilah couldn't hold back a small groan at that name, and her aunt smiled. "Yes, I know, dear. Elspeth Pierce is a dreadful gossip. But that's exactly why one mustn't get on her bad side."

"I suppose." She didn't really mind the woman's gossiping; it was the insipidity of her conversation that wore on Lilah's nerves. But her aunt was right; when Mrs. Pierce took a dislike to one, she was deadly.

"I really should call on the vicar's wife," Helena continued. "But their daughter is ill, so that will excuse us from that."

"It seems visiting people shouldn't be such . . . a chore."

Aunt Helena smiled. "It would be nice. But we cannot shirk one's social obligations, can we?"

Lilah thought somewhat resentfully that the Morelands seemed to be able to do so easily enough. But, of course, Lilah wouldn't want to be viewed as the Morelands were. She cast about for something to occupy her until this afternoon's calls.

"Perhaps I shall go to the bookstore first." Lilah popped up from the sofa as a sudden thought occurred to her. "On my way, I can drop off a book for Lady St. Leger. I have a Wilkie Collins she has not read yet, and I promised to lend it to her." Olivia wanted the book; it wouldn't be rude or out of place to visit the Morelands as long as she had a reason. Indeed, the proper behavior would be to take the book to Olivia, as Lilah had promised. And there was no reason to worry about running into Con; he was doubtless off on one of his adventures.

"Lady St. Leger?" Her aunt's forehead wrinkled a bit. "Do I know her?"

"She's one of Sabrina's sisters-in-law. She and her family came to stay at Broughton House for the wedding."

Her aunt's frown grew. "One of the Morelands? Dear, do you think that's wise?"

"I promised, Aunt Helena. I can hardly ignore a promise." Lilah was feeling more cheerful by the moment. It would be good to see Olivia again, to have a nice long chat about books. Much as she loved and respected her aunt, Helena was not a reader. Maybe Kyria would be there, too. Or the duchess.

"Of course not," her aunt agreed reluctantly. "I just thought now that the wedding is over, you wouldn't be seeing them as much."

"I haven't seen them. It's been four days," Lilah reminded her. "I should go now so I'll be back in time for our afternoon calls." She turned toward the door.

"It's rather early for paying a call, don't you think? Not yet noon."

"The Morelands pay no attention to things like that."

"I know," Aunt Helena said darkly. "Well, if you must go, take your maid with you."

"Aunt Helena . . . I hardly need a chaperone to go from here to Broughton House in broad daylight."

"Of course not, dear. It's how it would look."

"Society's rules are not so rigid anymore," Lilah protested.

"That may be. But that's no reason for us to lower our standards."

"Poppy has several things to do — um, mending my clothes and, uh . . ."

"I wish I hadn't sent Cuddington to the apothecary. She could accompany you."

"No, no, I'll take Poppy with me." The last thing Lilah wanted was to drag her aunt's dour maid along with her.

Lilah hurried upstairs, calling for her maid, and opened her wardrobe closet. Her casual morning dress would not do for paying a visit; it required something more stylish — this honey-colored walking dress with the rust-brown piping, for instance. It went well with the reddish-blond color of her hair, and the nipped-in waist gave her tall, willowy figure a more fashionable hourglass shape.

She could wear her new half boots. They were, perhaps, a trifle unusual, with their paisley print and curved line of gold buttons, but the colors went well with her dress, and anyway, no one would see them beneath her skirts. Well, except someone like Con, of course, who apparently made it a habit to keep an eye on ladies' ankles. But that sort of man was not interested in either fashion or propriety.

She set off for the Morelands' home, book in hand, Poppy trailing along a few steps behind her. It was annoying having to take her along. Perhaps Lilah should visit her home in Somerset, where she could hike wherever she wanted and not worry what society might think. It would provide her with an escape from the tedious round of courtesy calls — not to mention Sir Jasper's attentions. She could relieve her boredom.

The problem, of course, was that Aunt Vesta was there. Lilah hadn't stayed at Barrow House since her father's sister had returned. Lilah had been fond of her as a child, but children were so undiscerning, so easily pleased. And Aunt Vesta hadn't yet plunged the family into scandal.

Smeggars, the Morelands' butler, greeted

Lilah with a smile but said, "I fear the duchess is out today."

"It was actually Lady St. Leger I wished to see."

"Lady St. Leger is with the duchess."

"I'm sorry. I should have inquired before I came," Lilah said in disappointment.

"Perhaps you would like to speak with the duke or, um . . ."

"No, I'll just leave this," Lilah began, holding out the book.

At that moment Con came trotting lightly down the stairs. "Miss Holcutt." He grinned. "The ladies are all out. I'm afraid you'll have to make do with me." He turned to the butler. "I think tea would be in order."

"Of course, sir."

"No," Lilah protested as the butler left. "I mustn't stay. I was going to the bookstore, and I remembered that Olivia — Lady St. Leger, that is — had expressed an interest in reading one of my books." Lilah realized she was babbling and clamped her lips together. It was annoying that she should be so jittery and embarrassed at seeing Con again, whereas he was so obviously, so coolly unaffected.

"That sounds like Livvy." Con reached out and took the book from her hands. "Ah,

43

Wilkie Collins. Yes, she will enjoy reading it."

"She said his stories were favorites of hers, but she had not read this one."

"Please, sit down." He took her arm without asking and steered her down the hall toward the sitting room. "All the women except Anna left earlier. Anna had one of her terrible headaches and had to stay behind."

"I'm sorry." Lilah resisted the urge to sit down as he had suggested. There was no reason to stay. She had run her errand. She shouldn't sit down for a tête-à-tête alone with a man. Yet she lingered. "They're on a shopping expedition?"

Con let out a crack of laughter. "No, Mother's taken them to one of her suffragists' dos. They're standing vigil in front of Edmond Edmington's house."

"Edmond Edmington?" Lilah couldn't hold back a smile.

"Yes, he had alliterative if unimaginative parents. Sit down, Miss Holcutt, please. Smeggars will be crushed if you don't stay for tea and petits fours. He's always trying to turn Mother's meetings into parties, with little success."

"No, I should be going. I was just —" She gestured toward the door, taking a step backward.

"Going to the bookstore. Yes, I know." His eyes twinkled. "Come, Lilah, I won't make any unwanted advances . . . not with Smeggars lurking about."

What if they weren't unwanted, she thought, then blushed at her wayward mind. "You *would* make some jest about it."

"About what?" he asked innocently, moving closer.

"You know what." She scowled. "What we — the other evening on the terrace."

"Ah." He leaned in, far too close for polite behavior. "You mean when we talked?" His eyes widened in mock shock. "Unchaperoned."

"Yes." Her word came out in little more than a whisper. Irritated, she cleared her throat and went on in a firm voice. "No. I mean it was more than that. We were — we almost . . ."

"Yes?" His eyes danced. "We almost . . ."

She had known he would tease her. She should not have come here. "Oh, stop it. Just leave me alone."

"Of course." He sighed and stepped back. It was what she wanted, yet perversely she felt let down at his easy acquiescence.

She should go now. It was silly to be so reluctant. Lilah drew a breath to say goodbye but was brought up short by a shout from upstairs. "Reed! Someone!"

"Anna!" Con ran from the room.

Lilah followed him. When she reached the bottom of the staircase, Con was already halfway up the flight to his sister-in-law, who stood still and staring, her face deathly white.

"They've been taken!" Anna cried. "You have to save them."

She folded after that pronouncement, and Con grabbed her, easing her down to sit on the stairs. "Here, put your head down. Just breathe. Slowly now."

Steps pounded down the long stretch of the gallery, and Reed burst into view, his face almost as drained of color as his wife's. "Anna! What happened? What's the matter?"

Reed leaped up the stairs, pulling his wife into his arms and cradling her against his chest. Con stepped back. "Reed, she was saying — I think she's having one of her visions."

One of her visions?

Con's words didn't seem to shock Reed, who only cursed and continued to stroke Anna's back. "It's all right, sweetheart. Everything's fine."

"No!" Anna pulled back. She had regained

46

some of her color and her eyes were no longer wild, but she was clearly distressed. "You have to find them. You have to —"

"Who?" Con asked, his voice sharp. Lilah could see that his body was suddenly coiled tight as a spring. "*Who* is in trouble, Anna?"

"All of them!" She looked from her husband to Con and back. "The duchess. Kyria. Olivia. All of them. They've been kidnapped!"

CHAPTER FOUR

Con whirled and ran from the house. Lilah followed right on his heels. Signaling a hack, he ran out into the street and jumped into it before it completely stopped. Lilah climbed in after him. Con cast a glance at her, and for a moment Lilah thought he was going to protest her presence, but he only turned and called out an address to the driver.

He looked nothing like he usually did, his eyes as fierce as they were normally laughing, his mobile face stern and set, his body taut. He had undergone the same transformation two months ago when he had raced to free his twin.

Lilah wanted to ask him about Anna's bizarre pronouncement. Anna seemed the calmest of all the Morelands, but nothing could have been madder than her staring eyes and terrifying words. Yet Con and his brother Reed, while alarmed, had not appeared surprised. Moreover, it was clear that Con believed what she said, dashing off immediately to his mother and sisters.

But that was absurd. Wasn't it? Anna couldn't have actually seen something happening in another place. No doubt Lilah and Con would arrive at their destination to find the women unharmed and exactly where they were supposed to be. They would all laugh over it. "Anna must have had a nightmare. It was her headache. One often has strange dreams when one is ill."

Con shook his head. "She saw it."

That was nonsense of course, but she didn't want to argue when he was so worried. "Why would anyone want to harm the duchess?"

He cast her an eloquent glance.

"Well, yes, the duchess could have antagonized a number of people over the years, but surely not enough to harm her." Lilah frowned. "Do you think the police arrested the suffragists? For simply standing in front of someone's house?" She realized that now *she* was talking as if it had really happened.

"Lord only knows what they were doing. But no, I doubt it was the police," he replied grimly.

The carriage had been traveling at a fast clip but now, after careening around a corner, came to an abrupt stop. Lilah looked out the window and saw a number of women milling about in the street in front of a stately residence. Signs were tossed here and there, and everyone was talking excitedly. A policeman was arguing with one of the women, and several other women were clustered around something on the sidewalk. Was that a *body*?

Con let out an oath and threw open the carriage door, running to the constable. Lilah cast another quick glance around as she stepped down from the vehicle. She could see none of the Moreland women.

"Here, now!" The cabdriver protested at Con's abrupt departure without paying him.

"Stay here," Lilah ordered crisply. They would need transportation home as soon as Con found his family.

She caught up to Con at the side of the policeman. He was barking questions at the man. "What the devil happened here? Where is the duchess?"

"Wh-who? I don't know, sir! I just arrived."

The woman who had been talking to the constable, a solid woman dressed in the style of the rational dress movement, let out a snort. "You'd do better if you tried listening, young man."

"Mrs. Ellerby." Con moved to the woman's side.

"Lord Moreland! Thank heavens you're here. They attacked us!"

"Who?"

"The police, most likely." She turned to glare at the unfortunate policeman, who began to splutter.

"No, there weren't any uniforms!" another woman put in.

"It was a gang of ruffians! I saw them. All in black, with masks on."

"Oh, Ernestine, what rubbish," Mrs. Ellerby declared. "There weren't any masks, just caps pulled down so you could barely see their faces."

"They might as well have been masks."

"Mrs. Ellerby," Con said through clenched teeth. "*Where* is my mother?"

"She's gone! They drove up and jumped out and grabbed them. The duchess and her girls, all of them — except for Lady Raine." She gestured toward the women hovering over the thing on the sidewalk.

"Megan!" Con went pale and whipped around.

It *was* a body. Lilah's breath caught, and she ran after Con. The women stepped aside at Con's approach, revealing the woman on the ground. It was indeed Megan, but she

51

was now sitting up.

"Thank God. Megan." Con scooped Megan up and set her on the low stone wall that edged the property. He squatted down to look her in the eye. "Are you all right?"

"Of course she's not all right." Lilah sat down beside Megan. "Why do people always say that?"

Dirt and grit decorated Megan's dress. There was a large red spot on her cheekbone, and the skin around it had started to swell. The other side of her face was scraped and dirty. Her hat hung down, barely anchored by the long hatpin, along with strands of reddish-brown hair. Her eyes had a glassy look that worried Lilah. Lilah pulled out her handkerchief and began to gently brush the grime from Megan's face.

"Megan." Con took one of her hands. "Say something. Anything. Tell me to hush, even."

That brought a faint smile to Megan's lips. "I'm fine." She cleared her throat and straightened. "Really. I — I'm just a little woozy. I think I hit my head." She gestured toward the back of her head.

Lilah twisted around to look and let out a gasp. "Con! Her hair is bloody."

Con was instantly up and bending over Megan. He pulled out a pristine white handkerchief from his pocket and pressed it gently against Megan's wound. His voice was as gentle as his hand as he went on, "What happened, Megan?"

"I heard someone scream, and I turned around. And I saw these men — they'd grabbed Kyria, so all the others were trying to stop them. I ran to help, but I was too far away. So I picked up some rocks and started throwing them at the man Thisbe was fighting. Olivia was trying to free Kyria. Then he came after me and punched me."

Lilah saw fury light up in Con's eyes, but he kept his voice even. "He knocked you down?"

Megan nodded, then winced at the movement. "Yes. I hit the ground. I remember that but nothing afterward. I must have hit my head when I fell. Next thing I knew, I was lying on the ground and Miss Withers here was trying to awaken me."

Con looked at the other women. "What happened after that?"

"Those men threw all of them in the carriage and took off. They were gone before any of the rest of us could move a muscle. I'm so sorry." Tears sprang into Miss Withers's eyes. "I wasn't any use at all."

"Which way did they go?"

"Down the side street." She pointed.

"They turned left at the first street," one of the other women offered. "Then they were out of sight."

Con shoved the handkerchief into Lilah's hand and took off at a run.

"He won't see them. They must be long gone." Lilah watched Con as she held his handkerchief to Megan's head.

"That won't keep him from trying," Megan replied, a thread of amusement in her voice. Lilah looked into Megan's eyes and saw that they were clearer.

Con stopped at the end of the block and stood for a long moment, looking to his left, before he loped back to them. With Lilah's help, Megan rose to meet him.

Con's jaw was set and his eyes blazing. "Lilah, take Megan back to the house. I'm going after them."

"How do you intend to do that?" Lilah asked. "You don't know where they've gone."

"I'll figure it out."

"That sounds excellent," Lilah said crisply, taking Megan's elbow and turning toward the carriage. "Find a carriage and head off in the general direction they took sometime ago. No planning, no information, no idea what the duke or any of the other husbands think or why your mother and sisters were taken. I'm sure you will do wonderfully well."

Beside her, Megan snickered. Con's face was a study in frustration, but he scooped Megan up and strode toward the waiting hack, saying in an aggrieved tone, "Yes, I know. I'm impulsive and quick-tempered, and *you,* of course, are logical, rational and right."

The coach took off as soon as they were settled. Con leaned back against the seat, arms crossed, sunk in a deep study. The driver set a pace fast enough it made Megan wince as they rattled over the cobblestones, but she didn't protest. When they reached the house, Megan handed back Con's bloody handkerchief and insisted on walking into the house unaided.

"You are *not* carrying me in like some invalid. Theo will treat me as if I'm at death's door."

They found a thoroughly distressed Smeggars hovering in the entryway. He greeted them with a cry of delight and hustled them down to the Sultan Room. Even before they reached the salon, Lilah heard the agitated male voices. Inside, the room seemed to be filled with large men — standing, pacing, arguing, looking grim.

The butler, adept at gaining attention

from years spent in the Morelands' service, stepped in, announcing grandly, "Gentlemen! The Marchioness of Raine."

Silence fell instantly and they all swung around to stare at Megan, flanked by Lilah and Con.

"Thank God!" Theo crossed the room in two strides and pulled his wife into his arms, squeezing her so hard she let out a squeak of protest.

"What happened, Con? What's going on?" Reed came forward. Lilah saw for the first time that his wife, Anna, was also in the room, sitting against the wall. She was still pale, her face stamped with worry.

While Theo fussed over his wife's injuries, the rest of the men bombarded Con with questions. Lilah left him to the interrogation and made her way to Anna. "How are you?"

The other woman attempted a smile. "Better. The headache's gone. It usually disappears. But it always leaves me tired."

"Perhaps you should rest."

"Thank you. I'll be fine here. I couldn't lie down and sleep, knowing they were still out there. I feel so awful that I didn't go with them. If only I'd realized earlier —"

"You mustn't blame yourself. If you had been there, how could you have prevented

56

it? It's far better that you and Megan aren't missing, too."

"No doubt you're right. Tell me what happened. You found only Megan?"

Lilah related to her everything they had done and discovered, a good deal more quickly and in better order than Con was managing with the frantic and furious men across the room. Fortunately, Smeggars wheeled in the tea cart, along with iodine and bandages for Megan's injuries.

"This is no time for tea," Kyria's husband, Rafe McIntyre, protested.

"Oh, no, sir, I think you'll find it's exactly the right time." Smeggars smiled benignly.

"Yes, yes, you're right, Smeggars, as always," the duke agreed. "We're accomplishing nothing this way. Let's sit down and think this thing through. There has to be a way out of this. They won't hurt my girls."

Rafe started to object, but Stephen St. Leger clapped a hand on his shoulder and cast a meaningful glance at the duke. Rafe nodded and subsided.

"You're right, sir," Stephen said. "We shouldn't panic. That's what they want — to rattle us so much we can't think."

As Smeggars served the tea, Uncle Bellard slid forward on his chair, gazing at

57

Megan in his mild way. "Now, Megan, dear, is there anything else you can tell us about these men? Now that your mind is clearer. I'm sure your skills as a reporter enabled you to notice more details than the average person."

Megan took a breath. "You're right. I should think like a reporter." She closed her eyes. "There were three of them. They wore workingmen's sort of clothes, dark, and they had on soft caps, pulled low to conceal their faces. Their carriage — no, wait, it wasn't a carriage, it was more of a wagon. But enclosed like a . . ." Her eyes popped open and she sat up straight. "Like a Black Maria."

"A what?" The duke and others stared in confusion.

"A police wagon," Rafe explained. He set aside his tea and stood up, an almost-palpable energy pouring out of him. "It's a nickname in the United States for the vehicles they carry prisoners in. They're painted black, and they're made to keep prisoners from escaping. The doors in the back open from the outside only, and the windows are small, high and barred."

Megan nodded. "Yes. That's it. It was smaller than most I've seen, but I'm sure it had high barred windows."

"No wonder some of the women thought they were the police," Con commented. "But at least a vehicle like that should be easier to track."

"What else can you remember?" The usual lazy drawl was missing from Rafe's speech now, his words as hard and sharp as steel. He began to prowl around the room, reminding Lilah of a tiger in its cage. "Was it Kyria he was after? Con said he was dragging Kyria away."

"I — I'm not sure," Megan faltered. "When I first saw them, they were pulling Kyria and the duchess toward the wagon. Of course, they were all fighting them. I don't know if they meant to take one or two or everybody."

"It's clear it was planned," Reed said. "They had the prisoner wagon. They went straight for the Moreland women. They moved quickly."

"That sort of demonstration was an excellent place to take them. People thought they were the police, so they hesitated to step forward and stop it."

"One man stayed up on the wagon seat at first — I presume so they could get away quickly," Megan said. "He didn't get down until the women swarmed the first man. How could they think two men could take them all?"

"How could they think even three could?" Stephen spoke up. "There were four women — five counting you, and it would have been six if Anna had been there."

"Perhaps they didn't know the Moreland women well enough to realize they wouldn't go easily," Theo guessed. "They might have thought the ladies would be so shocked and frightened they wouldn't struggle."

"How did they take them?" Lilah, caught up in the conversation, jumped in. When the others turned to look at her, it occurred to her that she had crashed into the family discussion. "I'm sorry, I didn't mean to interrupt. It's just — how did they manage to fight five women and get four of them into the wagon so quickly?"

"True." The duke frowned.

"Chloroform!" Megan popped to her feet. "The man holding Kyria had his hand over her face. I thought he was trying to muffle her screams, but I remember now, there was a handkerchief in his hand. She went limp almost immediately."

"I'll kill that sorry son of a bitch," Rafe said in a low voice that was more frightening than a shout. He looked at the duke. "How long are we going to sit around here, yammering about it? I'm going after them."

"How do you intend to do that? We've no idea where they went, and they've a long head start on us," Reed said reasonably.

"I'll find someone who'll talk. Trust me, I can be very persuasive."

"Rafe, wait." Stephen stepped into his path.

"It's the Dearborns," Con said flatly.

"What?" Rafe swung around. "How do you know?"

"I don't *know*. But who has a grudge against the Morelands? Who is in desperate need of money? Who likes to abduct people to get their way? The answer to each of those questions is Niles Dearborn."

"I would have recognized the Dearborns," Megan pointed out.

"They wouldn't do it themselves. They hired someone."

"It's what they did with Alex," Theo agreed.

"Then that's my first stop," Rafe said.

Everyone began again to talk at once.

"Quiet!" Thisbe's husband, Desmond, jumped to his feet. He was normally such a quiet man that his outburst shocked all of them into silence. "We can't go running off in all directions. We need to get organized. Maybe it's the Dearborns and maybe it's just some men hoping to make a profit. We need to be ready for all contingencies, including a ransom demand. We haven't received one yet, but I would wager we will — no matter who took them. Let's divide up. Rafe, you and Stephen go confront the Dearborns. Theo, Alex showed you where they held him. You and Reed make sure they don't have Thisbe and the others there." The men left immediately as Desmond went on, "The duke should stay here because he'll be the one they ask for ransom. The same for Uncle Bellard because we need his brain."

"And you, as well," Con told him. "To keep us all straight."

Desmond sighed, casting a glance at the duke, who was pale and shaken. "Yes. I'm afraid I must stay. Con, can you follow the kidnappers?"

"I intend to. That wagon Megan described will make it easier."

"I'll go with you." Megan stood up.

"What?" Con whirled on her. "No. Absolutely not."

"Are you saying that I'm not capable?" Megan's chin thrust out. "That I'm too delicate?"

"I'm saying that Theo will have my head if I drag you around the city when you're bloody, bruised and concussed."

"That's — it's —"

"It's smart," Lilah said, rising to her feet. "Megan, you have been through enough today to fell anyone. You're sore. You're tired. You would slow Constantine down. Think of all the time and effort that would be wasted if you should lose consciousness again and he had to bring you back."

Megan regarded her stonily for a moment. "Oh, hell . . ." She sank back down on the couch.

"Anna, too," Lilah went on before Anna could speak. "You both need to recover."

"Exactly." Con turned toward the door.

"That's why *I* am going to accompany you," Lilah continued.

Con stopped abruptly. "No."

"Why not? I trust you're not going to say because I'm a woman."

Megan snorted with laughter. "Yes, Con, why not? I think she should. Don't you, Anna?"

"Yes, indeed."

"After all —" Lilah plowed ahead "— as you said, I am logical, rational and *right*. It will be an excellent counterpoint to your qualities."

Con glowered. "Blast it, Lilah, you'll slow me down. What if we catch up with them? What if there's a fight?"

"Then you'll have someone to help you. I kept up with you when we went looking for Alex, didn't I?"

"Yes, but . . . what about your aunt? Won't she wonder what's happened to you?"

"I can send my maid back to tell her I've been invited to stay for tea."

"I'll send her a note extending our invitation to you for dinner and the evening," Anna offered. "Or, even better, Megan can. A marchioness is much more impressive."

"There, you see? Think of the advantages if I go with you." Lilah continued her list of reasons. "You'll have another person to look for them, to question people. And —" Her face lit triumphantly. "If you find your mother and sisters and need reinforcements, you'll have someone who can go for help while you keep watch to make sure they don't escape."

"Oh, for . . ." Con looked at Desmond.

"I agree." Desmond shrugged. "It's better if you have two people."

"The devil." Con looked back at Lilah. "Very well. You're coming with me."

CHAPTER FIVE

It was a mistake to take her. Con knew it as soon as he said it. Lilah Holcutt never made anything easier. She would fuss; she would question; she would need looking after. But there was no way out of it now. Strangely, deep down it didn't really bother him.

Con sent a footman to have one of their vehicles brought round, then walked over to Anna. Squatting down beside her, he said, "I need you to tell me everything you remember about your vision."

Anna nodded. "I had a headache, so I was lying down. I dozed off, I think, because suddenly I woke up with a jolt. And I saw your mother and the others."

"You saw them being taken?" He was a little surprised to see Lilah sit down beside Anna and take her hand.

Anna shook her head. "No. I didn't realize that before. It wasn't in London. It was in the country. There were no other houses around, but there were trees. I saw Thisbe and Olivia being pulled out of — of something. It was rather dark inside the vehicle."

"A carriage?"

"I'm not sure. It was enclosed, but it opened in the back. It had a set of two doors, and they opened outward." She demonstrated. "Two men were carrying the duchess and Kyria. They were very still. I wasn't sure if they were asleep or —" Her voice caught.

"I'm sure they're fine," Con said soothingly. "Kyria was chloroformed. Probably Mother was, as well. The men want money for them. They wouldn't risk killing them."

She nodded. "Yes, you're right. There was a third man, who had a gun aimed at Thisbe and Olivia. They were all walking somewhere."

"Where? Could you see where they were?"

Anna shook her head. "There was a house, and I assume they were going there, but the vision ended before I could see them enter it."

"What did it look like?"

"Two floors tall, but not a big house. Very plain. It was stone — a beige sort of color — or maybe just aged and dirty white stone. There was an outbuilding, a shed or small barn, off to one side. There was ivy growing up one wall. It — I had the impression nobody lived in the house."

"Why?"

Anna shrugged. "I'm not sure. I . . . It looked untended. The smaller building was very weathered and leaned to one side. There wasn't any garden. The ground was dirt and weeds and such." She closed her eyes for a moment. "Oh! And there was a shutter half-off one of the downstairs windows."

"Did you have any idea what part of the country it was in?"

"No. I'm sorry. I'm afraid this isn't very helpful."

"It is. Every scrap of information will help me. Was there anything more you saw? You said there were trees."

"Yes, but not right next to the house. There was, um, a very large tree about twenty or thirty feet away. But in the distance I could see thicker trees. Like woods." She paused, thinking. "Oh! Right next to the vehicle was a large stump, as if a big tree had been cut down in the past."

"Good. That's terrific, a great help."

"I wish I could be of more use."

"Don't worry. This is good. I'll be able to recognize the house."

Con stood up and turned to Lilah, who had been watching their exchange with a baffled expression. No doubt she had decided both he and Anna belonged in an asylum. But to his surprise, Lilah said not a word.

Outside, the family's elegant small town carriage awaited them. The coachman stood at the horses' head, and he came toward Con now, saying, "They're in fine fettle, sir. They'll be wanting to move."

"Don't worry, Jenkins, I assure you I'll take care of the team."

"I've no doubt of that, sir." The man smiled.

"*You're* going to drive the carriage?" Lilah asked, staring.

"Yes." His smile held a little challenge. "Perhaps you'd like to ride inside. Or you could —"

"I am *not* staying here," Lilah replied crisply and went to the front of the carriage. "If you'd give me a hand up . . ."

Con simply took her by the waist and lifted her to the first step. Lilah grabbed the handhold and shot a dark look at him over her shoulder.

"The first step is rather high," he pointed out.

"Yes, and I am rather tall." Gripping the

bar, she lifted her skirt with the other hand and climbed up to the coachman's seat.

Con caught a glimpse of her stockings once again — an eye-searing yellow this time — and suppressed a smile as he scrambled up after her. The high seat was comfortable but, being built for one driver, it was not especially wide. Con could feel Lilah's arm against his jacket, the side of her leg touching his.

That was not a thing to be thinking of at a time like this. Taking the reins, Con started forward.

"Why are *you* driving the carriage?"

"Easier for me to follow that way." He shrugged. "I have a better view, and I don't have to yell to the coachman if I want to get down to look at something."

"Then why the carriage? Wouldn't a smaller vehicle be easier to handle?"

"I thought of taking my grandfather's old phaeton, actually. It'd be more maneuverable, lighter. But it's been some years since it's been driven — Father couldn't quite bring himself to get rid of it, but no one uses it anymore. It's too easy to grab a hansom or a seat on the omnibus."

"You travel by omnibus?"

"Sometimes." He grinned at the astonishment on her face. "Too plebian, you think?"

69

"No. It just surprises me."

"It's more convenient in certain parts of town. More in character sometimes."

"Such as when you're dressed as a quack medicine salesman?" A smile tugged at the corners of her mouth.

"Careful, you might actually grin."

The blue eyes narrowed, and she snapped her head around to look forward again. Con felt a pang of regret. After a moment, he picked back up their earlier topic of conversation in a conciliatory tone. "The carriage is more useful, too. We'll need to bring my mother and sisters back."

She cast a quick sideways glance up at him. He suspected the words *if we find them* were on the tip of Lilah's tongue, but she said nothing. They had reached the site of the abduction, and Con turned onto the street the kidnappers took. At the end of the block, he turned left and joined the jumble of traffic.

"Back there, at the house, how did Desmond know what to do? Who should go to the Dearborns and who should go to Alex's prison and so on. Nobody objected or discussed it."

"We know each other well. Rafe is the most intimidating. He's not as large as Theo, but his eyes can get this look that

70

chills one's blood. Having lived through a bloody war, then making a fortune in the Wild West, he has little regard for the niceties of gentlemanly behavior. Especially when Kyria's in danger. That's why he would be better able to get information from the Dearborns. Stephen is his friend — they were partners in a silver mine after the American Civil War. They understand and trust each other. Stephen will make sure Rafe doesn't get into trouble. Theo and Reed balance each other, as well. Reed's the levelheaded one. Theo's more one for action."

"Then I really do serve as your counterbalance." She shot him a sideways glance, and this time her smile won the battle.

Surprisingly, Con found he enjoyed having her along. Granted, Lilah questioned everything, but so far she had not been stuffy, and her conversation kept his mind off the worry gnawing inside him.

"Why were you chosen to follow the kidnappers?" Lilah asked.

"I'm better at that sort of thing. I can tell north from south. I've always been good at maps, and I'm familiar with the streets of London and the roads out of it. I've had experience, you see. That's what my agency does — locate lost or stolen objects, missing people. Alex often makes that easier, of course, with his ability. But I'm the one who tracks down the leads and decides where to go."

"I thought you investigated nonsensical things — ghosts and demons and whatnot."

"Mmm. I'm especially fond of whatnots." His words brought forth a laugh from her. "Sadly, though, there aren't that many supernatural possibilities to investigate. So I'm forced to fall back on something useful and mundane."

As they talked, Con had been weaving in and out of the heavy traffic, bypassing slower vehicles, but he also kept his eyes in motion, looking everywhere.

"What are we looking for?" Lilah asked.

"Any sign that a speeding vehicle might have gone this way."

"Which would be?"

"I'm not sure, really."

"That's certainly informative."

"I'm sorry. It's hard to describe — you can see from the way people act, the way things look, if there's been a disturbance. For instance, an angry seller whose cart has been overturned by a speeding vehicle. Or people talking excitedly. I don't imagine I'll find any, as it's been a good while since they passed by. But I'm hoping my sisters will help me out."

"What do you mean? They're captives. What could they do?"

"They're resourceful. I think they'll try to draw people's attention one way or another. Leave us a sign, perhaps."

"But how can you be certain you're on the right road? What if they've turned off?"

"I'm not certain. It's my best guess. There's no reason for them to twist and turn, trying to evade pursuers. No one was following them. They'd want to get to their target the fastest way possible, where they can secrete the women and get rid of or hide the vehicle. This is a major thoroughfare with a lot of vehicles. The more people, the more carriages and wagons, the less likely it is that anyone will notice or remember a certain one, even if it is uncommon. Also, eventually this street turns into the road to Tunbridge Wells. From what Anna said, the house they're using is in a rural area."

"Really, Constantine, don't tell me you believe in visions foretelling the future."

"Actually, in this case, it's more the present than the future." He glanced at her. "Why wouldn't I believe it? Anna's no liar. She wouldn't mislead us, especially about something important."

"I'm sure she isn't lying or trying to

mislead you. But it's far more likely that Anna dreamed it. She had a headache, lay down and fell asleep, and she had a nightmare. Dreams seem very real sometimes."

Con thought of a room with curving walls and clocks. "I know. But whether it came while she was asleep or awake, she saw that they were abducted. We know that was true. So it seems silly to ignore the rest of her vision."

"But how could anyone 'see' something happening miles away?"

"I've witnessed stranger —"

"Con!" Lilah grabbed his arm.

"What?" A little jolt ran through him. "What's the matter?" He glanced around.

"Stop. Stop. Look." Lilah pointed to a woman walking down the street. "That's Olivia's."

"What?" Con pulled back on the reins.

"That woman is wearing Olivia's scarf!"

CHAPTER SIX

Not waiting for him, Lilah scrambled down from the high seat on the other side, setting her foot on the front wheel, then jumping to the ground. She hurried after the woman, and a moment later, Con caught up with her. "Are you certain?"

She gave him an impatient glance. "Olivia was wearing it the other day. I remember because I particularly liked it. Besides, look at that woman. Does she look like that scarf belongs to her?"

The woman's clothes were worn and drab, her straw hat battered, but around her neck was draped a lovely red silk scarf.

"Ma'am." Con broke into a trot. "Wait. Just a moment."

The woman looked back over her shoulder and, seeing them, whirled around to run. She hadn't gone three steps before Con pulled her to a stop.

"I din't do nuffink. I din't steal it. It's mine."

"Calm down. I'm not accusing you of anything."

She tried to tug her arm from his grasp, clearly not believing him.

"Con, you're scaring her." Lilah laid a soothing hand on the woman's shoulder. "We aren't going to hurt you. All we want is information."

"Yes, sorry." Con eased his hold, though he did not release her. "I'm not trying to take your scarf from you. You can keep it. Just tell me where you got it."

"I din't steal it."

"I believe you. You found it, didn't you?"

" 'Twas just lying there. It din't belong to nobody."

"Where was it lying? Can you show me where you found it?"

She pointed back up the street. "Down there. It caught on the lamppost, see."

"Excellent." Con beamed and reached into his pocket for a coin. "Here's something for your information."

"Gor!" Her eyes widened as she snatched the coin from his hand. "Thankee, sir."

"Now, tell me, did you see where the scarf came from? You said it caught on the lamppost. Did you see it land there?"

No longer reluctant, she started to answer, then sighed and admitted, "No. It was just there at the bottom of the post. Nell went for it, but I got there first. An' we had a bit of scrap about it, an' I won. I saw it 'fore she did."

"How long ago was that? Since you found the scarf."

"Oh. Well . . ." She wrinkled her forehead in thought. "A while. I went in to get a little tipple, you see, 'cause of my luck. And then, um, I went down to Annie's to show her. A while."

"Thank you. You've been very helpful." Con smiled and swept her an elegant bow, which made the woman giggle and bob a curtsy back to him. Obviously Con was an expert at charming any woman.

It took only a few minutes of questioning the shopkeepers along the street before Con found one who remembered the black vehicle.

"Oh, aye, I saw it. Ugly thing, don't know why you'd want to paint your wagon black like that. Better something cheerful, I say. And why not a sign on it?"

"Did you hear anything?"

He looked puzzled. "It made a racket on the cobblestones, if that's what you mean. So loud I couldn't hear my customer. That's why I noticed it."

"How long ago was it?"

"Oh, some time now. An hour or two. Wait, I remember, it was just 'fore I ate. Around noon."

Con's eyes gleamed as he took Lilah's arm, propelling her back to the carriage. She could almost feel the renewed energy and hope surging in him.

"I knew it!" he said as they started forward again. "I knew they would find a way to help me."

"They'll have to divest themselves of a lot of garments to leave a good trail."

"There are four of them after all." He tossed a grin at her.

"It was very smart to do that."

"The family's had some experience," he said drily.

They kept a sharp eye on the street, hoping for another sign from the Moreland women. Every time they spied a possibility, Con would jump down to investigate, but none of the objects turned out to be anything belonging to Con's sisters. The problem was that any piece of clothing dropped on the street was likely to be picked up before Lilah and Con could find it. And how long could the ladies keep tossing out clues before one of their captors caught them?

The traffic and houses thinned out, which at least made it more likely that a discarded item might not be picked up immediately. Con spotted the next item, a crumpled straw bonnet that he thought might belong to Thisbe. "It's plain as she likes them."

Con fretted about the time as they continued at their slow pace. The sun had been growing steadily lower. Lilah decided it was best not to ask what they would do after darkness fell. Next they found a woman's jacket.

Lilah held it up, studying it. "It's very stylish."

"Kyria's then."

After a time, they came upon a handkerchief caught in a hedge. "Definitely Kyria's." Con spread it out on his knee. "See the monogram?"

Heartened by their finds, they pressed onward, passing fewer and fewer travelers. Whenever they came upon a slow cart or carriage, Con stopped to ask if the driver had seen the wagon they sought. One farm boy, walking placidly beside his ox-drawn cart, nodded, saying it had passed him not long out of the city.

"We're falling farther and farther behind," Con said grimly. "But I don't dare go faster or we might miss one of their clues."

After a while, Con stirred restlessly, looking around. "I'm not sure . . ."

"What is it?" Lilah half turned, putting
her hand on his arm.

Con glanced at her, startled, and Lilah
quickly withdrew her hand. "I think we may
be going wrong." He twisted around to look
behind him. "It's been a while since we've
found anything." He pulled to a stop. "We
crossed a road back there."

"You think we should have taken it?"

"I don't know. But at some point, they're
going to turn off. I doubt that cottage is on
the main road. And . . . this feels wrong."

He turned the carriage, a cumbersome
process, and headed back. When they
reached the intersection, he turned left
down the smaller road.

"Couldn't they have turned the other
way?"

"Yes. *If* they turned at all. I'll try the other
way next if — look." A white petticoat lay in
the muddy ditch. "They threw it out as soon
as they turned. Clever girls."

"We're gathering quite a collection."

"We're getting closer, I think, but it's taking too long." He cast a look at the gathering twilight around them and increased the
pace.

Lilah spotted a white handkerchief at the

juncture of a smaller lane. "Do you think she meant to stay on this road or turn?"

"It's ambiguous," Con agreed. "She could have tossed it out from either direction and it floated back here. I'm going to take the turn. Megan said the windows were high. I don't think they could see the road. They wouldn't know that the road turned off until they felt the wagon do so."

The overhang of trees turned the dusk into night. Lilah leaned forward, peering intently ahead. The carriage jarred as it passed over a rut, and she braced herself with a hand on Con's leg. Embarrassed, she straightened up quickly, glancing at Con. But he appeared not to even notice the inappropriately familiar touch as he stared, eyes narrowed, at a hedge-lined path.

"I think . . . I'm going to try this lane."

"It's more a track than a lane. Why do you think this is the way to go? Did you see something?"

"Not really. It's very nearly dark."

Very nearly? Lilah could barely even make out that there was a path. It was even darker along the lane, with the high encroaching hedges on either side. "Why do you think it's this way?"

"I'm not sure. This nearly hidden path made me think about what Anna said about it being secluded."

There was no point in getting into another discussion about the unreliability of Anna's "vision," so Lilah kept silent. It was fully night now; the moon was rising. Fortunately it was a full moon. The hedges ended, and the lane curved around a tree. Lilah could make out a dark shape ahead of them.

The night was hushed, the only sound the plodding of the horses' hooves and the carriage wheels turning, and even that was muffled by the dirt surface of the path. Neither Lilah nor Con spoke. The dark shape ahead resolved itself into a two-story cottage, a simple building of light-colored stone.

Lilah drew in her breath sharply, unconsciously grabbing Con's arm. A shutter hung askew beside a window, and a large tree stood not far from the house. In the other direction, Lilah could make out a small structure of some sort. Con looked at Lilah, then pointed to a large tree stump a few feet ahead of them.

It was exactly as Anna had described. A shiver ran through Lilah.

If they needed further proof, a dark wagon stood near the stump, with a pair of tethered horses grazing nearby. Con climbed down and took his horses by the head, walking them around so that the carriage faced the opposite direction.

As Lilah joined him, he murmured in explanation, "In case we need to make a quick escape."

"Then you plan to confront them?" she whispered back.

"There were only three men."

"And only one you," she retorted. "That's if they don't have accomplices who've joined them."

Con tilted his head, considering. "Still, I have the advantage of surprise, and my mother and sisters will help." His grin gleamed in the darkness. "You should see my mother brandish a cricket bat."

He reached up to pull the long carriage whip from its holder. "Unwieldy." He unscrewed the handle from the long supple stick and leather lash, leaving him with a sturdy truncheon capped by an ornamental brass knob. He turned to her. "Stay here. If things go wrong, run. They won't expect anyone else to be here."

"I'm going with you."

"What?" His eyebrows flew up. "You said you'd go for help if needed."

"No. I said I *could* go for help."

"Blast it!" he hissed. "You'll get in my way. I'll have to worry about protecting you.

Stay. Here."

"You said your mother and sisters would be a help to you." Lilah grabbed the longer, narrow end of the whip that ended in a leather lash, and faced him defiantly. "Are you going to tell me I am less capable than they?"

"Not when you've got that whip in your hand." Con started for the house. Lilah followed, her heart pounding. She stumbled over a root, nearly falling. Con swung around, and Lilah braced for a caustic remark, but to her surprise, he took her hand and leaned in to whisper, "Stay with me. I have good night vision."

"Of course you do," she replied waspishly, resenting the way the touch of his breath on her ear sent a shiver through her. This was no time to be thinking about things like that — or feeling that tremble of heat deep inside her.

Holding the front of her skirt off the ground with one hand, she went with him, surprised at how natural it was, how easy, to walk with him, shoulders almost touching, his fingers laced through hers. It made her feel faintly breathless — the warmth of him, the touch of his skin on hers — but somehow it steadied her, as well. She couldn't count on him to be appropriate in a drawing room or ballroom, but here, in a situation like this, she trusted him completely.

They skirted the edges of the yard, staying close to the shadows of trees and shrubs. Their care was probably unnecessary, for the front rooms of the house looked dark, but Con was clearly taking no chances. He edged up to the front window. "Nothing."

They slipped around the side. Light spilled from a window in a rear room. Con flattened himself against the wall and inched over, turning his head to peek inside. Pulling back, he whispered, "Two men at the kitchen table, playing dice."

"What's your plan?" she whispered back.

"Open the door and knock them in the head."

Before Lilah could point out that this was not much of a plan, he crouched down beneath the window and moved to the door. Lilah did her best to imitate him. It would be far easier if she weren't wearing a corset. As she stood up, Con took hold of the doorknob and slowly, silently turned it. The handle moved freely. Con raised his cudgel, knob end up, and looked questioningly at Lilah.

She nodded and took a firm grip on her whip. She'd never hit anyone with a stick before, but she was sure she could do it. In fact, she was rather looking forward to it.

Before Con could move, there was an explosion inside the house. Letting out an oath, Con flung open the door and charged inside.

CHAPTER SEVEN

In the kitchen, the two men jumped to their feet, turning toward the door. Several more bangs and crashes rang out upstairs as Con ran at the larger one of the men, swinging his whip handle like a club. The other man pulled a mug from the table and drew back to hurl it at Con, but Lilah swung the whip, cracking him smartly across the wrist. The mug fell to the ground, spilling ale over the floor. With a growl, he came at Lilah.

Lilah lashed the whip again, slashing across his torso, but the man grabbed the end of the stick and yanked it from her hand. Lilah jumped to the side as he slammed the stick down, hitting nothing but air. She darted away, grabbing a tin container from the counter as she ran, and whirled to throw the metal box at her pursuer.

He was quick enough to block the container with his arm, but the force of the blow popped off the lid, and flour exploded all over him. Coughing and cursing, he pawed at his eyes. Out of the corner of her eye, she could see Con exchanging punches with the other thug. No help there. She must do something herself.

Frantically she glanced around and saw a broom. Picking it up, she ran forward, wielding the long wooden handle like a knight with a lance, and rammed the end into the gut of her temporarily blinded opponent. He let out a *whoof,* clutching his stomach, and Lilah charged in, reversing the broom and hacking away at his head.

She was prepared for it this time when he tried to pull her weapon away, and she hung on as hard and long as she could. As she saw his muscles bunch to yank even harder, she released her hold, so that his momentum sent him staggering backward.

Lilah whirled, looking for a new weapon, and she smiled grimly when her eyes landed on a large iron skillet. But as she swung back to face her enemy, skillet upraised, she saw that Con, who had dispatched his foe, was running across the room at them. He slammed his truncheon down on the ruffian's head, and the man's eyes rolled up. He dropped to the floor.

"Con!" Lilah ran to him, flushed with

triumph, and Con, laughing, swooped her up and twirled her around. When he set her down, they remained that way for a long moment, Con's hands still at her waist, only inches between them. His eyes went to her mouth. Lilah's heart began to pound.

Just then, a man's scream pierced the air. Lilah and Con whipped around to see a man rolling down the hall staircase. He landed in a tangled heap at the bottom. His head and shoulders, Lilah noticed, were strangely wet. A moment later, the duchess trotted down after him, carrying a broken earthenware pitcher in one hand.

"Hello, Mother."

Emmeline Moreland glanced over and smiled. "Why, Con," she said, as if she were in a parlor instead of stepping over a body on the floor. "Dear boy. And Miss Holcutt. What a nice surprise." She kissed Con's cheek.

"Yes, you arrived just in time, Con," Kyria agreed as the duchess's daughters trooped down the stairs behind her. All of them carried makeshift weapons. Kyria studied the first man Con had dispatched. "Though I was looking forward to bashing that fellow in the head."

"You can have a go at him now, if you'd like," Con told her cheerfully.

"That hardly seems sporting."

Con hugged each of his sisters as they gathered in the kitchen, putting away their makeshift weapons. The Morelands, Lilah had noticed over the course of the past few weeks, were very prone to embracing one another. It had startled her at first, but Lilah was becoming accustomed to it now, and she was unsurprised when the women went on to hug her, too.

Thisbe patted Con on the cheek. "I knew you would find us, even though our trail must have been cold."

"We followed your bread crumbs."

"That was Olivia's idea," Thisbe said.

"A very good one." He embraced Olivia last, pulling the small woman up off her feet.

"I was afraid they would get blown away or trampled, but it was the best I could think of."

"You seem to have managed well on your own." Con cast a glance at the man who had fallen down the stairs. "I feel quite unnecessary."

"Oh, you'll be very useful," Olivia tossed back. "We need to tie up these men."

"Yes, starting with this one." Con pointed to the man he had fought, who had let out a groan and was now shifting restlessly. Con unfastened his cravat and squatted down to turn the man over and tie his hands behind his back. "What about him?" Con pointed to the ruffian who had come tumbling down the stairs. "Did you kill him?"

"Oh, no, he's breathing," Thisbe offered. "Mother just cracked him in the head with the washbasin pitcher."

"This is all of them?"

Thisbe explained, "No, there was another one who was here when we arrived, but he escaped out the window and down the drainpipe."

"How is Meg?" the duchess asked. "We weren't sure what happened to her."

"She's probably going to have a black eye, and she was unconscious for a while — she hit her head on the ground when the thug hit her. But she was able to tell us what happened."

They spent the next few minutes finding things with which to tie the men, who were beginning to awaken by the time they finished.

"What shall we do with them?" Kyria asked, using a glass-fronted cabinet as a mirror to repin the disarranged strands of her hair.

"I suspect your husbands would like to have a chat with them," Con said. "So we'd best load them into their van and take them back with us." He frowned. "Thing is, we have two vehicles. We could leave these chaps here while I drive you ladies home. Then Rafe and Stephen and I can come back to collect them later."

"Leave them here tied up all that time?" The duchess frowned. "That doesn't seem safe. What if something happened to them?"

"Mother, these chaps just abducted you and held you prisoner."

"Obviously, they are criminals, but the goal should be to reform, not just —"

"More important," Olivia put in before the duchess could gain steam, "they might manage to escape if we leave them alone here together."

"But if I take *them* back, you ladies will have to remain here," Con pointed out.

"Con, really, do you think I cannot drive a wagon?" Emmeline asked. "You know I was a country squire's daughter. I learned to drive all the wagons and carts on the farm."

Lilah doubted that driving wagons was part of the education of most country squires' daughters, but it was little surprise that the duchess had done so.

"You take the girls home in the carriage, and I'll follow you in the wagon," the duchess decreed.

"Very well, if you will agree to take some-one with you, just in case," Con countered, clearly accustomed to bargaining with his mother. "You have just been through an ordeal."

Con's mother gave him an indulgent smile. "Miss Holcutt can ride with me. She can take the reins if I grow too feeble, since she was not abducted."

"Though riding around with Con doubt-less qualifies as an ordeal," Kyria stuck in with a grin at her younger brother.

"Thank you, I would be happy to," Lilah told the duchess. It would be better not to spend the ride back to London with Con again. At least she wouldn't be lying when she told Aunt Helena that she spent the evening with the duchess.

"There. All settled. Let's get these fellows into the wagon and go home. I haven't eaten since breakfast, and I'm beginning to feel a mite peckish."

Con had bound the men's hands behind their backs and hobbled their feet, so they were able to march the still-dazed men out and load them into the wagon with only a little struggle. The duchess and Lilah climbed up onto the driver's seat, which was much higher but far less comfortable than the one on the carriage, and set off.

To Lilah's amazement, the duchess seemed cheerful, even invigorated. "Con's job is actually harder," she told Lilah, handling the reins with expertise. "Carriage horses are more mettlesome and easily spooked than these work horses. Though the carriage *is* better sprung," she added as they jounced over the rough dirt lane. "Would you like to learn? I could teach you when we get on a better road."

Lilah blinked. "I hadn't thought of it. But yes, I believe I would."

Her gloves, of course, were the wrong sort for the task, and she wasn't sure how she would explain the wear and smudges on them to her aunt, but Lilah thoroughly enjoyed the lesson. The duchess was a clear and patient teacher, if somewhat inclined to inattention, and the horses were as amiable and plodding as Emmeline had suggested, giving Lilah time to correct any mistake she made.

Her shoulders and arms began to ache after a while, and once again she found her stiff corset a nuisance, but she kept doggedly at it. The thought of Con's reaction to her newly minted driving skills was enough to keep her going.

The duchess took back the reins when traffic grew thicker as they neared London.

Lilah was astonished at how little time it had taken to drive the route, which had appeared so endless earlier.

A footman on the front stoop at Broughton House ran back inside as soon as he caught sight of them. By the time the duchess pulled up, welcoming relatives and servants had spilled out onto the street. They were swept inside in a hubbub of questions, embraces and laughter. After the initial greeting, most of the men went outside to deal with the kidnappers, while the women split up to go upstairs and change out of their grimy clothes.

Con turned to Lilah. "I told Jenkins to keep the carriage out front. I thought you would want to get home as soon as possible."

"Oh. Of course. It is terribly late."

Con was right. Aunt Helena was doubtless upset about Lilah's spending the day here in such an unplanned, casual way; arriving home later in the evening would be worse. Nor was there any reason to remain. Lilah had done all she could. And yet . . . Lilah felt disappointed at the way Con was rushing her out. Perhaps he thought she had no place here, that she had pushed her way into what was purely family business — which, of course, she had.

A faint flush rose in Lilah's cheeks. She had acted in an unaccustomedly inappropriate way. Awkwardly, she went on, "I shall take my leave. Please give my regards to your family. I'm very happy they are home safe." She started toward the door, glancing over at Con in surprise when he stayed by her side. "There's no need to escort me to the carriage."

"There is if I intend to get in it, too." He arched an eyebrow at her.

"You needn't see me home, Con — I mean, Lord Moreland."

"Really, *Miss Holcutt,* don't you think that after brawling together, we are well enough acquainted for you to call me by my given name?"

"Very well. Con." He was making jest of her, as he always did, and yet the sparkle in his eyes, the curve of his lips, made her want to smile back. Made her want to do things that were better left unmentioned. Being with Con was always so unsettling.

He paused, gazing at her significantly, and after a moment, he nudged, "And may I call you Lilah?"

"Oh. Yes." Her name sounded different when he said it, so silky smooth and rich. Whatever was the matter with her? She added tartly, "I am sure you have already."

"It's quite possible. You know how things are in the heat of the moment." His face was perfectly bland, making her uncertain whether he had meant to convey the double entendre. He went on smoothly, "And you are wrong. I do need to see you home. However unmannerly you think me, I am not ill enough behaved to send a lady off alone at night."

"I never said you were unmannerly," she protested as he handed her up into the vehicle, then swung in to sit down beside her.

"Did you not?" There was that "Con look" again, so inscrutable, yet somehow conveying laughter bubbling just beneath the surface. Lilah pressed her lips together. "Perhaps I might have. Sometime when you were being particularly outlandish. But I — it was said —"

"In the heat of the moment?"

She sent him a dagger glance. "Could you please, for just a few minutes, stop being so provoking?"

He chuckled. "I think I can." He leaned forward and took her hand. "I have to tell you how impressive you were this evening."

"I was?"

"Indeed. When I saw you whacking that

fellow with a broom, my heart swelled with pride."

"Hush." But she couldn't hold back a smile. "You're talking nonsense."

"You were a veritable Valkyrie. An Amazon. A warrior goddess come to life." His face turned serious. "You were a great deal of help today, and I apologize for ever thinking you would be a hindrance."

"Constantine . . ." It was foolish to feel so warmed by his words.

He leaned closer. "Tell me, Miss Holcutt, would you slap me this time if I kissed you?"

Lilah's heart skipped a beat. She should pull away from him. Toss back a sharp setdown for his boldness. But what came from her mouth was only a whispered "No, I wouldn't slap you."

He bent his head, and she closed her eyes, as if she could hide what she was doing from herself. Con's lips brushed over hers gently . . . once, twice. She felt his smile against her lips, then his mouth settled onto hers, his arms gliding around her, pulling her to him.

His kiss was slow and easy and thorough, his tongue stealing into her mouth and setting off a firestorm of pleasurable sensations. It was overwhelming, his kiss as dizzying as the champagne she'd drunk. Lilah was flooded with hunger. Urges she'd never imagined roiled inside her. She had no idea what to do, but she wanted to feel more, have more.

Lilah wasn't aware when she had put her hands on his arms, but now she dug her fingers into the cloth, holding on. It seemed like forever, yet it was over all too fast. Con raised his head and stared down at her, his expression caught somewhere between amazement and dismay.

Then his arms tightened around her, crushing her into him, and he pulled her into his lap. This time his kiss wasn't easy, wasn't gentle, but shockingly, Lilah welcomed it. She wrapped her arms around his neck and her lips answered his with abandon. Lilah's heart slammed in her chest, and her very blood seemed on fire. She felt reckless and wild, utterly unlike herself, and it was glorious.

Con's mouth left hers to kiss her cheek, her jaw, her throat. She shivered at the delicate touch on her sensitive skin. Someone moaned softly, and Lilah realized with a start that the sound had come from her. Con kissed his way downward, reaching the hollow of her throat. His tongue teased around the pearl drop there, tracing a circle. Her abdomen flooded with heat.

Her hands went to his shoulders —
whether to hold him off or hold on to him,
she wasn't sure. Right now Lilah wasn't sure
of anything . . . except the warmth of his
mouth, the velvet softness of his lips, the
touch of his hands upon her face. All she
knew was that she wanted this to go on and
on.

Too soon, Con pulled back, his eyes glittering in the dark, his breath uneven. For a
long moment, he simply looked at her. His
hands fell away. Clearing his throat, he said,
"We're here."

It was only then that Lilah realized the
carriage had stopped in front of her aunt's
house. How had they gotten here so quickly?
She heard the coachman climbing down
from his seat, and she hastily scrambled out
of Con's lap. Seconds later their driver
opened the door.

Lilah bolted out, keeping her head down,
afraid of what the servant might see in her
face. As Con started to follow her, she
turned, holding out her hand as if to ward
him off. "No, don't get out. I — well —
good night."

She hurried to the door and slipped
inside, her legs trembling beneath her. She
was careful not to look back.

CHAPTER EIGHT

By the time Con returned to the house, the wagon was gone, and he found his family seated around the dining table, polishing off the remains of the hasty meal Smeggars had brought in.

"Ah, there's the man of the hour," Theo said, smiling.

"Hardly. The ladies had already escaped on their own. All I did was drive them home."

"A good bit more than that," Thisbe protested. "You took care of the men downstairs. It would have been far different if we had had to overcome them, as well."

"I had a great deal of help from Lilah — um, Miss Holcutt." Con turned away, picking up a plate and beginning to fill it with food from the sideboard. "She went after one of them with the carriage whip, then a broom. Tossed a tin full of flour at him, as well."

"I *wondered* why he was covered in white powder," Olivia said, laughing.

"I was surprised to see her there," Thisbe said.

"She happened to be here at the time." Con kept his gaze on the dishes of food. "It was nothing, really."

"What was nothing? I thought you just said she was very helpful."

"She was. I didn't mean what she did was nothing." He toyed with the roll on his plate, then added another. "I meant her being here wasn't unusual. She came to see Olivia. Had a book for her."

"Did she?" Olivia's face lit up. "How nice. She had offered to lend me a book, but it was just in passing. I'm surprised she remembered."

"Miss Holcutt remembers everything," Con said darkly, bringing his plate to the table and sitting down.

"Goodness, Con, do you mean to eat all of that?" Kyria asked.

"What? Oh . . ." Con gazed at his plate in some surprise. "Well, I am hungry."

"I am not at all amazed that Lilah joined in," the duchess said. "I quite like her. She's a very nice girl, just a bit stiff. I blame her upbringing."

"Why?" Con asked. "What's odd about

her upbringing?"

"Nothing," his mother replied. "That is the point. She had the same sort of insubstantial education combined with an indoctrination into foolish rules that all young ladies do. It's a pity that a bright girl such as Lilah was forced into such a constricted position."

"I believe she was raised by her aunt," Kyria added. "Mrs. Summersley seems a nice enough woman, just a bit staid."

The duchess pointed at her daughter with her raised fork. "Exactly. Perpetuating a helpless, brainless vision of womanhood."

Con snorted. "I wouldn't call Lilah helpless or brainless."

"Yes, I have hope for the girl," Emmeline agreed. "Perhaps I should invite her to come to the next suffragists' meeting."

"I don't think our experience with the suffragists today would encourage her to accompany you," Olivia remarked.

"It isn't as if there are *always* abductions at them," the duchess protested.

"One would hope not," Reed commented drily.

"What did you find out from the kidnappers?" Con asked, turning toward Stephen and Rafe.

"Pah!" Kyria's husband let out an exclamation of disgust. "Nothing of any importance. They were hired hands."

"Nor were they particularly bright," Theo put in. "They had no idea why they were paid to abduct the women. They swore they didn't even know who the ladies were."

"He couldn't even give us a description of the man who hired them," Stephen added. "Said it was all done by way of letter, brought by a messenger."

Con cocked an eyebrow. "Do you believe that?"

"Strangely enough, we did." Theo shrugged his shoulders. "He seemed sufficiently demoralized. I think Mother terrified him more than Rafe. She does wield a wicked pitcher." Theo's green eyes twinkled.

"Really, Theo, you know I abhor violence. But I could hardly stand by when someone threatened my children."

"What did the Dearborns say?" Con asked.

"They vehemently denied it," Rafe said.

"Even when Rafe threatened them with various sorts of bodily harm," Stephen put in.

"I'm less certain that I believe *them,*" Rafe put in. "They let us search their house after a big show of British affront, but that only proves they were careful enough to keep their distance from the crime."

"I can't think of anyone else with a grudge against us," Reed said. "At least, no one who isn't already in jail."

"The Dearborns are obviously desperate for money."

"That's the peculiar thing." Uncle Bellard spoke up. "We never received a note asking for a ransom."

"It is odd," the duke agreed.

"Perhaps they didn't get a chance to send it before the ladies got away."

"Maybe," Megan said doubtfully. "But what sort of criminal wouldn't have the note ready to go as soon as they grabbed their victims?"

"An incompetent one," her husband suggested. "Which these men certainly seemed to be."

"Maybe they wanted to make Father wait and worry, so he'd be ready to give them whatever they asked for," Reed suggested.

"But I would have done that at once," the duke replied.

"I don't think they were after money." Every head in the room turned toward Olivia at her words. "They interrogated Kyria. Twice. They were after information."

"Interrogated you?" Rafe stiffened, looking at his wife in alarm. "What did they do

105

to you?"

"Nothing, really," Kyria said calmly. "So you needn't get murder in your eye. They shouted a good deal, but they didn't physically harm me. They just kept asking about the blasted key."

"Key? What key?" Rafe asked.

"Exactly." Kyria gave a sharp nod. "I asked them that very thing, but they had no response except to ask me again in a louder voice."

"Why didn't they describe it or tell you what it was for?" Desmond asked, frowning in puzzlement.

"They just said that I knew which key they meant. The one my father gave me."

"*I* gave you?" The duke's voice rose in astonishment. "Why would I have given you a key? To what? How very odd."

"That was my thought," Kyria agreed.

"I don't know anything about any key," the duke went on. "Except for a Greek key, of course, but I wouldn't think they were interested in ancient motifs."

"Perhaps they meant the key to your collections room," Bellard suggested.

"What would a gang of ruffians want with Greek and Roman pots?"

"And why would they target Kyria?" Con added. "Why would she have the key to

Father's collections room?"

"Maybe they didn't specifically target Kyria. Maybe they were told to grab one of the women, and any of them would have done."

"Then why didn't they ask the rest of us about it after Kyria proved recalcitrant?" Thisbe pointed out. "That would be the logical thing to do."

"Maybe they meant to take Emmeline," the duke suggested. "And they grabbed the wrong redhead."

The duchess smiled at her husband. "Dear Henry. I think even those men would have noticed that Kyria was far too young to be me."

"One of them had the nerve to say I was too *old*!" Kyria said indignantly.

Her brothers laughed, and Con said, "I suppose that's the one you wanted to bash over the head."

"It is. I heard them arguing in the hall after the last time he questioned me. One of them said some rather uncomplimentary things about my stubbornness, and the other said he could make me talk. But then Ruffian One — the one Mother demoralized — said that no, they couldn't hurt me. I think he had realized how much trouble they were in. That's when Ruffian Two said

I was too old. And the first one told him he was daft, and they fell into arguing over which of them was more stupid."

"Which would, admittedly, be hard to determine," Theo put in.

"They ended it with Ruffian Two stomping off downstairs. He was really a most obnoxious man. He kept complaining because Thisbe cracked him over the head with a parasol. I ask you, what did he think we were going to do?"

"I am sorry I broke Sabrina's parasol, though," Thisbe said. "It was such a pretty thing."

"I should have taken Papa's umbrella instead," Kyria mused. "It's much sturdier. Next time I'll know better."

Con frowned. "Wait. Kyria was carrying Sabrina's parasol?"

"Yes, I picked it up as we left the house because I'd forgotten mine."

"It's a very distinctive parasol, isn't it?"

"Yes, it has a lovely painted scene."

"So it's the sort of thing one might use to identify someone. And he said you were 'too old.' I think they took the wrong person. Maybe they meant to kidnap Sabrina."

Lilah went to bed thinking about Con's kiss and woke up with it still on her mind. It

108

was disturbing, even more so because it had also been so exciting. Con had a way of confusing things.

She disapproved of him. He was rash. He had the most outlandish notions. He didn't care a whit how he appeared to others. Indeed, he seemed to delight in making a spectacle of himself. She thought of the exaggerated mustache and garish suit she had seen him wear the first time she visited Broughton House. As if that weren't peculiar enough, he had been consorting with people who were certain the world was going to end that week.

What did it matter that he was handsome and witty or that his smile did the most peculiar things to her insides? It didn't make him any more normal or acceptable or dependable. He was, in short, *odd*. Just look at his name: Constantine. It was decidedly not British.

Con liked her no more than she did him. He considered her annoying and her beliefs antiquated. They could not be around each other for two minutes without finding something upon which to disagree.

Why had he kissed her? Why had he said he admired her? He had been teasing, she supposed, playing games with her. Yet he had seemed sincere. He had looked at her in a way that stole her breath.

Lilah was not a naive girl just making her debut. She knew better than to take compliments seriously — especially not the compliments of charming men like Constantine Moreland. She had done her best to learn all there was to know about Con, and she was well aware of his reputation as an inveterate flirt. He never pursued any particular young lady, dancing with this one, flirting with that one.

That was her answer, she supposed: Con had been flirting with her, and Lilah wasn't adept at flirting. She had taken him too seriously. Or else he had been testing her, seeing just how far he could push her sense of propriety. That was an irritating thought. Lowering, as well.

It would be better to just put him out of her mind. Especially since she had overslept and was in danger of being late to breakfast. It was always served promptly at eight o'clock. She rang for her maid and dressed quickly, doing her hair up in a simple knot. She stepped into the dining room at eight on the dot.

Uncle Horace looked up at her and smiled. "Ah, Delilah. Just in time."

"Good morning, Uncle. Aunt Helena." Her uncle was a good man, if somewhat

110

rigid about his schedule. He had taken on the raising of another's child, which could not have been an easy thing for a man who was accustomed to an orderly, childless life.

"Not much interesting in the newspaper today," Uncle Horace announced. It was his custom to read aloud to his wife and niece the stories he deemed suitable for the delicate ears of women, placidly unaware that after he left each morning, Lilah took the newspaper and read what she wanted. "I saw Sir Jasper at the club yesterday. I think he might drop in today."

Lilah maintained a polite expression, though inwardly she groaned. Her uncle proceeded to talk about this acquaintance and that. Aunt Helena related the elegance of Mrs. Baldwin's gown at the musicale the night before.

"Baldwin's a capital fellow," Uncle Horace stated. "Though I gather their youngest boy is a bit wild. Not the sort I would allow to court you of course." Uncle Horace patted Lilah's hand.

"No, naturally." Though Lilah had no desire to be courted by Terence Baldwin, finding him both a bore and a libertine, it scraped at her nerves whenever her uncle made such decisions for her. Lilah could just imagine what the duchess would say about Uncle Horace's pronouncement. She had to bring up her handkerchief to her mouth to hide a smile.

"Your aunt tells me you had dinner with the Duke and Duchess of Broughton last night."

"Lady Anna was kind enough to invite me to stay." Lilah avoided a direct lie.

"You really should not have, dear," Aunt Helena said, frowning. "Of course I could hardly refuse permission when Lady Moreland asked it, especially since she said it would please the duchess. But it's not the way things should be done."

Lilah felt another flash of annoyance. She was over twenty-one now; she scarcely needed her aunt's permission to do something.

"One would think a duchess would better understand the rules of polite behavior," Aunt Helena went on. "But then, of course, her family was only country gentry. Everyone was surprised when Broughton married her."

But she knew how to drive a wagon, Lilah thought, which had been more useful last night than needlepoint. Immediately she felt a twinge of guilt at even thinking something disloyal to her aunt.

"Odd lot, the Morelands," Uncle Horace

commented. "No finer lineage in England of course, but still . . . no denying they're peculiar." He then turned the conversation away from the Morelands, which was a relief to Lilah.

However, later, when Lilah and her aunt had settled down in the morning room, as was their daily custom, Aunt Helena turned to her with a worried frown. "Delilah . . . I cannot but wonder if it was a mistake to let you spend so much time with the Morelands."

Lilah swallowed her irritation. "But surely you cannot object. Uncle Horace said they're one of the best families in England."

"Yes, but it's a double-edged sword to be connected with that family. It raises your status, of course, to be on familiar terms with a duchess, but you run the risk of their reputation coloring yours."

Lilah stiffened. "You speak as if they weren't received."

"Of course they're received. But he is a duke. One has to do a great deal to be a duke and have society snub you. It's quite different for a young lady such as yourself."

"I think my reputation is undisputed. The Holcutts are an old family, too."

"Yes, but one must always be careful to maintain your reputation. You in particular must be especially circumspect, given the behavior of your father's sister."

"That was years ago. Surely it's been forgotten."

"And you must not do anything to cause people to remember." Her aunt leaned forward and took her hand. "I understand, sweetheart, that it is hard to have that sword of Damocles hanging over you. But we have been so careful to ensure your pristine reputation. I would hate to see you abandon it on a whim."

"I have not abandoned it, I assure you." Lilah's cheeks flamed with color. "I have done nothing wrong."

"I know. But your actions yesterday! Going to call on them, then staying over for supper on the spur of the moment. Why, you had nothing but your walking dress to wear to dinner."

"The Morelands are much more casual about such things."

"That is my point. I fear they are a terrible influence on you. Your actions yesterday were impulsive and inappropriate. You showed a lack of respect for me, which you have never done before." Tears glittered in her eyes before she blinked them away. "I fear that your Holcutt blood may lead you astray."

Lilah's resentment was washed away in a flood of remorse. "I'm sorry. I never intended any disrespect to you. I wouldn't hurt you for the world. I'm well aware of all you've done for me."

"Dearest girl, I do not ask your gratitude. I did it because I loved my sister, and I love you. I couldn't allow your father to ruin your chances. All I want is for you to make a good marriage and live a pleasant life."

"I know. I want that, as well." Her aunt was right; that was the sensible thing to do. That *was* what she wanted, too. The Morelands were exciting, but their life was too chaotic for her. Lilah wasn't herself around them. And she wasn't about to let the Holcutt in her come out. "I shan't call on them again."

CHAPTER NINE

Con was not going to think about Lilah Holcutt today. Nor was he going to dwell on that kiss. It had been a foolish thing for him to do. He had gotten caught up in the moment — and, yes, Lilah had looked damned desirable charging into battle, cheeks flushed and eyes glittering, without a care for how she looked or what others might think.

But kissing her had been a mistake. He had carefully avoided her since the wedding, and he'd reached the point where he hardly thought of her. Then, in one moment, he had dropped all his barriers and let her in again.

However different Lilah might have seemed during the rescue of his family, however much her kisses stirred him, she would go back to being herself. Disapproving. Rigid. Cold. Just she had been yesterday when Con entered the room. As if that moment of closeness on the terrace after the wedding had never happened, Lilah had turned her usual cool, measuring gaze on him. She had refused to even sit down with him to chat. Whereas he had come running like a puppy at the sound of her voice. He hoped she had not noticed the way he had rushed into the room.

How could the woman who had turned into flames in his arms last night manage to be all ice the rest of the time? She was a puzzle, so of course she intrigued him. But this was one conundrum that he must resist. One lock that he should not open.

He had better things to do today. The new threat to Sabrina needed his immediate and undivided attention. After breakfast, he headed to Morcland Investigations, the agency he had taken over from Olivia a few years ago. There, as he'd hoped, he found Tom Quick, the agency's employee of many years.

Quick was whip smart, cool under pressure and able to follow almost anyone without being noticed. He was also a wizard at picking pockets, having spent his early years on the streets, but that was a practice he had given up since he came to work for the Morelands. Though only a few years older than Con and Alex, Tom had been their mentor in subjects that were far more interesting to them than Ancient Greek or Philosophy.

Tom was appropriately incensed by Con's story of the ladies' kidnapping and rescue, though he had some reservations. "A key? You think they kidnapped your mum and sisters for a key?"

"Yes. I know it's odd."

Tom snorted. "That's true of anything connected with you lot. But a key is a small thing to risk prison for, and a parasol seems a flimsy clue."

"Perhaps, but it's the only one I have at the moment. Since Sabrina and Alex are off on their honeymoon, we can't ask her about it. But she is the heiress to her father's substantial estate, and she's already had Niles Dearborn and his son trying to get their hands on her money."

"Then you think it's the Dearborns."

"We know they're cheats and liars." Con ticked his points off on his fingers. "We know they still have a great many financial woes. They will resort to any method to get their hands on money. *And* they have twice abducted people."

"You've convinced me. But do you have any proof?"

"No," Con admitted. "That's why I'm going to pay a visit to the Dearborns this morning. Care to come along?"

Tom's ready grin was answer enough.

The footman who opened the Dearborns' door blanched at the sight of Con on the doorstep, but he quickly ushered them into Niles Dearborn's study. As they followed the man down the hall, Tom murmured, "I'd say that fellow remembers you."

"Is he the one I shoved aside?"

"You mean the one you punched? Yes, I think so."

Niles Dearborn looked equally alarmed when Con strode in on his servant's heels. He shot to his feet, sending a glare at the hapless footman. "What are you doing here, Moreland? You can't just barge in here."

"Apparently I can," Con returned.

"I told that maniac you sent over here yesterday that I had nothing to do with his wife's disappearance."

"Leave my father alone." Niles's son, Peter, hurried into the room. "Why can't you leave us alone?"

"Because you came after my brother's wife again."

"McIntyre said nothing about Sabrina," Niles protested. "He said it was the duke's wife and daughters."

"Is Sabrina all right?" Peter asked. "What

119

happened to her?"

"Nothing, for which you should be very grateful. The ladies are back, and your men are in jail. You might worry what information they'll give up about you."

"We don't have any men!" Niles barked. "I have no idea what you're talking about."

"Why would we kidnap your family?" Peter said reasonably. "Or Sabrina?"

"The same reason most kidnappers do," Con answered. "Money. Or perhaps you just wanted a key."

Both men gaped at him. "The key?" Niles asked.

"Her key?" Peter said at the same moment. The two men exchanged a glance.

"I don't know what you're talking about," Niles blustered. "Why would I want some key?"

"I don't know." Con's eyes narrowed. "But I think you do."

"Nonsense. We had nothing to do with any kidnapping, and I'm not looking for a key. Now, I'll thank you to get out of my house."

"Gladly," Con responded. "But before I go, let me remind you what Alex told you last time. If you try to harm Sabrina or anyone in his family, he'll come after you. And he won't be alone. You understand? Stay away from my family."

As soon as they stepped outside, Tom said, "He knew what you were talking about. I'd swear it. When you mentioned the key, there was a flash of something in his eyes."

"Yes. Until then, I was beginning to wonder if he was telling the truth. But it's clear we won't get any more information out of them. He knows we have no proof."

"What are you going to do, then?"

"I'm going to call on someone who knows the Dearborns and Sabrina very well."

"Dear, don't you think you ought to change?" Aunt Helena asked.

Surprised, Lilah looked up from her book. "I thought you had decided not to make calls this afternoon." She had looked forward to an afternoon spent in quiet comfort, reading.

"That's no reason to lounge about looking like that. Why, I don't believe you're wearing a corset."

"No," Lilah admitted. She had put on the loose sacque dress because it didn't require stays. She was a little bruised and sore from the constriction of the stiff corset during all the activity yesterday. "But there is no one here to see."

"I wouldn't be so sure of that," Aunt Helena said with a twinkle. "Your uncle mentioned that Sir Jasper might come to call, remember? And yesterday Mr. Tilden was very disappointed to find you not at home. I shouldn't be surprised if that young man wasn't on our doorstep again."

"Aunt Helena . . . I wish you would not encourage Mr. Tilden."

"Whyever not? He's a presentable young man. He has a tidy little fortune. He's amiable and educated — I have heard the two of you discussing Shakespeare."

"Only because he was shocked I had read the actual plays and not a bowdlerized version."

Her aunt frowned. "I'm still not sure it was wise for your academy to allow those plays around impressionable young girls. Not everyone has your strength of mind and moral certitude." Aunt Helena began to go through Lilah's wardrobe. "What about this russet silk moire? It's so pretty with your hair. These puffed sleeves are elegant."

Lilah sighed at the thought of climbing back into all those clothes — the small bustle in back, the corset to achieve the proper wasp waist, the boned sleeve supports to fill out the puffed sleeves, not to mention the petticoats and, over it all, the bodice and skirt. It was rather like donning armor. Social armor. But it *was* a lovely dress, and of course she couldn't receive guests in this softly draped morning gown.

"Yes, that will do nicely," she said and rang for her maid.

"If you haven't a preference for Mr. Tilden, there's always Sir Jasper," Aunt Helena said. "I think he's close to offering." So did Lilah; that was the problem. "He seems quite enamored of you."

"He's enamored of getting his hands on the estate my father left me."

"Lilah! What a thing to say. Sir Jasper isn't a fortune hunter. Your father left him that land in Yorkshire to go with the title, and I understand he has a nice income besides. In any case, it would be suitable to have the family seat and the title joined again. I never understood exactly why your father left the house to you instead of passing it with the title."

"Because I am his daughter. He wanted to leave me independent," Lilah said with some exasperation. "Because it was his home and he loved it. He didn't want to leave it to a man who was little more than a stranger. And since it wasn't entailed, he was free to do with it as he wished."

"Of course he wanted to provide for you, but still, it's unusual. If you married Sir Jasper, the estate would be whole again."

"That's hardly worth marrying someone for. Sir Jasper is older than I am."

"Only fifteen years. It's more comfortable to marry an older man. They are more stable. They're established in life."

"But we are related."

"Not to any significant degree," her aunt protested. "Sir Jasper may be the last male of the Holcutt line, but he's only a third cousin once removed, so there would be no reason not to marry."

"There's reason enough in the fact that I don't love him."

"Delilah . . . surely you don't mean that. You've always been so levelheaded. Reasonable."

"Isn't it reasonable to love the man you marry?"

"Yes, and I am sure you will come to love him in time. Love is the fruit from the seed of a good marriage. Only foolish girls marry because they fancy themselves in love with a man. It's infatuation, based on nothing more than the color of a man's eyes or the way he smiles or the lavish compliments he pays her."

"I hope I am not so shallow, Aunt, nor so unable to judge my own feelings. To know what is merely attraction, merely desire —" that was Con Moreland "— and what is true feeling." That was, well, she wasn't sure, for she had never felt it for any man.

"Of course you're not shallow. But you are young, and you have been influenced by the romance of Sabrina's wedding. But no one knows how that will end. You have seen only the excitement. There's a great deal more to life than that. A marriage needs a strong foundation — a suitable match of name and bloodline. A similarity of spirit. A husband who can provide and protect you, who is steady and high-minded. One of ir-reproachable reputation."

It sounded, Lilah thought, like a dull sort of marriage. But it was the kind her aunt herself had, so Lilah could hardly disparage it. She smiled and said teasingly, "Aunt Helena, you are going to make me think you want to get me off your hands."

Helena smiled fondly. "You know I would keep you with me forever if I thought only of myself. Your uncle would say the same. But I want what's best for you. I want you to have a good, happy life and a husband who can give you that."

"I know. I love you for it." Aunt Helena, having no children, looked upon Lilah as her own daughter, and she was the closest thing Lilah had to a mother, her own hav-ing died when Lilah was young.

125

Perhaps her aunt was right. Maybe it was foolish to hope to find love, to give a man her heart and hold the same from him. She wasn't even sure that love was something she was capable of. She'd never felt even a twinge of it for any of the young men with whom she had danced and conversed.

Maybe she should be practical. Find a man who embodied the qualities she admired, who was, as Aunt Helena said, steady and like-minded. Surely that would be better than falling into the trap her father had, holding his sad obsessive love to his heart all his life. Her aunt and uncle were happy in their marriage. As one grew old, it might be nicer to have a man to sit with by the fire than one who had made your heart beat faster.

But then she thought of Sabrina's face lighting up when Alex walked in. Or how Kyria and Rafe would look at each other across the room, as if no one else existed. The way the duke, after almost fifty years of marriage, still gazed at the duchess as if he'd just been given the most wonderful gift in the world. The thought of such love made her giddy. And terrified.

It was what she wanted. However fond of her aunt she was, Lilah was not going to marry anyone because it was appropriate or suitable. Still, she must be polite. Sorry that she had been irritated with Aunt Helena, Lilah decided that she would even do her best to see Sir Jasper's worthy qualities.

For that reason, an hour later she was sitting in the parlor, wearing the dark russet gown with the wasp waist and the puffed sleeves, as her aunt greeted Sir Jasper.

Her distant cousin was a nice-looking gentleman, and if his figure was not an imposing one, at least he was taller than she, which was more than she could say for her other suitor, Mr. Tilden. It was, she supposed, shallow of her that she could not marry a man to whom she must look down to speak. If only Sir Jasper smiled more or didn't talk in such a ponderous manner or if he made her laugh now and then, she might be able to think of him in a more romantic way.

"Sir Jasper." Lilah rose and smiled in a carefully modulated way — polite, but not too friendly, not too glad to see him. She would give him a chance, but she didn't want to encourage him.

"Please, you must call me Jasper. We are related after all." He gave her a stiff smile and bowed.

And that, Lilah thought, was the extent of Sir Jasper's sense of humor. Her own smile grew more forced. "Yes, of course, Cousin Jasper."

He frowned faintly at this reminder of their kinship, however distant, but said only, "Cousin Delilah."

Lilah's worst fears were realized when, after a few minutes of polite conversation, Aunt Helena excused herself from the room and went in search of her missing needle-work. Lilah knew she was clearing the way for Sir Jasper to propose.

Quickly, before her visitor could speak, Lilah said, "I hope the work on your house is proceeding well. I believe you said the banister was suffering from woodworms."

Sir Jasper looked a trifle taken aback at her choice of topic but said, "Yes. I hope to show it to you one day."

"I suppose it will be an extensive project." She wondered how long she could keep a conversation going about the renovation of a house she had never seen and had no interest in.

"I am sure it will." He cleared his throat. "Delilah. I believe you must be aware that I hold you in high esteem."

"Thank you," Lilah interrupted, desperately trying to think of a way to stave off his next words. With relief, she heard the sound of the front door opening and the butler's voice. Perhaps she would be rescued by another caller; at this point, she would welcome Mr. Tilden.

There were footsteps and the butler appeared in the doorway, saying with great pride, "Lord Moreland."

"Con!" Lilah jumped to her feet, smiling. There could be no greater disruption to any scene than Con Moreland.

Chapter Ten

Lilah realized that her smile was too glad and her greeting too familiar. She pulled her face back into order as she went forward to greet Con. "Lord Moreland. It's so good to see you again." As if it had been ages since last they'd met.

Con's eyes twinkled. Lilah had little doubt that he had immediately read the situation. He bowed over her hand and said in a syrupy voice, "Miss Holcutt. How could I stay away when all I can think about are a pair of sky blue eyes?" He all but fluttered his lashes.

Trust Con to overplay it. She shot him a stern glance, which only caused him to grin. She realized that he was still holding her hand. Jerking her hand back, she turned aside. "Allow me to introduce you. Sir Jasper, this is Constantine, Lord Moreland."

The two men greeted each other, Sir Jasper stiffly and Con graciously.

"Were you a friend of Miss Holcutt's father?" Con asked with great innocence. "How good of you to pay a visit to his daughter."

Sir Jasper looked as if he were about to swallow his tongue. Lilah jumped into the silence. "Sir Jasper is related to me."

"Ah, I understand. At first I feared you were unchaperoned. But with your uncle here, it is quite appropriate."

"I'm a very distant relation," Sir Jasper said with a forced levity that made him sound as avuncular as Con had suggested.

"You must have had the pleasure of knowing Miss Holcutt since she was in pigtails and pinafores," Con said as Sir Jasper and Lilah took their seats.

Instead of sitting in the vacant chair beside Sir Jasper, Con chose to sit on a nearby hassock, only a foot away from Lilah. Lounging there, athletically graceful and utterly at ease, in contrast to Sir Jasper's increasing stiffness, Con proceeded to flirt with Lilah so outrageously that it was difficult for her not to burst into laughter.

It became obvious that neither man was going to give up any ground. After a few minutes of paying Lilah ever more fulsome compliments, Con let out a dramatic sigh and said, "Alas, Miss Holcutt, I can see that

131

you have forgotten your promise."

"My promise?" Lilah asked warily.

"Why, yes, you told my nieces you would accompany us for ices at Gunter's and a walk in the park." He adopted a doleful expression. "Poor Brigid and Athena, they will be sorely disappointed."

"Oh, my goodness," Lilah exclaimed in equally stagy tones, one hand to her heart. Clearly her aunt was right: Con Moreland was a bad influence. "We cannot have that, now, can we? Of course, we must go. I am so sorry to have forgotten." She stood up and turned to Sir Jasper. "I do hope you will forgive me, Cousin Jasper. I must leave. Brigid and Athena are such adorable little moppets." They were also wild as March hares, but Lilah saw no reason to mention that. She barely waited for Sir Jasper's polite agreement before turning to Con. "Just let me fetch my hat and give the butler a message for my aunt."

She hurried out the door, the men trailing after her. Sir Jasper walked with them to the street, and Lilah feared that he might decide to stroll along with them. She turned to him, holding out her hand and saying, "Goodbye, Cousin Jasper. It was good to speak with you."

He could do little but take his leave of

them. "Good day. I am sure I will see you again soon, Cousin Delilah."

Blast the man. He had called her by her full name. She sneaked a sideways glance at Con. Of course he *would* catch that. Lilah pivoted and started off at a quick pace, but Con kept up with her easily. His eyes brimming with laughter, his tone rich with wicked delight, he said, "*Delilah?* Your name is Delilah?"

Lilah let out a huff of annoyance. "Yes. It is. You're a fine one to talk . . . *Constantine.*"

He chuckled. "I rather like being an emperor."

"It's a good deal less embarrassing than being a . . . a . . ."

"Temptress?" He grinned. "Seductress?"

She gave him a freezing look, her former good humor with him gone. "Deceiver. Liar. Betrayer."

"You're none of those things. Though I imagine you could bring a man to his knees." When she made no answer, he went on meditatively, "I should probably be afraid of you. But I believe I'll risk it."

"You are a perfectly annoying man."

"So you've told me. It's a wonder you're willing to go anywhere with me."

"I was in desperate straits."

He laughed. "I could tell. Was he about to

ask for your hand?"

Lilah let out a gusty sigh, and the knot she hadn't even realized was in her chest loosened. She slowed her steps. "I didn't want to risk it."

"I should think not. I'm surprised you didn't ward him off with a chaperone. There are several old ladies in my family whom I would be happy to lend you."

"Thank you, but that's not necessary. Ordinarily my aunt is there. But I believe she hoped Sir Jasper would make an offer."

"She favors his suit."

"Yes. She thinks it would be a most appropriate marriage."

"Egad."

"Just so. It would be convenient."

"I can't see how. He seemed a dead bore."

"He inherited my father's title. But Father left the main house to me. It's the family seat — the Holcutts have owned it for ages. So marrying him would reunite the estate and the title. Everything would be in the direct line once again."

"That scarcely seems a reason to marry."

"Not in my opinion. Though perhaps he is less stiff once one gets to know him."

Con frowned. "Don't let them talk you into accepting him. It would be a terrible waste," he said, his voice unaccustomedly serious.

Lilah glanced at him, surprised. "I would have thought you'd say the two of us were well matched."

"Lord, no. You are aggravating but never boring." He grinned. "I am always available to chase off suitors, should you need me."

A laugh bubbled up out of her throat. "You seemed quite adept at it. Though I must say you overdid it. Eyes as blue as the sky?"

"In my defense, I was unprepared. But you are right, your eyes are more the color of the ocean." His irrepressible grin flashed. "A stormy ocean."

"Nor are they like stars in the velvet sky. And hair like the sunset? Really, now . . ."

"But that is the truth." His eyes went to her hair, his expression changing subtly. "Your hair is beautiful. It's what first drew my eye."

"I thought that was my lilac stockings," Lilah said drily, struggling to ignore the hot, jittery feeling the look on his face evoked in her.

"No. Your lilac stockings were why I followed you. Your hair was why I was I watching you closely enough to spy your lilac stockings."

"You have no absolutely no shame, do you?"

"I'm sure I must. Somewhere."

"It's well hidden."

Con turned into a small park, little more than an oasis of grass and a few trees in the midst of the city, and led her to a wrought iron bench in the shade of one of the trees. She sat down, and Con took his seat beside her, his expression so serious it raised a faint twinge of alarm in Lilah.

"Con, what is it? Why did you call on me today?"

"I came to ask a favor of you."

He had surprised her again. "What? Surely no one in your family has been abducted again already."

"No. It's about Sabrina." He looked into her eyes. "I need your help."

"Yes, of course. Anything."

"You know her better than any of us do. Can you tell me about her key?"

Lilah stared at him blankly. "Key? What key? I don't understand."

"Damn. I'd hoped it would be something you recognized." Con leaned back with a sigh. "We think the ruffians yesterday were actually after Sabrina."

"What? Why?"

"They seemed to be interested only in

Kyria. I think they probably hadn't expected the other women to fight them, and in the course of trying to subdue them, they threw them in the wagon, too. But Kyria is the only one they questioned. They asked her repeatedly about a key. Kyria had no idea what they were talking about. There was never a demand for a ransom, as one would expect from kidnappers. This key seems to be all they wanted."

"It's certainly peculiar, but what does that have to do with Sabrina?"

"Kyria was carrying Sabrina's parasol. It's very distinctive."

"The white one with the painted blue scene and the Fabergé handle?"

He nodded. "I don't know if it's Fabergé, but the handle is carved out of some blue stone."

"Lapis lazuli."

"Kyria says Sabrina carries it often."

"She loves it. Her mother gave it to her. But are you saying the men mistook Kyria for Sabrina because she was carrying Sabrina's parasol? That's a bit of a leap, isn't it? Why would Sabrina know anything about this key?"

"I don't know. That's what I hoped you could tell me. Kyria's interrogator insisted her father had given it to her. But our father never gave Kyria any key."

"But that doesn't mean they thought she was Sabrina."

"Who then? The men were just hired help. No doubt they were told when and where to abduct her — my mother's plan to attend that meeting with her daughters and daughters-in-law was well-known. But they would have to have been able to identify their target. So, a certain parasol, one that was easy to recognize . . ."

"Yes, I can see that. Did you ask the kidnappers why they picked Kyria?"

"No," he said in disgusted tones. "Kyria told us about it after they'd already hauled the men off to jail. I'll try to question them at the jail, but I have nothing else to use to threaten them, so I doubt they'll be willing to talk."

"Still . . ."

"Who has been in danger recently? Who is an heiress? Who is it that already has a set of enemies?"

"I know you suspect the Dearborns, but . . ."

"It *is* the Dearborns. Alex let them go before because he didn't want any scandal attached to Sabrina. They might think they could get away with it again. They have a grudge against the Morelands, Sabrina and

Alex in particular. And they're still in great need of money to pay their debts."

"But that's a rather circular argument. You say Sabrina was the target because she has the Dearborns as enemies and that the Dearborns are the ones who orchestrated it because the victim was Sabrina."

"Why are you always so bent on defending them?" Con scowled.

"I'm not. Don't growl at me because you have a weak argument."

"I'm not growling. I'm grinding my teeth."

Lilah ignored his interjection. "The Dearborns acted in a villainous manner to Sabrina. I shall never forgive them for that. And it does seem likely they might be behind it."

"Aha! You see? You think it was them, too. You just want to argue."

"I think it's important to approach it in a logical manner," she corrected. "To think it through before you rush off to accuse the Dearborns."

"I already accused the Dearborns."

Lilah sighed. "Naturally. I do hope you didn't blacken that poor footman's eye this time."

"No, I did not." He adopted a dignified look. "I was quiet and restrained."

"So, in the face of your quiet restraint,

they must have admitted their guilt."

"Of course they didn't," he replied cheerfully. "However . . ." He held up a finger like a professor making a point. "When I brought up the matter of a key, it was clear they knew what I was talking about."

"They told you what the key opened?"

"No. But when I said the men were looking for a key, Niles said, 'The key?' And Dearborn the Younger said, 'Her key?' Not *a* key, but *her* key. *The* key. As one would say about a specific object. There was this look in their eyes — it wasn't bewilderment, as yours was a moment ago. It was knowledge. Tom Quick saw, too. Even if — and it's a very unlikely if — they were not the ones who seized the ladies, I am certain they know about that key."

Lilah knotted her brow, thinking. "What kind of key are we talking about? What would it open?"

"Something that contains money. Why else would the Dearborns be interested? A safe? A room? A chest full of gold doubloons?"

"That's what this is all about." Lilah narrowed her eyes. "You want to hunt for pirates' treasure."

"Aye, matey." He gave her an unrepentant grin.

"Oh, hush."

"I'd make a grand pirate, I think. I could get an eye patch. I already have the parrot."

Lilah began to laugh. "Are you never serious?"

"Only when it's absolutely necessary." But his face turned serious again. "That fourth kidnapper got away. He's still out there. What if he tries again? What if he is still looking for the key? Whether I'm right about Niles Dearborn or not, someone hired those men, and I'm sure he's still looking for this key. I have no intention of letting him steal something from Sabrina. Besides, the man's dangerous, and if I find what he wants, he hasn't any reason to go after Sabrina — or my mother and sisters — again."

"If you have it, he'll go after you."

"Exactly." His smile this time held no humor.

"But if you don't know what the key looks like or what it unlocks, how are you going to find it?"

"That's why I came to you. You know Sabrina and her father and the Dearborns better than I. You'll be a great help when I search Sabrina's house."

Lilah stared at him blankly. "Carmoor?"

"No, the Blair house here in town. I'm going there this afternoon."

"But I haven't a key to it. Do you?"

"No. I'll pick the lock."

CHAPTER ELEVEN

Con reached inside his jacket, bringing out a small leather case and opening it to show her the two narrow metal rods inside.

"Con!" Lilah said, aghast. "That's illegal."

"You know Alex and Sabrina wouldn't mind."

"It's still illegal."

"That's why I plan to not get caught." Con grinned at her as he slipped the lock picks back into his pocket. He shouldn't tease Lilah — she always took things so seriously, and he *was* asking for her help. But when she was on the edge of temper, cheeks flushed and eyes snapping, it sent a primitive thrill through him.

Lilah gave him a reproving look — which he also somehow found perversely enjoyable — but she said, "Well, if Mr. Blair hid anything, I don't think you'll find it at the town house. It would be at his country estate."

"Why?"

"That's where he preferred to live." She began to tick off the points on her fingers. "There are many more hiding places at Carmoor. The house is larger, and there's the land around it, as well. Most of all, that's the house Sabrina knows well. She never lived at the town house. I'm not sure she even visited there."

"You're right." Con considered her words.

"Anyway, Con, this is absurd. Why would Mr. Blair stick some gold in a chest, lock it up and hide it somewhere?"

"I refuse to give up on my buried treasure," Con said. "But I admit it's odd. What if it — whatever *it* is — wasn't Mr. Blair's? He and Dearborn were friends, weren't they?"

"Yes, they were all three friends — Mr. Dearborn, Mr. Blair and my father."

"If Sabrina's father was close enough that when he died he entrusted his daughter to Dearborn, might he not have been holding some family heirloom or other valuable for Dearborn?"

"Why?"

"I don't know. Maybe Dearborn was smart enough to know he couldn't keep from spending it if he held it himself. Or maybe he gave Blair money to invest for

144

him, Blair obviously being better with money than he. Now, with creditors at his heels and Sabrina's fortune no longer there for him to ransack, Dearborn wants to get whatever it is back. 'Family honor be damned. I need cash in hand.' "

Lilah drew breath to speak, but Con held up an admonitory finger. "*However* . . . his friend Blair hid it away safely somewhere, hid the key, then died without telling Dearborn where it was. Sabrina's father died unexpectedly, didn't he?"

"Yes. Apoplexy, I believe."

"There you are. Blair was young to die, had no reason to think he would, and so he didn't tell Dearborn where he hid the key. He didn't even think to leave a letter."

"But why did he find it necessary to not only store this unknown 'thing' in a secret place but also to hide the key?"

"Fear of thieves," Con replied airily.

"You should write novels."

Con laughed. "I doubt I have the patience for it. Besides, I understand it requires at least a modicum of skill."

"If you're right, that makes it even more likely that he would hide it in the country. That's where they always met."

"Met?" Con's curiosity was piqued.

"The Dearborns regularly came to visit

Sabrina's family for a week or two."

"A house party?"

"I'm not sure you'd call it that — they didn't invite any other guests. There weren't hunts or organized entertainments. It was just our families. They'd have dinner, play cards, that sort of thing. Mr. Blair and Mr. Dearborn often rode over to our house for an evening — I presume so they could leave their wives behind and have a cozy time drinking and chatting. Sometimes Mrs. Blair would host a ball and invite some of the local people, but most of the time it was just them and my father and aunt."

"Mrs. Summersley lived with you?"

"No, no." Lilah chuckled. "My father's sister, Aunt Vesta."

"Aunt Vesta — now there's a name with a ring to it."

"No doubt you would like her," Lilah said bitingly.

"I'd wager she had a hand in naming you Delilah." Lilah didn't deign to respond to that, and Con went on, "They did this often?"

"Oh, yes, I'd say three or four times a year."

"Good Lord — even Aunt Hermione only dropped in once a year to bedevil us."

"It's odd," Lilah mused. "I don't think my

father liked Mr. Dearborn."

"Discerning man. Why do you think he disliked him?"

"I'm not sure that he *dis*liked him. But I never had the impression that Father was fond of him. They didn't correspond, and Father never went to London to see him, whereas he and Mr. Blair called on each other often. My father and Niles were very different."

"Fortunately for you."

"I don't mean only that the Dearborns are cheats and liars and Father was not — though that is true. But they didn't enjoy the same pursuits. My father was a solitary man. He was quiet and stayed at home, rarely went to London. Niles Dearborn, on the other hand, thrives on social activities. I understand his parties are lavish. He spends a great deal of time in the city — going to his club and parties and the theater. Gambling."

"Perhaps your father and Dearborn were each friends with Sabrina's father, so they were simply thrown together."

"But Father and Mr. Dearborn continued to get together even after Mr. Blair's death. Father mentioned them sometimes in his letters, and I remember seeing the Dearborns at the house once when I was at

Barrow House visiting my father."

"Visiting?" Con glanced at her, startled. "You didn't live with your father?"

"No." Her face returned to its usual cool expression. "When I was twelve, he and Aunt Helena agreed that it would be better if I lived with her. A woman's touch, you know."

Con suspected there was some story hidden there, but he said only, "So if they weren't friends, what if they met for some other reason? Like business?"

"What business?"

"I don't know. But meeting as regularly as that doesn't sound social — or, at least, not only social. It's more like meetings of a board. Father is on the board of trustees for a charity. They meet quarterly to discuss it — make rules or allot the money. Uncle Bellard belongs to a society of historians that meets every month, and twice a year they also have a meeting of their board."

"So you think they met because they were trustees of . . . something?"

"It could have been a business their fathers owned jointly."

"If they did, it's not something my Father passed on to me. Perhaps he gave it to Sir Jasper, though I'm not sure why he would. He resented having to leave the title to him, as I remember."

"I examined the books on Sabrina's estate when we were investigating Dearborn's guardianship of her," Con said. "I don't remember her father sharing any possession with your father and Dearborn — though Dearborn could have already stolen it from her." He frowned. "I should dig further back."

"You looked into the fraud?" Her eyebrows rose.

"Yes. You always seem surprised by my investigations. You must not think my agency does much work."

"I presumed Mr. Quick did most of it."

"And I just put on costumes and beards and chase bizarre things."

"Well . . . yes."

"Your faith in me is astounding. But I'll ignore that. Going back to the subject at hand, they didn't have to share a business. It could have been a charity. Or a club — that could involve a key. Some clubs have silly ceremonies, don't they? Maybe this key opens the place where they meet — like the Hellfire Club."

"The Hellfire Club!" Lilah goggled at him.

"Yes, it was a club where, uh . . . ." He stopped, realizing it was going to be difficult to explain the subject genteelly.

"I know what the Hellfire Club was," Lilah retorted. "And I can assure you that my father would *never* have —" She blushed. "Or Mr. Blair either."

"No, of course not." How was it that he always managed to say the wrong thing to this woman? Maybe it was because there were so few things she considered right. "I didn't mean they were engaged in anything nefarious. I just meant a club in a secret place out in the country. You said there was ample land on Mr. Blair's estate."

"Yes, and ours too, but there aren't any caves. And what kind of club would have only three members?"

"Good points. Well, we'll find out all that later. Right now I must go to Carmoor to search."

"But Carmoor is closed."

"So is the town house," he reminded her.

"I realize that you can continue your criminal career in Somerset if you wish. What I meant was, there's no place for you to stay."

He cast a sideways grin at her. "Why, Miss Holcutt, I was rather hoping for an invitation from you."

"Me?" Her voice rose.

"Yes. Your home is near Sabrina's, I thought." He looked at her quizzically. What had brought that sudden look of panic to her face?

"Well, yes, it is. We were neighbors. But, um, I'm not *at* Barrow House."

"I've heard that trains are quite handy for taking one from one place to another."

"Yes, but that's a long way to go, and you don't even know that the key is at Carmoor."

"You just said that was the most likely place for it. And I think we can survive a trip to the wilds of Somerset." How very curious. Lilah's manner was almost furtive.

"It's so sudden. Impulsive. There are things I would have to do — pack and, um, well, we should consider it before we act. It would be rude, just to drop in like that. I haven't even written my aunt."

"Oh. It's your aunt's estate? I thought it belonged to you."

"It does. But my father's sister is living there now."

"That's all to the good, then. You'll have a chaperone, so it will be proper."

"You clearly don't know Aunt Vesta." Lilah's laced her fingers together tightly. "The thing is, Barrow House is old and . . . Well, you wouldn't care for it. It's old-fashioned. Uncomfortable."

"I can sleep anywhere. I've even been

151

known to sleep in a tent in a field." He studied her face. "You don't want me there, do you?" The idea shouldn't cause this pang in his chest; he was aware of Lilah's antipathy. Con took cover in a comically tragic expression. "Miss Holcutt . . . I am devastated at your unkindness. You will have me sleeping in a ditch."

Lilah rolled her eyes. "Con . . . you are the most egregious overactor."

"I? Miss Holcutt!"

"Stop calling me Miss Holcutt every other sentence."

"But I do think Lilah would be much too familiar, given your lack of welcome, don't you? But perhaps you would prefer Delilah." He wiggled his eyebrows ludicrously.

"If you don't cease this nonsense, I think I may hit you."

"Now I'm all aquake." But Con found that he was tired of playing this game. It wasn't as if he could force Lilah into liking him. "I'm sorry. I shouldn't tease you." He gave her an easy, impersonal smile to show his lack of resentment and stood up. "I'm sure there's an inn in the village where I can stay."

Lilah got to her feet, as well. "It isn't really an inn. Only a couple of rooms above the tavern. It's doubtless noisy."

Now what was the problem? "I can sleep through anything." He began to walk to the park's exit.

Lilah followed. "I doubt it's comfortable. Maybe not even clean."

"Lilah . . ." He turned on her in exasperation. "You told me the key was most likely to be at Carmoor, so why the devil are you so eager now to keep me from searching the place?"

"I'm not. It's just . . . You'll break in and get caught. You're always so rash."

Con looked at her. There was something more here. It wasn't just that Lilah wasn't fond of him — or at least it wasn't *all* that. She was pale, almost frightened. His face softened, and he started toward her. "Lilah, what's the matter? Why are you afraid?"

"Afraid!" She bristled, taking a step backward. "What nonsense." She spun on her heel and marched off. "Blast!" She swung back to face him. "Oh, very well. You may stay at Barrow House."

Con's eyebrows soared even higher, and he began to laugh. "Why, Miss Holcutt, how could I refuse such a gracious invitation?"

CHAPTER TWELVE

Lilah regretted her decision immediately. She couldn't take Con home. She thought of Barrow House; she thought of him meeting her aunt. He would tease Lilah mercilessly. There'd been no reason to give in to him. He hadn't argued or even continued to tease her. Instead, he had given her a polite, pleasant smile that she had never seen on his face before. The sort of smile he might show a stranger. And it had pierced her.

It was absurd to worry that she had hurt his feelings. He was a man whom barbs bounced from. Yet she had felt like a selfish wretch.

It was silly; Con was always annoyed with her anyway. Indeed, once he'd thought about it, he would have been relieved to be free of Lilah's interference. He could happily explore the house by himself, poking into every nook and cranny.

While she stayed here, making calls and receiving visitors, warding off Sir Jasper's proposal. She had said she would do anything to help Sabrina, and yet she was refusing to even visit her own home in an effort to help Sabrina. What sort of a friend was she?

It was that thought that had made her give in. For an instant, watching him laugh, she'd been happy, almost eager. But now, as Con chatted amiably about timetables and train tickets, all Lilah could think was what her aunt would say. Aunt Helena disliked her seeing the Morelands, yet here Lilah was, jaunting off to Somerset with the worst of the lot.

She had promised only to not call on the Moreland family, so this trip to Barrow House didn't break the letter of their agreement, but it certainly trespassed against the spirit of it. Nor could Lilah reveal to Aunt Helena the real purpose of their trip; that would only make things worse. She would be aghast at the notion of Lilah running about the countryside, tracking down clues to a doubtlessly apocryphal treasure.

Much to Lilah's chagrin, Con insisted on seeing her to the door, and her aunt immediately popped out of the drawing room as they walked in, as if she'd been watching for them. Lilah forced a smile. "Aunt Helena."

"Delilah." Yes, her aunt was displeased. Aunt Helena's eyes went to Con and narrowed.

There was nothing for it but to introduce Con. He swept her an elegant bow. "Mrs. Summersley, it's such a pleasure to meet you. It's clear now that beauty must run in Miss Holcutt's family."

To Lilah's surprise, her aunt softened, and she extended her hand to Con. Apparently she was no more immune to Con's charm than other women. "Lord Moreland, how kind of you. I regret that I was momentarily out of the room when you called earlier. I wish Lilah had sent for me." She cast a dark look at her niece. "I fear you must think me lax in my chaperonage."

"Not at all. Miss Holcutt's uncle — or was it her cousin? — was there, so it was all very proper," Con assured her.

"I apologize for leaving the house so abruptly," Lilah told her. "I had forgotten I had promised Lord Raine's children that I would have ices at Gunter's with them."

"My nieces would have been most upset." Con continued on his good behavior for the next ten minutes, sitting down in the drawing room to exchange meaningless pleasantries. He ended his visit, however, by saying, "Your niece has been so kind as to invite me for a visit to Barrow House." Ignoring Aunt Helena's stunned expression, he went on, "I look forward to meeting Miss Holcutt's other aunt."

"Oh. I — how unexpected." Aunt Helena swung her gaze to Lilah.

"Yes, C— Lord Moreland is interested in the architecture of Barrow House." Hastily Lilah added, "Elizabethan architecture is one of his . . . um, interests."

"Indeed," Con agreed. "One of my passions, even." He directed a dazzling smile at Lilah's aunt. "I do hope you will forgive me for stealing your niece away for a few days."

"Yes. Of course," Aunt Helena replied weakly.

"I'm sorry that you must take your leave of us so soon, Lord Moreland," Lilah said, jumping to her feet. "But I know you are pressed for time."

Con sent an amused glance at Lilah, but he rose to his feet and said, "Thank you for reminding me, Miss Holcutt. There is much to do if we are to leave in two days."

"Two days?" Her aunt goggled.

He smiled winningly at Helena. "Yes. Your niece is a model of efficiency."

"Of course," Aunt Helena replied, looking

157

confused. "But I don't understand the need for such a rush."

Con started to speak, but Lilah tucked her hand in his arm and gave it a little tug. "I'll let Miss Holcutt explain that," Con said. "I must leave. I'm sorry. It's been a pleasure meeting you, Mrs. Summersley. I hope to see you again soon."

Con bowed over her aunt's hand. Lilah dug her fingers into his sleeve and pulled. "I'll see you to the door."

They walked back into the entry hall. Con bent his head toward Lilah and murmured, "I fear you're leaving bruises, my dear Miss Holcutt."

"What? Oh." She glanced down at her tight grip on his arm and dropped it. "I'm sorry. I have never told so many lies in one afternoon in my life."

"Don't worry. You'll grow accustomed to it."

"I don't want to grow accustomed to it." She stopped and turned to him. "I'm not sure this is a good idea."

"Don't back out on me now, Lilah." He smiled down at her. "Think of it this way — at least you'll avoid Sir Jasper's proposal."

It was doubtless wrong of her, but Lilah chuckled. "Just go."

He took her hand and bowed over it, but

he didn't release it immediately, instead leaning forward until his lips were only inches from her ear. His breath on her skin sent a shiver through her. "I promise I won't importune you . . . at least, not much."

Her aunt was waiting for her in the drawing room, arms crossed, her face stern. "Lilah . . . have you run mad? First, you sneak out of this house with a man, completely unchaperoned and without my knowledge."

Temper sparked in Lilah, but she firmly shoved it back down. "I am over twenty-one. Surely I don't need your permission to leave the house."

"Courtesy should impel you to at least tell me you were leaving."

"I left you a message. As for being unchaperoned, you thought it was all right for me to be alone with a man when you left the drawing room."

"It was Sir Jasper. That's an entirely different matter."

"Why?"

"Because Sir Jasper isn't a temptation," Helena said with far more candor than was customary. She sighed. "Hopefully no one will learn of this afternoon's misstep. We can count on Sir Jasper not to say anything.

But now you're proposing to hare off to Somerset with Constantine Moreland! To stay in the same house with him!"

"People frequently invite both men and women to house parties. Even unmarried men and women."

"But they are chaperoned. There are other people there."

"We will be chaperoned. My aunt lives there."

"Vesta?" Helena made a noise that would have been termed a snort in anyone less refined. "Your father's sister is no chaperone. She's worse than no chaperone. She's the one who created the storm to begin with. And the way she's been flaunting herself all over Europe since then! Calling herself Madame LeClaire, though everyone is certain she's never been married."

"I won't be swayed by Aunt Vesta. And I should hope that I have established a good enough reputation that it won't be tarnished by being in the same household with my aunt for a week or two."

"I would never question your morality, dear. But it's how it will *look*."

"Isn't the important thing how it will *be*?" Lilah shot back. "Don't you care about that?"

Helena's eyes widened in shock. "Lilah,

how can you question that?"

"I'm sorry. Truly. I don't question your love or concern. But I do think that I should be able to have some freedom." The feelings she'd been having the past few days — no, weeks — welled up. "To decide for myself what to do."

"I have no desire to *cage* you. But I worry about you. I remember how unhappy and frightened you were when I first brought you here to live. The times you awakened from nightmares. The tears you cried."

Some of the tears had been for her father and her home, though she doubted Aunt Helena ever realized that. But Lilah remembered, too, how Aunt Helena had awakened her from her nightmares and held her, how she had sheltered and protected her. Lilah smoothed down her irritation.

"I know. But I'm not a child anymore, Aunt Helena, and you don't have to shield me. Aunt Vesta has written me several times, asking me to come see her."

Aunt Helena let out an indelicate snort. "No doubt because she wants something from you. That woman cares only about herself."

"I am well aware of that. But she is, after all, my father's sister, and as such I must show her respect. It has been rude of me not to go there." This, more than anything, would sway Aunt Helena's mind. "I won't be influenced or hurt by Aunt Vesta. Nor am I weak and silly enough to allow Con to take liberties." She already had of course, but there was no need to tell Aunt Helena that. "Don't you trust me?"

"Of course I trust you." Aunt Helena took her hand. "It's Lord Moreland I don't trust. I've heard he behaves most peculiarly. That agency he runs — they say he dresses up in disguises, pretends to be all sorts of low creatures. You know that people call them the Mad Morelands."

"That's most unfair and unkind," Lilah protested hotly. "They are not mad."

"They're odd. They don't behave as they should. They're *different*." Aunt Helena turned away with a gusty sigh and dropped back down into her chair. "How I wish you had never gotten tangled up with the Morelands. Why couldn't Sabrina have married a nice, normal young man?"

"Alex is normal."

"I fear he will lead you on and break your heart."

"Con?" Lilah let out a short laugh. "There's little danger of that."

"He's a very personable young man, handsome, as all the Morelands seem to be, and he has that dash of something wild about him that's so intriguing."

"Aunt Helena!" Lilah gaped at her aunt, mildly shocked.

Her aunt made a little moue. "Do you think I don't remember what it was like to be a young girl? How alluring a rogue can seem? I also know that's the sort who will leave you weeping. He is friends with that Hetherton set, and they're interested only in having a good time. I fear he's not looking for marriage."

"Then it's fortunate that I am not looking for marriage either. I know Con flits from girl to girl like a butterfly. But he's no deceiver. He's honest, even rudely blunt. I shan't swoon over him. He and I have managed to get along, after a fashion, since Sabrina married his brother, but that is the extent of our 'friendship.' "

"Then why are you running off to Somerset with him?" Aunt Helena narrowed her eyes at Lilah. "And don't try to fob me off with that silly story about the architecture of that monstrosity of a house."

Lilah's mind raced furiously. "No, that's not the real reason. It's the official story, the one we are putting about. It concerns Sabrina, so we didn't want to make it known." That much, at least was the truth.

"Sabrina?" Her aunt frowned. "But Sabrina isn't even here."

"No, and that is exactly why he must go there." Her aunt's words gave her inspiration. "With Alex gone, Constantine is the manager of his twin's affairs. That now includes Sabrina's matters, as well." That, too, hovered in the vicinity of the truth.

"But what does that have to do with you and Barrow House?"

"Apparently someone has broken into Carmoor. More than once." Lilah hated lying to her aunt, but she couldn't tell her the truth. It was too outlandish. It was typical of Con that the truth would sound more unlikely than a falsehood. Aunt Helena wouldn't consider looking for a key as an acceptable reason to hasten off to Somerset with Con Moreland.

"Thieves? What is the world coming to? What happened? Did they take anything?"

Her aunt looked so concerned that Lilah was swept with guilt. Lies were coming to her far too easily. "I'm not sure. Lord Moreland didn't tell me the details. He was reluctant, naturally, to frighten me." That was the biggest untruth of them all.

"Naturally."

"But he is worried about it. He must leave immediately to look over things. He can hardly stay at Carmoor — there are no servants, and it's been closed up for years. The inn in the village would be entirely unsuitable for a duke's son."

"Yes, I can see that you would feel obliged to ask him to Barrow House, but you needn't go with him."

"But I must. I can't let him meet Aunt Vesta on his own. Imagine what he'd think."

"Oh. Yes, you're right." Aunt Helena appeared more alarmed by this possibility than she had by thieves. Her aunt sighed. "I suppose you must accompany him, but it's most worrisome." She squared her shoulders. "Perhaps I should go with you."

Lilah almost laughed at her aunt's martyred expression. "No, that's very kind of you, but I would not subject you to spending all that time in Aunt Vesta's company." To say that the two of them did not get along well was a vast understatement. "We would all be miserable."

Her aunt's face brightened. "You must take Cuddington with you."

"Your maid?" Lilah asked in horror. Cuddington was as sour a person as existed, stiff and critical.

"Yes." Aunt Helena nodded her head, pleased with her idea. "I will rest much easier, knowing you have Cuddington along."

"But what will you do without her?" Lilah protested. "I'll take Poppy with me."

"I'll manage," her aunt said determinedly. "Poppy is a sweet girl, but far too young and easily charmed. Cuddington is the answer."

Lilah sighed. "Very well. I'll take her with me."

It did afford her some amusement to think of Con's expression when he met Cuddington.

CHAPTER THIRTEEN

Con lounged against a pillar, watching the flow of travelers into Paddington Station. He had arrived too early. After buying the tickets, he'd had nothing to do except wait, which he had never been good at. He wished that he'd picked Lilah up from her house rather than meeting her at the station.

But there was no need to worry. He pulled out his pocket watch, then checked it against the large clock hanging in the station. Lilah wasn't late; the fact that she hadn't yet arrived didn't mean she was backing out on him. She had said she would go, and she would keep her word — even if she didn't really want him in her home.

Her reluctance to invite him had been rather lowering. It wasn't as if they got along well of course — in fact, she was frequently bloody irritating — but still, he hadn't thought she disliked him that much. Women

167

usually enjoyed his company. They might rap his knuckles and tell him he was naughty — that seemed to be a favorite word of ladies old and young — but they always smiled when they said it. They flirted with him, danced with him, hung on his arm. Indeed, some of them had even been the ones to lure *him* into an alcove for a stolen kiss.

But Lilah was not among those women. She was stubbornly immune to his charm. She seized every opportunity to criticize him. Con annoyed her. He angered her. Indeed, the only thing about him that pleased her was his kiss.

Con smiled to himself. That was one thing he was certain about. He suspected that she would deny it, but he had felt her response — the flare of heat in her skin, the way her body melted into him, the way her mouth moved against his.

He straightened, pulling his mind back from where it had wandered. It didn't matter that Lilah enjoyed their kisses. Physical pleasure would not weigh enough with Lilah to balance her disapproval of him. It shouldn't have come as a shock that she would recoil at the thought of being trapped for days in the same house with him.

Nor should it have caused that twist of

hurt inside his chest.

It wasn't as if Con wanted to be saddled with Lilah either. She was rigid and judgmental. Argumentative, obstructive, unimaginative . . . and seemingly lacking any sense of fun. It was entertaining to exchange barbs with her, to see her eyes flash with temper and to startle a smile or a laugh from her, but he was sure her company would become tiresome after a while.

Nor was he usually bothered by other people's opinions. He and Alex had a number of cousins who thoroughly disliked them — admittedly with some justification — as well as scores of tutors they'd driven off, not to mention the neighboring squire, who had termed them "imps of Satan."

Their dislike had never bothered him. Not once had he cared that any of the charlatans he'd exposed had spewed venom at him. Never had he felt that odd ache or wished that things were different.

Women had rejected him before. There was that languid Farthingham girl, for instance, who told him he was too tiring, and Genevieve Winters had been prone to pout because he didn't pay her as much attention as other young men. And others — he knew there were others. But none of them had caused him even a twinge of pain.

Pain was a thing that came from the people one loved — the disappointment in his father's eye when Con created trouble or the sorrow on his mother's face when her brother died or the emptiness in the house when his siblings married and moved away. The cut of separation when Alex married. Pain was hard and it was deep, not something he wasted on people who didn't matter.

Against all reason, in some perverse way he liked Lilah Holcutt, but she was not someone who mattered to him. Who could matter to him. She was on the periphery of his life. His sister-in-law's friend.

Con straightened, pushing away from the pillar. She was here. Lilah walked toward him, followed by not only her aunt, but also a portly middle-aged gentleman and a tall spare woman in black.

The little lines between Lilah's eyes were pinched, her mouth tight, her pace fast. She was simmering, he thought, and for some reason that made him smile. Assuming his blandest, most innocuous expression, Con went forward to greet them.

Lilah made impressively quick work of the introductions and goodbyes. The thin woman in black stood apart the entire time, her glacial eyes boring holes in Con. Her face was long, her lips narrow, and her eyebrows, stark black in her otherwise-pale face, seemed to perpetually pull together. Lilah didn't introduce her, and that, along with her stance behind the group, made him assume she was a servant.

He felt a decidedly dark premonition of her purpose there, confirmed when Lilah's aunt and uncle returned to their carriage, leaving the woman behind, along with Lilah's baggage. Con looked from her to Lilah.

The corner of Lilah's mouth twitched — he wasn't sure if it was in amusement or irritation — and she said, "Cuddington is my aunt's maid. She'll be traveling with us."

"Ah. How very proper." Con tried a smile. Cuddington's face remained stony.

"I'll get our tickets and see to your things, miss," Cuddington told Lilah and turned to summon a porter.

Con brought out the tickets he had already purchased, admitting that he had not gotten one for Cuddington, as well. "I'm sorry," he told Lilah, watching the other woman bustle off with Lilah's trunk and a porter in tow. "I didn't realize you would bring your duenna."

"Surely you knew I would bring my maid."

"Maybe, but I didn't know she would be

171

a gorgon," he replied. They started walking to the platform where their train awaited. "I was beginning to think you had decided not to go after all."

She glanced at him in surprise. "I told you I would."

"I know. But . . ." He glanced at her. "I didn't mean it, you know — what I said to you as I left. I won't bother you with my attentions. I was only . . ."

"Making jest of me?"

"I wasn't —"

"No?" She raised an eyebrow. "You weren't lampooning my prudish ways? My silly regard for society's rules? You weren't laughing at my desire to maintain my reputation?"

Con floundered for something to say. He supposed he'd been making light of those things. But he hadn't meant it the way she made it sound.

"Don't worry," Lilah said crisply. "I never take what you say seriously."

Con realized he didn't like that idea any better. He strode along in silence, wondering what was making him feel so aggrieved. Lilah, naturally, seemed fine with the lack of conversation, glancing around the station, anywhere but at him. She was stiff, that coiled tension still inside her. Something had roused her anger; no doubt it was him.

They found their compartment on the train. The little room seemed somehow smaller than usual, and Con thought he probably should not have shut the door behind them. But he was damned if he was going to turn around and open it. They stood together awkwardly. Then, with a grimace, Con turned away to look out their window. There was no sign of the maid. Perhaps she would miss the train; the thought lightened his spirits a bit.

"I don't suppose there's any hope that your maid will sit somewhere else."

"That would hardly serve the purpose," Lilah responded.

"We won't be able to talk in front of her."

"Don't be absurd."

"Not about anything important. I can imagine how well your aunt would receive a report of hidden keys or kidnappers."

"Cuddington isn't reporting to Aunt Helena about me." Her voice faltered at the end, but she added sharply, "You are in a foul mood today."

"I wanted to leave yesterday." Con realized that he sounded petulant, but he couldn't seem to pull his mood into something more pleasant. "Don't you ever get tired of someone trailing after you everywhere you go?"

"Of course I do!"

There was such heartfelt irritation in her voice that he turned to her, surprised. "Then why do you do it? I can scarcely imagine that you're so meek your aunt dictates your every move."

"Of course not. I don't *always* take my maid."

"I see. So it's just with me, then." He started to turn back to the window. "Damn it, Lilah!" Somehow he couldn't make himself ignore it, couldn't stop the words from leaping out of his mouth. "Why the devil do you dislike me so much? Why am I so repugnant to you?"

She gaped at him. "Don't be ridiculous."

Lilah turned away, but Con circled around to stand in front of her again. "I'm not. It's clear. You aren't rude to anyone else. You don't take Alex's head off if he makes a joke."

"I don't do that to you."

"Oh, yes, sometimes you'll laugh, as if it's been torn out of you against your will. You'll smile, but then you turn away, as you just did. You appear to like everyone else in my family. You're sweet as honey when you speak to my father. But you're an ice queen

174

with me."

"Your father is a wonderful man."

"Yes, he is. That's not the point."

"What *is* the point?" Lilah's eyes were snapping now, which gave him some satisfaction. She might disdain him, but he could always break her calm.

"You're polite to others. Not friendly of course, but you're pleasant. You don't question their every statement, don't argue about each last thing. So what is it that makes you disdain me so? I am usually considered a pretty good fellow. Women don't flee from me."

"They're all mad for you, I'm sure."

"I didn't say —"

"You obviously have a very high opinion of yourself. No doubt the fact that I don't pursue you like all the others wounds your pride." She clenched her fists, her arms stiff at her side, and moved away again. This time he did not follow. "No. I *refuse* to let you draw me. I will not let you goad me into creating a scene."

"Why not? Maybe it would do you good to set yourself free for once and stop being so bloody straitlaced."

She whipped back around, eyes blazing, cheeks flushed, and even in the midst of his anger, Con could not help but think how glorious she looked. "Very well. You want to know why I am not taken by your charms? I'll tell you."

Con had a sudden doubt — perhaps he didn't really want to know, but he set his jaw and waited for her cannonade.

"You're like all the other wealthy, aimless young men who waste their lives on idiotic pursuits, pulling silly stunts, playing pointless jokes. You're part of Hetherton's set — not a care for the gossip you create or your effect on other people."

"You're blaming me for what other men do? You're judging me by Freddy Hetherton? The fact that I have talked to them or laughed with them doesn't make me part of that set."

"You're charming. You're all flirtation and meaningless compliments and stolen kisses in the moonlight."

"So now my sin is being charming."

"It's that you fly from one young lady to the next, never staying, never caring."

"You think it would be better if I avidly pursued a girl, opening her up to gossip and speculation?"

"I think it would be better if you showed some steadfastness! Some depth of feeling. You're forever dissembling, adopting disguises, lying for this reason or that or, apparently, just for fun. I don't know whether anything about you is true."

"You don't trust me?" Her words hit him like a blow.

"How could anyone? You make jest of everything. You're impulsive. Chasing down a rumor of ghosts or pursuing some insane theory that the world is about to end. You have no dignity at all. It's an embarrassment to your family."

"My family doesn't give a flip about dignity. They aren't embarrassed. It's only you who is."

"I would be if I cared." She lifted her chin pugnaciously.

A fierce white heat speared him. "I'm well aware that you don't care for me. But you sure as hell have a lot of opinions about someone you don't even know. How could you know about my feelings or my loyalty or that precious 'steadfastness' of yours when you avoid me like the plague?"

"*I* avoid *you*? That's rich." She took a step forward. "You are the one who jumps up and leaves the room whenever I come in. The one who wouldn't even sleep in his own house because I was staying there."

Con flushed, knowing that he had indeed done those things during the weeks before the wedding, when Lilah had been constantly around. "I was trying to maintain harmony in the house. I thought you would appreciate my absence, given your dislike of me."

"I did."

"Then I wonder why you're complaining."

"I'm not —"

"And it's a lie to say I haven't spent time with you. We spent half a day together chasing down the kidnappers."

"Because I forced my way in. It's not as if you wanted me along. You made that quite clear."

"What about asking you to search Sabrina's house? What about now — I'm heading off to bloody Somerset with you."

"Yes, when you need something from me."

"I am not using you," Con shot back, taut as a bowstring, fury coursing in him. "I could easily have gone to Carmoor and searched it myself. I don't need you to accompany me. In fact, everything would be a damn sight easier if you weren't here. You're bloody infuriating, and I was a fool to ask you."

"Then why did you?" Her eyes shimmered, and there was a look on her face that made him ache.

"Because I was idiotic enough to want you with me."

Lilah drew in her breath.

He was being stupid. Utterly stupid. Con knew it and yet he couldn't help himself. He pulled her into his arms and kissed her.

Lilah stiffened, then melted into him, her mouth opening to receive him. Her arms slid beneath his jacket, and he shuddered, swept with lust. The scent of her, the feel of her, the taste of her filled his head. There was no thought in him, only heat and yearning, only pulsing need. He could not stop kissing her longer than to change the angle of his mouth.

Con had no awareness of moving, but suddenly they were up against the door, his body pressing into hers. His hand came up, fingers thrusting into her hair. He heard the ping of hairpins hitting the floor. It wasn't enough, not nearly enough. He kissed her mouth and cheek, caught the fleshy lobe of her ear in a tiny nip, and her startled gasp that turned into a moan almost undid him. He envisioned sliding down to the floor with her, but some faint remnant of sanity stopped him. Instead, he began to kiss his way down the column of her throat.

The sensitive skin was so soft, so smooth, so warm. He felt the tiny beat of her pulse against his lips. His other hand slid up to cup the soft swell of her breast. He would have given anything to be someplace else with her, somewhere he could follow the course of his yearning to the heart of it. He knew he must stop, must pull back.

In a moment, just one moment.

The train whistle blasted through the air. Con froze. It came again, cutting through the haze in his brain. He pulled himself away, turning to the window and running a shaky hand through his hair. He tugged at his waistcoat, his cuffs. He could see Lilah's reflection in the window. She was frantically repinning the strands of hair his fingers had loosened. He flexed his hands, itching to sink them into her hair again.

Con took a deep breath, trying to force calm though him. Half turning, he glanced over at Lilah. She looked flustered and breathless. It made him want her even more. He had no idea what he should say. What he should do. He was utterly at sea.

A sharp rap sounded on the door and an instant later, Cuddington entered the room, looking stern and suspicious. It was, he thought, going to be an infernally long trip.

CHAPTER FOURTEEN

The trip to Somerset was every bit as terrible as Lilah had imagined it would be. Worse. She had envisioned a stilted and dull conversation with Cuddington present. She had not bargained for the wealth of sensations roiling around in her, seeking escape.

Con was no help. He took up a seat by the window and brooded. It was not a look she'd seen on Con before . . . and one she hoped never to see again. It was strangely disturbing to see his mobile face turn dark and stony. This wasn't the Constantine Moreland she knew, the one she . . . Yes, very well, she was forced to admit it: the Con Moreland she *liked.*

Despite all she'd said, the truth was that she enjoyed being with him. Whenever Con entered the room, it became more lively, more fun. Everything was more uncertain around him; one never knew what he might do or say. It was, of course, unnerving and not the way a gentleman should behave. But it was also exciting. Con carried the possibility of adventure with him.

It was wrong of her. She should not be drawn to someone who alarmed her. He was the opposite of the man she'd dreamed of — no rock-solid anchor, but fireworks that burst beautifully in the air and were gone.

But there no escaping it. She wanted Con. She wanted that face, those hands that he used to punctuate his words, that long, lean body that fitted so perfectly against hers. She desired him the way she imagined an opium eater must desire the drug, knowing it was wrong and impermanent but oh-so-pleasurable.

She sneaked a sideways glance at him. What was it about Con that stirred her so? The glint in his eyes? The way his mouth quirked up as he awaited her response to his teasing?

Her cheeks burned as she thought about his kisses a few minutes earlier and the way her body had flamed into response. The way he'd touched her had been shocking, his hand roaming over her, covering her breast, but it had aroused her even more than it astonished her. Just the memory of it made her nerves dance. Con had the ability to turn her into a different person.

Look at the way she'd jumped at the chance to leave the house with him the other day. And little as she wanted Con at Barrow House, the thought of going there with him had thrilled her. It was, she knew, the main reason her aunt's insistence that she bring Cuddington had chafed so. Her own maid, Poppy, would have readily agreed to taking a seat in the other car by herself.

What was she to do the rest of the visit? They would be thrown together, but she had ruined that. After the things she'd said to him, Con wouldn't want her to accompany him when he broke into Carmoor. And wasn't regretting the opportunity to commit a crime proof of just how much Con turned her into a different person!

She wished she hadn't said what she had. He *was* inconstant, always moving from one thing to another; he believed in all that otherworldly nonsense. His teasing made her yearn to slap him sometimes. But maybe she and her aunt were wrong about him being part of Hetherton's set. She'd seen him talking and laughing with them at parties; she'd heard of some of the ridiculous practical jokes they'd played. But she hadn't seen any sign of their wildest sorts of behavior in Con, and it had been some time since she'd heard of him engaging in one of their stunts.

The last few months, being around him more, she had begun to wonder if what she had taken as impulsivity was actually an ability to think and act quickly. If one looked at his flirtations in a different way, it was good of him not to pursue anyone so intensely that it raised expectations or caused gossip. Of course, why he felt the need to flirt with every woman alive was a mystery — and rather irritating, as well — but it didn't rise to the level of wickedness. He was quite loyal, at least to certain people.

She had just been so angry at her aunt for not only saddling her with Cuddington, but also dawdling so much Lilah had almost been late to the station. Then Con had kept goading her until finally she exploded. She wished she could have her words back, but they were irretrievable. He would remember them no matter how much she might try to explain or apologize — and really, apologizing to Con was not something she looked forward to. She would do it of course, because that was polite, but Con would make it difficult.

It was foolish to be so downcast. It wasn't as if Con had liked her before her angry, impulsive statement. He found her staid, stuffy and dull. He seized any opportunity to make light of her, always prodding and poking. And, whatever he said, he *had* avoided her the entire time Lilah had stayed at Broughton House when they'd helped Alex and Sabrina escape.

But why had he said that at the end? After telling her what a nuisance she was, he'd admitted he'd wanted her with him. He didn't mean that — but it had shot out of him as if he couldn't keep from saying it. As if he hadn't wanted to feel it.

Then he had pulled her into his embrace and kissed her until she couldn't think straight — which, admittedly, had not taken long. If she couldn't deny her attraction to Con, neither could he deny his desire for her. She remembered the heat in his eyes, the hunger with which he'd kissed her, his hard body pressing her against the door.

If Cuddington hadn't come in, there was no knowing what might have happened. Lilah supposed that was a good reason to have the woman along, but she couldn't summon up any gratitude. She wanted to know what Con would have said. What he would have done.

Any chance of finding out was gone now. Con was deep in gloomy thoughts, not even speaking to her. There was little chance he would kiss her again. Which, of course, was all to the good. She shouldn't ache for a

185

repetition of the incident. It went so far beyond inappropriate that she scarcely knew what to call it. Vulgar? Licentious? Scandalous?

What if she was like Aunt Vesta? That was a worrisome thought. No. She wasn't. Even if she did have these improper feelings, Lilah could control them. Other people must have felt this way and not given in to it. So could she. The current awkwardness between her and Con would help her to do so. She should be glad of it. Really.

Lilah leaned her head against the cushioned back and closed her eyes. At least she could avoid the heavy silence by pretending to sleep. To her surprise, her pretense turned to reality, but she awakened when the train stopped. She glanced around, disoriented. "What — are we to Bath already?"

"No." Con shook his head. "Just a stop to pick up passengers." He pulled out his watch and opened it. "Still some distance from it, if their schedule is correct."

"I see." She wondered if she'd disarranged any of her hair as she was sleeping. She tugged at the hem of her jacket. At least Con was talking to her. "The weather has been nice."

This was precisely the sort of polite social chitchat Con abhorred, but what else could she do under Cuddington's basilisk gaze? She wondered if the woman really did have instructions from her aunt to report Lilah's behavior. Con made a noncommittal noise, but apparently he decided to make an effort as well, for a moment later he said, "What is your home like? Barrow House, isn't it?"

"Yes." She wished he had chosen something else to talk about. "Well, um . . ." She picked an invisible bit of lint from her skirt. "It's in the Levels. Do you know anything about them?"

"Bogs? They were drained, weren't they, as the Fens were?"

"Yes. It's all farms now where there used to be marshes. The land's flat and crossed with rhynes — that's what they call the canals."

"But what about your home itself? What is it like?"

Why did he insist on talking about Barrow House? "It's, um, a little hard to describe." That was putting it mildly. "It was built during the Tudor era. Actually, it was erected on the foundation of an old castle. It sits on one of the few elevated places in the Levels. You can see Glastonbury Tor from our land — if it isn't too foggy. We're not too far from Wells. Wells is quite lovely." She launched into a description of the history of both the town and the cathedral.

Apparently the flood of words ended Con's interest in the subject of her house, and he settled back into silence, though now he studied her rather than the view out the window. Lilah shifted uncomfortably and wondered what he was thinking.

It was a relief to reach Bath, where they had to change trains. Only one trip a day was scheduled for the short spur to Wells, which meant a two-hour wait, and by the time they reached Wells, it was late afternoon. She was pleased that the only vehicle they could hire was a one-horse trap that seated only two people, leaving the maid to ride in the hired cart with the luggage.

Glad as she was to be free of Cuddington's gloomy presence, the knot in Lilah's chest grew with every minute as they drew closer to her home. It was all dearly, hauntingly familiar. Twilight fog crept in as they drove, gathering above the rhynes and obscuring the road beneath their wheels. Willow trees planted in rows beside the numerous waterways rose above the mist, their drooping branches stirring in the evening air.

The land rose gradually, and the low-lying fog became patches of mist drifting across the ground. They turned onto the drive leading to the house, and the ache in Lilah's chest swelled. There it was: Barrow House, looming before them in all its hulking, shopworn grandiosity, a testimony to the conceit of successive generations of Holcutts.

The house had started as a standard Tudor design in the shape of an H, but the family extended one leg of the H. A later Holcutt had added on another wing perpendicular to the extension, so that now the mansion was a rectangle with a chunk missing in the center of one side, looking more like a blocky backward C. It was as if three separate houses had been awkwardly mashed together.

All the wings faced inward to the hidden central courtyard, so that from whatever direction one came, the visitor was presented with the rear of the house, giving it a closed, secretive look. It was erected on a foundation of stone, in a flamboyantly Tudor style, the first two sections built of plaster and black wood beams forming geometric designs. The last wing was half-timbered, the lower section dark stone and the upper part decorated with black wooden shutters, carvings and window tracery, heightening the sinister appearance of the place.

Tudor arches, Tudor roses, trefoils and quatrefoils were everywhere, and slender ornamental brick chimneys forested the roofs. Oriel windows jutted out here and there, dozens of gables faced in all directions, and it was difficult to see how any more glass windows could have been crammed into the walls.

The gap between the top and bottom of the C opened to the inner courtyard. On the far side of that gap, the original wing jettied, each floor sticking out beyond the one below it. Like many Tudor buildings, it had come to warp and sag under the weight of the third floor, giving it a vaguely drunken appearance. An incongruous round stone tower bulged from its side.

In the bright sun of day, it was a decidedly peculiar house, but now, with dusk falling and fog wafting about, it was eerie, as well. Con let out an exclamation, and Lilah glanced warily at him. He was staring raptly at Barrow House, his hands loose on the reins.

"This is where you grew up?" he asked.

"Yes."

"Amazing." He looked at her speculatively.

Lilah felt her cheeks flush, and she turned her head away, chagrined.

"How could you bear to leave it?" Con

went on.

"You *would* like it," Lilah said darkly. She had known he would bedevil her about Barrow House. Whether he scorned her home or delighted in it, it would provide him plenty of fodder for his quips.

"Of course." He resumed his study of the house. "It's fantastical, the sort of place where you can imagine anything happening."

"I fear I haven't much imagination," Lilah responded crisply. "It's too large. The floors are uneven, the rooms massive and impossible to heat. It's an absolute monster of a house."

"Yes." Con's eyes gleamed.

They pulled into the large cobblestoned courtyard and rolled to a stop. She saw Con gazing around him with interest, taking in the out-of-place yew tree growing there, the dark stone fountain spouting water from the mouth of a Green Man face and the three sets of grand double-doored entries.

"Please tell me that if I pick the wrong door, I won't fall into a pit."

"We use the middle one," Lilah said shortly and got out of the vehicle.

A startled footman came hurrying out to greet Lilah. Con left the trap to him and caught up with her. Bending close, he murmured, "It's this house, isn't it? That's why you were so reluctant for me to stay here."

Lilah stopped, meeting his all too knowing eyes. "Don't be absurd."

He started to reply, but at that moment the front door burst open and a woman swept out. Her face was stamped with surprised delight, and she spread out her arms in welcome. "Dilly! Oh, Dilly, my pet."

"Dilly?" Con's eyebrow quirked up.

"Don't. You. Dare," Lilah hissed at him and hastily shifted aside to avoid her aunt's embrace.

The move was unsuccessful, and Aunt Vesta enveloped her in a hug. Though it had been almost ten years, it was painfully familiar. She smelled of the same heavy exotic scent and her embrace was as emphatic. Lilah stood stiffly in her arms. "Hello, Aunt Vesta."

Even softened by age, Vesta still cut a dramatic figure. As tall as Lilah, she was considerably larger, her bosom jutting out like the prow of a ship above her corset. Ten years ago her hair had been a lighter gold than Lilah's, but now it was jet-black, pulled up into an enormous pompadour and adorned with a curling feather.

A diamond clip anchored the feather to

her hair, and more diamonds winked at her ears, wrists and neck. Her dress was black satin, with red and gold flowers embroidered in a diagonal slash across the front. The sweetheart neckline exposed much of her impressive bosom. In one hand she held a fan of white feathers to match the one in her hair.

Vesta stepped back, holding Lilah's hands and beaming. "I cannot believe that you are here. What a wonderful surprise! But of course, things always work out just as they ought, don't they? I'm so happy to see you again. It's been far, far too long."

Lilah refrained from pointing out that it had been Aunt Vesta who had left so abruptly and remained away so long. "It's good to see you, too."

"And who is your young beau?" Vesta cast a flirtatious sideways look at Con.

Lilah colored. "He's not my beau."

"Constantine Moreland, madam." Con swept her aunt a bow as grandiose as the lady herself. "At your service."

"Oh, my." Aunt Vesta dimpled at Con, wafting her fan flirtatiously. "You have caught yourself a prize, Dilly."

"Aunt Vesta! He's not —"

Con, of course, ignored Lilah's words and flashed a dazzling smile at Vesta. "No, ma'am, it is your niece who is the prize. I was merely lucky enough to be where Dilly could stumble over me."

"Con . . ." Lilah gritted her teeth.

"Come in, come in." Aunt Vesta hooked her arm through Con's and swept him into the house. "I do hope you will call me Aunt Vesta. I feel so close to you already. I can tell that we are kindred spirits."

Sourly, Lilah followed them inside.

"You must be exhausted after that terrible trip," her aunt said, as if they had trekked through the desert rather than ridden a train for a few hours. "I know you must be famished. I will tell the kitchen to prepare an early supper. But first, no doubt, you'll be eager to freshen up."

Vesta whisked them up the stairs and down the hall. "Here, of course, is Delilah's room. Ruggins sees to it that it's always kept as if you'd just stepped out. Now, you, dear boy — I'm sure Ruggins will have the maids up here any moment to set up your room." She smiled waggishly. "Across the hall and a proper distance away of course. We must observe the proprieties."

"Must we?" Con responded in the same teasing tone.

"I am along there." Vesta waved vaguely down the long hall. "I have moved into your mother's old room, dear. I hope you don't mind."

Lilah did mind. She minded a good deal. "Of course not."

"It faces the yew, you see, which of course is vital."

"Naturally." Lilah didn't look at her or Con, just hurried into her room and closed the door behind her.

She leaned back against the door, letting the tension drain from her. It was blessedly quiet, and though she had not been here since her father's death two years ago, it was cozy and familiar. The bookcase still held her childhood books. If she opened the small door on one wall, she would find a cunning little playroom tucked in behind a gable, doubtless still filled with her dolls and toys.

She thought of just staying here and not going down to supper. But that would leave her aunt alone with Con, and God only knew what bizarre thing Aunt Vesta might tell him. Con, of course, would encourage her to talk. No, Lilah had to be there to steer the conversation away from all the topics it would be better to avoid.

Turning away, she went to the water basin to wash away the dust and grime of the road, doing her best to brush it off her skirts, as well. Still she lingered, drifting about the room, touching her old jewelry box, the crudely stitched sampler that had been her first attempt at needlepoint, the glass dish shaped like a lady's hand that had held stray buttons and pins, the small chest of her mother's that had sat for years in her father's room and had been moved to hers after his death.

Lilah moved aside the chair that now sat in front of the small door to her playroom, and, ducking her head, she stepped inside. It was dim, lit only from the bedroom behind her, but that was enough to make out the row of dolls sitting on the shelves and the hoop leaning against it. A large trunk beneath the window held her toys; she had often sat there, looking out. On the wall opposite was an elaborate dollhouse atop a child-size table, a matching chair beside it. She had loved that dollhouse; it had been so wonderfully normal, so completely unlike her own jumbled home.

The air was stale, smelling of the dust that layered everything. Light glinted on the glass eye of a doll. Lilah's heart clenched inside her chest. This was a house of sorrow. Her father gone. A mother she had never known. This little room, holding the lifeless remnants of the child she had been.

She left, closing the door behind her and returning the chair to its position in front of the door. This house, this land, might pull her in some visceral way, but Lilah was certain she no longer belonged here.

CHAPTER FIFTEEN

Lilah didn't need to steer the conversation around treacherous waters, for her aunt didn't even mention Barrow House or the Holcutt family. Instead, Vesta and Con kept up a steady stream of chatter about London. What was the gossip? What plays were at the theaters? Who was fashionable and who was not? Judging by their laughter, the chatter kept them thoroughly entertained. It made Lilah twitchy.

It was a relief when her aunt's idea of a simple meal — only six courses — came to an end. Con turned down Aunt Vesta's invitation to an evening of cards and conversation and climbed the stairs with Lilah. At the top of the stairs, when Lilah started to bid him good-night and turn toward her room, Con wrapped his hand around her wrist, saying, "Wait. I wanted to talk to you."

Nerves coiled in Lilah's stomach, but she joined him on the seat at the oriel window.

What was he going to ask her? She had been a fool to hope she could keep Con from learning everything about her family. Obviously he and her aunt were quickly becoming great chums.

"Lilah . . ." Con sat down beside her, hesitated, then stood up. "I acted abominably this morning on the train. I must apologize for my ungentlemanly behavior." His words sounded stilted and rehearsed. "For the way I . . ." Uncharacteristically, he groped for words.

"Kissed me?" Lilah was swept with relief. *This* was what he wanted to talk about?

He relaxed, too, and sat down beside her again. "No, I'd never regret that. It was far too enjoyable."

"I have to say, then, it scarcely seems a sincere apology."

"I regret that I offended you. I'm sorry that I alarmed or distressed you. That I was boorish or rough. I am not usually so clumsy. I lost my temper."

"I don't understand why getting angry would cause you to kiss a person. I would think that disliking someone would make you want to *not* kiss her."

"One would think." With a long sigh, he leaned back against the glass. "The truth is, you tangle me up inside. I don't understand it. I don't like it any more than you do. But I can't seem to help myself." He paused, then added quietly, "If I avoided you before, it wasn't because I dislike you."

"No?" Her eyebrows shot up.

"No. I like you more than I should for my own peace of mind."

"If you like me, then why do you tease me all the time?"

He looked startled. "It's clear that you grew up without a brother. Didn't any boy ever tug your pigtails because he liked you?"

Lilah stared. "Well, I . . . I don't know." She shook her head. "Not really. Anyway, that makes no sense. Why would you want to irritate someone if you like her?"

"I tease you because . . . I enjoy the way your eyes sparkle and your cheeks flush."

"But it's because I'm angry!"

"Perverse, isn't it?" He leaned in. "I like your snapping at me. Your humor. That frown you make, with the little lines right here." He brushed his fingertip between her eyes. "It's fun to see your real self pop out from behind that social mask." He took her chin between his thumb and forefinger. "I love causing you to lose your vaunted control. Making you as stirred up and uneasy and confused as you make me."

He dropped his hand and pulled back.

Silence stretched between them. Lilah thought perhaps Con was as surprised by his words as she was. Finally, pulling her thoughts together, she said tartly, "Then you have certainly succeeded."

"I've spent a lifetime perfecting that particular skill." He smiled and stood up, reaching a hand down to her.

Lilah took his hand. He held it too long, but she didn't mind. As they strolled down the corridor to her door, she said, "I apologize, too. I said a number of things I used to believe about you, but I don't really think them any longer. You're inordinately irritating, but . . ." She raised her eyes to his as they stopped outside her bedroom door. "You have a good heart and a good mind. And I don't dislike you either."

Con laughed. "I'll take that as high praise from you." He released her hand, stepping back. "Good night. Sleep well."

"Con . . ." Lilah said as he started away, and he turned back, his eyebrows raised in question. "Today on the train . . . when you kissed me? I enjoyed it, too."

Lilah turned and slipped inside her bedroom.

Well, that certainly destroyed any chance he had of going to sleep quickly.

He had kissed Lilah before and thoroughly enjoyed it. But it was one thing to steal a few kisses, to tease her into blushing and taste the sweetness of her mouth. This morning's kisses had been something else altogether. Passion had roared up in him so hard and fast, so hungry, that for a few minutes, he had been oblivious to the world.

Knowing that Lilah enjoyed it, having felt her flame up in ardor, absolutely incandescent . . . well, that changed everything. Before it had been flirtation and fun. This was dangerous. This was the sort of hunger that turned a man blind and stupid, that sent him rushing toward something he knew was absolutely wrong.

Everything inside him thrummed with the desire to follow his instincts. But all the complications and barriers that made wooing Lilah a dangerous proposition were still there. If she were anyone else . . . but she was not. However rash Lilah might think him, this was one time when he had to be careful. It was no longer only he who might suffer. There was his brother. Sabrina. Lilah herself.

He took off his jacket and cravat and unbuttoned his waistcoat, then poured a glass of whiskey from the decanter Vesta had thoughtfully provided. Dropping into the chair, he considered the puzzle of Lilah Holcutt. Con had never been able to resist a puzzle.

How the devil could the practical, sensible, self-admittedly unimaginative Lilah have sprung from this fantastical home? It was too bad this wasn't the place they must search. It was bound to have secret staircases and hidden rooms. Priest holes. Doors behind tapestries, bookshelves that swung out. Even dungeons — after all, Lilah said it was built on top of an ancient castle.

Come to think of it, perhaps Lilah wasn't all that different from her home. She had the same quality of secrecy, of things hidden beneath the surface. He had seen glimpses of the personality beneath her polite mask — in her laughter, in the way she joined in his hunt for the kidnappers. Most of all, in the heat and hunger of her kiss. The longer he knew her and the closer he came to her, the more he discovered that he didn't really know her at all.

Why did she never visit this house? Yes, it was strange, which would not appeal to Lilah, but it was her childhood home, which usually made a person fond of a place. Then there was the way she had acted with her aunt. Vesta had seemed overjoyed to see Lilah, but Lilah had been distant.

He remembered the sight of her standing stiff in Vesta's arms, enduring her embrace, not welcoming it. Vesta was the sort of flamboyant character who would discomfit Lilah. But there had been more there than embarrassment. Not exactly dislike, but something . . . hard.

And why had Lilah, at the age of twelve, gone to live with her other aunt in London? Lilah had said it was because her father felt she needed a woman's guidance. But why, when she already had an aunt living with her?

He wondered how Lilah had felt, what she thought about being sent away. She seemed fond of her Aunt Helena, but still, it must have been painful. Lilah said little about her father. Indeed, she rarely talked about her family or childhood at all. Wasn't that a trifle strange in itself?

Con had given her half a dozen stories about his family and childhood on that long ride in pursuit of the kidnappers. Lilah had told him nothing. The only reason he'd learned anything about her father was because he'd questioned her about the key.

Lilah hadn't wanted him to see her house; he'd seen the mortification on her face. He was certain it was the reason for her reluctance to invite him. That was a relief, of course, but now he had to wonder why it embarrassed her so.

Barrow House was peculiar, obviously, but he couldn't imagine why she would think a Moreland would object to oddity. Least of all him. But perhaps it was the opposite — that she feared he would be attracted to it, that it would rouse his curiosity. Or that he would see something in Lilah, too, some aspect she didn't want revealed.

That was an intriguing thought, and he spent the rest of his drink on it. After that he went to bed. He fell asleep thinking of Lilah.

He wasn't sure what awakened him, but his eyes popped open and he lay for a moment, listening. There was nothing but silence. Only the creaks and noises of an unfamiliar house. But he was wide-awake now. With a sigh, he swung out of bed and went to the dresser to open his pocket watch. Two o'clock.

Going to the window, he pushed aside the drapes and gazed out at the night. The moon was almost full, palely lighting the landscape below him. He could make out the dark shapes of trees and shrubbery, the broad pathway leading into the center of the garden.

A white figure moved below him. His

heart gave a jump, then he smiled at himself. It was a real person, no phantom, just a woman in a white nightgown. He leaned closer to the glass. Why was a woman walking in the garden in the middle of the night?

It was Lilah. She was too far away and the light too faint to see her clearly, but he recognized that fall of hair even in the fainter light from the moon. What the devil was Lilah doing outside at two o'clock in the morning? And dressed only in her nightgown?

Stunned, he watched her move along the path, then turn left and walk out of sight into the shadows and trees. She was not hurrying, but neither was it the ambling, aimless walk of a person taking a stroll. She had a destination. But what? Why? Even on a warm summer night, what would make the very proper Lilah leave her bedroom wearing only a simple shift?

His first thought, his only thought, was that she was meeting someone. Meeting a man — one she knew quite well if she was wearing nothing but a nightgown. Something hot and acidic bloomed in his chest, such an unfamiliar feeling that it took a moment to recognize it as jealousy.

Con pulled out his shirt and began to dress, then stopped. What was he doing?

Was he actually going to follow her? And what did he intend to do if he found her in the embrace of a lover? He had no claim on Lilah.

He turned back to the window, torn. It wasn't jealousy, just his usual insatiable need to know. He had no right to be jealous, no hold on Lilah. A few kisses, no matter how torrid, did not make a relationship. Oh, the devil. Of course he was jealous.

At that moment, she walked back into view. He let out a breath, the knot in his chest easing. Thank goodness he hadn't made an idiot of himself by running out after her. But why had she sneaked out of the house at this hour, only to stay no more than five minutes?

If she had met a lover, surely she would do more than exchange a few kisses with him. For that matter, if she had a lover here, why hadn't she come to Barrow House in the last two years? But if not a lover, who then? And why?

CHAPTER SIXTEEN

Lilah crawled out of bed the next morning, feeling almost as tired as when she'd lain down. But she was determined to be at breakfast. As taken as Aunt Vesta had been with Con, Lilah wasn't going to count on her aunt sleeping late.

She rang for Cuddington to help her dress, and to Lilah's surprise, the sour-visaged maid turned out to be an artist with hairstyles. She rolled Lilah's hair into one of the popular new pompadour styles, and though Lilah had not yet worn her hair that way — she never liked to draw attention to herself by being on the front edge of fashion — she was as eager as Cuddington to try it out here in the country, where no one would see. Except Con.

The result was enough to make even Cuddington smile, and the expression on Con's face when she walked into the dining room was deeply gratifying. He came around the table to pull out her chair, his eyes straying back again and again to her hair.

"Good morning, Miss Holcutt. It promises to be a lovely day."

"The fog has lifted?" Lilah asked.

"It's absolutely sunny out there, but I was referring more to being with you all day."

Lilah raised a disbelieving eyebrow, but she couldn't hold back her smile. Had Con meant it last night when he said he liked her? Or maybe that wasn't what he said; maybe he had just told her he didn't *dis*like her. It was so distracting talking to Con that sometimes she lost track of what he was saying.

It was impossible to carry on a private conversation with the butler and a footman bustling in and out with breakfast, so Lilah made no mention of their purpose or plans. "I trust you had a pleasant sleep."

Con made an affirmative noise and fixed an oddly intent gaze on her. "What about you? Were you up and about last night?"

"Goodness, no, I retired for the night as soon as we parted."

"The moon was almost full. It was so bright I could clearly see the garden, even in the middle of the night." He paused, almost as if waiting for something, then continued. "So I got up and spent a few

209

minutes looking at it."

"Indecd?"

"Yes. It was bright enough to have taken a stroll."

"Was it? I'm afraid I've never been out in the garden so late." Lilah was finding this chitchat hard going. She wished the servants would leave.

"You haven't? I thought I saw you there."

"Me?" Startled, Lilah glanced up at him. "I wasn't in the garden." A frown began to form between her eyes. "I can't imagine who would have been. One of the servants, I suppose."

Con simply looked at her for a long moment, then shrugged. "Perhaps I was dreaming."

"Yes, that's probably it." Lilah sent the butler for more toast, and after he left the room, she swung back to Con. "I do hope you won't mention that again. The servants will be sure to decide you saw a ghost. They're dreadfully superstitious here."

His look was assessing, but he said only, "No, of course. I shan't say a thing."

They fell silent as they ate. Lilah felt his eyes on her, but she did her best to ignore it. She wondered if there had actually been someone there . . . perhaps some maid having a tryst with a lover? Lilah hoped Con would keep his promise and not quiz the servants about it. Even worse, what if he broached the matter to Aunt Vesta? God only knows what sort of story she would concoct.

"I thought we'd ride over to Carmoor this morning." The sooner she could get him away from her aunt, the better.

"Why don't you show me around Barrow House first?"

"Here? But why? That will hardly help us find the, um —" She paused, remembering the butler, who was once again standing by the door. "What we're looking for."

Con grinned, leaning forward to murmur, "Very stealthy, Delilah." He settled back and, returning to his normal voice, said, "It helps to get the lay of the land first, before one starts an investigation. Besides, Barrow House is interesting. We could explore the maze."

"How did you know there was a maze?"

"I took a turn around the garden before breakfast and saw the hedges. Thought it must be a maze."

"It's completely overgrown," Lilah protested. "It's not safe. I was never allowed to go in there by myself."

"Then you must be eager to see it now."

"Not really." There was something unnerving about the maze's dark green depths, the ever-narrowing passages. "Why would anyone want to get lost?"

"I think the idea is more to find what's hidden at the center. Aren't you curious?"

"No." She fixed him with an exasperated gaze. How was it that Con always managed to bring up bothersome topics? "My father took me in there once because I kept insisting." She remembered her anxiety, the hedges looming so high, so dark around her, the untrimmed branches and twigs reaching out to snag her. Her chest tightened. "There's nothing there to see."

"Very well." He shrugged. "I'll explore the maze later myself."

"Con, no. You'll get lost."

"I never get lost. You know, perhaps we should talk to your aunt before we go."

She should have foreseen this. Of course he would want to talk to Aunt Vesta, and God only knew where that would lead. It would be impossible to keep him away from her aunt. But at least she could delay it. "No, let's explore the maze."

Con looked faintly surprised at her reversal but said nothing. Later that morning, Lilah led Con out to the maze. The hedges had grown taller, their branches straggling out every which way and turning the walkways even darker.

Branches stretched and curled from either side, narrowing the pathway, in some places even knitting together enough that Con had to push them aside in order to pass through. An odd, stifling feeling settled over Lilah, confirming her dislike of this place.

"Lilah, you need not come," Con said softly. "I can go on alone."

Lilah stiffened her spine. "Nonsense. I can't have you vanishing in the maze."

His eyes drifted over her face. "Very well." They started forward again, Con taking the lead. "Tell me about this maze. Who built it?"

"I don't really know. It was here when my father was young. He got lost in it once as a child. That's why he wouldn't let me into it alone. Weren't mazes popular during the last century?"

Con shrugged. "No doubt Alex could tell you better than I. But I think they've been around long before that. Didn't the Tudors have them?"

"Then perhaps it was planted by the first Holcutt." Lilah was glad Con had thrown out a conversational gambit. While she concentrated on his questions, she could ignore the tightness in her chest, only vaguely aware of the twists and turns Con took.

They reached an intersecting path, and Con paused, frowning faintly as he looked first one way then the next. Lilah pointed straight ahead and started forward. "I think this is the correct way."

"No. We should turn here." He took her arm, halting her. An odd look crossed his face. "Yes. I'm sure. It's this way."

"How could you possibly know?" Lilah asked. Confidence was one thing, but Con could be annoyingly stubborn in his certainty.

"It just makes sense," Con replied vaguely.

With a shrug, Lilah followed him. It was small of her, she knew, but a part of her hoped they would find themselves in a leafy dead end. Con released her arm, but he kept his hand on the back of her waist in a gesture Lilah found oddly — and irritatingly — reassuring.

They turned again, and there, in front of them was the center of the maze. A sundial marked the spot, a wrought iron bench facing it. The bench had been overgrown by ivy, and the vine had inched over the stone foundation on which the sundial sat. Tendrils crawled up the pedestal.

Lilah turned to Con in astonishment.

214

"How did you do that?"

"Do what?"

"Go directly to the center. Not even one wrong turn. Father told me no one ever managed it on the first try." Lilah narrowed her eyes. "Did you come here this morning and figure it out beforehand?"

Con burst into laughter. "Delilah Holcutt. You are an exceedingly suspicious soul." He moved closer, smiling down at her. "No. I didn't sneak in earlier so that I could astound you with my directional skills. I told you I was good with maps and directions. I generally can tell which way is north."

"There is no map of the maze." Lilah planted her hands on her hips. "And I don't see how knowing east from west could help you work your way through a maze."

"Then I suppose it must be luck." He grinned. "Or maybe I do have a mystical ability after all. I'm a human compass." As Lilah rolled her eyes, Con turned to examine the sundial. The pedestal was made of stone, the face of copper, long since oxidized. "I wouldn't think a sundial would work very well, here in the middle of these hedges."

"No." Lilah joined him at the edge of the triangular stone slab on which the sundial sat.

Con squatted down and pushed aside the creeping strands of ivy. A figure of three spirals fused into a triangular shape was carved into the corner. He tore more ivy away to reveal the carving repeated at regular intervals around the edge. Con ran a fingertip around one of the spirals.

"The mystical number of three," he murmured. "Look. One at each of the three corners, two more along each side, making a total of nine — three times three."

"They're triskeles," Lilah told him. "They're on some ancient artifacts found in this area. I believe the spirals represent eternity. I suppose three is the Holy Trinity." She wrinkled her brow. "Though I think the artifacts are older than Christianity."

Lilah glanced around her. The looming hedges cast too many shadows; the walls felt like a prison. "Con, there's no reason to stay here. I'm tired."

"What?" Con turned. "Oh. Yes, of course." They started back the way they had come. "Something about this place bothers you. What is it that makes that little pulse in your throat jump? I dare not hope it's excitement at being around me."

"I assure you, it has nothing to do with you." Lilah sent him a repressive look.

Con grinned. "You're a harsh woman, De-lilah."

"Would you please not call me that?"

"I like it. It fairly rolls off the tongue. Dilly, now, is rather charming, but it doesn't have the same grand effect."

"If you start calling me Dilly, I swear I will lure you down to the dungeons and lock you up."

"So there *are* dungeons. We'll have to try them next."

Lilah laughed. "You *do* remember we are here to search Sabrina's house, don't you?"

They had reached the entrance to the maze, but Con grabbed her wrist and pulled her back into the shelter of the hedges. "When you laugh like that, I have the devil of a time sticking to my promise."

Lilah's heart began to thunder in a way that had nothing to do with the maze. She watched his eyes darken, saw his mouth curve wickedly. She knew as he bent toward her that he was about to kiss her. And that she was not going to pull away.

"Lilah?" Aunt Vesta's voice floated through the air. "Where are you, dear? It's time for a cup of tea, don't you think?"

Con murmured something under his breath that Lilah was sure she should be glad she couldn't understand, and his hand

217

fell away from her.

"Yes, Aunt, I know," she called. "We're coming."

"It's such a lovely day." Aunt Vesta smiled at Con, pouring the tea as they approached. "I have felt the ancient power of the earth all day. Can't you sense it?"

"No," Lilah said quickly. "I've been showing Lord Moreland around."

"The maze," Aunt Vesta sent Lilah a sly look. "Couples often enjoy a walk there."

Lilah caught her aunt's meaning, and she began to blush. A glance at Con told her that he, too, understood her aunt's implication, though *he,* of course, just grinned.

"Do you know who built the maze, Miss Holcutt?" Con asked Aunt Vesta, reaching out to take the cup she offered.

"It's Mrs. LeClaire, dear. I am a widow, you see." She gave him a wistful smile. "Poor dear Henri."

"I beg your pardon. Mrs. LeClaire." He frowned, looking thoughtful.

"I told Con that I didn't know which of our ancestors installed the maze. Do you, Aunt Vesta?"

"No, it's been there for . . . oh, ages and ages. Dear Papa loved it. He would often go there to contemplate life. But he didn't create it. I believe he put in the little area in the center — the bench and so on."

"He placed the sundial?" Con asked. "I was very interested in those figures in the stone around it."

"Yes, yes." Vesta nodded her head as if Con had made a telling point. "Triskeles. They are very powerful symbols. I believe Papa had a connection with the Other Side, too."

"I thought Con and I would take a ride tomorrow morning." Early. Before Aunt Vesta arose.

"How delightful! There are so many important sites to show him. That ancient barrow. And Holy Well, though that's perhaps too far. You'd have to have Cook pack you a lunch."

"Holy Well?" Con asked, looking interested.

"Yes, it's said that Joseph of Arimathea visited there, but of course Glastonbury was a sacred place to the ancients long before that."

"Ah . . . the Holy Grail," Con said.

Lilah suppressed a sigh. At least they were off the subject of the Other Side.

"Then you know about it!" Vesta cried with delight.

"Indeed. The legend is that Joseph of Arimathea sailed here to Britain and buried the holy chalice at Glastonbury Tor."

"Yes. Some say that Glastonbury Tor was the isle of Avalon, where King Arthur was borne on his funeral barge, but of course that is all nonsense."

"Is it?" Con leaned in, food forgotten on his plate.

Vesta nodded emphatically. "Glastonbury Tor was once an island, but it wasn't Avalon. It was the Western Isle, where dead souls traveled to meet their reward."

Lilah cleared her throat. "We aren't going to the Holy Well. We're planning to ride to Carmoor."

"Carmoor!" Aunt Vesta stared at her. "But why? It's just a house." She looked over at Con. "There are so many more interesting places around here. There's the Faerie Track. That's not far."

"The Faerie Track? I've never heard of that."

Vesta nodded. "Yes, some call it the Fae Path or the Silver Way — it's said it gleams silver to those who have the ability to 'see.' It's ancient, very ancient. A safe passage through the bogs."

"We are going to Carmoor," Lilah reiterated firmly. "Con has business there. His brother, you know, is married to Sabrina, and Con is here to monitor the house for them. To make sure everything is all right."

"Little Sabrina. Such a sweet child." Vesta sighed. "I so missed the two of you."

Lilah bit back the words that rose in her throat. *Then why did you stay away for nine years?*

"Miss Holcutt is correct," Con said. "But I look forward to exploring this area. It seems to be a very special place."

"Con . . . I . . . um —"

Vesta nodded enthusiastically. "It is indeed. It has been a place of power for thousands of years. The old ones knew this. Glastonbury Tor, you know, forms a triangle with Stonehenge and the standing stones at Avebury. And, of course, three . . ."

"Is a mystical number," Con finished.

Vesta waved her hand around vaguely. "The paths all run through here."

"Like this track you mentioned, the Fae Path?"

"There are no paths," Lilah said flatly. "Aunt Vesta, please . . ." Did her aunt not realize, did she not see, how foolish she appeared? But Con, of course, would encourage her.

"Oh, no, I didn't mean the Faerie Track." Vesta leaned forward, happy to expound. "Although it must lie atop one. I'm talking about the channels in the earth. The power that lies beneath us. It courses in Lines, many Lines, from Cornwall to London and beyond. From the Channel into Scotland. It is mystical power."

"Mystical power?" Con asked encouragingly.

"Yes. One can almost feel it pulsing beneath one's feet. Some people call it magic, which is sheer foolishness. The Lines are the connection to the Source. It's the essence of life. Most people cannot feel it, never realize it. But those of us who have ability, we know." She reached over and patted Con's hand. "You feel it. You have the ability."

"No, I fear not," Con replied.

"Oh, you do." She wagged a playful finger at him. "You just haven't realized it yet. But I can sense it in you."

"Tell me more about these Lines. They come from Glastonbury Tor?"

"As I told you, it's an ancient holy place. A multitude of channels course through it. Glastonbury is a crossroads, a place of power, but it's not the source of it. That comes from the earth itself and spans the globe." She held up her hands in a circle, fingertips interlacing. "A web, you see. One can draw on the power from anywhere, but it is stronger when you are on a strand of the web. And it is very mighty at one of the hubs." She paused. "That is why I returned."

Lilah tightened all over, her hands knotting into fists in her lap, but she could think of no way to stop her aunt.

"Because this area is powerful?" Con asked.

Aunt Vesta leaned forward, confiding, "Because Barrow House is." She tapped the table. "This land beneath us. We sit on a tor, smaller by far than Glastonbury but a crossroads nevertheless. Many lines intersect here. Long ago, I didn't understand what fueled my abilities. I thought it all lay within me." She smiled deprecatingly. "Vanity of course. I left here, full of pride, emboldened by my success. But I learned I didn't have the same power anywhere else. I was still connected to the spirits of course. I could call on them and they would answer. But it wasn't the same."

"Aunt Vesta, no, please . . ." Lilah wasn't sure what she pleaded for. She held her hand against her roiling stomach, as if she could keep it all locked in. She could not bring herself to look at Con.

Vesta paid no attention to her as she rolled on. "But finally, I understood. I held great ability because I was born here, atop this hub, this center. That was why I was able to use the power to such an extent. That was why I could call forth Brockminster and he would respond."

"Brockminster?" Con straightened. "Elmont Brockminster? Good Lord — you're Madame LeClaire!"

Aunt Vesta beamed. "Yes. Dear boy, how astonishing that you remember!"

"How could I not? I can't believe I didn't recognize your name at once. The Brockminster Séance was a sensation."

"It was astonishing," Vesta agreed. "You cannot imagine what power surged through me. It was like ice and fire all at once. That was when I knew, really knew, what I was capable of."

"Stop!" Lilah shoved back her chair so hard it almost toppled over. Her face was stark white, her eyes full of storm. "Why can't you just leave it alone?" Anger and resentment choked her throat. She knew she was making a bad scene even worse, but Lilah couldn't stop herself. With an inarticulate cry, she turned and ran from the room.

CHAPTER SEVENTEEN

"Lilah —" Con jumped to his feet, alarmed at the look on Lilah's face. "Lilah, wait." He took a step toward her, but she was already gone. Con muttered a curse beneath his breath and started after her.

"Don't," Vesta told him, reaching out. "Let her have a little time alone. It's never wise to push Dilly."

Con hesitated. Her aunt was probably right. He had enough experience with Lilah to know that if he pursued her, she would lash out in anger. And while he didn't mind a good argument, he had no wish to upset her more.

"Mrs. LeClaire, I'm sorry." He turned to her. "I didn't mean to distress Lilah. I was just startled when I realized who you were."

"That's perfectly fine. Poor Lilah . . ." She sighed heavily. "I'm afraid she has little tolerance for what she doesn't understand.

Sadly, she didn't inherit any of the family talent."

"There were others in the family with, um, your ability?"

"Not to the extent I had." She preened a little. "But the Holcutts have always been attuned to the world of the spirit. Of course, many of them attributed everything to accepted theological beliefs, but there were others who were more adventurous."

Barrow House and its occupants were growing more fascinating by the moment. Why had Lilah never mentioned any of this? Well, no, he knew the answer to that. It was because it went against her view of the world. But why had she turned out so differently from the rest of her family? And, most of all, why did it give her the pain he had seen just now in her eyes?

As soon as he could extricate himself from Vesta's conversational clutches, Con went searching for Lilah. He had heard the door out to the garden slam a moment after she ran from the room, so he turned in that direction. He could not find her in the garden, but as he emerged at the other end, he saw Lilah standing in the distance. Her arms were crossed, and she stared out broodingly over the landscape.

He followed her. Lilah heard his approach

and glanced back, then turned away without speaking. Con decided that was as good as an invitation, and he joined her. Lilah stood on the edge of the promontory on which the house sat. As Lilah's aunt had said the tor wasn't high, but it was taller than anything else around and gave a panoramic view of the Levels. Con could see all the way to Glastonbury Tor, rising dramatically far off in the distance.

Perfectly flat, the farmland below them was laced with short, straight waterways. Willow trees grew in straight rows along the embankments, and here and there he could see a marshy spot, where ferns and reeds grew wild. The late-afternoon sun washed it all with a pale golden light, but fog was already beginning to ooze in along the canals and around the base of Glastonbury Tor.

There was an odd, eerie beauty to the place. It was a far cry from the rolling, green land of the Moreland country estate, with its grand old trees and pastures dotted with wildflowers. But the Levels held a magnificence all their own, still and timeless.

"Are you all right?" Con asked. It was a foolish question because obviously she was not, but he knew he must tread carefully here.

"Yes, of course." Lilah glanced at him, her face reverting to its polite public mask. "I apologize for leaving so abruptly." She turned back to her contemplation of the view, clearly done with the topic.

He decided to try a different path. "I like it here. There's something about it that draws one." When she made no reply, he went on, "Do you feel that way? Doesn't it tug at you?"

"You've been listening too much to my aunt," Lilah said tartly. "It's just land, not some sentient being or ancient holy ground." She let out a sigh. "But yes, I love it. I feel at home here. That's only natural. I grew up here."

"So you don't believe that it's the pull of Glastonbury Tor?" Con knew that would light a fire in her. That was exactly what he wanted. It seemed the only way he could pierce the polite calm she used as a shield.

He was right. Lilah's eyes darkened. "Of course not. Aunt Vesta can make herself believe anything she wants to believe, no matter how flimsy the reasons. You can draw a line from anywhere to anywhere. It's not magic. As for that ludicrous triangle linking Stonehenge, Glastonbury and Avebury, well, of course a continuous line to three places will form a triangle. You could do the same with any spots!"

"True."

"And you, of course, encouraged her. Tell me about the power. What of the Fae Path?" She was building up steam now. "There is no Source. No power running beneath our feet. And the Faerie Track is nothing but a safe passage through the bogs built by the people who dwelled here long ago. It's clever. It's interesting. But it is not supernatural." She flung her hands out wide.

"I suppose you have a logical explanation for what happened at the Brockminster Séance."

"How could you know about that? It happened nine years ago. You were scarcely out of short pants."

Con laughed. "As it happens, the length of my trousers had little to do with what I learned. However, I read about it two or three years ago when I took over the agency. In Olivia's collected accounts of . . ."

"Hoaxes? Charlatans?"

"I was going to say unusual occurrences. There were a number of stories about that séance. It caught the newspapers' attention. It's not often you have a pack of peers sitting around a table summoning spirits. It's even more unusual when those spirits come crashing into the room, shattering the

229

windows and plunging the whole room into darkness. As I heard it, the air fairly crackled with energy, and everyone's hair stood on end."

Lilah made a disgusted sound. "What nonsense. It was only a storm. They held a séance in the midst of a storm, and the wind shattered one of the old windows. The room was lit by only candles — for the proper atmosphere, you see — so it's no surprise that the gust of wind blew out all the lights. I know. I was there."

Con's eyebrows shot up. "*You* were at the Brockminster Séance? But you were only . . . What? Twelve?"

"I was often at Aunt Vesta's séances." Her mouth twisted. "Father thought my presence might make my dead mother more willing to come back."

"I see." And he did. This news made a lot of things clearer.

"I knew you would."

"And that is why you tried so hard to dissuade me from coming here. You were embarrassed not only about the house, but also your aunt."

"My whole family," she tossed back. "Of course I was embarrassed. Barrow House looks as if it was built by a madman. And it probably was. The Holcutts always had a reputation for being peculiar. My aunt thinks she's connected to some unearthly force. My father spent my whole life trying to communicate with his dead wife." For an instant, tears glittered in her eyes before she blinked them away.

"Lilah . . ." Con's voice was soft. He stepped forward and placed his hands on her arms, moving them up and down in a soothing manner. "There was no need to worry about my reaction. I am the least likely person in the world to be shocked by the Holcutts. My family is known all over England as the Mad Morelands after all."

Lilah jerked out of his grasp. "Yes, but you didn't have an aunt who created an enormous scandal by holding an infamous séance, then adopted the name Madame Le-Claire, declared herself a psychic and ran off to Europe with Brockminster's nephew."

"Abandoning you," Con added. His heart twisted a little, thinking of the girl, little more than a child, going through what must have been a frightening experience, however much Lilah discounted it — and then losing the aunt who had always taken care of her.

Lilah waved his comment away. "That didn't matter."

"I think it mattered quite a bit," Con

replied. "She must have been in the place of a mother to you since your own mother died young."

"Aunt Vesta is hardly a maternal sort. She may have lived with me, but I wouldn't call her influence as being like a mother. That role belongs to my other aunt, the normal one. Aunt Helena took me to live with her in order to preserve my reputation. She knew my name would be tainted with scandal if I remained here with no better influence than a father who spent all his time trying to commune with the dead. Worse, Aunt Vesta could have come back at any time. Even my father saw how bad it would be for me. I could never have made a good marriage. As soon as I made my debut, the rumors would be flying. 'You remember her aunt, don't you? Cut from the same cloth, I warrant.' "

"I understand it now." And he did. Motherless, largely ignored by her father, deserted — however Lilah might deny it — by the aunt who had raised her, Lilah had been cast adrift. Her rule-abiding aunt Helena had saved her, but it had meant leaving her home and breaking away from everything she had known. "Your antipathy to the occult, the way you stay away from your home, your abhorrence of scandal. It's no wonder you're so insistent on following the rules."

"Of course I want to follow the rules. Of course I abhor creating a scandal. Who doesn't? Everyone does. Except you." She turned and started away, then swung back to say, "I am planning to ride to Carmoor first thing tomorrow."

He executed a little bow. "I will be there."

Con watched as Lilah strode away. It was no wonder the woman was such a study in contrasts. Imagine living half one's life in a completely unconventional manner, going to séances, trying to contact their dead mother's spirit. Then living the other half in the most conventional, rigid, rule-abiding style.

Lilah regarded Aunt Helena as having saved her. Perhaps she had, at least from a torrent of gossip. But Con could not but think that the woman had stifled Lilah's spirit, as well. It came out in flashes — when Lilah laughed without thinking how it looked, when she was hot on the chase after the kidnappers, when some idea sparked the light of interest in her eyes.

There was far more to Lilah than the shell her aunt had sought to create around her. And Con was becoming very interested in discovering what lay beneath it.

CHAPTER EIGHTEEN

Lilah could scarcely believe she had said all that — and to Con of all people. He thought he understood her because his own family was odd. But that was precisely why he could not understand what she felt — the shame and anger, the resentment, the hunger to fit in, the determination to be so good, so right, that no one would even think of her as one of *those* Holcutts.

Con felt none of those things. The Morelands didn't embarrass him; he reveled in their reputation. Happy and secure in the midst of his loyal, loving family, he had never felt the weight of others' opinions. With his twin beside him, he had never been lonely. God knows, he certainly had never been afraid. Even when he was a child he and Alex had sailed into any danger, confident that they would win out — or if they did not, their older siblings would rescue them.

She hadn't feared he would be appalled by her story. What she dreaded was his amusement. Con would consider her narrow-minded and rigid to be embarrassed by her aunt's behavior. He would love the irony that the straitlaced, oh-so-proper Lilah Holcutt had a family as bizarre as his.

Now he would tease her about Aunt Vesta and her séance or the oddities of Barrow House. He had admitted that he enjoyed annoying her — and she *still* did not understand that — and this knowledge gave him plentiful ammunition.

What if he found it such an entertaining story that he told it to others? He would certainly tell Alex; that wouldn't be too bad since Sabrina already knew Lilah's family. But what if he recounted it to the others in his family? The women with whom Lilah had become tentative friends: Olivia, who had once occupied herself with revealing fraudulent mediums, his outspoken mother and — worst of all — Megan, a journalist! She must persuade him to keep the story to himself.

Lilah came downstairs the next morning already dressed in her riding habit. It was a bottle green that went well with her hair. Though the style was plain, as habits usually were, it was set off by the unusual fastening of four large wooden buttons running diagonally across the front. The finishing touch was a small hat accented by a green-and-blue feather that curled forward, almost touching her face.

Con jumped to his feet when she walked in, his eyes lighting in a way that made her pulse speed up. As they rode to Carmoor, Lilah rehearsed what she would say to him. It was difficult to ask anyone for a favor, but with Con, she was doubly reluctant. She wasn't sure why, since he had a generous, easygoing nature, but the words stuck in her throat.

Finally, when they reached Carmoor and stabled their horses, she pulled together her courage and said, "I'm sorry."

He glanced at her in surprise. "For what?"

"Snapping at you last night. I shouldn't take my irritation with my aunt out on you."

He shrugged. "I am immune to insults. Remember, I have three sisters whom I've aggravated even more frequently than I do you. I've weathered many a feminine bad temper."

"I hope — that is, I want to ask you a favor." Again she paused.

"Lilah, what is it? Surely you know I would help you in any way I can."

"Yes, I know." She did, really; the sudden

realization filled her with warmth. "I would ask you not to tell anyone about . . . all this." She waved a hand vaguely in the direction of her home.

"All what?"

"My family. My aunt. What happened nine years ago."

"Did you think I was going to gossip about you?" Con's voice turned sharp. "Do you know me so little you think I would do anything to hurt you?"

"No." She took his arm, pulling him to a halt. "I know you would not set out to hurt me. But it is the sort of thing that intrigues you, and I'm afraid you might tell your family because it makes interesting conversation. They might repeat it. Or you might mention it to someone else, at your club, perhaps. A jest. A comment. I fear you don't understand how important it is that no one know."

"I don't understand why it worries you so much, but —"

"I've been so careful," she told him urgently. "I've worked hard to be above reproach. Aunt Helena has taken great care to make sure that the taint of scandal doesn't cling to me. She wants so much for me to make a good marriage." Con's lips twitched in irritation, and she hurried on,

"I know that isn't something that you would care about. But if that scandal came out again, it would hurt not only my reputation but hers, as well. I could not bear it if Aunt Helena suffered because of me, if people whispered behind her back or snubbed her."

"Lilah!" Con stared. "That was almost ten years ago, and the scandal was your aunt's. Society has forgotten about it. In any case, it wasn't your fault or Mrs. Summersley's. Why would it hurt your reputation? How would it keep you from making a 'good' marriage?"

"You don't know society very well if you think that. Ask your sister Kyria. She'll tell you I'm right. If the subject of my aunt and her peculiarity was raised, the old scandal would be taken out and dusted off. It would be new fodder for gossip. They'd recall that the Holcutts had always been peculiar. 'Remember what her aunt did. Lilah may be circumspect now, but what if she changes? What if she turns out to be the same?' Worse, the story would grow with each recounting. Faulty memories would be embellished. Soon people would whisper about bad blood and how I might taint a family line."

"I know how important an appropriate marriage is to you," Con said tightly. "But any man who wouldn't marry you because of your aunt's old scandal wouldn't be worth marrying anyway." His face softened, and he laid his hand against her cheek. "You needn't worry. I will say nothing about you or your aunt to anyone. I wouldn't have anyway. This isn't just an interesting story. It concerns you."

"Con . . ." The tightness in Lilah's chest began to dissolve. Inexplicably, tears welled in her eyes.

Con swept his thumb across her cheek, catching a tear. He bent to kiss her tenderly. When he raised his head, gazing into her eyes for a long moment, the world seemed still and timeless around them, as if they stood poised on the brink.

Con stepped back, and the moment was gone. "We should . . . The house." He gestured toward the redbrick mansion before them. His movements were a trifle jerky, his voice raw.

"Yes. Of course." Lilah pulled herself together. "The key."

They walked through the untended gardens, growing in a riot of color, intermingled with weeds, vines and limbs inching into walkways and obscuring statuary. Clearly the house had been closed for some years. The rear door was locked, but Con pulled out his lock picks and had it open in a minute.

Their steps echoed on the slate floor as they walked down the hall, peering into rooms. If the gardens had not shown the house was un-lived-in, the film of dust over everything would have. Carpets had been rolled up and stowed against the walls, and most of the furniture was shrouded with dustcovers. Tables and shelves stood bare of ornamentation. There was an empty, dead feeling to the house that sent a shiver down Lilah's spine.

"I — this feels wrong," Lilah said, her voice hushed. "We're intruding."

"I know." Con nodded. "But if Sabrina and Alex weren't gone, they'd be here, searching with us. I want to find out what's going on and put a stop to the Dearborns before Sabrina and Alex return."

Lilah nodded. "You're right. They shouldn't have to deal with the Dearborns again."

The first room they explored was Mr. Blair's office. They roamed around the large room, taking off the desk's dustcover to go through the desk drawers and searching through the bookcases. Lilah went down the rows of books, uncertain what she was looking for. Now and then, she glanced back at

Con, who was inspecting the mantel and fireplace, testing various embellishments for hidden levers. It was hard to keep her mind on what she was doing; it kept drifting back to that tender kiss Con had given her, the depths of his eyes, the touch of his hand upon her cheek.

She turned and looked at him again. He had left the fireplace and was at the desk, rummaging through empty drawers. A lock of hair had fallen across his forehead; he wore his hair too long and shaggy. But it was hard to pull her eyes away from the way it curled against his collar. As if he felt her gaze, he glanced up. Lilah flushed, embarrassed at being caught watching him — or perhaps the heat was from something else entirely, for there was a look in his eyes, a certain set of his mouth that made her knees want to buckle.

Lilah whirled away and blindly searched the shelves. Behind her she heard Con close a drawer sharply and walk away. It took a few minutes for her heart to regain its steady rhythm. She moved to another bookcase. Across the room, Con said, "Nothing."

He spent a few minutes going down the line of shelves, tilting back two or three books at a time. Lilah stopped what she was doing to watch him in puzzlement. "What are you doing?"

"Easy way to set up a hidden door. Especially here, where he's got so many volumes. You attach one of the books to a latch so that when you tilt the book back like this, it unfastens the latch. The whole bookcase is attached to the door, hiding it, and the case swings out."

Lilah knelt at the farthest end of the shelves, her skirts pooling around her, and began to make her way toward him. She could hear the continued *chunk-chunk-chunk* of the books as he dropped them back in place.

The small thuds became more erratic, then stopped altogether for so long that Lilah glanced up in curiosity. Con was watching her, his hand still on one of the books, and there was a look in his eyes that made her words die in her throat.

Con pivoted abruptly and walked to another bookcase. His face turned in the opposite direction, he started down the row. Lilah went back to her task, moving rapidly, as if she could outrun the turbulent sensations inside her. Perhaps they should take different rooms. It would be easier not to think about Con if he weren't right there, and there was the practical notion that it would halve their work time. But Lilah couldn't bring herself to offer the solution, nor did Con suggest it.

They moved through the other rooms downstairs. Lilah was ever aware of Con's movements behind her, and she could not keep from glancing over at him. It grew warmer as they continued to work, and Con shrugged out of his jacket, tossing it over the back of a sofa. He unfastened his cuff links and dropped them in a pocket, then rolled up his sleeves.

There was something primitively arousing about watching him begin to undress, and Lilah found it difficult to pull her gaze away. She couldn't recall ever seeing a man do anything like this. Of course, it was highly improper to be in one's shirtsleeves in company — naturally Con didn't feel himself bound by such rules.

She pulled her eyes back to her task, though at the moment she couldn't remember exactly what she had been doing. *Oh, yes, the piano.* Somewhat shakily, she straightened the pages of sheet music before her, though it didn't need it. She hoped Con had no idea what she had felt watching him. What she still felt.

It was a relief when they left the room and went upstairs. She realized that was a mistake, though, as soon as she stepped foot inside the first bedroom. The room was dark, the draperies shut, giving the place an enclosed, almost-intimate atmosphere. The large bed seemed to take up all the space.

She could feel a blush rising up her throat and she sneaked a glance at Con to find him, too, staring at the bed. He jerked his eyes away and strode to the far wall to begin his search. Lilah opened the draperies, but it offered little more light, for the shutters outside were closed. It was still too cave-like, too much like night.

Con let out a muffled exclamation, causing Lilah to jump, and she whirled around to look at him. Con was taking down a painting on the opposite wall, revealing behind it a square metal door embedded in the wall. Lilah hurried over to join him, glad to have her mind once again on what they were supposed to be doing rather than thinking about Con.

"This may take a while," Con said, glancing at her. "I'm not as good at combinations." He leaned closer to the safe, listening, as he turned the knob.

Lilah inched in, watching his fingers, anticipation rising in her. Con turned the knob this way and that, and after a moment, he leaned his forehead against the safe, drumming his fingers on the wall. "Lilah."

"What?"

"You're distracting me."

He turned his face toward her, and she realized, startled, that she was only inches away from him. Her breath caught in her throat. His eyes were hot, his voice husky. "I can feel your breath on my neck, and I can't remember a bloody thing."

"Oh. I'm sorry." Lilah blushed and started to step back, but his hand cupped the nape of her neck, holding her in place.

"I like it."

As her mind whirled, trying to come up with a response, Con kissed her.

His lips weren't tender as they had been earlier in the garden. They were hot and seeking, persuasive, charming her very will from her. Her body was suddenly warm and pliant. Lilah thought she might melt all over, but the idea didn't bother her. Melting into Con seemed like a very nice thing to do.

His hands went to her waist, pulling her into his body, and he reeled back against the wall, clamping his arms around her, as his mouth plundered hers. She could feel his body against hers, no longer encumbered by his jacket. He was hard, all bone and muscle against her softness, and Lilah pressed her body against his, twisting as if she could move into him. He made an odd noise deep in his throat and turned, so that it was her back against the wall and he sank into her, moving more boldly than she had.

Lilah dug her fingers into his hair, shaken by the swirl of sensations inside her. Everything was so fast, so shimmering, so turbulent, she could not take it all in. She wanted to slow down, to savor it, yet at the same time she ached to have more, feel more. Con broke their kiss to trail his mouth across her face, down her throat. She could feel his breath, quick and a little shaky, upon her skin, in a seductive combination with his lips. His skin was scorching, matching the heat that boiled up inside her.

His hand went to the large round buttons that slanted across her chest. "I've been thinking about undoing these all morning. These buttons . . ." His lips found the hollow of her throat. "God, these buttons made my fingers itch."

Lilah couldn't manage more than an incoherent murmur. His fingers were sliding beneath her riding habit, gliding across the bare flesh of her chest in a way she'd never felt, never imagined. The tips of his fingers brushed the row of lace at the top of her chemise, then slipped beneath it, startling her so much she froze. She stayed that way, not wanting to move, even to twitch, lest he stop the delicious exploration.

The flesh of his fingers was harder than hers, slightly calloused, his touch so light it made her shiver, and all the while his mouth roamed her neck, the flat hard plane of her chest. And then his hand was cupping her breast, his lips edging onto its soft curve.

It was shocking. She should be shocked. She was certain she should not make that moaning sound and dig her hand into his shoulder. "Con . . ." Her breath caught in her throat. She had no idea what she wanted other than that she didn't want him to stop. She never wanted him to stop.

But when he did stop, it was only to seek her mouth again, and that was equally entrancing. His hands roamed down her body, over the thin cloth of her chemise, rounding down over her buttocks. His fingertips dug in then, lifting her into him, so that she felt him pulse against her. The only coherent thought Lilah had was how glad she was that she never wore a corset with her riding habit.

Lilah's hands were at his waist, and she slid them up over the soft silk of his waistcoat, wishing she could slide her palms over his bare skin, as he had done to her. Still, it was good to have only his silk waistcoat and shirt between them. Even better, in the wide V made by his waistcoat, there was only his shirt between his skin and hers. She could feel the form of him, the bone overlaid by muscle. And, she noted, it seemed to please him, for his kiss turned hotter, more consuming. She eased her fingertips under the sides of his vest, and that made him shudder.

Con took her jacket in his hands and pulled it back and down, allowing his hands to roam freely over her. He kissed her lips, her face, her throat, his teeth toying with her earlobes, while his hands delved beneath the thin cotton chemise, caressing every inch of her skin. Deep within Lilah, an ache blossomed, flooding her with desire.

He bent his head to her breast, teasing the nipple with the tip of his tongue and shooting bright shards of pleasure through her. Lilah drew in her breath, shocked, and then, startling her even more, his mouth settled on her breast, pulling the sensitive bud into it. She sagged against the wall, her mind floating away as pleasure washed over her.

Lilah had never felt like this before, never ached and throbbed and hungered all over. And when he slipped his hand between her legs, with only the fabric of her skirt between them, she had to clamp her lips together to keep from crying out. His mouth pulled at her, his fingers moved against her core, and inside her the heat built until finally the oddest little burst of pleasure rippled up through her.

She could not hold back the faint cry that came to her lips. "Con!"

He planted his hands on the wall on either side of her head and pushed himself back from her. For a long moment they didn't move, could only stare at each other. Con's eyes were glazed and hot, his lips reddened from their kisses, and tension radiated from him. The sight of him made desire coil inside Lilah again. She wanted more. She wanted him.

"Lilah . . . We can't . . . I shouldn't."

"I don't care." Lilah shoved her fingers into his hair and moved into him, fastening her lips to his.

CHAPTER NINETEEN

After that, he said nothing, merely tore at his clothes as they continued to kiss, moving blindly across the floor. Unwilling to part, they jerked and twisted and shoved at their clothes, leaving bits and pieces of them scattered across the floor in a meandering trail to the bed.

When they finally reached the bed, they tumbled backward onto it, shedding their last remnants of clothing. They rolled across the bed, kissing, stroking, reveling in the feel of naked skin on skin. Con's body was heavy on hers, and the very weight of him was another pleasure.

He slid down her, cupping her breasts to feast on them. Every tug of his mouth, every velvet caress of his tongue sent another twisting thread through her, tightening the tangle of desire deep within her. As his mouth worked its magic on her, he explored her body, moving with a featherlight touch that left a shiver in its wake.

His fingertips slid across her stomach and down onto her thigh, and then, startling her, insinuated themselves between her legs and drifted upward over the soft skin of her inner thigh. She was lost, breathless in anticipation as he teased ever closer, until at last he settled in that most intimate of places.

Con's lips returned to hers in a deep, slow kiss as his fingers caressed her. Lilah would have been embarrassed had there been any room inside her for anything but passion. She felt in that moment utterly open and exposed to him, naked in every way, and she reveled in it, at once so free and yet so caught. Transfixed, transformed, she drank him in.

Hunger grew and pulsed, and she moved her legs restlessly against the bed, aching for completion. The knot of desire deep in her abdomen became ever tighter, and suddenly pleasure exploded through her, waves of it sweeping outward and leaving her shaking.

There was still more, for Con moved between her legs, opening her to him. His hard length pulsed against her sensitive skin, probing, easing inside. She drew in a gasp, amazed and eager, and then he was thrusting into her. There was a flash of pain, but it was stifled under the bone-deep satisfaction as he filled her, stretching her in a way that made her want to purr beneath him.

Lilah dug her fingers into his back, flooded with an elemental hunger, a deep primitive need to surround him, possess him, be taken by him. With every stroke, every hard, hot breath he took, the wild hunger built in her. Unbelievably, it broke through her again, crashing through all barriers, all resistance. She shook under the force of the feeling, clinging to him, as he emptied himself into her.

In that moment, it was so fulfilling, so achingly pleasurable, so shattering, that tears welled in her eyes.

Con collapsed against her, his face in the crook of her neck, his breathing ragged. Pressing a gentle kiss on the soft skin of her neck, he rolled onto his side, sliding an arm beneath her head and with the other, tucking her into him.

She was enveloped in his warmth, her chest swelling with emotions she could not express, could not even identify, and somehow that spilled more tears out of her eyes. Con's arm tightened beneath her head. "Are you *crying*?"

No, no, don't, Lilah thought helplessly, as he reared up on his elbow, gazing down at her with something like . . . horror.

"Oh, my God, Lilah." He sat up, pulling his arm from beneath her head.

Lilah swiped at her eyes. "No." Her voice came out hoarse, and she had to clear her throat. "Don't be silly."

"I'm sorry. Lilah, I — please, forgive me. I thought you wanted — no, that's no excuse, I know." He closed his eyes, shoving his hands back into his hair. "I was wrong, so wrong. You're — you didn't know really, and I should have —" He muttered a curse.

Lilah lay there, looking up at him, tears gone, along with the achingly sweet, wonderful moment. Now she was aware of the air upon her bare breasts, and shame washed through her. What had she done? She thought of the way she had acted, throwing herself at Con — it was no wonder he thought she had wanted to do this. She had. She'd been utterly brazen.

Lilah crossed her arms over her chest, wishing desperately for clothes, a blanket, anything to cover her nakedness. But her clothes were thrown everywhere, and even though Con had obviously seen her naked, had touched her and done the most intimate things, somehow she couldn't bear to hop out of bed and run about naked in front of him, picking up her skirt and bodice and —

oh, Lord — her various undergarments. She and Con were lying atop the dustcover over the bed, and she reached out to pull it across her, covering herself as best she could.

"I shall marry you of course." Con squared his shoulders, his face, for once, tight and inexpressive. Like a child offering to take his punishment. A man facing the firing squad.

His words froze her. Lilah sat up, keeping the dustcover wrapped across her front. "I think not."

Con sighed, his face changing from the blankness into a kind of sorrow, an expression equally unfamiliar on him and somehow even worse. "Lilah . . . I know you're angry at me, and you have every right to be. I should have been more careful. I knew it was a mistake. I knew, deep down, that you didn't realize what you were agreeing to."

A mistake. That inexpressible, heart-piercing joy she had felt, that new and wonderful experience, was a mistake to him.

"I'm not a child, Con. Of course I realized what I was doing." It made Lilah feel a little better that she could still pull her armor into place. Whatever else she might be, she would not be weak. "I'm surprised that your

mother's son would make such a condescending statement."

"It's not condescending!" he protested,
looking offended. "You are an innocent, and
I am not. I am at fault."

"This is a perfectly nonsensical thing to
be arguing about," Lilah said crisply. She
was on firmer ground now, at least, with
Con glowering at her.

"Blast it, Lilah, be reasonable. It's all very
well to believe in women's equality, but you
know as well as I do that it's the woman
who suffers."

"I have no intention of suffering."

"I am talking about your precious reputation — you know, that thing you were so
worried about a couple of hours ago."

Lilah wanted to lash out, toss back some
withering retort, but unfortunately Con's
barb had hit the mark. She had been a
complete hypocrite, whining about her aunt
causing a scandal and a few minutes later
acting like a . . . a hussy. The moment a
man kissed her, apparently she turned to
jelly. "I am a bit surprised to find you so
concerned about propriety."

"I don't give a damn about propriety, and
you know it." He swung off the bed — obviously *he* had no qualms about his nudity —
and began to pick up his clothes. Back

turned to her as he yanked on his trousers, he said roughly, "I just don't want to see you hurt."

It was too late for that, Lilah thought. But she had brought it on herself. She had been willful and reckless, and she wanted more than anything to burst into tears. But she wasn't about to let him see that her spirit was bruised. She was thankful that he wasn't looking at her. "This will doubtless surprise you, but I don't want to marry you any more than you want to marry me."

"Less, I'd say, since you're turning down my proposal."

"And I won't be hurt unless you plan to bruit this about to your cronies."

"Lilah!" Con swung around indignantly, his fingers stilled in the process of refastening his shirt. "I would never! How can you even think that?" His temper was well up now, which, really, Lilah preferred to that regret that had sat so incongruously on his face earlier.

"I didn't think you would. I was simply pointing out that no one will talk about it because no one will know."

"And what if you're pregnant?"

Lilah blushed at his blunt words and looked away. "Well, of course, then it would be a different matter. It would be necessary for us to — to —"

"Sacrifice ourselves?" he asked sarcastically.

"Don't you dare!" Lilah flared, almost dropping her concealing dustcover in her anger. "Don't you dare pretend that you are a wounded party here. As if you wanted to marry me. You would be miserable if I had said yes. You're glad not to marry me. You're just pouting because I don't want to marry you either."

He glared at her for a moment, jaw clenched, then let out an explosive sigh and dropped down onto a chair to pull on his boots. Giving an extra — and in Lilah's opinion, entirely unnecessary — stomp to fit his feet into them, he stood up and began to pick up Lilah's clothes. It put a strange lump in her throat to see his hands holding her things.

"Here," he said in a far more conciliatory tone, setting her clothes on the bed beside her. "You're right of course. You are being rational. We would never suit. I just . . . I want you to know that I am sorry." He raised his head and looked into her eyes. "I didn't intend for this to happen. I didn't set out to seduce you. And I truly regret if I have caused you pain or regret."

"I know." It was impossible not to believe

Con. Impossible not to like him. But it was equally impossible to admit that she was so brazen that she didn't even regret what they had done. "I am a grown woman, Con. I am responsible for what I do."

He nodded. "I . . . um, I shall go search another room."

"Very well. It's . . . I think it's best if I go home now."

Well, he'd certainly mucked that up, Con thought as he strode down the corridor. What in the hell was the matter with him? Yes, he had always been a bit impulsive, but he'd never before been so seemingly unable to control himself. Certainly never before had his lovemaking made a woman *cry*.

His stomach twisted as he remembered turning to look at her, feeling so deeply, amazingly replete, and saw that she was in tears. Had he physically hurt her? Of course, how was it any better if her tears had been those of remorse and regret?

Con rubbed his hands over his face now, feeling again the bite of guilt. Whatever Lilah said, she was far too naive to have really known what she was getting into. Even though she had flung herself into his arms and kissed him, he had taken advantage of her. Deep down, he'd known he was

258

taking advantage. He shouldn't have accepted her "yes" as consent.

Con reached the end of the hallway, so he turned into the last room and went through the motions of searching it for hiding places, though at the moment he couldn't bring himself to care about finding some benighted key. He was too busy brooding over Lilah.

She'd been most forgiving about it — which did not really seem like Lilah at all. He would have expected — if he had thought about it — that she would make him pay for breaking so cardinal a rule. Worse, for tempting her into breaking a rule. Truthfully, he wished she had. It would have been far easier to take if she had rung a peal over his head or taken a swing at him.

She'd been so reasonable. So calm and dispassionate. The thing that had apparently roused her ire had been his offering to marry her — and where was the sense in that? While he would not classify his irritation as "pouting," as Lilah had termed it, he had to admit it had stung a bit when she'd said she didn't want to marry him.

She was right; he didn't want to marry her either, but she needn't have been so bloody adamant about it. It wasn't as if he were some penniless mountebank. Or some mad relative who'd been hidden away in the attic. He was generally considered something of a catch. He had ample money, and he was the son of a duke. And he had only to look at Alex to know that he wasn't bad-looking. You'd think a woman who was so rational, so respectful of social mores, would be agreeable to making an advantageous marriage.

But oh, no, marrying him was apparently horrifying and to be done only in the most extreme emergency. Of course, to be reasonable, what woman would want to marry a man whose lovemaking reduced her to tears?

Why had she cried? What had he done? Until that moment, he would have sworn that Lilah had been as deep in the throes of passion as he. The way she had kissed him, touched him. He thought of the way her hands had slid beneath his waistcoat.

Con braced his hands on the mantel and stared down at the cold fireplace, his search forgotten. The devil of it was he was aching for her all over again. It seemed the bitterest irony that he should feel this way about Lilah Holcutt.

Why was it that her cool, calm, so carefully polite face set him on fire? That when she looked at him in her disapproving way, he could think of nothing but turning that look into passion? That he couldn't look at her without wanting to take down that mass of bright hair and bury his face in it?

God, she was beautiful. It was a crime she was so beautiful. And if he had thought so before, now that he had seen that slim white body, now that he had felt her move beneath him, she dazzled him even more.

He rested his forehead against the edge of the mantel. The truth was, he had never before been so shaken, so turned inside out, so shattered and put back together again as he had just now with Lilah. It had been a storm of heat and hunger, and when he had sheathed himself in her warmth, when he'd come to climax inside her, her voice a soft moan in his ear, it had been like coming home. No, that was far too tame a term. He had felt . . . perfect.

And wasn't that mad? To feel such desire, such pleasure, in a woman who was so absolutely wrong for him.

He should leave. He didn't have to find the key now. There wasn't any immediate danger. In fact, he had the feeling that if he really examined his motive in coming here to find the key, it might have more to do with that wrongheaded desire for Lilah Hol-cutt than it did with solving the mystery.

The wise thing to do was to remove himself from temptation. No doubt Lilah would prefer not to have him around. Indeed, now that he thought about it, Lilah might very well ask him to leave.

That idea brought up a surge of alarm. However perverse it was, he didn't want to go. He *liked* it here. He wanted to explore Lilah's odd house; he wanted to see the Levels up close. He wanted to go through that maze again. The mystery of the key intrigued him even if it wasn't necessary to resolve it right now. He wanted to figure out why Dearborn was so eager to get his hands on it.

The truth was, at the bottom of it, he didn't want to leave Lilah. He liked looking at her. He enjoyed being around her, even if she was as frustrating as the devil. He could control his desire. It wasn't as if he was some lust-craved maniac. After all, desire for her had been a low, nagging heat in him these past months, but he'd not done anything. He wouldn't have done anything today if Lilah hadn't been so willing, even eager. He doubted that she would be so receptive again. One could count on Lilah not to throw out teasing lures.

If she wanted him to leave, that would be a different matter . . . though he thought he could talk his way out of that. His mood brightened a bit. He worked his way down the hall, finding nothing, and finally, he decided to stop for the day. It was time for tea, and frankly, it was boring to search the rooms alone. Besides, he needed to check on Lilah, make sure she was all right.

To his surprise, he found Lilah sitting on a bench in the hall below, idly twirling her riding crop in her hand. Con eyed her somewhat warily. "Come to take the crop to me?"

Lilah, who had been looking down the hall the other way, started in surprise and turned to him. "What? Oh. No, of course not." She rose to her feet, dropping the crop on the bench beside her.

"I thought you had gone home." Con went down the last few steps.

"I decided not to. I walked around a bit and . . . and I thought."

Con tightened, marshaling his arguments against returning to London.

"I hope that you will stay and continue to look for the key," Lilah said, leaving him speechless. "I don't want what happened today to put an end to our project."

"Neither do I." She had obviously tried to do her hair up again without a mirror, and it looked endearingly messy. Alluring. Con

263

thought it best not to mention that. "I assure you that I won't repeat my behavior."

"Nor will I." She tugged at the waist of her jacket. "We were . . . taken by surprise. In the future we'll be more careful. We can agree that today was an unfortunate mistake, and there's no need for blame or apology or protestations of feelings that don't exist." She looked at him uncertainly. "I don't suppose one could call us friends exactly, but . . . I want things to be as they were between us."

"So do I." He smiled. "And I think we qualify as friends . . . just friends who disagree a bit."

"Yes. Just so." Lilah smiled, and Con realized that it was going to be damned difficult to stick to his promise.

They rode home, at first silent and ill at ease. Lilah brought up the topic of their search, and as they talked, the awkwardness gradually faded. Neither of them had discovered anything useful, and they agreed that their search was proving to be a daunting task.

"When you think about it," Lilah said. "The thing could be almost anywhere. He didn't even necessarily hide it in his house. It could be stuck under a rock somewhere."

"We should ask your aunt about it."

Lilah looked at him skeptically. "I doubt she would be of much help. She wasn't even living here when Mr. Blair died."

"Still, she must have known those three men better than we do. They all grew up together after all." He flashed a sideways grin at her. "And you no longer have to try to keep me from talking to her."

When they sat down to tea, Lilah brought up the subject. "Aunt Vesta, Con and I had a reason for coming here."

Vesta gave a tinkling little laugh. "I *knew* that. Come, Lilah, I'm not that foolish. I've been home over a year, and you've never felt the need to visit before. What I don't understand is why the two of you are at Carmoor."

"We're looking for a key," Con said. "The Dearborns —"

"Niles Dearborn? That dreadful little man. I never did like him. He looks like a weasel. Have you noticed?"

"I share your opinion, ma'am. The thing is, the Dearborns are after a key. We think it's something to do with the three men — your brother, Dearborn and Mr. Blair."

"But why would you look for it at Carmoor?" She looked at him blankly. "They always met here. Surely Virgil would have been the one to hold a key."

"You know about the key?" Lilah asked in surprise.

"I don't know about any key, but it would only make sense that your father would —"

"Good God!" Realization rushed through Con. He jumped to his feet, sending his chair wobbling backward. "How could I have been so blind?"

"What are you talking about?" Lilah asked, vaguely alarmed.

"Lilah, those men weren't trying to kidnap Sabrina. It's obvious. They were after you!"

Chapter Twenty

Lilah gaped at him.

"Kidnap!" Aunt Vesta gasped and turned to her niece. "Someone kidnapped you?"

"No. They got the wrong person, and it wasn't me they wanted." Lilah frowned at Con. "Sabrina's parasol —"

"The devil with Sabrina's parasol. The important thing is your hair."

"My hair!"

"Yes, what color is it? Do people ever call it red?"

"Yes. Often," Lilah responded with obvious annoyance. "But it's not."

"Well, it does have reddish tones," Aunt Vesta mused.

Lilah frowned. "It's strawber—"

"Never mind that," Con waved aside their disagreement. "The point I'm trying to make is that if someone was identifying a woman to, say, some dull-witted ruffians, he would describe the most obvious things about her. Hair color. Height. However distinctive that parasol is, it wouldn't be more important than a physical description. And no one, not even an idiot, could think Kyria is black-haired and short like Sabrina. But if this fellow had said, take the tall redhead . . ."

Lilah's face paled. And suddenly, Con's excitement was replaced by dread as the implications sank in on him. Lilah was in danger. "Oh, God. He's still out there."

"Who?"

"The other kidnapper — the one my sisters said escaped through the window." He cursed under his breath. "I should have gone after him."

"Don't be silly," Lilah said. "You couldn't have found him. It was night, and he probably went into those woods behind the house. Besides, the important thing was to get your mother and sisters home."

"Yes, but he's free. He could come after you again."

"What man? Someone wants to hurt Lilah?" Vesta's voice rose in alarm. "What is this all about? I don't understand."

Con pushed down his anxiety. He was frightening Lilah's aunt, and if he kept on, he was going to scare Lilah, too. *Let her remain unworried.* He would make damn sure nothing happened to her. Forcing a soothing note into his voice, he said, "I'm sorry, Mrs. LeClaire. You mustn't fret. Lilah is perfectly safe here. Let me explain."

He recounted their chase to Lilah's aunt, making it sound far more amusing than it had been, ending with their decision to find the key. Aunt Vesta listened with wide eyes, and when he finished, she clasped her hand to her chest, saying, "Oh, my, a treasure hunt. How exciting!"

"Con, this doesn't make sense," Lilah said. "Why would they think I was with your mother and sisters?"

"You've spent a good deal of time with them recently," he pointed out. "They might have assumed you would be with them, and that would be a good way to obscure the fact that it was you they wanted."

"Before this, you were sure it was Sabrina."

"I jumped to a conclusion — you know, that quality you say is my besetting sin." He gave her a wry smile. "I let myself be distracted by that blasted parasol."

"But what does Niles have to do with it?" Aunt Vesta asked. "Why does he want this key?"

"We assume there must be some money involved. Mr. Dearborn's in financial difficulty," Lilah told her.

"He was always one for gambling and, well, other sorts of things I cannot speak of in front of you, dear. I warned Alma not to marry him. Kalhoul told me what —"

"Who?" Con blurted.

"Kalhoul — he is my contact on the Other Side. My mentor and adviser."

"Ah. I see."

"But of course Alma paid no attention to me. They never do, you know. It's the curse of Cassandra." She shook her head.

Con pulled the conversation back on course. "Mrs. LeClaire, why did you say it made sense that the key would belong to Lilah's father? What does it open?"

"I don't know." Vesta shrugged. "I just assumed . . . because Barrow House was where the Brotherhood always met."

"The Brotherhood?" Con straightened.

"Yes. Niles, Virgil and Hamilton. They called themselves some silly name. The Brothers of the Blessed. The Blessed Brotherhood. Something like that."

"What was this brotherhood? What did they do?" Con asked, the familiar excitement of having found a trail rising in him.

"I've no idea." Vesta spread her hands out, palms up.

"It sounds like something religious," Lilah

offered. "The Blessed."

"Niles?" Aunt Vesta chuckled. "I wouldn't think so. No, I think it was just some foolishness that started with our fathers."

"So their fathers started the Brother-hood?" Con asked.

"I think so, and the boys continued it. Family tradition . . . that sort of thing. Papa was great chums with their fathers. I'm sure they wanted their sons to continue. And, of course, men do love their little clubs and rituals, don't they? I'm sure you understand, dear boy." She smiled archly at Con. "It wasn't as if the club was a great chore. They simply met on the old festivals every year."

"The old festivals?" Con asked.

"Yes, you know. All Hallows' Eve, Mid-summer's Eve, winter solstice, spring equi-nox."

Con's jaw dropped. "They were, um . . ."

"Witches?" Vesta laughed. "Oh, no, I wouldn't think so. But Papa had a great respect for the old ways, the ancient reli-gions. I imagine he thought it appropriate to gather then. Of course, it's true that one feels the Source's power more at those times."

"You said they had rituals," Con put in before Vesta could launch into a discourse about mystical forces. "What sort of rituals?"

"I don't know, really. I just meant in general secret societies have handshakes, passwords, rings, that sort of thing, don't they? But I've no idea what Virgil and his friends did. I was a great deal younger than they of course." She gave a dimpling smile to Con, but it was bitterness that tinged her tone as she went on, "And they would never include a mere female into their little circle."

"My father never told you anything about it?" Lilah asked. "Never gave a hint?"

Vesta tilted her head to the side, thinking. "No, dear. I'm sorry, but Virgil rarely said anything about the visits except that sometimes he complained because it interfered with his plans. I assumed they just drank themselves silly."

"A key would be the sort of thing a group like this would have," Con mused. "To the entrance to a ceremonial room, perhaps."

"A secret room?" Vesta glowed. "How exciting."

"I should have realized. When I first saw this house, I thought it would be the perfect place to hide something. Forget Carmoor." Con grinned at Lilah. "Tomorrow we're going to explore Barrow House."

Lilah and Con began their search the next day in the newest wing of the house, going into every room, examining mantels and knocking on walls. By the end of the afternoon, even Con was tiring of the task.

"It would take us years to find anything in here," Lilah said, sinking down onto one of the chairs. "We haven't even finished this wing."

"The house does have a great many nooks and crannies," Con agreed. "And your family had an inordinate fondness for stairs. Perhaps we should narrow our focus tomorrow." He reached out his hand to her. "But come. I'm sure your aunt is waiting for us."

As Con had predicted, Aunt Vesta was sitting by the tea cart, ready to pepper them with questions about their search.

"I'm afraid it won't be fast or easy," Con told her after he'd described their search. "What's the likeliest room for your brother to hide something?"

"His bedroom?" Vesta shrugged. "He kept things in that box on top of his dresser. And of course there was the little chest of your mother's things. Virgil was always a secretive boy. I remember he used to hide a cache of sweets behind books in the library. He thought I didn't know it." She grinned mischievously. "But of course I did. I just didn't filch enough that he would notice."

"No hidden staircases?" Con asked. "Secret rooms? Priest holes?"

"Wouldn't that be marvelous?" Vesta said wistfully. "If there are, I've never found them."

They were just finishing their tea when there was a cannonade of pounding on the front door. The three of them looked at each other in mystification. A moment later, Ruggins let out an exclamation, followed by a crash, and heavy footsteps thundered down the hall.

"Sir! No! Please allow me to announce you" came the butler's voice. "Sir, please . . . You cannot simply barge in."

"The hell I can't!"

"But, sir — it's the middle of tea!"

"Moreland! Damn you, where are you?"

"Isn't that —" Vesta began, turning toward the others.

"Niles Dearborn," Con finished grimly, shoving back his chair and standing up.

As Con came around the table, Lilah stood up, as well. "Con . . . ."

"I shan't break any of your furniture," Con told her.

"Ha! There you are!" Dearborn charged into the room. "How dare you break in? How dare you steal my key? Give it back at once!"

"Your key!" Con gazed at him in astonishment. Had the man run mad?

"Yes, my key!" The blank looks on everyone's faces seemed to enrage him further. He shook his fist, his face turning red. "Did you think I wouldn't know you took it?"

"Mr. Dearborn," Lilah said pacifically, stepping forward to take his arm. "Come. Sit down and calm yourself."

"I don't want to sit down!" Niles jerked his arm from Lilah's grasp and turned his wrath on her. "Do *you* have it? Is that it? Did you think to have it all for yourself?"

Con quickly stepped between Lilah and the older man. His eyes bored into Niles as he said in a deadly level tone, "You will not speak that way to Miss Holcutt."

Niles let out a snort of disgust but moved back. "You're nothing but a ruffian, no matter how high your father's title is." He straightened his waistcoat, making a visible effort to subdue his temper. "I want my key back. You had no right to take it."

"I *didn't* take it." Con folded his arms. "Are you saying someone stole your key?"

"Of course that's what I'm saying. Are you daft?"

"No. But I'm inclined to think you are. Why would I take your key?"

"Do you think I'm stupid? First you come around, blustering about kidnapping and Sabrina's key. Then suddenly you're here at Barrow House, and the keys are gone. It's obvious you took them," Dearborn said scornfully.

"*Keys,* you said." Con seized on his word. "There are three keys, aren't there? And you naturally stole Sabrina's, so you had two of them."

"I didn't steal it. She couldn't use it." Dearborn narrowed his eyes. "That's it, isn't it? You and your brother want to use the girls' keys yourselves."

"Mr. Dearborn." Lilah stepped up beside Con. "If we wanted to use the keys, we *girls* would do it ourselves. But we do not have your key." She spoke the last few words with slow, heavy emphasis.

"Why should I believe you?" Dearborn shot back. "You're clearly under *his* spell." He jerked a thumb at Con. His gaze swung toward Aunt Vesta, who sat watching them raptly. "You!" he sneered. "No doubt *you're* the one who told them about it. They wouldn't have known otherwise."

"Told them about what?" Vesta pushed up out of her seat. Jaw set, she looked a more imposing figure than usual.

"The Brotherhood! The keys to the Sanctuary!"

"How could I possibly tell them about that?" Vesta shot back bitterly. "I know nothing about it. None of you would let me join you. You wouldn't tell me anything. I was just a *girl* after all."

"You couldn't be in it. You were a fool to think you could. It was a *Brother* hood. Only sons can join it."

"Why?" Con asked. "What were the rules? What did the Brotherhood do?"

Dearborn started to speak, then stopped and looked from one to the other, his eyes shrewd. "You don't know anything about it, do you? You haven't the least idea what you're dealing with."

"Why don't you tell us?"

Dearborn let out a short sharp laugh. "Don't think you can weasel information out of me so you can use the keys. But I'll tell you this — I'm the only one here who can handle what's going to happen in two weeks."

"And what is that?"

"Oh, no." Dearborn wagged his finger. "You bring me those keys — all three of them, and I'll stop it. Otherwise . . . Midsummer Day, the Sanctuary will unleash holy hell on the world." With that pronouncement, he turned and walked out of the room.

Con let out a curse and ran after him, reaching out to pull Dearborn to a halt. "Tell us what the devil you're talking about."

"Or what?" Dearborn taunted. "You'll kill me? You'd never get the answer then, would you? Or maybe you'll turn me over to the constable. I can imagine how well the law would respond to your tale of magical keys and hidden rooms."

"I don't need the law to help me."

"You plan to thrash it out of me? Torture me into telling you? You don't have the stomach, boy." His gaze flickered toward Lilah, who had followed them into the hallway. "And how do you think the proper Lilah Holcutt would like that? I'll tell you this, as a gift — every three years on Midsummer Day, you have to renew the bond or else it will be freed. And it's been three years now since we did so." He pulled away. "You give me back the keys, and I'll stop it."

"*What* will be freed?" Con ground out.

"Destruction. More power than you've ever dreamed of." Dearborn grinned and nodded toward Lilah. "Your lot called it the goddess. I'd say it was the devil himself."

CHAPTER TWENTY-ONE

Dearborn stormed out the door, and Lilah turned to Con, then Vesta. Both wore the same stunned expression that Lilah was sure was on her own face.

"I never liked Niles," Vesta said prosaically.

The very ordinariness of her words after the scene that had just taken place made Lilah laugh. Hearing the hysterical note in the sound, she reined it in. "What in the world was Mr. Dearborn talking about? Aunt Vesta, do you have any idea? He spoke of a sanctuary — do you know where that was?"

Her aunt shook her head somewhat doubtfully. "I — no, Papa never said anything about a sanctuary. He used to talk about a great force beneath the earth. I remember once he told Virgil to be cautious — or was it wise? Anyway, he saw that I was there and stopped talking." Her mouth fell into a pout.

"What about this renewal?" Con asked. "Did your father or brother ever mention that? What did they renew? What was this 'bond' Dearborn mentioned?"

"I don't know." Uneasily she went on, "But clearly we must do something soon. Midsummer is only two weeks away."

"Ten days, to be exact," Con said grimly. "That doesn't leave us much time."

"What if we can't find it before then?" Vesta's unease was turning into panic. "What will we do?"

"Aunt Vesta, stay calm," Lilah said firmly. "You are assuming that Mr. Dearborn is right. There's no reason to believe that some magical sanctuary is going to explode — or whatever it was he was predicting. It sounds like superstitious nonsense to me."

"Oh, Lilah, your stubborn resistance to the Truth will be the ruin of you," Vesta moaned. "Of all of us."

Lilah had a strong desire to shake her aunt. Before she could speak, Con said soothingly, "Mrs. LeClaire, Lilah has a good point. We all know Dearborn wouldn't hesitate to lie to get what he wants. What if he invented this story about the dire consequences that would befall us unless we gave him the key? Don't you think that the, um, *presence* you sense beneath the ground is more benign than that?"

Con's words had the desired effect on Vesta. She looked much struck. "Dear boy, of course. There's no wickedness there. It's a force for good."

"You see? No need to be worried. We must simply continue to work as hard as we can to find the key." Con took Vesta's hand and patted it. "This has been a dreadful experience for you. Perhaps you should go upstairs and rest a bit."

Vesta beamed at him. "Lilah, this boy is a treasure. You must keep him. He's right. The dark emanations Niles emits have sadly depleted my energy."

As Aunt Vesta went up the stairs, Con grabbed Lilah's arm and whisked her into the sitting room. She frowned at him. "Must you encourage her foolish notions?"

"Where's the harm? You told me yourself your aunt believes what she wants to. And it will be easier to talk about it without her here."

Lilah had to admit that. "I hope *you* don't believe what Mr. Dearborn said."

"You mean, that we're all going to disappear on Midsummer Day? Barrow House will be destroyed? It seems unlikely."

Thank heavens Con was being sensible.

"Do you think his keys really were stolen?"

"His anger certainly seemed sincere. Still, I'm more inclined to believe he made up the story."

"But why would he pretend they were stolen?"

"To trick you into letting him have your key. He hoped you'd show it to him or give away where it's hidden. Or that he might coerce you into handing your key over to him by accusing you of theft. When he realized we knew next to nothing, he made up a tale about impending doom to frighten you into giving it to him — only he could save us all from destruction, et cetera."

"But what if he was telling the truth about the keys being stolen? What if Mr. Dearborn didn't order that kidnapping and there's somebody else involved here?"

"And that someone is responsible for both the kidnapping attempt and the theft of Dearborn's keys?" Con looked thoughtful. "That's certainly a possibility."

"But who would have wanted those keys?" Lilah asked. "What good would they do anyone else? How would anyone even know about them?"

"I suppose his son could have robbed him."

"Peter?" Lilah asked skeptically. "I can't

imagine him going against his father. He's always been cowed by him. Anyway, what would be the point?"

"Perhaps he finally decided to rebel. Or he thinks he could get you and Sabrina to join him. After all, that trio would have someone from each of the three families. Maybe that's important, or at least they believe it's important."

"But his father won't consider it because we are appallingly female," Lilah finished. "So Peter is defying him." She paused, thinking. "Truthfully, I do seem the likeliest suspect. Or you. But neither one of us stole them." She looked over at him warily. "You didn't, did you?"

"Alas, no. It would certainly make all this easier if I had. Do you suppose each person had a key to the same lock? Or that it took three keys together to get in?"

"It seems more likely one would need all of them. Why else would he have been holding Sabrina's key, as well?"

"True. If there was a club of only three people and they had a secret meeting room — I presume that must be what this sanctuary he mentioned was — then it makes sense that they might set it up in a way that took three keys to open. I've seen locks that required two keys to open. I suppose you could make one that needs three. Or have three separate locks."

"Wonderful. Now we have *three* keys to find." Lilah sighed.

"It certainly makes our quest more challenging. Especially now that we have a time limit."

"I thought you said you didn't believe that we had to find the key by Midsummer Day or we'd all be destroyed."

"I don't," Con replied. "But personally, I'd rather not put it to the test."

Con paced his room. It was one o'clock, and he had yet to get into bed. It was pointless; he knew he wouldn't be able to sleep. He had downed a whiskey; he'd tried to read; he'd listed all the Roman emperors in his head — in order; he'd had another drink. Even when he set his mind to the puzzle of the keys, that brought him right back to Lilah and the danger she was under. Nothing could distract him from his thoughts of Lilah.

Just looking at his bed brought up memories of making love with Lilah yesterday, and passion surged in him all over again. Passion, which, of course, he was not going to give in to. He would not think about those long shapely legs and the way they had felt locked around him. Nor the rose-tipped breasts that fitted so perfectly in his palm. The way she moved beneath him, shy but eager.

Blast it. This was getting him nowhere. He gave up, lit a candle and, not bothering to pull on his boots again, went down to the library. The library was stocked primarily with books on philosophy, religion and history, but he was intrigued by one entitled *The Ancient Mysteries of Somerset.* He suspected it belonged to Aunt Vesta.

He settled down in one of the chairs and spent the next hour reading about symbols, legends, barrows and ancient tracks — the Fae Path, sadly, was not mentioned. Most of it was about Glastonbury Tor, but in one chapter, Barrow Tor was mentioned as a "holy" site, though no reason was given for it.

Picking up the candle, he headed for the oldest part of the house, which he and Lilah had not yet explored. It was this section, the one that sagged drunkenly under its own weight, that intrigued him the most. And since they were going to spend the next day more pragmatically searching her father's room, this seemed a likely time to get a look at the old wing.

At the end of the hall, he turned left and

opened the door, stepping into what could only be the Great Hall of the original home. Dark and massive, the room rose to the full height of the house. His candle cast only a small circle of light in the vast black void.

A dark figure waited in the shadows, giving him a start before he realized it was only a suit of armor. One wall held a stone fireplace, deep and wide enough to roast an ox.

He crossed the hall and opened a door, revealing another corridor. The rooms were dark and empty, giving the place a funereal air. Con climbed a set of winding stone steps to the next floor and found a similar corridor of rooms with uneven floors and a drunkenly tilted fireplace.

Alex would love this place. They would have to invite the newlyweds here as soon as they returned from their honeymoon. Belatedly, he realized that he was thinking of Barrow House as his and Lilah's, the invitation *theirs,* not his. That was an unsettling thought.

Con left the hall and went up to the top floor. Here was the long gallery, added on years later. This floor, at least, had light, for windows lined the wall. But the pale glow of the moon only served to make the dust and cobwebs more visible, the emptiness more tangible.

Portraits of dead Holcutts hung on the long wall opposite the windows, gazing out from the shadows. Everything was coated with a layer of dust, and a deathly silence hung in the air. Con started forward quietly, as if not to disturb anyone.

Something caught the corner of his eye, and he turned toward the window. It looked out on the wide swath of grass separating the house from the untended maze. In the silvery moonlight, a white figure moved across the grass.

Lilah. The old glass distorted his view, but he was certain it was she . . . once again roaming about outside at midnight. What the devil was she doing? The suspicion that she was meeting someone flared in him anew, but he could not imagine who it could be. It was also difficult to believe that Lilah was carrying on any sort of deception at all.

As he watched, she stopped in front of the entrance to the maze. He waited for someone to join her, for her to go inside, for something to happen, but she only stood, still as a statue. Finally, she turned and started back toward the house.

Con whirled around and hurried back down the stairs. Blast it, he was going to find out what was going on. His candle flickered wildly, creating dancing shadows on the walls around him. Two flights of steps — why had he had to climb all the way to the top floor? He ached to run, but that would be suicidal on these narrow, uneven steps.

When he reached the hallway, he broke into a run. And that was his mistake. The rush of air blew out his candle, plunging him into the utter gloom of the Great Hall. He stopped, then started forward more slowly, one hand stretched out in front of him. The door into the other wing was directly across the room; as long as he walked in a straight line, he couldn't miss it.

He made it across without running into anything, but it had cost him precious time. He trotted down the long hall. Thanks to the lamp he'd left burning in the library, the hall was illuminated enough to see his way. Con turned and went to the back door, coming out of the house onto the terrace. He looked toward the maze, but there was no sign of Lilah. Had she been that fast? He stood for a moment, listening. There was nothing but silence.

It occurred to him that he was acting the fool, running around all over the house, trying to find a woman who obviously did not want to be found. Lilah had a right to her secrets. If she wanted to ramble around the grounds at midnight, it had nothing to do with him. Turning, he went back into the house.

The hall was quiet, as was the corridor above. Lilah's door was closed, no sign of light beneath it. Determined to put the whole thing out of his mind, he began to undress. Just as he was about to blow out the candle and get into bed, he heard something. Had that been the click of a latch? Turning, he opened the door. But the hall remained still and dark.

CHAPTER TWENTY-TWO

Lilah came down to breakfast in a cheerful mood, eager to get started. Unnaturally silent, Con fiddled with his spoon, watching her with an assessing gaze. Lilah shifted, faintly uneasy.

"I saw you last night," Con said abruptly.

"Of course you did. We spent the evening together." Whatever was the matter with him?

"I'm talking about later. I looked out and saw you standing at the entrance to the maze." His eyes were focused intently on her face.

Lilah went cold. "That's impossible. I haven't been near the maze — other than when you and I went the other day."

"Lilah . . . I *saw* you. There you were, in your nightgown, staring into the maze. Then you turned to come back in."

She could feel, literally feel, the blood draining from her face. "You're mad. I wasn't. It was a . . . a trick of the moonlight. Why didn't you come out and ask me what I was doing?"

"I tried, but you were gone by the time I got out there."

"So you saw a figure flitting about outside, and then it vanished." She felt on surer ground. "Con, you were dreaming."

"It was not a dream. Unless I dreamed sitting in the library, reading *The Ancient Mysteries of Somerset,* as well."

"No wonder you had a bizarre dream if you fell asleep reading that."

"It was not a dream." Con finished his words with a rap of his spoon against the table.

"If there was actually someone there, it must have been my aunt — she was probably out talking to the goddess of the moon. Or maybe it was one of the maids sneaking out to meet a man." Lilah pushed back her chair and popped up. She no longer had an appetite. "I was in bed asleep. All night."

Con frowned at her for a moment, then shrugged. "Very well. Let's talk of something else. Are you ready to look into your father's room?"

"What? Oh. Yes. I — I must, um, put on other shoes. I'll join you in a few minutes."

Lilah fled from the room. It wasn't true.

Con was mistaken. Or maybe he was playing a joke on her; he had an odd sense of humor. She'd been asleep. She ran up the stairs and into her bedroom, where she startled one of the chambermaids.

Dropping down onto the hassock, she whipped off one of her soft-soled slippers. The sole of her foot was dirty. Her heart began to hammer. No, it couldn't be . . .

She glanced around the room, panic fizzing inside her. "My nightgown. Where's my nightgown?"

The maid stared. "I think your lady's maid took it to the laundry room."

Lilah shoved her foot back into the slipper and flew out of the room and down the back staircase. In the laundry room, the maid at the washtub gaped at her. No doubt she thought Lilah was even madder than the upstairs chambermaid did.

"I — I'm just looking for — there." She pounced on her nightgown, lying atop a basket.

It was no wonder Cuddington had taken it to the laundry. Blades of grass clung to the dirty hem. Lilah stared at it blindly; she couldn't breathe. It couldn't be. This could not be happening again. Not after all these years. She was past that. Her life was neat. Calm. Orderly.

She dropped the gown and walked away, clenching her trembling hands in her skirts. What was she to do? Lilah fought down the panic in her chest. It was an aberration. Just a momentary relapse, brought on by being in the old surroundings. She had been tired last night, and there had been that tumultuous scene with Mr. Dearborn. That moment — no, that life-altering event — with Con at Carmoor.

It was no wonder she had let her guard down. Nor was there any reason to panic. She was no longer a child. She was in command of herself, and, now that she was aware of it, she would control it. Just as she would control that strange, wayward hunger for Con Moreland. She refused to be ruled by her clearly unhealthy instincts.

Hurrying back upstairs, she found Con loitering in the hall outside her chamber. "What are you doing here?"

"Waiting for you." Con glanced down the hallway from which she'd come, then at her feet. Lilah realized that she hadn't changed her shoes. She tried to think of some excuse, some reason. For a wild moment, she even thought of blurting it all out to him.

But she managed to restrain herself. She had already revealed far too much to Con. She decided to simply ignore the inconsistencies. "Are you ready?"

"Yes." Con swept his arm out for her to precede him. "We need to find two things, you know. The key and the door it opens."

"To this sanctuary?" Thank goodness, Con had decided to ignore the situation, as well. There was something to be said for a man who was accustomed to eccentric behavior. "I can't imagine where that could be — an old building on the estate? In town? It sounds religious, but I can't imagine it being at a church."

"No, I wouldn't think a church — unless perhaps there is some old abandoned ruin of one somewhere near." He raised his eyebrows in question.

Lilah shook her head. "I've never heard of one."

"I think religious-sounding phrases are common in secret societies — it gives them weight. Dignity. All it has to be is a room, a hut, just a place where they conducted their . . . whatever it was they did."

"What *do* secret societies do?" Lilah asked.

"I've never belonged to one. Aunt Vesta would think me a poor example of manhood. But from what I've heard, it seems mostly to involve solemn oaths, passwords and secret handshakes. Wearing silly hats."

"That sounds like exactly your sort of activity. I'm surprised you haven't joined one." But Lilah smiled as she said it.

Inside her father's bedchamber, Lilah pulled open the draperies, letting in a flood of sunlight. "His sitting room is through this door."

Con trailed after her into the small enclosed room and went over to a large portrait of a young woman. "Is this your mother?"

"Yes. Her name was Eva."

"She was beautiful." He glanced back. "You look very much like her."

"Thank you." Lilah felt herself blushing and turned away. "Why don't you go through his desk? I'll, um, look in this cabinet." It would be better to work at some distance from Con. Standing close to him was exactly how she'd gotten in trouble the other day.

She tried to concentrate on her task, but after a moment, she realized that she had stopped working and was watching Con instead. He had run his hands through his thick dark hair, leaving it sticking out everywhere in a way that was somehow endearing. Her fingers itched to reach out and brush it back into place. She remembered the feel of his hair between her fingers, soft as silk. She thought of his lips, reddened from kissing her, the hard line of his collarbone, the taut skin stretched across it.

And this was exactly what she needed to avoid. Lilah walked over to the window, staring out until her pulse settled down. Surely she could manage to control her lust. Con was not the only handsome man in the world. His was not the only man's touch she would ever feel; someday she would marry. She tried to think of another man's hand sliding over her naked skin, and the only feeling it evoked was repulsion.

It wouldn't be that way, though. She would be in love with her future husband. He would be a man who loved and respected her. Who *wanted* to marry her. She would make love with him, and it wouldn't be a mistake. The problem was that when she tried to picture such a man, he had black hair and green eyes and an engaging grin.

Con looked over at her, as if he had felt her gaze. His eyes darkened, and his hand stilled. For a heartbeat they gazed at each other. Con took a step, and Lilah whipped around to stare out the window again. Con stopped and returned to looking through the desk.

They worked their way through the office bit by bit. Con found one carved wooden box that proved to have a puzzle of sliding pieces, exciting their interest, but it proved to have nothing inside it but a woman's glove and a curl of reddish-gold hair bound with a blue ribbon.

"Your mother's, I presume," Con said, touching the lock of hair, his face unaccustomedly sad. "He must have loved her very much."

"He loved her more than anything. He wasted his life away, trying to call her back to him." Lilah heard the touch of bitterness in her voice. "I'm sorry. It's wrong of me, I know, to resent his abiding love, his grief."

"No, it's not." Con set the box aside. "He should have been devoted to raising you, not chasing after her memory. I'm sorry he was obsessed." His face hardened. "I despise the frauds who prey on the grief of those like him, the mediums who claim they can contact dead loved ones."

Lilah raised her eyebrows, surprised. "But you believe in that sort of thing."

"No. I am open to belief, but I've never yet come across a medium who was anything but a swindler using a bag of tricks. Some may actually believe they can contact the dead. But I've never found one who had any real proof. Olivia used to investigate mediums. There was a wave of them a few years back."

"I know," Lilah replied drily.

"Of course. Your aunt." He paused. "Mrs. LeClaire seems to believe it. Perhaps she'll prove me wrong."

"I doubt it. She lives in a world of her own making."

They continued to work through the day but had found nothing by the time they stopped for tea. Lilah was dispirited. "I had hoped we would find something here — the key, a location . . ."

"We'll find them," Con assured her with his usual confidence, but he frowned. "Hopefully soon. I worry . . ."

"What?" Lilah asked. "Don't tell me Mr. Dearborn's deadline matters."

"No. Well, perhaps, some. The thing is, as long as this remains undiscovered, there's still a threat to you." He looked into her face searchingly. "Lilah, is there something more going on here that I don't know about?"

"No." Her answer was quick, and she firmly suppressed the flicker of guilt. Last night had nothing to do with the search or the key. "Of course not. And I doubt that there's any danger to me. Mr. Dearborn has threatened us with doom — what else can he offer?" She put up what she hoped was an insouciant smile.

Con nodded, but he didn't look entirely convinced. She could hardly blame him. Whatever she said, Lilah could not deny that now there was something awful hanging over her head.

As they made their way downstairs for tea, Lilah was surprised to hear her aunt talking and the murmur of a male voice in response. Lilah glanced at Con, who returned her puzzled look. "Don't tell me Dearborn's returned."

Their steps quickened, but when they reached the open doorway of the drawing room, they came to an abrupt halt. Con muttered, "What the devil is *he* doing here?"

"Lilah, dearest!" Her aunt rose. "Look who's come to visit us!"

Lilah forced a smile. "Sir Jasper."

"It's wonderful how popular Barrow House has become," Aunt Vesta said blandly.

"Yes, isn't it?" Lilah walked forward, extending her hand to her cousin. "This is indeed unexpected, Sir Jasper." Drat the man. How could they talk about the key, much less hunt for it, with Sir Jasper hanging about?

"I do hope you will forgive me for not sending notice," Sir Jasper responded. "Mrs. Summersley urged me to come. She feared you might be lonely on your own."

"As you can see, I'm not alone." What was Aunt Helena thinking, to thrust Sir Jasper on them like this? It certainly would not further Sir Jasper's suit to be placed in constant comparison to Con. "You remember Lord Moreland."

"Yes, of course. Sir." Jasper's stiff nod toward Con conveyed little joy at the memory.

Con took Lilah's arm in a proprietary way. "Sir Jasper. The depth of your devotion to your family is astounding."

"It's so nice to have the company of young people." Aunt Vesta beamed. "Makes one feel less old. No doubt you think the same, Sir Jasper."

Lilah hid a smile. Clearly Con had a champion in Aunt Vesta.

"Are you on your way home, Sir Jasper?" Con asked as Lilah sat down. He took a chair between Lilah and the other man.

"Sir Jasper lives in Yorkshire," Lilah put in.

"Ah, then you are indeed a good cousin

to go so far out of your way."

The conversation limped along. Aunt Vesta filled in most of the empty stretches. Lilah wondered how long Sir Jasper meant to remain. It was unfair of Aunt Helena to interfere in her life this way. She'd already saddled Lilah with her dour maid. Why couldn't she trust Lilah to do the proper thing?

Lilah knew the answer to that — however much Aunt Helena hid it from her, deep down she feared that some wild Holcutt behavior would surface in Lilah before Helena could get her safely wed to a respectable gentleman.

Guilt swept Lilah immediately. She shouldn't be irritated at Aunt Helena. After all, perhaps she was right to worry, given Lilah's recent behavior. Lilah told herself she should make more effort with Sir Jasper. She sat down to tea, putting on as agreeable an expression as she could muster. Con, she noticed, made no such effort but sat, staring a hole in the man the whole time.

Lilah came up with a few pleasantries about Sir Jasper's journey, to which he responded in far greater detail than she would have wished. After that, conversation lagged. For once, Con and even Aunt Vesta said little, leaving an awkward silence.

"Barrow House is quite, um, interesting," Sir Jasper said finally. "I should enjoy seeing more of it. Delilah, perhaps you could show me about the place after tea."

"Well, um, I —"

"Oh, but surely you would rather take a rest first, wouldn't you, Sir Jasper?" Vesta put in sweetly.

"After that arduous journey," Con added.

Sir Jasper gave a forced laugh. "It takes much more than that to tire me, sir." He gave Lilah an admiring look. "And no journey is too long with such a reward as Delilah at the end."

Con choked on his tea and gave way to a long fit of coughing. Lilah swallowed a laugh, feeling obligated to send Con an admonitory look. She hoped that the subject of a house tour was over, but unfortunately, when they stood up later, Sir Jasper said, "I believe you were going to show me the house now, Delilah."

"Yes, of course."

She had the unpleasant fear that Con would desert her to continue their search alone, but Con said cheerfully, "A tour of the house sounds delightful. I've a mind to join you."

Sir Jasper glared at Con, but before he

could say anything, Lilah gratefully accepted Con's offer. She led the way out the door, pretending not to notice the arm Sir Jasper extended for her. Con, sauntering along behind them, said, "We should see the kitchens, don't you think?"

"The kitchens!" Sir Jasper turned to stare at him. "Good Gad, why would we go there?"

"I always find the servants' areas interesting. One can tell a good deal about someone from the kitchens. The laundry, the still-room."

"I'm surprised you don't want to see the smokehouse," Jasper grumbled.

"Oh, the smokehouse would be much too hot in the summer," Con replied earnestly.

Lilah swallowed a giggle. "I believe we'll stay with the main area. It's a large house."

"Yes, difficult to heat, I'll warrant," Sir Jasper said.

They moved along the corridor, slowed by Sir Jasper's thorough perusal of each room. He interspersed his frequent and flowery compliments to Lilah with didactic pronouncements on the many defects of Barrow House: the stairs were oddly placed; there were too many windows, which, of course, was the reason the carpets were sadly faded; this room was too small, that one too large, and the smoking parlor would do well turned into a billiards room.

Lilah began to think it would serve the man right if she did drag him through the kitchens and laundry. But she couldn't risk the cook leaving when Jasper began to correct her method of baking.

"You certainly have a lot of plans for a house that isn't yours," Con commented acidly.

Sir Jasper preened, Con's sarcasm sailing past him. "Yes, well, I have a bit of an architectural bent." He surveyed the library in which they were now standing. "This room, you see, has far too many books."

"It's a *library*." Lilah looked over at Con, who had let out a snort and turned away, his shoulders shaking with muffled laughter. She wasn't sure which was more exasperating, Sir Jasper's presumptuous statements or the way Con tempted her to laugh at every turn. "Gentlemen, I'm sorry, but I think that's enough of a tour for one day. I believe I must rest before supper. I have contracted a headache." That was certainly true.

She gave Sir Jasper a brief insincere smile and walked away. She didn't dare even glance at Con.

The evening passed in a similarly annoying manner. After supper, Aunt Vesta decreed that Lilah should entertain them by playing the piano. Sir Jasper was quick to offer to stand beside her and turn the pages, and the piano turned out to be sadly out of tune. But at least there was no need for conversation.

None too soon for Lilah, Aunt Vesta, her eyes glazing over in boredom, announced that she was retiring. Lilah seized the opportunity to go to her room, as well. In the end, all four of them tramped up the stairs together. Sir Jasper said a prolonged goodnight to her, bowing over her hand and holding it far too long. Lilah snatched her hand back and hurried into her room. Sir Jasper's visit could not end soon enough.

Con opened his door a crack and, positioning a chair where he could see Lilah's closed door, settled down to wait. He hadn't believed Lilah's denials this morning for a second. He was certain that the figure he had seen was Lilah.

Lilah would have his head if she found him spying on her. It made him feel a little guilty; she was entitled to her privacy. But whatever she was doing was dangerous. The escaped kidnapper could be lurking out there in the dark, waiting for an opportunity to grab the right woman this time. Or Niles Dearborn. He might very well still be around. And there had to be something wrong with whatever Lilah was doing or she wouldn't be this secretive about it.

The click of a door opening brought Con out of his thoughts. He leaned closer, watching Lilah, clad in her nightgown, walk down the hall away from him. Con waited until her head disappeared down the stairs, then eased out of his room and followed her. He crept down the stairs, careful to avoid each spot where he had discovered a board would creak. His heart was beating faster, the atmosphere of mystery heightened by the dark silence all around him.

When he reached the foot of the staircase, he hung back in the shadows, watching Lilah. He expected her to turn down the cross corridor leading to the rear door, but to his surprise, she walked past it without a glance. Now he was even more intrigued.

She passed the library and the dining room in the same unhurried way, neither dawdling nor rushing. It was riskier to follow her here, where he would be exposed if she glanced back, but she had not looked around her yet, and the hall was dim, the only light the moonlight coming through intermittent windows. Con kept in the shadows well behind her, matching his pace to hers. When she reached the end of the corridor, she turned, clearly heading into the oldest wing of Barrow House.

Con sped up the steps, and as he pulled open the door into the Great Hall, he saw the door opposite him shutting. Where was she going? He tried to remember if he had seen an outside door in this section. If so, it would certainly explain why he'd missed her yesterday when he ran to the garden entrance. It was almost pitch-black in the hall, but there was the faintest glimmer of moonlight before him that he hadn't noticed last night. It was hardly worth calling a light, but it enough to allow him to keep up his speed.

When he emerged from the Great Hall, there was no sign of Lilah. He instinctively turned to the stairs. It was so quiet in the narrow stairwell that he thought he could hear her breathing. She kept climbing, and he realized that she must be going to the top floor. It was perhaps the last place he had suspected as her destination. Hard to imagine that she paid a visit to her ancestors' portraits at midnight.

He paused at the top of the stairs. Lilah was only a few feet ahead of him, strolling down the gallery at that same even pace.

The long gallery had been an eerie scene the night before, desolate in its emptiness, its gloom crossed by patches of moonlight through the windows. It was even more chilling now to see Lilah's ghostly white figure gliding along, never glancing right or left as she moved from shadow through moonlight and back into shadow again. An icy finger trailed down Con's spine.

He started after her, a strange dread, almost panic, seeping into him. Lilah stopped at the end of the gallery in front of the high, wide windows. Moonlight cascaded over her. Con realized too late that when she turned back, he would be directly in her line of vision. There were no doorways to take shelter in along this long, unbroken corridor.

Lilah turned slowly, and for the first time Con saw her face. Her eyes were blank, her face empty. She looked straight through him.

CHAPTER TWENTY-THREE

An atavistic dread froze Con in his tracks. He could only watch as Lilah turned and opened a door he hadn't noticed before. She walked through it, as emotionless, as mindless as an automaton. Lilah was walking in her sleep.

The almost-inhuman blankness of her face, the utter lack of recognition or response, was enough to make Con shiver, but now he understood it. No wonder she had denied her trip to the maze last night; she didn't remember her nightly rambles. With a start, Con realized that Lilah had disappeared through the doorway while he stood here like a dolt.

He rushed after her and came to an abrupt halt, stunned. Lilah stood in a round room. On the left was a staircase leading downward. The curving walls around her were covered in clocks. Large, small, of every sort, they covered the walls and filled the cabinets. It was the room of his nightmare.

Con let out a loud and profane exclamation, and Lilah whirled around with a shriek.

"Lilah. It's me. Just me." He held out his hands in a pacific gesture. "You were walking in your sleep."

Lilah stared at him, then looked all around the room, confusion and panic mingling in her expression. "Where — no, oh, no . . ." With a moan, she sank down onto the floor, covering her face with her hands. "I thought it was gone. I thought I could manage it." Lilah glanced around and shivered. "Please. Let's go somewhere else."

"Of course." Con took her arm and pulled her up; she was cold as ice. He infused warm good humor into his voice. "I would offer to sweep you up in my arms like any worthwhile hero and carry you to your room, but I fear we might wind up in a messy heap at the foot of that staircase."

He was rewarded by her breathy little laugh. "I'd rather not. I'm not a wilting damsel in distress anyway. Just a fool who has no control over what she does," she finished bitterly.

"Nonsense." Con put his arm around her shoulders and pulled her to his side as they walked down the gallery. "You are without a doubt the most controlled woman I know. Perhaps sometimes you just need to escape those shackles you bind yourself with."

"You can see why I have to keep them there. God only knows what I might do otherwise."

"Trust me. You won't act like a madwoman."

"Really?" She gave him a skeptical look and pulled away, starting down the stairs. "Look at what I've done — apparently I wandered out to the maze last night, and tonight I wound up in Grandfather's tower."

"What is that place anyway?" Con said, only in part to divert her from her self-criticism.

"It's the tower room where my grandfather kept his collection. All his clocks and compasses."

Con remembered the smaller dials scattered among the clocks. There had been compasses in his dream, as well. It was the very same room. He would swear to it. The thought didn't bring him any comfort. "Ah, yes, the tower — that tumorous growth at the end of the house."

"Yes." Lilah continued, "Whatever hapless ancestor added the gallery stuck on the tower as well — obviously someone with no understanding of architecture."

"Or taste." Con's mind buzzed with questions about the bizarre room, but this was hardly the time to interrogate Lilah. He needed to get her warm again, to soothe her shaken nerves. Underlying that was a driving need to take her in his arms and hold her, but he couldn't let himself do that.

Con thought of whisking her upstairs to her bedroom, but, considering how it had felt to have her body pressing against his side, he thought her bedchamber might prove to be a dangerous place. Besides, he wanted to talk to her without risking anyone waking up and finding them. God only knew what her idiot cousin would do upon finding Con in Lilah's bedroom. Probably challenge him to a duel.

Con thought of the smoking room Sir Jasper envisioned turning into his billiards room. It sat handily near the end of the main corridor. He led Lilah there, closing the door behind them, and knelt to light a fire. Rising, he poured them both a brandy. Lilah still stood in the middle of the room, arms wrapped around herself, looking lost.

"Here." Con couldn't stop himself. Setting the glasses on a small table he scooped Lilah up and sat down in the chair by the fire to cradle Lilah in his lap.

With a tiny sigh that shivered all through

313

Con, Lilah relaxed and rested her head on his shoulder. Con slid his hand up and down her arm to warm her. He tried not to think about the fact that only a thin layer of cotton separated her bare skin from his touch. Lilah was vulnerable; she required tender attention, not lustful thoughts.

It was doubtless an indictment of his character that his thoughts strayed that way. But it was damnably hard not to notice the dark circles of her nipples faintly visible beneath the white cloth. Or the inches of leg her rumpled gown revealed.

Con picked up one of the glasses from the side table and downed a gulp. He handed the other to Lilah. "Here. This will warm you up."

With meek obedience that it pained Con to see, Lilah took a swallow. She shuddered, her eyes watering, and shot him an accusatory look that reassured him somewhat about her emotional state. But she didn't leave his lap.

"I haven't done that in years — walk in my sleep, I mean," she said, surprising Con by offering the information without being asked. "It stopped after I went to live with Aunt Helena."

"Did you do it frequently before that?"

Lilah shrugged. "Not at all when I was

314

small. It began as I got older, and at the end, it was happening once or twice a week. That's one reason why Papa sent me away." Con wasn't sure if Lilah realized that she sighed.

"It must have been terrifying for a young girl."

"It's terrifying for a grown woman."

"I'm sure it is." He pressed his lips to her hair. When she didn't pull away, he rested his cheek against her head. Her hair was soft and fine, like silk beneath his skin. He wondered how desire could beat in him like a drum even as he wanted to shelter her. Reluctantly Con lifted his head. "When I asked you this morning, you were unaware you had gone to the maze last night?"

"I didn't remember it. But when you said that, I couldn't help but suspect."

"Why didn't you tell me?"

"It's embarrassing. I thought about confessing, but I told myself I could control it now that I was aware of what I had done." She sighed and said in a lower tone, "I didn't want it to be true. I didn't want you to know, to think . . ."

"To think what?" he prompted gently when she stopped.

"That I'm mad." The words were almost a whisper.

"You're not mad. You're not even approaching the edge of madness. Trust me."

"But how can I sleep so heavily that I don't wake up through all that? I don't understand how I could make my way to the Clock Room and not awaken. Not be aware of it. Or go out to the maze. It's as if I'm drugged."

Con stiffened. "Do you think you were?"

"No." She sighed. "It would be a handy excuse. But it's ridiculous. They would have had to drug me when I was a child, too."

"Were you dreaming?"

"While I strolled along? No. At least, I don't remember it. It's as great a mystery to me as it is to you. And why, after all this time, did it start again?" She sat up straight, turning to look him in the face. "I'm not a child anymore. I should be able to control what I do."

"You were asleep, Lilah."

"But I'm still *me.* How can I do things and not even know about it?"

"I've no idea. But you aren't the only one who's ever walked in her sleep. It doesn't happen because one is weak-minded," he added when he saw she was about to protest. "People aren't in control of their dreams. I think this must be very much like a dream, only stronger."

"It scares me, Con. What might I do without even knowing it? What *have* I done?"

"Nothing reprehensible, if that is what worries you."

"You don't know that."

"I know you. I'm sure you wouldn't do anything immoral. As you just said, you are still you, even when you're asleep. And you are a good person — not because you abide by the rules, but because that's what you are inside. You wouldn't hurt anyone or commit any other sin."

Lilah relaxed, snuggling back into him, and he curled his arms around her. This was dangerous. *She* was dangerous, though not in any of the ways Lilah was thinking of.

He wanted far too much to hold her, protect her, keep her from harm. He wanted, in short, to coddle her, something he'd never felt before in his life. *Her. Lilah Holcutt.* Who was about as cuddly and in need of protection as a hedgehog.

Why did it have to be Lilah for whom he felt this bone-deep need? Con had buried that hunger for her, ignored it, rejected it, but nothing seemed to eliminate it. It lay there like a banked fire, waiting to be fanned back to life. It had been there since he had kissed Lilah after the chase.

317

If he was honest with himself, it had been there long before that. Whatever his excuses had been for avoiding Lilah throughout the wedding preparations, at the root of it was the fact that when Con was around her, his thoughts went in a direction that was unacceptable. Indeed, perhaps it had begun even longer ago than that, from the very first moment when he had glimpsed those shapely legs clad in unexpected lilac stockings. It wasn't a momentary whim that caused that explosion of passion the other day at Carmoor. It wasn't the circumstances.

Con glanced down at Lilah. She had fallen asleep, her head on his chest. He could feel her breath against him with each exhalation, and it set every nerve in his body dancing.

But he had given his word not to touch her again. Just because he hadn't realized how damnably hard it would be didn't mean he could break the vow. However much he might want to sweep her up and take her to his bed. To kiss her, caress her, sink deep within her.

Con muttered a curse. "Lilah? Wake up. You'd best go back to bed now."

Lilah awakened the next morning feeling almost lighthearted. It seemed strange, given that Con had discovered her sleep-walking. But, just as when Con had found about her aunt and the scandal, it was a relief.

He was privy to all her secrets now. She no longer had to pretend with him. And her secret was safe; she needn't worry. She knew Con now — no matter how often he might break the rules, he held to his standards. He was, above all else, loyal.

To her dismay, she found Sir Jasper, not Con, in the dining room. "Ah, Delilah." He rose and pulled out a chair for her, saying to the butler, "You may bring Miss Holcutt's breakfast now."

From the butler's expression, Lilah guessed that he appreciated Sir Jasper issuing commands as little as she did. And what made Jasper presume that he could take his seat at the head of the table? She turned to the butler, defiantly waiting for her command. "Yes, that would be nice, Ruggins, but I'd like a cup of tea first."

"It's a lovely day," Sir Jasper announced. "I took a stroll about the garden this morning. It's been sadly neglected."

"I rather like a rustic look." Next he would be telling her what should be done to spruce it up.

Jasper smiled benignly. "Rustic, yes, but

not, I think, *wild.*"

"That's something you'll have to take up with my aunt."

"But surely Barrow House is your home."

"Yes, but my aunt is living here. I leave the affairs of the house in her hands."

He looked taken aback by the firmness of Lilah's tone, but he shrugged it aside. "I thought, Delilah, given that it's such a pleasant morning, you might show me about the estate."

"Yes, *Delilah.*" Con's mocking voice came from the doorway behind her. Lilah thought that she had never been so glad to hear his teasing voice. "That sounds like a capital idea. I'd love to get a closer look at the Levels, too." Con gave Sir Jasper a toothy grin.

Sir Jasper scowled, but there was little he could say without being impolite. Later, as they rode down to the Levels, Con was at his most annoying, effectively managing to wedge his horse between Lilah and her cousin while he kept up a light, nonsensical chatter, needling Sir Jasper until Lilah almost felt sorry for the man.

Sir Jasper's expression grew steadily stonier, and when Lilah suggested an early return to the house, he was happy to agree. Aunt Vesta was up by the time they came back, and she pulled Sir Jasper into a conversation, giving Lilah and Con a chance to escape.

"You are a terrible man," Lilah told Con as he steered her back outside.

"I know. Aren't you glad?" He grinned.

"Rather. Where are we going?"

"To the maze."

"Why? Con, I've no desire to go back into the maze."

"Just bear with me. I have something I want to try out. Besides, Sir Jasper can't see us there. I don't want him interrupting. I have something to discuss with you."

"What?" Lilah asked, a frisson of alarm going through her at the serious look on Con's face.

"I think I know why you've been walking in your sleep. You're being called to the maze."

CHAPTER TWENTY-FOUR

"What? Con, really . . ."

"No, wait, hear me out." He raised his hands conciliatorily. "You said yourself you hadn't walked in your sleep in ages, but it started after we arrived here. Maybe it's because we're searching for the key."

"How could it possibly have anything to do with that?"

"What if you heard or saw something about the key when you were very young, and you've forgotten it over the years? You might not have realized it was important. But that knowledge is buried deep in your memory, and your sleeping mind remembers it."

"My mind is sending me to retrieve your key?" Lilah asked skeptically.

"It's not my key. It's yours. Maybe you have a connection to it."

"The key is not calling to me to find it," Lilah retorted flatly. "I would know if I had some connection to it."

He shrugged. "Maybe. But there's a reason you started sleepwalking again when you returned to this house."

"The house is making me walk in my sleep? It has some kind of power over me? You sound like Aunt Vesta."

"Maybe she has a point. What if there is a force at work here that we don't recognize? Or don't understand?" He reached out and took her hands, saying seriously, "Don't dismiss what I'm about to tell you. I'll swear on anything you want that I'm not playing a bizarre jest. I'm serious."

"Very well." Lilah regarded him warily.

"That room last night in the tower — I recognized it."

"What? How could you —" Lilah's chest tightened.

"I've dreamed about it. Many times."

"I don't understand. You'd never seen it before. How could you dream about it?"

"Exactly . . . How did I know what it looked like? Why did I dream about it?"

She frowned. "Are you sure? Sometimes I'll feel as if I've had a dream before, but I can't remember when. I think it's just some trick of the mind."

"This is no trick of the mind. I've dreamed about that room. Ask Alex when he returns.

I've described it to him. I had it the night before he got married and several times before that. Because of the clocks and the . . . the feeling of panic, I dismissed it as nerves. I assumed I was worried about being late, doing something wrong and spoiling Alex's wedding ceremony."

"That's understandable. When you walked into the tower, you saw a room full of clocks, and it reminded you of the one in your dream."

"It didn't remind me of it. It *was* the room in my dream. The walls were all curved. There were clocks on the walls and in cabinets. I saw that window, that desk. The only thing different was the staircase. In my dream, there was no way out."

"But, Con . . ."

He quirked an eyebrow. "Do you think I'm lying?"

"No! No, I don't, but . . . There must be some explanation."

"I'm sure there is. But not the rational, cut-and-dried explanation you would accept. I think I was meant to see it."

Lilah grimaced. "Meant by whom?"

"Or what."

"You think the *house* reached out to you? That it has some power? Or maybe one of Aunt Vesta's buried strands of energy sent a

324

message to you?"

"I don't know. What I do know is that it happened, and I can't find any logical, scientific explanation for it. So I think we must consider that it may have been something more. Lilah, however much you want to discount it, the people in my family sometimes have dreams that are . . . significant, for want of a better word. Reed dreamed that Anna was in danger, and she was. Kyria had dreams about an ancient ceremony even though she knew nothing about it."

Lilah shook her head. The knot in her chest grew bigger.

"Lilah . . . you know my sister Olivia. She wouldn't make such things up. Yet she will tell you that she saw ghosts at Stephen's home. She dreamed about them. Saw what had happened to them. And Megan — you couldn't ask for anyone more skeptical than a journalist. But she and Theo saw each other in a dream, a mutual dream, ten years before they met. So I have to believe that my recurring dream about the Clock Room means something."

"You told me that you didn't have any of the talents that the others in your family seem to."

"I've always thought so. But now, I'm

beginning to wonder. I spent a lot of time thinking last night as I was sitting there, waiting for you to leave your room."

"You mean while you were spying on me."

Con ignored her interjection. "You aren't going to distract me. I thought about our conversation in the maze a few days ago. I made a joke about it, but I'm beginning to wonder if I actually have an ability."

"You're saying you *are* a human compass?" Lilah began to chuckle.

"Yes, I know, as supernatural talents go, it's not impressive. But you can't believe I would make up something so lacking in drama."

"No, probably not."

"I've never thought of it as anything unusual. I assumed I was just better at directions and maps or making deductions."

"Because you think you're smarter than others."

"Well, yes . . ." He looked at her sheepishly.

"You *are* smarter than a great many people," Lilah said simply.

Con looked extravagantly shocked. "Did you just pay me a compliment?"

"I think I did." She smiled.

"The thing is — other people in my family are smart, too, but they can't find things as well as I can. I've realized that it's more than figuring out which way a person went. I can *sense* it. Last night, for instance, when I went from the Great Hall into that next corridor, there was no sign of you, but I was certain you had gone up the stairs. And it's odd, isn't it, that I know which way is true north? I can find my way around a place even though it's not familiar. You said yourself that it was unusual for someone to find his way to the center of the maze on the first try. Besides, I noticed something in the maze."

"What?" In spite of herself, Lilah's curiosity was aroused. That was the thing about Con: he always managed to catch her interest.

"It's better if I show you. Besides, I want to test it." They had been standing near the entrance to the maze, but he went more deeply into it now.

"Test what?"

"As we were walking through here, I had that surety that I was going the right way, but it was stronger than usual. When I took your arm, I felt this — this sort of tingling, but not on my skin. Inside me. Suddenly I was more . . . aware. It was like turning up a lamp, and everything's suddenly brighter. More visible."

"A tingling?"

"When I touched you, it was immediately clear which way I should go. It was so strong that I noticed it. That was what set me thinking. I remembered how easily we followed those kidnappers."

"Because your sisters threw us clues."

"But we were already on the right path by the time we saw the first one. And remember when I realized we were going the wrong way? You were close beside me."

"So you're telling me that you have this special ability to . . . to follow people." She crossed her arms pugnaciously. "And I am, what, your battery?"

Con grinned. "I would say more of a conduit, but . . . yes, I think that you . . . amplify this ability. Make it stronger."

"There are often people who understand maps better, who have a good sense of direction."

"That doesn't disprove it. On the contrary, if you can believe that someone can innately have a good sense of direction, why couldn't it follow that others might have an innate ability that's even stronger?"

"But people have different areas in which they excel — mathematics, say, or painting or playing the piano. That doesn't make it *mystical.* It doesn't mean that there's some sort of otherworldly force beneath in the ground. And it certainly doesn't mean that I can increase your talent for directions." The knot in her chest, which had relaxed, was now back in full force.

"Why are you so set against the possibility of there being powers we don't know about? Just because you can't see it, it doesn't mean it's not there. The same is true for air."

"But, Con, really — magic? Séances? Unseen forces controlling us? What's next? Witches?" Lilah took a step back. Why was he being so stubborn about this? So serious? The knot twisted tighter.

"I said nothing about magic or witches. My point is that there are things we don't know, don't understand, but they're still there. If you had shown an electric light to someone in the 1600s, they would have labeled it witchery. It's easy to dismiss something as magic just because you don't understand it."

"Electricity can be explained. Understood. It can be proved. But the idea that some unknown, unseen force is sending you nightmares about the Clock Room or calling me there in the middle of the night is ludicrous." Why must he keep on with this?

"That doesn't mean it's not true. As for

proof, you've seen inexplicable powers at work. What about the link between Alex and me? How do he and I know when the other one is in trouble? He and Sabrina have the same sort of connection. Alex could picture Sabrina's house from holding her father's pocket watch. You saw Anna's vision about the kidnapping. You heard her describe the place. And when we got there, you *saw* that it looked exactly the way she had described it."

Lilah crossed her arms, feeling trapped. "I don't know! I don't know what to think about any of those things. But I cannot believe in this whimsical . . . nonsense."

"You mean you *won't* believe it." Con shoved one hand back into his hair. "You are so bloody stubborn."

"So if I don't believe what you want me to, I'm stubborn?"

"And if you don't want to believe in something, it's nonsense."

"Why do you harp on this? Why do you have to push and push —"

Con overrode her words. "The real question is, why do you continue to deny the existence of things you've witnessed? You refuse to accept it because it upsets the pleasant, orderly fantasy you have fashioned for your life. You might have to admit that

Vesta could be right. Maybe her séance wasn't a humbug."

"You're wrong!" Anger surged in Lilah, shooting through her veins like wildfire. At the same time, she wanted to run away, as far and as fast as she could. "Stop! Just stop."

But Con pressed on, throwing his arms out wide, "If you weren't so bloody narrow-minded, you'd admit the world isn't as tidy as your Aunt Helena would want you to believe. The rules don't always apply, Lilah."

"No!" For the second time in her life, Lilah slapped him.

CHAPTER TWENTY-FIVE

Con gaped at her in astonishment, but he could not have been more surprised than Lilah herself. Letting out a choked moan of dismay, she covered her face with her hands.

"I'm sorry." The words came out in little more than a whisper. She dropped her hands, but she couldn't yet bring herself to look into his eyes. Clearing her throat, Lilah said, more firmly, "Please accept my apologies. I — I don't know how I could have acted in such a way."

"That's twice, you know." There was an odd note in Con's voice, not anger, really. It sounded more like . . .

Lilah lifted her head. "Are you *laughing*?"

"No. Never." His eyes twinkled with amusement. "Tell me, am I the only person you thrash on a regular basis?"

"I have never hit anyone else in my life," Lilah said indignantly.

"I'm special to you, then." A smile teased

at his lips.

"You are the only one who's that infuriating," she responded, beginning to relax. "Honestly, Con, how can you laugh?"

"I have three sisters. I've been hit any number of times. It happens when one is, as you said, 'that infuriating.' "

"I doubt they slapped you."

"True. But Olivia once chased me down the hall, wielding a hairbrush. She's faster than you'd think."

"You must have been a terrible child."

"There you are. A smile." He laid a caressing hand on her cheek.

"I don't know how you can be so pleasant after I hit you."

"Well, I'd prefer you didn't make a habit of it. But you didn't hit me that hard. I need to teach you how to punch properly. And I should have had my guard up. It's embarrassing, really." He wrapped his arms around her.

"I truly am sorry, Con. It was rude and uncalled for." It felt so good to stand like this, his chest warm and firm beneath her cheek, his heart steadily thumping.

"It *was* rather impolite." Con kissed the top of her head and stepped back. "I'm sorry, too. I was bullying you. And I shouldn't have mentioned your aunt."

Lilah felt the loss of his embrace, but she couldn't let him see that. "Which one? Helena or Vesta?"

"Either. Both. I shouldn't get angry because you don't believe what I do."

"I don't normally act that way, though I can hardly expect you to believe that."

"I believe you. Have you ever seen a cork shoot out of a champagne bottle?"

"Now I'm like a cork?"

"Tightly sealed things sometimes explode. You're worried by your sleepwalking. Peculiar things are happening. I'm pressing you. Your ardent, elderly suitor pursued you here."

"Hush." Lilah chuckled. "Sir Jasper isn't elderly."

"He will be."

"So will you."

"Yes, but I'm not trying to manacle you to me for the rest of my life."

There was no reason his remark should hurt. She wanted to be tied to Con no more than he did to her.

Con tucked her hand into his arm, and they strolled out of the maze. "Let's say I'm wrong and there is no mysterious energy at work. I'll set aside the fact that I dreamed about the place. There is still this indisputable fact — you walked in your sleep to that room. Another thing we agree on is that your grandfather's Clock Room is unusual. Last, but not least, that room is precisely the sort of place where one might expect to find a hidden key."

Lilah looked up at him and smiled. "Then I suggest we go through the tower so we won't run into Sir Jasper."

They cut across the grass and around the end of the house and entered the tower through a sturdy wooden door. The tower was empty save for stone steps against the wall, curving upward. They began to climb.

Con glanced around as they went past the next floor, also empty. "There's no door. Isn't this the level below the gallery?"

Lilah nodded. "The tower doesn't open into the house anywhere except the top floor." She waved off his question before he could ask. "I don't know why."

"I'd say your ancestor was trying to hide something."

"Probably."

"What do you think it was?" he asked cheerfully. "Mad relative? Secret trysts?"

"Maybe he just liked to read undisturbed."

"Well, that would be disappointing."

When they reached the Clock Room, Con took a long, slow look around, still amazed by how close it was to his dream. "Do you see anything different?"

"I wouldn't know. I haven't seen it in ages. Even when I lived here, I was rarely in this room. It wasn't forbidden like the maze, but the door was kept closed, and my governess didn't like to be in this part of the house. She said it was because I might get lost, but I think that it was more that she found this wing eerie."

They moved methodically around the room, checking the wall for a safe and examining the clocks for hidden compartments. It was a time-consuming process, and by the time they had to leave to dress for tea, they had made their way through only a third of it. They hadn't even looked in the cabinets.

Lilah sighed, wiping the dust from her fingers. "This will take days. It's going to be very difficult to search with Sir Jasper hanging about."

"I've been thinking about him."

"Jasper? Why?"

"Don't you think it's suspicious that your cousin showed up at your house right now?"

"Not really. It's clear Aunt Helena sent him. She worried that I'll fall prey to your lures." She stopped abruptly, blushing. That was exactly what she had done.

A light flared briefly in Con's eyes, but he

said only, "Maybe not. Sir Jasper would make an ideal culprit for stealing Dearborn's keys."

"Sir Jasper?" Her voice rose in incredulity. "Why?"

"He's male and he's a Holcutt. He took over your father's title."

"You think he wants to join the Brotherhood." Lilah considered his words. "I don't know. It seems little to go on."

"It would explain his determination to marry you."

Lilah lifted her brows. "I'm glad you don't feel the need to flatter me."

"My dear Lilah, I am sure that your beautiful face and impeccable reputation — not to mention your compliant nature — would sweeten the pot for him. But the man is bloody persistent. He's more or less forced a visit on you without invitation. He keeps pursuing you even in the face of your obvious disinterest. I have never seen you give him the slightest encouragement."

"I haven't."

"It's not normal behavior. Most men would have given up by now and gone on their way, brokenhearted." He laid his palm on his chest, looking melancholy.

"Oh, stop." Lilah grimaced at him. "I have wondered why he keeps on. I thought he

337

must simply be obtuse."

"That much is clear. But I think he's also eager to be in possession of this house."

"I assumed his suit was spurred by his desire for Barrow House, but that doesn't mean he wants the key, too," Lilah pointed out.

"He's excessively interested in the layout of this house. Last night, while he and I were having our manly after-dinner port, Jasper was interrogating poor Ruggins about where this was and that was . . . *and* —" he paused for emphasis "— he wondered if Sir Virgil used the office downstairs."

"What? That *is* odd, even for him."

"Ruggins was tight-lipped of course. 'I'm sure I couldn't say, sir.' Jasper said he wondered because the office appeared to be unused, and it seemed a waste."

"Maybe he wants to turn it into a billiards room," Lilah said sourly.

"And what about that inspection tour of the house yesterday? He was examining it far more closely than would be polite."

"He was looking at it as a future owner."

"Or he was hoping to find the key's hiding place."

"Very well. His actions are suspicious," Lilah agreed. "But how would he even know about the keys? About any of it?"

"Maybe your father told him."

"I suppose it's possible," Lilah said doubtfully. "But my father had no liking for Jasper. And why wouldn't he have simply given him the key if he thought Jasper should have it?"

"Maybe Dearborn told Jasper. He seemed wedded to the idea of only male descendants qualifying for his very exclusive club. Perhaps it was another requirement that there be three of them. There were three men to begin with, then the next generation of three. Dearborn might have wanted to bring in Sir Jasper as the third man after your father passed on. Dearborn isn't inclined to share, but he might if he thinks it's the only way to get what he wants. But Sir Jasper decided he'd rather have it all — whatever *it* is — to himself. He could marry you to acquire one key and steal the others. You're resisting, so now he is storming the ramparts."

"Perhaps. But I think you just don't like him, so you made him a villain."

"I don't like him," Con agreed. "But it doesn't mean he's not a villain. I think he warrants keeping an eye on."

"I agree." Lilah sighed. "I wish Sir Jasper would go home."

"Perhaps you should tell him to."

"I can't. That would be rude."

Con lifted his eyebrows. "You've managed being rude well enough with me."

"Yes, but that's you. You're . . ."

"Annoying?" he supplied.

"No. Well, yes, you often are, but I didn't mean that. I meant . . ." Lilah shrugged. "I don't have to mince words with you. You aren't one to take offense. You don't care if something I say isn't proper or I sound too bold."

"The bolder the better, as far as I'm concerned."

"*That* is what I mean. You aren't shocked if I know things or dispute what you say."

"I'd be shocked if you didn't dispute what I say." Con grinned. "As for avoiding your cousin, I suggest we return after he's gone to bed."

"Sneak out of my room to meet you in the middle of the night? I-it would be most improper." If Aunt Helena knew about it, she would be horrified.

"I know. Sounds like fun, doesn't it?" He crossed his arms and leaned his shoulder against the wall, his familiar half smile on his lips.

Lilah wanted suddenly, shockingly, to take that plump lower lip between her teeth and nibble at it. She drew in a sharp little breath and whipped around, heading to the stairs.

"Well?" Con levered himself away from the wall. "Will you be here tonight?"

Lilah paused on the steps. She didn't turn around; she hated to think what Con's sharp eyes might see on her face. "You know I will."

The evening dragged, and Lilah retired to her room as soon as she could without causing comment. Cuddington was something of a problem; she would find it decidedly odd if Lilah didn't change out of her evening dress. In the end, Lilah rang for the maid and went through her usual nighttime ritual.

After she left, Lilah changed back into a comfortable sacque dress, which she could fasten herself and wrapped her hair up into a knot atop her head. It was messier than Cuddington's creations and listed a bit to one side, but it would have to do.

Lilah turned out her lamp and sat down to wait. Sitting here in the darkness, listening for the sounds of the others coming up to bed, she had nothing to do but think about what she was doing. It was foolish. Unnecessary. Dangerous.

All the same things could be said for Con.

It was a welcome reprieve from her thoughts when footsteps sounded on the stairs. She heard Aunt Vesta's voice saying a cheery good-night and Sir Jasper's polite response, then Con's. Doors closed. But still, she waited to make sure that everyone was safely in bed.

Finally she opened her door, unable to bear it any longer, and slipped down the shadowed, silent corridor. She had worn her soft bedroom slippers, and she would have gotten down the staircase without a sound if she hadn't stepped on a tread that squeaked.

Freezing, she waited, then continued in the same stealthy manner. It occurred to her that it was absurd to be sneaking about like a thief in her own house. The soft glow of light from the library told her that Con was already waiting for her there. The man must move like a cat; she hadn't heard a sound.

Con was, indeed, lolling in a chair without a jacket, waistcoat or tie, his shirtsleeves rolled up to his elbows. Lilah's eyes went involuntarily to the small V that showed at his neck, the shadowy, almost-vulnerable hollow of his throat in sharp contrast to the hard line of his collarbone. She had the most shocking urge to press her lips against it, to trace the shallow dip with her tongue.

Con rose to meet her, picking up the small

kerosene lamp from the table. Walking down the hushed corridor with Con seemed furtive, even illicit, and the atmosphere was only accentuated by the flickering shadows cast by the lamplight. Lilah knew she should be appalled by her actions, but what she felt was excitement.

Inside the tower room, Con set the lamp on the desk and began his search there. As Con ransacked the drawers, looking for hidden compartments, Lilah started on a nearby cabinet. It was a mundane task, but the hush, the time of night, their secrecy lent it all an eerie quality.

Lilah went through one cabinet, which contained only more compasses. She moved on to a short cabinet beside the desk, but when she tried to open the door, it stayed firmly shut. She tugged on the handle again. "Con . . . This one's locked."

"That sounds promising." Con fished around in the drawers of the desk. "No key in here. Damn. I should have brought my lock picks."

"Surely this can't be the key we're looking for."

"I doubt it." Con glanced around and picked up a letter opener, then sat down on the floor to work on the lock. "If it is, it's a severe disappointment because this lock is easy." He opened the door.

"Oh. It's only books."

"Don't discount it. Books can be handy hiding spaces." Con began to pull out the volumes and set them on the floor beside him.

Lilah joined him on the floor, picking up the top book of the stack. She went still when she saw the one below it. It was bound in dark green leather; on the cover, printed in gilt, was a circle filled with tangled branches. Three triple spirals were evenly spaced above the figure. A leather strap fastened with a metal clasp held the book closed.

"Con . . ." Lilah reached down to touch the cover. "Look."

"Those spirals. Triskeles. What's this in the middle that looks like branches or maybe roots?"

"Both. Branches above and roots below. It's the Tree of Life. That's another thing you'll find on artifacts around here." Her stomach quivered, and she felt a trifle breathless.

"You think it's something to do with the key?" Con was watching her rather than the book. "Lilah, you sense something about this book."

"No. I don't know." She found herself

curiously reluctant to open it.

Con had no such qualms. Flipping up the little latch, he opened the book, fanning through it. "No cutout with a key inside. Just a lot of writing . . . by hand, it's not printed. You think it's your grandfather's journal?" His voice rose with interest. "Your aunt said he was interested in the ancient religions."

"I don't know." Lilah leaned closer to him, turning to the frontispiece. The Tree of Life was printed here as well, but beneath it, cupping the circle, were three words in Latin: *Fortis Voluntas Fratronis.*

"The strong will of brotherhood." He looked at Lilah. "Aunt Vesta said they called themselves the Brothers of something."

"The Brotherhood of the Blessed," Lilah said.

"Is that what she said?"

"No. It's right here." Lilah had turned the page. She pointed to the first words written.

"We are the Brotherhood of the Blessed, given the fortune granted to only the few who know the way."

"This is their agreement, the charter of their club," Con said, excitement in his voice.

Lilah skimmed her eyes down the page. "Actually, I think it's their bible."

CHAPTER TWENTY-SIX

"Or, at least, a thesis on their spiritual beliefs," Lilah clarified. She began to read.

"Gods once walked upon this land, and men understood the pattern of life. Their names are long forgotten, both gods and men, but the truth of the world will always remain.

"Like the spiral, we are never ending. Birth, life, death are but three phases of the same being. There are three realms: land, sea and sky. There are three Brothers. There are three aspects of our nature: mind, body and spirit."

"That explains the triskeles," Lilah interjected.

"To those who have opened the Gateway, as foreseen, the Goddess grants the further blessings of their natures."

"I presume your grandfather and his friends opened this 'Gateway,' whatever that is," Con said. "But what does 'the blessings of their natures' mean?"

"He called the mind, the body and the spirit the 'three aspects of our nature.' So I would think he means the blessings are of those three things. Maybe health for the body — everyone says that my grandfather was very ill when young and made a miraculous improvement. Maybe that is his blessing."

"Is he the only one who received a blessing? They're a brotherhood, and he says 'to those who have opened the Gateway.' Wouldn't each of them be blessed?"

"Let's say my grandfather got health, and I think obviously Mr. Blair would be the mind. He would want wisdom."

"Leaving Niles Dearborn for the spirit?" Con asked skeptically.

"Hmm. Doesn't seem likely. Let's go on." She turned the page. "Here. He calls the three natures head, heart and hand." She continued to read.

"The hand belongs to the material world and as such lies within the realm of the earth, whereas the sky is the ruler of the head, the intellect, and the heart, or spiritual, dwells within the sea. We, the Brothers, embody these realms."

"The old boy didn't suffer from a lack of pride, did he?"

"I'd say not. As best I can tell, he's identifying himself as the spiritual aspect — yes, here he says he has long 'suffered from an affliction of the spirit.' "

"What was his illness?"

"I've no idea. I never knew him. He died years before I was born." She paused, thinking. "I can't remember who told me about his illness. It was simply one of those family stories. But I had the impression it involved a weakness, a lack of stamina — maybe his heart or lungs."

"That would fit. Your grandfather, Sir Ambrose, received relief from his weakness of the heart or 'affliction of the spirit.' Mr. Blair took wisdom, and Dearborn got material things. Makes sense — at one time, Niles's father made a great deal of money off some investments."

"Oh!" Lilah exclaimed, her eyes widening as she scanned the rest of the page. "Con, look. Here he says, 'We are the Defenders of the Gateway. We are the Keepers of the Keys.' "

"What!" Con leaned over to look at the

words himself. " 'Keepers of the Keys.' " He looked up at her, his face only inches from hers. Lilah's heart began to pound. Con pulled his eyes away and sat back.

"But why do they want the key to this meeting place so badly? Surely they're not kidnapping people because they want a blessing?"

"If the Dearborns believe their ability to make money is tied to this place, they'd do anything to get in."

"It's hard for me to imagine Mr. Dearborn actually believing in all this."

"I doubt he believes in this 'three realms' spiritual dogma. But gamblers believe in luck, and he's a gambler. He wants his luck back."

Lilah nodded and went back to the book. She turned the page. "This just looks like a list of Latin words. Some have a word beside it like *healing* or *war.*"

Con looked at the page. "I recognize some of these. They're the deities of ancient Britain — though most of these are the romanized versions of their names. Sulis — the goddess of the healing spring at Bath. Latis. Cuda, the mother goddess. Belatucadros — that one really trips off the tongue, doesn't it?"

Lilah stared at him. "How do you know

all this?"

"You know my father is mad about any-thing Greek or Roman. He might not be interested in ancient Britain, much less the present one, but he was keen on the Roman rule in England. It was part of our studies. Contrary to what some believe, I did actu-ally study now and then." He tapped his finger on one of the words. "The Matres. That's another triple concept. They were three goddesses, always pictured together."

"Like the three Fates. What were they god-desses of?"

He shrugged. "They're shown carrying fruit, so they probably have something to do with the harvest. Fertility. But they also seem to have some connection to death and the afterlife." He laughed at Lilah's amazed expression. "The Matres were described in that book I read the other night."

She contemplated the list of names. "Are these the gods he thinks once walked the land?"

"I suppose. I would guess that this gateway must lead to the gods."

"My grandfather must have been quite mad. Ancient gods and gateways."

Con shrugged. "Maybe. But it also could have been just some silly thing three idle and bored young men came up with to pass the time. I think a number of the secret societies have religious or mystical themes. Things like that help with rituals. I suspect it's the rituals they like, more than the religion." He paused, then went on, "And if Sir Ambrose was insane, Sabrina's and Peter's grandfathers must have been, as well."

"I suppose that's reassuring."

"What else is in there?" Con leaned in to turn the page. Their heads almost touched; their bodies were so close Lilah could feel his heat. "This supports the barrow idea." Con pointed at the objects drawn on the next page. "That looks like a statue. A bowl. An earring. I'm fairly certain that is a torque."

"What do you think this statue is?" Lilah peered at the ink drawing.

"A rotund and rather frightening woman. Is that a snake in her hand? But see, in her other arm, she's carrying a basket or a bowl."

"It's like the Matres you were talking about, though there's only one instead of three."

Con nodded. "My guess is a fertility figure, though the snake usually has some connotation of death or the afterlife."

The next page was a listing of dates.

"Records of their meetings," Con suggested. "They start in June 1841. At first they're irregular, then they become four each year."

Lilah paged through the book. "Look how many there are."

The next page was blank. Con turned back to the listings. "Look at these last couple of pages. The dates are haphazard again."

Lilah studied the entries. "This is around the time my grandfather died. My father took over, and he wouldn't have been faithful in keeping the accounts." She sighed and set the book aside, turning to Con. "What are we going to do? I feel as though we just discovered a great deal, but I can't see that we're any further along in finding the key. Or where it goes."

"I feel exceedingly odd saying this to you, but I think we must be patient." Con took her hand. "We *do* know a great deal more, and understanding what they were doing will help us. Your grandfather was much more involved in this than your father, so I think we should focus on him after we finish here."

"You're right." Con had not released her hand, but Lilah didn't want to point that out. Reluctantly she said, "I suppose we

353

should stop. It's getting rather late."

Con gazed intently into her eyes, his thumb tracing her fingers. "Do you — would you like me to keep watch tonight?"

"Keep watch? For wh— oh, you mean to catch me if I start roaming about in the middle of the night?"

"Yes."

Lilah squeezed his hand, warmed by his concern. "That's very good of you, but I have solved the problem. I shall lock my door and put the key away."

"Very well, but if you need me . . ."

"I know." Lilah's chest was suddenly full and aching. For the first time she could remember, she wished that she was different. That she was a woman who didn't worry or plan, who wasn't skeptical and bound by convention. The sort of woman who could ignore the conventions and not think of the consequences. The sort of woman Con could care for.

"Lilah . . ." Con stopped, his face troubled. "You aren't . . . You wouldn't seriously consider marrying that man, would you?"

"Sir Jasper? I think that's clear from the way I've been avoiding him."

"But I know your aunt Helena favors him, and you trust and rely on her. I thought she might persuade you. That you might give in because it's 'appropriate.' I should hate to see you tied to someone like him."

"Would you?" Lilah held her breath. What was Con saying?

"You deserve so much more. You should have a man who will treasure you."

The way you do not? But she did not say it. Con leaned closer.

"Delilah!" They whirled around. Sir Jasper stood in the doorway, looking horrified. "What in the name of all that's holy is going on?"

CHAPTER TWENTY-SEVEN

Sir Jasper presented such a comical figure, standing there in his brocade dressing gown, matching nightcap askew on his head and candlestick in hand, that Lilah struggled not to smile.

"Lord Moreland! Explain yourself. What are you doing here with Delilah in the middle of the night? Not wearing a jacket! And sitting on the floor!"

"At least I'm not wearing my night-clothes." Con rose to his feet, a dangerous light in his eyes. "Why are you roaming about Miss Holcutt's home, spying on her?"

"Spying!" Jasper's face turned scarlet. "How dare you, sir! I am Miss Holcutt's only male relative, which gives me every right to question your conduct and motives."

"And here I would have sworn your motives were something other than familial."

"Con, stop." Lilah turned toward the

older man. "We were going through some of my grandfather's things."

"At this hour?"

"Yes, isn't it amazing?" Aunt Vesta's voice came from the inner staircase, making everyone jump. "Young people have so much energy."

They turned to see Vesta standing at the top of the stairs, a hand on her ample bosom as she caught her breath. Unsurprisingly, she was a startling vision in a bed robe of vivid purple embroidered with golden dragons. Her too-black hair streamed down her back. Not content with a single candlestick, she carried a candelabra with three tapers.

"Good God." Sir Jasper goggled at her. "Where the devil did you come from?"

"Why, from the floor below, Jasper, where else? And, really, I'm surprised to hear you curse in the presence of ladies."

As Jasper fumbled for words, Lilah said, "Hello, Aunt Vesta."

"Mrs. LeClaire." Con embellished his greeting with an extravagant bow, which made Vesta giggle.

"Sorry to be running late," Vesta said, adding in an aside to Jasper, "The children are helping me go through my father's things. It is something of a task, as you can see."

"Good God," Jasper said again, looking around him at the room for the first time. "What a bizarre place."

"Sir Ambrose was fond of clocks and compasses," Aunt Vesta said in a vast understatement. "He said he always wanted to know when and where he was."

"Yes, I can see."

"I'm so sorry that we bothered you, Sir Jasper," Lilah said.

"I beg your pardon for awakening you," Con added insincerely. "You must sleep very lightly indeed to have heard us from your bedchamber."

The other man replied stiffly, "I happened to be up and saw the light in this tower. I thought it best to investigate. It could have been robbers."

"Mmm. One never knows whom one might find creeping about the house," Con said.

Red flared along Sir Jasper's cheekbones, and Lilah said hastily, "It was very thoughtful of you, Sir Jasper. We appreciate your concern very much. Don't we, Aunt Vesta?"

"What?" Aunt Vesta had wandered over to the pile of books on the floor. "Oh, yes, of course."

After a long, uncomfortable silence, Sir Jasper said, "Yes, well . . . um . . . then I shall bid you good-night and leave you to . . . your work." His eyes flickered over the opened cabinet, the books piled on the floor and the objects Con had discarded on the desk.

Turning on his heel, he left the room. The other three stood, listening to the ring of his retreating footsteps until they were gone. Lilah relaxed, letting out a sigh.

"I must say," Aunt Vesta offered. "It seems most peculiar that Sir Jasper is sneaking about the house in the dark."

"I think he hopes one day to be master here," Con replied.

"Is that why he's here?" Aunt Vesta asked. "I wondered. I suppose Helena encouraged his suit. I can't imagine why. He hasn't the slightest interest in anything but the mundane." She shrugged. "Of course, neither does Helena. Your mother was always so much livelier. No, no, dear, no need to fire up." She waved a dismissive hand as Lilah frowned. "I know she is your beloved aunt."

Lilah heard the faint stress on the word *beloved.* She wondered if Vesta was jealous of Aunt Helena. Had Vesta really expected to pick up with Lilah where she left off, after all these years?

"How did you know we were in trouble?" Con asked.

"I actually *did* look out the window and saw the light. I knew it must be you. Then I heard Sir Jasper going down the stairs, so I followed and saw him disappearing into the old wing. Well, I guessed he must be coming here to investigate, so I cut across the courtyard. I thought I might beat him here, but, my! Those stairs!" She placed her hand over her heart dramatically. "I'm not the slip of a girl I used to be."

Con, as expected, gallantly protested her statement. "Those stairs would lay anyone low."

"Have you found anything?" Vesta asked, looking around.

"A book," Con told her. "Did your father never discuss his beliefs about the old gods and such?"

"He may have." She frowned in thought. "I remember him talking about old legends. King Arthur and Merlin. The Holy Grail. He used to speak very reverently about a goddess. Once he told me that this tor was sacred. He said we drew our life from it. He meant the channels of energy in the earth of course, but I didn't realize that until later. He often spoke of the miracle of his cure."

"Do you know how that happened exactly?" Lilah asked. "What was wrong with him?"

"He had a terrible, long-lasting fever when he was young, and the doctors told him it had damaged his heart. He had . . . attacks of some sort."

"Heart attacks?"

"No, not his heart stopping. He said his heart would 'go mad.' Sometimes it skipped and other times it pounded so hard and fast, he feared it would explode. He didn't say how he was cured. He would just say that he went 'to the heart of the tor,' and it gave him back his heart. That was when he told me the tor was sacred and that our family's life comes from it." She looked at Con. "Do you think that's where the key goes? To this place that's 'the heart of the tor'?"

"I would think so," Con agreed.

"He never said anything specific about where it was located? Inside the house? On the grounds?" Lilah pressed.

Vesta shook her head. "Not that I remember. I was still quite young when he died. He may have discussed such things with Virgil. But Virgil had just married your mother, so of course he was much more interested in love."

"Unfortunately, the book doesn't say anything about where he might have hidden the key," Lilah said, bending down to pick up her grandfather's book.

"We'll start again tomorrow," Con said with his usual confidence.

Lilah nodded. "And I don't intend to waste time trying to entertain Sir Jasper."

"Yes," Aunt Vesta agreed. "It's my opinion, dear, that if a man takes it upon himself to drop in on people, he can hardly complain about rudeness."

As they started toward the door, Con glanced at the book Lilah cradled in her arm. "You're taking the book with you?"

"Yes. I —" Lilah looked down at the volume. She wasn't sure why, but she felt the need to keep it with her . . . Though she wasn't about to admit that to either of these two. "I think that's safest."

Though her eyes were shadowed from lack of sleep, Lilah was brimming with enthusiasm as she went down to breakfast the next morning. She had locked the door the night before, which had prevented her from walking in her sleep, but her night had been restless. She had awakened several times, disoriented in the darkness, her heart pounding. Finally, she got up and spent the rest of the night poring over her grandfather's book. She was eager to tell Con what she'd found.

Unfortunately, Sir Jasper was seated at the

table with Con, spoiling her plans. Lilah shot a glance at Con and sat down. Con drew up straighter, and his voice was tinged with question. "Lilah."

"Constantine." A smile tugged at the corner of her mouth.

"You seem chipper this morning."

"Do I?" Lilah let her smile broaden.

"Chipper!" Sir Jasper exclaimed. "I say, Moreland, have you no eyes? Delilah, you look worn through."

Con brows rose, but he made no comment.

"Why, thank you, Sir Jasper. It's nice to know I look haggard."

"I did not mean — of course you look lovely. You could appear nothing else. But it's clear you have taxed yourself. I fear these late hours are too much for your constitution."

"My constitution is fine, Sir Jasper."

"Now, now," he said in a jovial tone. "I can't have you coming down ill now, can I?"

Con cleared his throat and settled back to watch. Lilah fixed her coolest look on Sir Jasper. "*You* 'can't have' it? I fail to see what business it is of yours."

Jasper blinked. "Well, um, that is . . ." He shot a resentful glance at Con, as if he had caused the problem.

Lilah pushed her tea away. "Con, if you would excuse us, I believe Sir Jasper and I need to have a discussion."

Con looked from Lilah to Jasper and back. "But of course." He rose to his feet, snagging a piece of bacon from his plate, and strolled from the room. "Ruggins, I believe we aren't needed here."

The butler followed him, and Lilah closed the door. She turned back to Sir Jasper, who had risen to his feet.

"Thank you, Lilah, for asking that chap to leave. It's time to put a stop to his hanging about. The attentions of a duke's son are doubtless flattering, but it will cause talk if he remains here. And your Aunt Vesta is, um, well, not someone whom I would consider an adequate chaperone."

"Thank you for your concern, but I assure you, it is unwarranted. And unwelcome." Lilah felt her hand knotting into a fist by her side and unclenched it. "I don't know what Aunt Helena told you that caused you to visit."

"Mrs. Summersley is naturally worried about you being here with a man of a certain reputation paying court to you and only Mrs. LeClaire to chaperone."

"Constantine Moreland is not 'paying

court' to me. He is related by marriage to my dearest friend and is a friend to me, as well." Lilah ignored his dismissive grunt. "Moreover, I have never heard of him putting a young lady's good name in danger."

"He has no substance, no gravitas. His father may be a duke, but it's well-known that his entire family is peculiar."

"I might remind you that the Holcutt family is not known for its normality."

"That is why it's especially important that you and I are careful not to lend credence to the rumors."

"There is no 'you and I,' " Lilah snapped, goaded.

He smiled benignly. "I hope that condition will change."

"There is no reason to."

"Delilah, my dear, you are young. It's entirely understandable that you enjoy the round of parties, the attention of many young gentlemen. But such things cannot go on forever. You will soon embark on your adult life. A woman on her own has no place in the world. She must have a husband to protect and take care of her, children to nurture, a home to call her own."

"I have a home to call my own. We're standing in it. And I don't need someone to protect or take care of me."

"My dear . . ." His smile, his tone, were so patient and condescending that it made Lilah clench her teeth.

"Sir Jasper! If Aunt Helena gave you reason to hope your suit would be successful, I am truly sorry. She had no right to encourage you."

He looked taken aback. "But, Lilah . . . we make an excellent match. It will reunite our lands. I am devoted to you."

"I don't love you, and I'm certain that you don't love me either."

"I am most fond of you, my dear, and I'm sure in time you will come to feel the same."

"I doubt it, as I am growing less fond of you by the moment." Lilah drew in a calming breath. "I'm sorry to be discourteous, but my subtler efforts haven't been met with success. So I must tell you as directly as possible that I have no intention of marrying you. Now or ever."

He scowled. "If you are clinging to girlish dreams of a love match, you are most foolish. Love is much overrated."

"It probably is. Certainly, it is rare, and I have no expectation of such. But I must have something more than 'a good match.' "

"I would think carefully if I were you," Jasper said tightly. "Given the situation in which you are living here, your reputation could be very much at stake. I am willing to put your actions down to naïveté and girlish silliness, but not everyone will be as generous."

Fury shot through Lilah. "Are you threatening me?"

"It's no threat. I'm simply stating the realities you should be aware of. You won't get an offer from that duke's son, if that is what you're holding out for. It's clear the fellow is merely trifling with you."

For an instant Lilah wished Con *had* shown her how to throw a proper punch. But she held on to her control and said only, "I think it's time you left this house, Sir Jasper."

Jasper blinked at her bluntness. "I see. Well, then, I will take my leave of you. Pray give my regards to your aunt." He started toward the door, then swung back. "I feel it is my duty to speak to Mrs. Summersley about the situation here. I fear she will be severely disappointed."

Lilah's stomach knotted at his words. He was right, and she could not help but feel guilty. She had strayed far from her aunt's precepts. Worse, she had enjoyed it deeply. "Aunt Helena's primary concern is my happiness."

Unfortunately, she wasn't any longer sure that she believed her words.

CHAPTER TWENTY-EIGHT

Con refrained from lurking about in the hall, much as he wanted to hear what Lilah said to Sir Jasper. From the expression on her face, he had the strong suspicion it wouldn't end well for Sir Jasper. It was probably petty of him to find satisfaction in that outcome, but he did.

Retreating to the library, he spent his time idly pulling on books to see if they triggered the opening of a secret door. A few minutes later, when he heard the rush of heavy footsteps down the hall, he returned to the dining room.

Lilah was standing at the windows, and the sun lit her hair in a flame of red and gold. She was ramrod straight, and her face was stony, but it was such a pleasure to look at her long slim body and bright hair that Con just leaned against the door frame for a moment, enjoying the view.

Lilah turned. "Oh. I didn't realize you

were there."

"I take it your swain was not best pleased by your conversation."

"No." Lilah sighed and sat down, picking at the toast on the plate before her. "Why is it so hard to know what's right?"

"I never thought I'd hear you admit you didn't know the right thing to do." Con sat down beside her.

"I used to." Lilah rested her chin on her hand.

"You can blame it on me. I'm a bad influence."

Lilah gave him a glimmer of a smile. "You are."

"Dare I hope Sir Jasper is leaving us?"

"As soon as he can, I imagine." Her look hardened. "He'll run straight back to Aunt Helena. I hope she doesn't decide she needs to come down here herself to straighten things out."

"What is so tangled that it needs straightening?"

She gave a half shrug. "Me, I suppose."

"You don't need straightening." Con thought how she had changed recently, her beauty blossoming with each smile, each laugh, each wayward thought. He suspected she wouldn't want to hear it. "Why don't you tell me what you were itching to say when you walked in this morning?"

"How do you know I wanted to say anything?" She smiled teasingly, and the now-familiar warmth stole through him.

Con had a strong urge to lean over and kiss her, but he said only, "Because I'm not as blind as Sir Jasper. Did you find something in that book?"

"I did. The last page had another Latin phrase printed on it. *'Fortis quam germanitas nullum est vinculum.'*"

" 'No bond is greater than that of brotherhood.' They certainly are fascinated by that idea, aren't they?"

"But that is not the main thing. This was folded and stuck between the last few pages." She pulled a sheet of paper from her pocket and spread it out on the table.

Excitement flared in him. "The designs for the keys!"

"Look at the different heads on the keys. One has the spoked wheel one often finds on the artifacts around here. I think that's a symbol for the sun. And above it a yellow citrine."

"So it stands for the sky? Intellect? Blair's key. The three parallel undulating lines . . ." Con pointed to another of the drawings. "The sea?"

Lilah nodded. "A sapphire for it. My

grandfather's."

"So this last one with the obsidian decoration and, fittingly, twisting snakes would have been Dearborn's." Con drummed his fingers absently on the table. "You'd think he would have written more about what he believed."

"Perhaps he did. We didn't finish searching the Clock Room last night. There may be more in those cabinets."

"Then let's go back."

They spent the rest of the morning rummaging through the things in her grandfather's desk and cabinets. Late in the morning, Con, to his great delight, found a carved spiral embellishment on one of the drawers that he was able to push to the side. Beneath it lay a smaller strip of wood. When he turned it, there was an audible click.

"I knew it! A secret drawer." He felt beneath desk and found a shallow drawer that slid out. He pulled it out and set it down on the desk. "Lilah, come look. I've found something."

Together they bent their heads over the piece of paper lying inside. Lilah had come to recognize her grandfather's spidery handwriting by now. She read out loud.

"All that we have, we owe to you. All that

we are, we offer to you. Out of fear and darkness, you revealed your glorious being and entrusted to us the knowledge of the Otherworld. In humility and joy, we give you this, our sacred vow:

"We pledge to you our lives and our devotion. We honor the old ways. We revere the ancient gods. We believe in a life renewing. We are forever the holders of the Gateway, the guardians of the Path. We stand constant in our faith, knowing that for eternity we shall be blessed to reside in peace with you."

"Their creed. Fascinating." Con reached down to pick up the paper. "Look. There's another page."

"It's their order of worship."

We march in solemn procession.
Unlocking of the door in unison.
Assemble at the altar.
Presentation of sacrifice.
Offer of blood.
We lay hands upon the altar and recite the creed.
Receiving of gifts.
Final prayer.
Recessional.

"Sacrifice. That's a bit frightening." Lilah

turned to Con. "You don't think they were . . . sacrificing animals there, do you?" Her stomach began to churn.

"I doubt it. Sacrifices could be anything — gifts of fruit, for all we know. Or even giving up certain things, as with Lent. 'I swear to forgo cigars the next three months.' "

"But what about this 'offer of blood'?" Lilah pointed out.

"Sounds like it was in addition to the sacrifice. My guess is they made a small cut on their wrists or hands, say, and all three of them dripped a bit of blood onto the altar. Blood oaths, that sort of thing."

"Then they put their hands on the altar and said their creed. And look . . ." Lilah pointed at the bottom of the page. "Here's a drawing." She frowned over the rectangle with three circles grouped around it.

"The way they stood at the altar," Con said. "And this is no doubt the final prayer. 'O Gracious Mother, we thank thee for these, thy gifts. Renewed, we go forth, confident in thy bounty and in the fullness of thy love.' Amazing how a ritual makes one go back to *thee* and *thy,* isn't it?" Con mused.

"I like the way he underlined *solemn procession.*"

"Pointed at Dearborn, you think?" Con grinned. "Sir Ambrose was certainly a dictatorial sort."

"Don't you dare say it runs in the family." Lilah gave him a stern frown.

"Wouldn't dream of it." With a wink, he turned back to his search.

The rest of the day proved fruitless, though they kept at it doggedly, breaking only for tea. Finally, Con sat down with a sigh and leaned back against the cabinet. "I think we have covered — or uncovered — every square inch of this room."

"I think it's safe to say there's nothing else to be gleaned here." Lilah sat down beside him.

"Where shall we look next?" Con asked. "We can't afford to waste too much time."

"Con, really, if you start talking about Mr. Dearborn's calamity on Midsummer Day . . ."

"But doesn't that seem more likely — less absurd, at least — now that we've found all this?" He waved his hand vaguely around the office. "Doesn't it sound like what these fellows would have dreamed up — 'we meet and renew every three years or else the gods will curse us.' Only with more *thees* and *thou shalts.*"

"Yes, it sounds precisely like them. And

the important part of your sentence is *dreamed up.* They concocted this religion purely out of their imagination. It doesn't make it real." Lilah wasn't about to admit that despite her words, she felt a strange tug of urgency deep inside her.

"Well, Dearborn and Sir Jasper are quite real — and one or the other, or both, is after the key. We must find it."

"We've already searched my father's room. There's my grandfather's office. I don't know, Con. A key is such a small thing. It could be hidden anywhere."

"We must also find the Sanctuary," Con pointed out. "If we could see the door, we'd have a better idea what we're looking for."

"Yes, but we know even less about its location."

"Let's think about it." Con leaned his head back and closed his eyes. "These men get together and prime the pump with a few glasses of port or brandy. Then they tromp off to this room, open it with their three keys and have a ceremony. Or perhaps they do the drinking there as part of the ceremony."

"Perhaps we should look for their 'silly hats.' "

"Oh, I think these were hooded robes kind of chaps." Con opened his eyes. "How did they stumble upon this 'Gateway'? It can't be readily apparent or others would have found it. We have three young blades, stuck in the country, miles from entertainment. Even given your grandfather's ill health and Blair's preference for intellectual pursuits, they must have been inclined to have some fun, go adventuring."

"Probably. You think that's what they were doing when they found their sanctuary?"

"Yes. Where would they go around here for an adventure? A cave, perhaps?"

"There aren't any nearby."

"Some old ruins?"

"The barrow is miles away, and the Holy Well even farther."

Con's eyes lit up. "Ah, but there are some ruins right here, aren't there?" He pointed downward. "Didn't you say this part of the house was built on the ruins of an old castle?"

"The cellars!" Lilah brightened. "You're right. That sounds exactly the thing to intrigue a group of young men."

"Exactly. Dank, dark cells. Skeletons in chains. We should go down to the dungeons."

"They aren't dungeons. They're just cellars . . . but I understand they are very extensive."

"The cellars it is, then." He stood up and offered her his hand.

"It's too late to start now. That's an all-day task."

"You're right. Much as it grieves me to be prudent, we'll start tomorrow."

Con took up his post by his door again that night. Lilah had not asked him to keep watch, and hopefully her remedy of locking her door would keep her from wandering, but he couldn't just go to bed, knowing that she might put herself in danger.

He had done it last night as well, after they'd returned to their rooms, not going to bed until the servants were up. His lack of sleep was telling on him. Now, as he sat there, he kept slipping into a doze, then awakening with a start.

It began to rain and the sound soothed him, lulling him to sleep. He woke up with a start at a clap of thunder. Groggily, he peered down the hall at Lilah's closed door, then got up and went to the window. The rain had turned into a storm, clouds covering the moon, turning the night pitch-black until lightning flashed, illuminating the garden.

He glanced at the time. It was almost three. He wondered if it was safe to give up his watch now; the other times Lilah had gone out had been before this. Going to the door, he took another look down the hall. He stiffened. There was, he saw now, a thin line of black separating her door from its frame.

Heart hammering, he crossed the corridor. The door stood a trifle ajar. He pushed it open cautiously — the last thing he wanted was Lilah waking up and screaming at the presence of a man in her bedchamber.

But there was no possibility of that. Her bedcovers were turned back, her bed empty. The door key lay on the floor at his feet. Con turned and ran down the stairs. He told himself there was no reason to worry. She had done this several times now without coming to any harm. Her senses and instincts seemed to work even though her mind was unknowing. But Con could not subdue this feeling of urgency.

He cursed himself for falling asleep. Had her door been ajar when he woke up and he hadn't noticed it in his stupor? Or had it been closed and she had left just a moment ago, while he was staring out the window?

He intended to go to the tower, but he pulled up short when he crossed the hall leading to the back door. Logic told him

Lilah would have headed for the tower, as she had last night. But something else tugged at him, and he turned toward the back door. The loosening in his chest told him he was right.

He realized that between him and the door lay — not a light or a vision — just the hint of a disturbance in the air. The closest he could come to describing it was a faint shimmer or ripple, akin to the distortion of heat waves above a fire.

His steps quickened. This faint glimmer was what he had seen last night in the Great Hall, not light, when he had followed Lilah through the darkness. He burst out the door and began to run, following the indistinct ripple that stayed steadily before him. She had gone to the maze.

Thunder rumbled; the rain soaked him. And Lilah was out here in only her nightgown. She would come down sick. She could slip on the wet grass. She could lose herself in the maze. He charged into the tangled hedges. The glimmer flowed, not toward the center, but away from it, and he turned in that direction.

Lilah hadn't gotten far. He found her in one of the blind alleys, the thick shrubbery looming around her, tiny branches reaching out like fingers toward her. She was on her knees beside a bench, her nightgown soaked through, her hair streaming water. She sobbed, hands over her face, her whole torso shaking under the force of her sobs.

"Lilah!" He ran to her.

She lifted her head. "Con. Oh, Con!" She threw herself into his arms, clinging, her face buried in his chest.

Con wrapped his arms around her, hugging her to him, searching frantically for what to say, what to do, to ease her pain. He murmured her name and kissed her head, saying helplessly, uselessly, "Shh, darling, it's all right. I'm here. Don't cry. You're safe. I won't let anything hurt you."

"No," she moaned, her arms tightening around his waist. "It's not. You don't know —"

"Tell me. Tell me what's wrong. What can I do?"

"Nothing." She pulled back, gazing up into his face. Her eyes were huge and wounded in the darkness. Rain ran down her face, mingling with her tears. "There's nothing anyone can do. It's in me. Oh, Con, it's true! It's all true!"

"What's true?"

"The séance. This house."

Nothing she could have said would have surprised him more. For a moment, he could only stare at her, speechless.

"I've been hiding and lying all these years." Her words were rapid, panicked. "But it's here and it — it's going to take me over. It's going to destroy me. It's going to destroy us all."

CHAPTER TWENTY-NINE

Lilah's words were met with a stunned silence. In the dark she couldn't make out Con's expression; she had no idea what he thought or felt. At the moment, she was too numb and drained to care. She shivered.

"Lilah . . ." She felt his hand stroke her head, and she leaned into Con, wanting the heat of him, the steady thumping of his heart. He scooped her up in his arms. "You're freezing. Let's get you inside."

Con carried Lilah into the enormous kitchen and set her down on the wide stone hearth. Stirring the fire to life, he looked around and found a rough jacket hanging on a hook beside the door. He wrapped it around her. "This will help warm you while I get you something dry to wear."

Lilah watched him leave. The room seemed colder without him. She wrapped the coat more tightly around her and huddled close to the flames. She couldn't stop shivering. It wasn't just the wet clothes that chilled her. It was that horror of waking up in the maze, thunder rumbling through her and that thing, that power, pulling at her. In that moment, she knew. She remembered it all.

When Con returned, he carried a pile of blankets and clothing, and he had obviously changed into dry clothes. His shirt, hanging outside his trousers, was simple, with loose sleeves and unfastened ties at the neck. His hair was damp and tumbled. He looked vaguely disreputable. Utterly desirable.

Con set a stack of folded blankets beside her. Atop it lay a nightgown and robe. The thought of his hands sifting through her gowns and undergarments sent a shiver through Lilah that owed nothing to being chilled. How could she be thinking such things at a time like this?

"Put these on. I won't look." He took the jacket from her and began to make tea, carefully keeping his back to her.

Lilah whisked off her nightgown, feeling exposed — and strangely a little aroused by that — and put on the dry one. Wrapping her dressing gown around her, she pulled a blanket around her as well and sat down once again by the fire.

Con brought her a cup of steaming tea

and pulled up a low stool to sit down facing her. He sipped at his own tea, watching her, then set the cup aside and leaned forward. "Tell me what happened."

"I don't know where to begin."

"Start with what happened tonight," he told her, taking one of her hands in his.

"Clearly I walked in my sleep again. I must have taken the key out of my jewelry box and unlocked the door, unbelievable as it seems."

"Were you dreaming?"

"I — I'm not sure. I was aware of being . . . *pulled*. I couldn't quite catch my breath, and I had to go somewhere, though I had no sense of where it was."

"Had to? You dreamed someone was forcing you?" Con asked.

"No. I *needed* to. I felt driven."

"And then . . ."

"Suddenly there was a clap of thunder, and I woke up. I saw where I was, and I realized that I'd walked in my sleep again. And . . . perhaps it was the storm, the thunder and lightning, I'm not sure, but suddenly I remembered." She pulled in a shaky breath, her hands trembling slightly. "Oh, Con, I've been so wrong and foolish. *So blind.*"

"It's all right." He took her hands between

his. "What did you remember?"

"What happened that night. At the sé-ance." She wet her lips. She wanted to tell him, needed to, yet she could hardly force out the words. "A man Aunt Vesta knew — someone she loved, I think — wanted to contact his great-uncle. It was important to her, so she wanted me there. She used to say that the spirits yearned to be with children. I didn't want to go. The séances scared me — the dark and the candles and the ghostly talk."

"Sounds enough to scare any child."

"But she was insistent. It meant so much to her. And I . . ." Lilah pressed her lips together, pushing back the tears. "I loved Aunt Vesta. You were right. She was the clos-est thing I had to a mother. She was fun. She came to my pretend tea parties. She liked to braid my hair. She said she had always envied my mother's hair."

"I'm sorry she left." Con raised her hand to kiss it. "I'm sure it had nothing to do with her feelings for you. That séance drew such attention. She wanted the life that beckoned."

"The fame and fortune. I know." Lilah sighed. "And that was my fault. The séance was . . . I did it."

"Did what?" Con frowned. "Caused the

386

window to explode? Lilah, as you said, that was exaggerated. It was the storm."

"No. It wasn't." Lilah braced herself, looking Con in the eye. Her heart pounded madly. "There was rain that night, but it wasn't a ferocious storm. At least, it wasn't before the séance."

Con stared. "You're telling me you think a vengeful spirit appeared? That you brought it back from the dead?"

"Do you not believe me?"

"Of course I believe you." Lilah relaxed, warmed by his swift response. "Lilah, I know you don't lie. And if *you* believe a spirit appeared, so do I. But I don't understand. Why do you think you're at fault?"

"I was the one who attracted it. There was something wrong with me."

"Lilah, no, there's nothing wrong with you."

"There was. I knew. I felt it. It had gotten worse that last year. That was when I started sleepwalking. I had no memory of what I did, but sometimes, when I was jarred awake in the midst of it, I had that feeling I had tonight. I felt . . . pulled."

"And in the séances?"

"It was the opposite there. I felt as if I were drawing something out. I'd have a tightness here." She tapped her chest. "Like

387

a fist clenching inside me, pulling this . . . this power into me. I was responsible, but I had no control over it. It controlled me."

"You were a child, Lilah. You didn't know what to do. If there is blame, it should be Vesta's. She used you."

"I'm not sure she realized how much was my doing. She thought it was all her. I was more a good-luck charm."

"Exactly what happened at this séance?"

"Aunt Vesta had the servants set up a table in the Great Hall. I sat between her and Father. There were several people there, and we all held hands. When Aunt Vesta called to her spirit guide, that knot began in my chest. It grew stronger and tighter, and that power began to flow into me. It spread throughout my body, expanding and rising. It was like floating in the ocean and being lifted by a wave. It was exhilarating."

"I can imagine."

"But it frightened me, too. As it poured into me, the rain outside turned into a storm. I tried to fight it, to push back the energy, but I couldn't. I felt as if it were going to consume me, smother me. Then it exploded, flooding out of me like water breaking through a dam. That's when the window broke and the storm rushed in. I don't know what happened after that because I fainted."

"It must have terrified you."

"It did. I didn't wake up until the next afternoon. My father came into my room, and — oh, Con, the expression on his face." Unconsciously Lilah squeezed his hand. "He was happy and relieved, but also shocked, even a bit awestruck. Beneath it all was fear. And that frightened me even more. After that, he never looked at me the way he had before. It was as if he loved me, but I was a stranger to him. A dangerous stranger."

"I'm so sorry, love." Con reached out, pulling her into his lap. He cradled her, his head against hers. "He was worried about you, afraid *for* you, not *of* you."

"Perhaps. But he gave me to Aunt Helena."

His arms tightened around her. "I'm sure he thought he needed to get you out of this house for your own protection. You'd been walking in your sleep, and then this wild séance rendered you unconscious for hours. No doubt he feared that if you stayed, something even worse might happen to you. If you were away from this 'force' and under the care of your aunt Helena, not his sister, Vesta, you would be safe."

"You're kind. But there's no need to feel

sorry for me. My father and I had never been close before that either." She sighed, nestling into him. "How could I have forgotten such a thing? I *thought* I remembered it, but it was all wrong."

"You had a horrifying experience. You wanted to forget it. So you created a better memory."

"I don't know what to think anymore. I feel as if I've built my life on a foundation of sand. Has everything I've believed been wrong? Who am I really? What if this thing overtakes me again? It controls me. I cannot keep myself from walking in my sleep. I have no power over it or over myself. I fear that it will consume me, and I — I won't exist anymore. That I will be nothing but an empty shell, a body, and inside me will be only . . . *it*."

"Nonsense," Con said crisply, taking her by the shoulders and looking into her eyes. "Being mistaken about a childhood memory doesn't make you someone else. Whether Lilah, Delilah or Dilly, you are and always have been *you*. You have spine. You have principles. You're steady. You're calm. You're skeptical. You think things through. None of that changes."

"I sound a dull sort."

"Anything but. You're also clever and

beautiful and adventurous."

"Adventurous? Really, Con . . ."

"You are," he insisted. "You've just tried to avoid that the last ten years." He curled his arm around her again, gently pushing her head back against his shoulder. "Nothing is going to take you over. You are stronger than any force. And if it tries to harm you, I won't allow it."

Lilah smiled. "Ah, well, then, I feel better." Her voice was teasing, but the truth was, she did feel better. She trusted Con. And somehow she believed him — with Con beside her, she could fight any battle. It felt so good, so right, to rest here in the circle of his arms, as if . . . as if she belonged here. That was a thought that should have shaken Lilah to the core. But strangely it did not. What she felt was freed. Even buoyant.

She had been much ruled by her mind these past few years — her memories hidden, all her actions, her attitudes devoted to creating a personality of reason and control. Perhaps it was time she let her instincts have their way.

She sat up and looked at Con, taking in those leaf-green eyes, the mobile, sensual mouth, the jet-black hair that tumbled around his face. His morning beard was showing through, giving his well-modeled face a hint of roughness that made him even more desirable. Lilah reached out to cup his cheek.

Con's eyes widened when she touched him, but he said nothing, his body utterly still beneath her. Lilah stroked her thumb across his cheek, following its path with her eyes. She caressed his lip in the same way, luxuriating in its velvet smoothness. She could see the pulse leaping in his neck. She dragged her thumb down his neck to rest on that hard, fast pulse, awakening an answering throb deep inside her.

She leaned in to kiss him. Con's fists clenched in the fabric of her gown, his body taut and unmoving, but his mouth welcomed her. Warm and soft, hungry but patient, his lips moved on hers. Lilah thought she could sit here all night kissing him. But she wanted more.

Lilah pulled back and gazed into his eyes. "Take me to bed, Con."

CHAPTER THIRTY

It was a wonder he didn't choke on his lust.
It surged in him so hard and fast. Con
wanted nothing more than to do as Lilah
asked. No, as she commanded — which
made it all the more arousing. For a few
minutes, she had been almost broken, her
confidence shaken, but here she was, Lilah
once more, sure and compelling. The depth
of his need for her was frightening. It was
also almost unbearably erotic.

"Lilah, no . . ." he murmured. How the
devil was he supposed to resist this?

"Don't tell me you don't want to." She
wiggled her hips, proving her point as his
traitorous flesh leaped in response.

"You're upset. You're acting impulsively."

Her lips curved up in a knowing way that
staggered him. "I am." She stood up and
stretched her hand out to him. "Come."

Con followed her. They climbed the stairs,
Lilah before him, and Con could not look

away from the sway of her hips, the delectable curve of her derriere. It would be wrong of him to make love to Lilah. He'd promised her, and Con never broke a promise. But he'd never before been faced with a force as strong as the desire clawing at him now.

At the top of the stairs, the door to Lilah's room stood ajar, the dark interior beckoning. He was having more and more trouble remembering why he could not do this. Con paused in the doorway. Stepping inside seemed to be crossing a line, an action he could never call back. "Lilah, no. I promised you I would not."

"I release you from your promise." Lilah gave him that soul-stealing smile again and laid her hands on his chest. Their heat seared through his shirt; he ached to feel them against his skin.

"You will hate me," he murmured.

"I don't think so." Her hands went to the hem of his shirt, gathering the cloth and climbing upward.

When she reached his waist, she slipped her hands beneath the fabric. He jerked as if he'd been stung, and reached out to grasp the door frame on each side — he wasn't sure whether it was to hold him back or to hold him up. He dropped his head, resting it against hers, drinking in the scent of her even as he struggled to retain the last remnant of his control.

"Think." He made a final effort. "You'll regret it."

"I won't." Her hands glided over his ribs, circled his nipples. She went up on her toes, her mouth seeking his.

And Con was lost.

He seized her by the waist and pulled her into him, holding her hard and fast as his mouth consumed hers. All thought of codes of conduct, gentlemanly behavior, even honor, were swept aside by desire. He had to have her. And he would make damn sure she didn't regret it.

Unwilling to let her go, Con lifted her and walked into the room, pushing the door closed with his foot. This time undressing was an easier task, with only their hastily donned clothes to whisk off. The first time Con had enjoyed seeing Lilah naked in the light of day, but the darkness now was seductive, entangling, heightening his senses. The sound of rain on the windows mingled with Lilah's faint murmurs and moans, sweet and soft in his ears.

Her skin was like velvet beneath his fingertips. He wanted to linger over every inch, but he wanted even more to feel her beneath his lips. He ached with need, yet it was so sweet he savored it. The empty bed that had so alarmed him earlier was now an invitation, and he made his way to it, falling back upon it and taking her with him. He loved the weight of her body on his, the feel of her against him all the way up and down.

He slid his hands down her back, curving over her rounded bottom and her thighs. Slipping a hand between their bodies, Con edged his fingers between her legs and had the satisfaction of her opening to him. Her slick heat was enough to drive him mad, but wanting more, he rolled over onto his side and began a long, thorough exploration of her body.

Every muffled gasp, every moan, every movement of her body in response sent another shaft of desire spiraling through him, his hunger building and building until he thought he must explode. But still he held it leashed to have the pleasure of making love to her, the barbed thrill of watching her take what he gave her.

Lilah circled her hips, urging him on, and only then did he begin to hasten the movement of his fingers. He watched her, his own flesh tightening in response, as she arched up, pressing herself against his hand, then trembled as the pleasure took her.

She went limp all over and opened lambent eyes to gaze at him, her mouth curling in a satisfied way. She reached up and stroked his arm. "But . . . what about . . . you know, the rest of it? What about you?"

"Oh, we'll get there, never fear." He smiled. "We're just taking the long way around."

He kissed her lightly, his fingertips skimming over her, teasing at her breasts, her stomach, her legs. Soft as a feather, he slid his fingers up the inside of one leg, moving closer and closer to her core without touching it, then drifting back down her other thigh.

He kissed her mouth, long and thoroughly, before moving down over her neck and chest. He devoted extra time and care to her breasts, caressing and teasing, until her breath came short and sharp in her throat. His lips moved downward, over her ribs and onto her stomach, her abdomen. Lilah moved restlessly, murmuring his name, but still he lingered, opening her legs to kiss the insides of her thighs. Then, finally, his settled his mouth on her.

Lilah twitched and gasped. "Con! I . . . Ohhh." She dug her hands into the sheet beneath her. Then it was a moaning "yes" that fell from her lips as pleasure rippled through her once again.

At last he parted her legs wider and moved between them, lifting her hips to receive him. He pushed into her slowly, watching the play of expressions across her face, savoring the sensation of her closing tight and hot around him. He thought he could stay here forever, but need drove him on. He thrust and retreated in an ageless rhythm, pumping harder, faster, as the pleasure gripped him. Everything inside him shattered, and a delight so wild, so deep, so intense that he could scarcely breathe, swept through him.

Con sank back onto the bed, breathless and beyond speech. Curling an arm around Lilah, he snuggled her close, nuzzling into her hair. He felt as if he'd been turned inside out. Tomorrow he might count himself a fool or the luckiest man on earth, he wasn't sure. But right now, his whole world, his life, was here, wrapped in his arms.

Lilah woke up, disoriented and groggy, as the bed moved beneath her. She rolled, snuggling into the warmth, and realized it was gone. She opened her eyes to see Con sitting up and turning away. There was little light to see him, but Lilah's memory supplied the rest. She knew each curve of muscle, each line of bone. Indeed, she was certain she would know Con even if she could not see at all.

She reached out and laid her hand upon his back. He turned his head, sweeping his tangled hair back from his face. "Sorry, I didn't mean to wake you."

"It's all right." Lilah could not keep from caressing his back. "Are you leaving?"

"I must." He dropped back down on his elbow, slipping his hand beneath the covers and spreading it out across her stomach. "Can't have Cuddington coming in and finding me in your bed."

"No." Lilah giggled at the thought of her somber maid's horrified face. "I suppose not."

She curved her hand over his cheek, the bristle of his morning stubble prickly beneath her touch. She wanted to ask him to stay, wanted to snuggle into the warm bed, pulling the covers up over them to shield them from the world. But she had done that last night, and she couldn't ask again.

She wondered what he thought, how he felt, if he regretted coming to her bed, if he still thought this a mistake. But she didn't ask. No longer on the firm ground of the old rules, uncertain of the future, she had only what she had here and now. She would live only in the moment and say nothing to spoil it.

Con leaned down to kiss her, and when he raised his head, his eyes had a heavy, slumberous look. His hand glided over her stomach and up to cup her breast. He propped his head on his hand, gazing at her, as he caressed her skin. He looked about to speak, but instead he bent again and kissed her again.

Nuzzling into her hair, he murmured, "Tell me you don't hate me, Lilah."

"I don't hate you, Con." Lilah smiled to herself, sliding her hand up and down his arm lazily.

"Tell me you don't regret last night."

"I don't regret it." She felt his small sigh of relief upon her ear. Imagine that, the cocksure Con Moreland uncertain.

"Good." There was a hint of smug satisfaction in his voice now, but Lilah didn't mind. Somehow it was arousing. Almost as arousing as his fingertip circling her nipple. "We must talk more about this house, you know. What you felt."

"I know. We will. Just . . . not right now."

"No." He smiled and kissed the side of her neck, his hand slipping between her legs. Lilah drew in a sharp little breath as he began to stroke her. "Right now I have something else altogether on my mind."

His mouth came back to hers, and all conversation ceased.

When Lilah awakened again, Con was gone. He had to leave; she knew that. He was protecting her. But still, she missed his presence. She lay for a few moments, letting herself drift in the pleasure of last night, taking each kiss, each caress, each electric thrill, and turning it over in her mind.

She felt limber and languid, stretched, filled, even thoroughly used in a titillating way. It made her blush to think of the things Con had done, the way she had reveled in it. She was discovering herself in all sorts of ways, and she wasn't sure what to make of it. What she thought about herself. But she was eager to find out.

Down the hall, she heard a maid's voice and Cuddington's sharper one. Lilah jumped out of bed and flung on her nightgown, throwing the dressing gown onto the chair. She thought with horror of the sodden nightgown she had dropped on the floor of the kitchen. What had the servants made of that? Lilah turned as Cuddington entered, hoping she didn't look as guilty as felt. Perhaps, she thought, she should start making changes in her life now.

"Cuddington," she said in a casual voice

401

as she pulled on her dressing gown. "You must miss London and Aunt Helena. Perhaps you should go back. Poppy can come down instead or one of the girls here could help me dress."

"But, miss . . . who will do your hair?"

"Oh. Well, I'm sure one of the others —"

"Are you displeased with me, miss?" The woman drew herself up in righteous indignation.

"No, of course not. You're an artist with hair, and you take excellent care of everything." All that was true; she actually would miss Cuddington's skills. But the danger of her finding out about Con and relaying that to Aunt Helena was too great.

"Then why are you sending me away?" Cuddington looked, amazingly, hurt.

"You're Aunt Helena's maid," Lilah said reasonably. "Surely you want to get back — make sure her clothes have been handled correctly. You must find it dull here. The people are strangers."

"Not all of them." Her face softened a little, surprising Lilah even more. "I lived here before. Did Mrs. Summersley never tell you? I was your mother's maid."

Lilah stared. "You were?"

"Yes. From the time she was old enough to wear long skirts." For the first time Lilah could remember, Cuddington smiled. "She was a sweet girl, so lovely, and her hair! It was just like yours, miss, and she loved to try out different styles. I was young then, too, and we, well, we enjoyed changing it up. People noticed because her hair drew one's eye. Lady Battenborough even asked her one night who arranged her hair."

"I . . . I never knew." Lilah sank down onto the stool by the vanity. Was nothing what she'd thought?

Cuddington picked up the silver-backed brush and began to brush Lilah's hair. "You were just a babe. You wouldn't remember me. Mrs. Summersley was good enough to take me with her when she came to your mother's funeral. She knew me well of course, and I'd helped her, too, in the course of my duties for Miss Eva. Your aunt is a good woman. I owe her a great deal."

"Cuddington." Lilah turned to face her. "Will you tell me honestly? Did my aunt send you to report back to her on what I did?"

"No! Miss, how can you think that? Mrs. Summersley wouldn't ask that of me, nor would I agree to it. You're Miss Eva's child. That's why I came. To make sure you were safe." She scowled. "So nothing foolish might happen."

Lilah's eyebrows shot up. "Safe? You mean, from Con?"

The older woman's face turned prim. "He's a devilishly handsome man, miss."

Lilah chuckled. "He is that. But Con wouldn't harm me." She turned back to face the mirror. "Then you would prefer to stay here?"

"Unless you wish me to leave." She added reluctantly, "Mrs. Summersley is a saint, but she is very devoted to one fashion of hair."

"No. If you want to stay, then you should." Lilah had decided she would look at the world with new eyes. Perhaps she should do so with Cuddington. The woman was something of a dragon, but clearly she had hidden depths. After a moment, as Cuddington continued brushing her hair, Lilah said, "You knew my father as well then."

"Oh, yes, Miss Eva loved that man. Sir Virgil was head over heels for her, too. He was in such a state when Miss Eva passed on. Roberts — that was his valet, miss —" Cuddington's cheeks turned a little pink, surprising Lilah once again. "Roberts feared the master might do himself harm."

"What of my grandfather? Was he still alive when you came here?"

"Oh, yes, but we didn't see much of him.

He spent his days in his office. Or up in that room of his. He liked to walk the maze. Your father, now, didn't like that maze, and it scared Miss Eva. That's why he let it go to ruin after Sir Ambrose died." She paused, then went on in a confiding voice, "It's my opinion Sir Virgil didn't like his father much either. The man was barely cold in the ground and the master had Sir Ambrose's things packed away in trunks."

"All of them?"

Cuddington tilted her head, thinking. "I'm not sure, miss. That was when Miss Eva was in the family way, and I paid more attention to her than anything else. Poor thing, she could scarcely keep down anything but toast and water. But I remember Sir Virgil clearing out his father's room. He even did some of the packing himself."

That was interesting. "What did my father do with the trunks?"

"Why, I don't know, miss. The attic perhaps?"

"Ask Ruggins about those trunks, would you? I would like very much to look in them."

"Yes, miss." Cuddington twisted Lilah's hair up and secured it in a casual knot. "There now. I'll just go and draw the water for your bath." She started to the door, then stopped and turned back. "You know, Miss Lilah, if you're wanting to know more about your grandfather, Roberts might be of some help. He did everything for your father for years."

"Yes, I remember him."

"Before he was Sir Virgil's man, he was a footman here. He would know a good deal about Sir Ambrose, as well."

"He's still here?"

"Not working in the house, but he has a cottage on the estate." Cuddington's blush returned. "Your father left him a bit of money and the cottage when he passed on, so Roberts retired."

"Cuddington, you're a jewel." Lilah silently took back all the bad things she had said about her aunt's maid — well, her maid now, apparently.

CHAPTER THIRTY-ONE

Lilah had thought that she might feel a little awkward, even embarrassed, when she saw Con again at breakfast. But as it turned out, all she felt was a rush of happiness when she walked into the dining room, and he jumped up to greet her.

He pulled her into his arms and kissed her, and it took all her willpower to pull back. "Con, the door is open."

"Devil take the door." He reached for her waist.

"We must talk." Lilah drew a shaky breath.

"Must we?" He lowered his head, tantalizingly close.

"Yes." She infused her voice with as much determination as she could. "You said so yourself."

Con heaved a dramatic sigh and turned away. "Very well." He pulled out her chair and took his own seat again. "I have some questions about last night." When Lilah arched her brows, his eyes twinkled. "Not about that. I think I have that down."

"You want to talk about my problem."

"About your *gift,*" he corrected firmly. "At that séance, the way you summoned this spirit —"

"I didn't summon him. I had no conscious thought about him or anything else. It just swept into me. Much as I hate to admit it, I think you were right in what you said that day in the maze. I was a conduit for the energy. It went through me, but Aunt Vesta used it to summon him."

"Did you feel that way in the maze? When I touched you?"

"I don't know. I may have. I wasn't paying attention to it at the time. I was . . . um, rather resistant." She ignored Con's snort. "What I felt in the maze with you certainly wasn't the same feeling I had at the séance. I didn't feel pushed."

Con reached across the table and took her hand experimentally. Lilah tried to open herself to any sensation, but in fact all she felt was the same flutter of sensual excitement she did whenever Con touched her. She shook her head. "There's nothing different. Just . . ."

His eyes darkened. "I know." He cleared his throat and released her hand. "Perhaps I don't feel anything unless you are actively using your ability. Let's say this power comes from some source here, the house or whatever. And that energy flows into you and out into the other person. Maybe you felt it so strongly that night because your aunt has a great deal of power. Whereas my directional talent is a pretty mild thing."

"It could be the opposite — if the person's ability is stronger, he doesn't need to pull as much from me, so it's not as noticeable."

"I wonder . . . That day when the women were kidnapped and Anna had such a vision, didn't you take her hand? Do you suppose that was what made her vision so strong, so coherent?" He stuck his hands into his pockets and rose to pace about. "This is fascinating. When we get back to London, we need to research this."

When we get back to London. As if they would be together. As if it were a given. But no, she wouldn't think that way. No plans, no building castles in the air, no thinking about consequences. Only now, only here.

Con stopped, waving his words aside. "But that's for the future. Why were you pulled to the maze?"

"But I don't know if I was pulled there because I wanted it, needed it, the way one is drawn to the fire when it's cold. Or was I

409

being dragged there against my will? I'm not sure." She shook her head. "I cannot believe I am seriously considering such things."

"You'll get used to it." Con grinned. "The question is, what is calling to you? This sanctuary of the Brotherhood?"

"The real question is, how are we going to stop it?" Lilah responded. "If the Sanctuary exists and the men tapped into it, then perhaps what Mr. Dearborn told us is also true."

"That the . . . the contract, I suppose you'd call it, with the Sanctuary has to be renewed every three years?"

"Yes. And that if it is not renewed by Midsummer Day, something horrid is going to happen — that this force is going to be set free."

" 'Unleash holy hell,' " Con quoted.

"I have felt that power, Con, and it is unbelievably strong. I terrifies me to think of what it might do." Her insides were suddenly like ice. "And it's only a little over a week until Midsummer Day."

They looked at each other in stark silence for a moment. Con said, "Then I guess we'd better get to work."

They decided to continue with their plan to

search the cellars. Given Lilah's experiences with the Sanctuary's power, Con was sure the first course of action was to pinpoint its location. When they asked Ruggins for a pair of lanterns so they could explore the cellars, he looked aghast and began to issue dire warnings about getting lost in the vast underground area, but they ignored his protests and ventured down into the cellars.

Close to the steps, the area was clean, the stonewalled rooms filled with wine, food-stuffs and supplies. As they went on, the walkway grew narrower and split off into different paths. They wound their way through them, peering into rooms, some containing rubble and others merely dust and spiderwebs. Now and then there was a squeak or the scrabbling of paws that brought Lilah closer to his side.

Con smiled. He enjoyed the darkness and the hint of danger, the lure of the unknown. It was made even better by Lilah's near-ness, her body soft and warm, almost touch-ing his, the scent of lilacs clinging to her hair.

"Ruggins was right," Lilah said. "I never realized how huge the cellars were." She cast him a sideways glance, a teasing sparkle in her eyes that made him want to kiss her. "Let's hope your human compass is working today."

"Never fear. I have you with me." Because it gave him the excuse to do so, he took her hand.

It hadn't been his imagination. A ripple of awareness ran through him, and everything was suddenly, subtly, clearer. Sharper. Con hadn't feared getting lost; the way back was obvious to him. But now he sensed something else, something more — a tickle at the back of his mind that made him turn around and return to the dark room they'd just passed.

"What is it?"

"I'm not sure. This place . . ." He raised the lantern and walked farther in. Dust coated the floor like a carpet, and great spiderwebs hung in the corners, dust gathering on their silken threads. There was a pile of stones at the other end, as if part of a wall had come down.

"Ah." Con skirted the rubble and there, almost hidden in the dimness, was a recess in the wall. A closer look showed a gaping hole.

"What is it?" Lilah asked. "The wall caved in?"

"I think perhaps it was torn down. See how rectangular the hole is? I think it's a door that had been blocked, and the stones were moved away." He held the lantern inside the hole, lighting another stone wall beyond it.

"A passageway?" Lilah breathed.

Con grinned. "A *hidden* passageway." Ducking his head, he stepped through the doorway.

Lilah followed him, taking a firm grasp of his jacket, and peered over his shoulder. "It's not a tunnel after all."

"No," he said, gazing at the worn stone steps curving down into the darkness before them. "Even better. It's a hidden staircase."

Con started down the stairs cautiously. The steps were so worn that in some places they almost disappeared, as if the rock around them was swallowing them, and the circular staircase was so narrow that Con all but filled it. Lilah stuck close behind him, her hand on his shoulder.

The stairs seemed to go forever, spiraling into the darkness in a way that was dizzying, but Con had a sense of the strata beneath them, almost a map in his head of the tunnel that lay at the bottom of the stairs. They emerged into a tunnel far narrower than any in the cellars above and with such a low ceiling that Con could not stand completely upright. It was unnerving to be so deep in the earth, surrounded by stone.

Lilah linked her arm through his. "I think we *have* found the dungeons."

"Mmm. Hopefully no skeletons in chains." He held the lantern higher, but it lit up the stygian darkness for only a few feet. "Shall we go on?"

"Of course." Lilah looked at him indignantly. "I didn't climb down those wretched stairs just to turn around and go back."

Con grinned and started forward, holding the lantern out in front of him. "Watch out for holes. I'd hate to tumble into some oubliette."

"I'm more worried about the tunnel collapsing on us."

They came upon a few small rooms, empty of all but dirt and rubble.

"I wonder where we are," Lilah commented. "It seems as if we must be beyond the house."

"The castle may have been laid out somewhat differently than Barrow House. By and large, we've been heading east, in the direction of the maze, but I believe this tunnel is going back under the house."

"I wish I had some idea whether you actually know these things or are bluffing."

He laughed. "I'm fairly certain. And you can't deny you have a powerful effect on me." He couldn't resist dipping his head and planting a firm kiss on her mouth. They walked on, but at last they came to an abrupt stop at a blank wall. "It seems we've reached the end of the road. Quite literally."

No amount of searching the cracks and crevices of the stone turned up a latch or lever. Nor could they find any line of separation, however thin, that might betoken a door set into the wall. At last they were forced to admit defeat, and they turned around to trudge back up the stairs to the cellars.

It was a relief to exit the cramped space of the staircase. The cellars might be dirty and often odorous, but at least one could stand up straight. Con started toward the path back but stopped and pointed in the opposite direction. "We didn't finish going through the cellars. I got distracted by the staircase. Shall we continue?" He looked at Lilah. "Or perhaps you're tired. I'm afraid we went straight through luncheon."

"No, let's see the rest of it. I don't want to wonder if we missed it because we didn't bother to finish."

Con nodded and set off. The pathway ended in a series of connecting rooms, arched doorways leading from one to another. The first room had nothing in it but dirt. The next held a few wooden kegs, one broken, as well as some discarded furniture and a very old chest. They passed through two more, both empty.

"No doorways, hidden or otherwise." Con sighed. "If your grandfather found a sanctuary down here, he's better at searching than I. I fear we've wasted this day."

"There's still my grandfather's office to look through," Lilah said encouragingly, taking his hand.

Con smiled down at her, touched by her attempt to buoy his feelings. He squeezed her hand. "Yes. I'm sure we'll find the key."

"And there are the trunks."

"What trunks?"

"Cuddington also told me this morning that my father had all Sir Ambrose's things packed in trunks and stored away. Personal things from his bedchamber. Father even did some of it himself."

"You think then that he packed things he didn't want anyone else to see? That sounds promising."

"I thought so. I told Cuddington to have Ruggins find them and bring them down from the attic." She came to a stop. "Con . . . There are trunks down here."

"You mean that old chest in the room back there?" Con looked doubtful.

"No, it's too old. And why stick it way

back there? But closer to the stairs into the house, after the wine cellar and the storerooms for foodstuffs, there were some rooms filled with odds and ends. I'm sure I saw chests and boxes in there."

They turned back, heading toward the stairs, and as Lilah had remembered, near the front, they came upon a storeroom containing a number of trunks as well as old furniture. The trunks were of varying sizes and shapes, but all were covered in a uniform dust of disuse. Con opened the closest and found a stack of old clothing and shoes. Lilah wound her way through them and stopped beside a humpbacked trunk. Leaning down, she wiped away the dust on the center of the top. "Con."

Her voice was sharp, and Con's head snapped up. "What?" He stepped across a trunk and around another to join her.

"Look." She pointed to the symbol of a triskele adorning the top of the chest.

A slow grin spread across his face. "Lilah, my love, you're a wonder."

He tried to lift the lid, but it wouldn't move. He squatted down beside it, examining the keyhole on the front side. "I think I can open this, if you'll lend me a couple of hairpins."

After a moment, the lock clicked, and Con

opened the lid. A square of folded white material lay on top, covering the other contents. Con took it out and stood up, letting the fabric unfold. It was a long loose-fitting garment made of white linen, slightly yellowed with time, that fell past Con's knees. The sleeves were long and bell-shaped, tapering to a point, and embroidered spirals marched down the front.

"I think we've found it."

CHAPTER THIRTY-TWO

"It's a surplice," Lilah said, reaching out to touch it. Her pulse raced.

"A priest's clothes?"

"Yes, the vestment that's worn over the cassock. But obviously not a normal priest's surplice." Lilah ran her hand over the embroidered triskeles on the shoulders, one on each side and a third one high on the back. Multiple spirals were sewn down the left side of the robe.

"What do you want to wager there are twenty-seven of these spirals on the front?" Con asked. "Three times three times three."

Con folded the garment and handed it to Lilah, then rummaged in the trunk again. "There are two more robes in here. Aha. And here are some candles. Ceremonial, I'd guess. Some books."

"If this was where they stored their paraphernalia, they would be likely keep the key in here, too, wouldn't they?"

"One hopes. We need to take everything out of this trunk and examine it." He cast a glance around the dusty room. "But not here."

"You're right. I'll tell Ruggins to have it brought up to — where should we do this? The library?"

"How about Sir Jasper's billiards room?" Con suggested.

"The smoking room?" Lilah asked, surprised.

"Yes. It's one of the few rooms in this house that actually has a key. I think we may want to lock these things up." He delved into the trunk again and came up with two small bundles of papers, wrapped round with ribbons. "But these, I think, we'll take up and look at now."

"Letters?"

"Hopefully very informative letters." Con handed her one of the bundles, returning the surplice to the trunk.

Lilah hurried back up the stairs, filled with anticipation. She wondered if this was what Con felt when he was on the trail of a clue in one of his investigations. She could understand why he enjoyed it. The hunt was exhilarating.

Inside the smoking room, Con shucked off his jacket as he was wont to when he began work. Lilah watched him roll up his sleeves, and heat curled deep inside her in response to the sight, just as it had the other day. But now she knew what lay beneath his clothes, the pleasures hinted at.

She remembered the different textures of his skin — his stomach smooth as satin, the firm, fleshy nipples, the prickle of hair on his chest — and she remembered, too, that intriguing way the hair narrowed to a thin line leading downward. She thought of her forefinger trailing down it.

As if feeling her gaze, Con looked over at her. His face shifted subtly. "If you continue to look at me that way, we'd better lock the door."

For a moment, Lilah was tempted to do just that, which went to prove how very deeply she was in trouble, but she recovered her wits and shook her head. Con sat down on the floor and untied the ribbon on his bundle, spilling the letters out in front of him. Con had a peculiar propensity for sitting on the floor, but she could see the sense in it here. She sat down beside him and began to go through her batch of letters in a more orderly fashion, laying them out in neat piles beside her.

"All these are from Sabrina's grandfather Emory."

"Mine are from Bertram Dearborn." Con looked at his much smaller stack. "Clearly our Bertie was not much of a correspondent." He watched her organize her letters. "Tell me, what are you doing?"

Lilah looked up. "Separating them by dates. I'm putting the ones dating from before Ambrose's book in one pile, the much later ones in another, and these are the ones from right around the beginning of the Brotherhood." She frowned at his grin. "What are you laughing at?"

"Not laughing, sweet Lilah. I just enjoy watching you work. You're so orderly." He reached out to take her hand and bring it up to kiss.

Lilah couldn't suppress the little shiver that ran through her at the touch of lips on her skin, but she covered with a tart response. "Yours, I see, are rather more haphazard." She nodded at the pile spread out in front of him.

He kissed her hand again and released it, then turned back to his task, plucking out a letter from the pile and scanning it rapidly. Lilah, too, began to read, starting with the letters around the first dates in the book.

"I found something," Lilah announced triumphantly. "This is from Emory at Oxford. He talks about school, but then he says how much he's looking forward to the holiday and 'going on a lark with you and Bertie.' " She added her own emphasis to the last few words. "*And* he wonders whether they will 'stumble over any skeletons down there.' "

"Sounds like they were going down into the dungeons, doesn't it? We may have to check it again. Perhaps we should take more lanterns."

Lilah returned to her stack. "Emory starts writing again after he returns to Oxford. He references their 'discovery.' So they found it between —" she checked the dates of the two letters "— December 5, 1840, and January 19, 1841. The first recorded date in my grandfather's book was in June of 1841."

"It took Ambrose a few months to cook up his theories and start conducting ceremonies. They found it close to the winter solstice. So that might be why they decided to tie the ceremonies to those four times. What does he say about their discovery?"

"Nothing helpful. He doesn't say what it is or where they found it." Lilah handed Con the letter and picked up another. "Here he's making plans to 'try it again.' That's three months later."

"Here's one from Bertie — the man was not good about dating his missives. He goes on and on about how his luck at the tables has changed." He scanned a few more pages. "This one calls the idea of the keys a 'bang-up notion.' Next he's talking about an investment and attributing it to — I'm not sure of this word — *Mattie,* I think."

"*Matres,* perhaps?" Lilah answered. "Emory has a pretty long discourse on Ambrose's theory about 'Matres' in this letter. Wasn't that in the book?"

"Yes. The three goddesses grouped together like the Fates."

Lilah began to read Emory's letter aloud. " 'I agree with your theory regarding the connection of the Matres to the Sanctuary.' He talks about the importance of the sacred power of threes. Then he says, 'However, I am not convinced that the Matres was three goddesses in one in the same way as Hecate. But like her, they were connected to the Otherworld, in particular guiding lost souls through the Gateway.' "

"Pedantic sort, wasn't he?" Con said wryly.

"Yes. One could wish that they'd been a bit more specific about what they found and where it was, instead of philosophizing."

"Even though Bertie's 'not one for religion' and Blair seems to regard it more as an intellectual exercise than faith, they seemed to believe in the blessings. It makes it more understandable that they kept up with it over the years and were insistent that their sons carry it on, but —"

"But it doesn't help us find either the place or the key," Lilah finished for him.

"That's it for Bertie. At least he wasn't long-winded." Con restacked the letters and tied them. "Perhaps we should look at the earlier letters from Emory since he was more assiduous at corresponding. It sounded from that first letter you read that they had some idea where they were going. Perhaps they've discussed it earlier." Lilah handed him one of her stacks, and he continued to read. "Hmm. Listen to this. 'I am concerned about the disturbing dreams you have been having.' Perhaps your grandfather was being pulled by this force, as you were. Guided to it, so to speak."

"I wish it would tell *me* where it is, then."

"You're pulled to the maze," Con pointed out.

"But how could the maze be the Sanctuary? It's hardly a secret. And there's no door."

"It could be underneath the maze. A trapdoor."

"I thought your theory was they were talking about the subcellars."

425

"Yes, but I'm always open to other ideas. Beneath the maze, you'd still have the idea of the underworld, which seems to figure into their belief. This gateway they're guarding could be the gateway to the dead." He tilted his head, thinking. "Maybe the maze sits on top of some ancient burial ground."

"A bit gruesome, meeting in the midst of the dead bodies."

"We're talking about university-age lads. I suspect the grue would be one of its appeals."

"The more you say about young men, the gladder I am that I'm female."

Con laughed. "So am I, my dear."

They went back to reading, and the room was silent until Con said, "Lost John — who the devil is that?"

Lilah stared at him blankly for a moment, then began to laugh. "Last John, I imagine, not Lost. Why on earth were they discussing him?"

"Your grandfather found some journal written by him, which influenced his thinking."

"Really?" Lilah said doubtfully. "It would have been terribly old."

"Blair was skeptical, as well."

"Last John was an ancestor. There were three Sir Johns in a row before the grandson got more creative and named his son William. The family refers to them as John Major, John Minor and Last John."

"Well, apparently Ambrose wrote Blair, saying he'd found this Last John's journal, and it revealed that there were tunnels beneath the house — I can't tell if he means the dungeons or something besides that. Ambrose believed that your ancestor found a secret passageway. Not only that, John added to it."

"This is all so bizarre." Lilah shook her head. "Secret passageways. Ancient gods. A gateway to the Underworld. How am I to believe this?"

"It does sound like something out of one of those books you and Liv like." He shrugged. "I don't know that it's true. But if it was all a mad delusion, what did the young men do? Why did they meet for so many years? Why does Dearborn believe in it? There must be a sanctuary."

"Yes, one that's going to destroy us all in a few days." Lilah grimaced and returned to reading the letters. "I'm finding almost nothing in these newer letters." She picked up the last one in the stack. "This isn't from Emory — oh, I see. It's from Hamilton — Sabrina's father. It's after Hamilton's father died, thanking Ambrose for his condolences."

Con flicked a finger at the date. "Look. Emory died at a young age, too."

"Yes, I suppose it was. They found the Sanctuary while he was in university, so he must have been around twenty. That would have made him only forty-eight or so when he died."

"Don't you find it odd? Emory's son Hamilton, Sabrina's father, died when she was twelve or thirteen, so he must have been in his forties, as well. Your father passed on at . . ."

"Forty-four."

"You said Sir Ambrose died before you were born, which would make him around fifty. I don't know when Bertram Dearborn died, but he's obviously gone, as well. Of these six men of the Brotherhood, only Niles Dearborn is still alive."

"You think Niles killed them all? I can't believe that."

"No, I don't think so. His crimes are generally smaller. I'm just pointing out that it's peculiar for this many men to die before their time."

"We don't *know* how old Mr. Dearborn's father was when he died."

"Do you remember him meeting with

your father and Dearborn?"

"I don't remember him at all."

"Then at best, he must have died when you were still a child. Five men — and for all we know, Niles could be at death's door. That's a very great coincidence."

"What are you saying? That they died because of . . . all this?" She made a vague gesture at the letters before them. "That the Sanctuary killed them?"

He shrugged. "I don't know. But we have to consider the possibility."

"No . . ." Lilah groaned. "Now you're going to tell me that this is a . . . a . . ."

He nodded, finishing her sentence, "A curse."

CHAPTER THIRTY-THREE

"No." Lilah jumped to her feet. "I cannot. I have reached my limit. It is difficult enough to accept that I have this bizarre ability. It's even harder to conceive that my grandfather and father followed a religion my grandfather dreamed up and held strange ceremonies in some secret place, where they recited incantations about ancient gods. But curses are simply more than I can agree to."

Con went to Lilah, taking her in his loose embrace. "I have trouble believing all of this myself. I don't really mean a curse, not in the way of 'you have disturbed this ancient resting place, and now you will be eternally cursed.' It's just that it seems the two things — the Sanctuary and their early deaths — must have some connection. Either circumstance is odd, but the two things together is — well, that's pushing *my* limit."

"But what could possibly be the connection between their early deaths and this

'Sanctuary'?" Lilah pulled away and began to pace. "How could finding that place or participating in these rituals cause someone to die years later?"

He thought for a moment. "What if there was something in the room, poison in the air or on an object they touched? Maybe there's a well that they drank from, and it contained . . . something dangerous."

"Years later?"

"Like arsenic — it built up over time as they continued to visit, until finally it killed them."

"But if it was a poison, wouldn't their deaths be similar? My father died of a heart attack, but Sabrina's had apoplexy."

"I've no idea," Con admitted.

"We don't have anything that really connects the two," Lilah went on, gaining steam. "We don't know when or how Niles's father died, and Niles is still alive. Second, it's possible that my family and Sabrina's don't have long life spans. Perhaps many of our ancestors died young. It's a strange coincidence but not impossible."

"We should talk to Aunt Vesta. We can look into the family histories. See if all your ancestors met early deaths. Perhaps this valet you talked about could tell us."

Lilah said quietly, "If you are right about

431

this, if the early deaths somehow happened because our grandfathers found the Sanctuary, then Sabrina and I —"

She saw the realization hit Con, too. "No. No. It doesn't mean that." He went to her and took her arms, looking intently into her face. "If a poison in the Sanctuary killed them, you and Sabrina wouldn't be affected. Neither of you have ever been there. Anyway, you're right. A curse is ridiculous. You are *not* going to die." He set his jaw in such a pugnacious way that Lilah had to smile.

"Well . . . if you forbid it . . ."

"I do." He kissed her, hard and quick. "Come, let's find out what your aunt can tell us."

As it turned out, Aunt Vesta could tell them very little. She couldn't remember when Bertram Dearborn died or how, and she was equally ignorant about Sabrina's grandfather. "And Papa simply didn't wake up one morning. I was quite young, you understand, when they died. But I cannot imagine that a holy place would make anyone die. It's a Sanctuary."

"They *called* it that," Lilah said. "It doesn't mean it actually is."

"Oh, no, no, I am sure Papa was right if he said it was a sacred spot. He was sensitive to such things. That's where I got it.

Your father, sadly, was not." She gave a little sigh at the thought of her brother's lack of discernment. "Besides, the Goddess wouldn't harm her faithful servants. She's a kind and loving being. She *blessed* them."

"You knew about the goddess? The Matres?" Even Con sounded a trifle exasperated. "Your father told you about his religion?"

"No, only in a general way — 'one mustn't forget the old gods,' that sort of thing. But of course the Sanctuary would belong to the Goddess. She is the giver of all life after all. Mother Earth, you understand. Obviously she must be the source of the power."

"Well, I wish she'd use her power to show us where the key is," Lilah retorted.

"Oh, no, dear girl." Aunt Vesta shook her head gravely. "Those from the beyond are never forthright. They move on a different plane. That is why we have to interpret their messages. Never give up hope, Dilly. I am sure it will come clear to you. Although . . ." She frowned. "The Goddess may reveal herself only to a believer."

"I think I have become one," Lilah admitted in a less-than-happy voice.

"What? Do not tell me — you have awakened to the Truth?"

"I don't know about that, but I started

walking in my sleep again. And, well . . ." Lilah sighed. "I sensed some sort of energy."

"It speaks to you?" Aunt Vesta gaped at her.

"I wouldn't call it that," Lilah demurred. "I am just . . . aware of it."

"She is crying out," Vesta exclaimed, clutching her hands to her chest. "Clearly the Goddess wants her Sanctuary to be found." She paused. "Hmm. Perhaps if we three believers . . ."

"I am *not* going to participate in a summoning ceremony," Lilah said flatly.

"In any case, I doubt it would work without the key." Vesta patted Lilah's hand. "I am sure you will come up with the answer."

Lilah was far less certain of that.

When Lilah and Con returned to the smoking room, they found that the servants had placed the trunk, now wiped free of dust, in the middle of the floor. Con knelt down next to it, Lilah beside him, and they began to empty the chest. Lilah set the white robes aside on one of the chairs. Beneath them were several books on ancient British religions as well as other pantheons of the Norse or Celts. Lilah picked up a hard rectangular object, wrapped in velvet, which turned out to be another book, worn with age and bound with a leather tie.

"This is really old." With great care, Lilah set it, velvet and all, in her lap. "Do you think this is Last John's journal?"

"One hopes." Con leaned over to watch as she opened it. The top page was splotched with mildew and various stains, and the ink was so faded the words were almost invisible.

"If it is, I'm not sure we can get anything from it. It's in terrible shape." Lilah turned the page, and the corner crumbled in her hands. She closed the book and rewrapped it, setting it aside. "We'll have to read that with the utmost care."

Con turned back to the trunk, pulling out the other books and several candles, as well as a humidor — empty — and a case containing a pair of spectacles. Watching him, Lilah thought how much she would like to run her hand down his arm or across his shoulders, to lean her head against him. Even better would be to snuggle against his side, his arm curling around her shoulder. It wasn't passion — though she suspected it might quickly turn into that — but a happy, almost giddy desire to be close to him, to link the two of them together in even a small way.

Unaware of her thoughts, Con continued to fish around in the chest. Finally, he pulled out a small wooden box.

Lilah's eyes widened. "The key? Open it."

"No, it's yours." He held it out to her.

Her pulse tripping, Lilah lifted the lid. Her shoulders sagged in disappointment. "No, just some odds and ends. A button, a little rock. A ring and tiepin."

"Look at this ring," Con said, plucking it from the box and showing it to her. The top of the ring was a tiny compass.

Lilah laughed. "I wonder why Sir Ambrose was so fascinated with compasses and clocks."

"Maybe he didn't want to be late," Con joked. "Or he was afraid of getting lost. Though he wouldn't have gotten far with this one. It doesn't work. It's frozen on southwest. Still clever, though. Wait, this looks like . . ." He pressed his fingernail against the side. The top of the ring opened, and a tiny triangle popped up on the flat face.

"A sundial!"

"Like a poison ring," Con commented.

"But far nicer."

"Yes. I wonder if you can do it with the same hand." Con closed the compass and slid it onto his finger, using his thumb to open the ring again.

Lilah watched Con's face, bright with his usual delight in something clever, and her heart rolled in her chest. He closed the lid and started to slide off the ring, but Lilah stopped him, her hand closing over the ring and his hand. "No. Don't. It's yours."

"But, Lilah . . ."

"I want you to have it."

"You're giving it to me?" His face changed subtly.

She nodded, her hand dropping away. In the next moment Lilah realized how inappropriately she'd acted. A lady would never give such a gift to a gentleman who wasn't her husband or a member of her family. Jewelry was too valuable, too personal, especially a ring, hinting as it did of commitment.

She blushed vividly. "Oh. I'm sorry. That was so forward. I shouldn't —"

"No, you don't." Con tucked his hand behind his back. His eyes danced wickedly, matching his smile. "You can't take it back now. It's mine now, Miss Holcutt."

"Yes, it is," she murmured. As he was hers. Wherever he might go or whatever he might do or be, he was hers. Even if she never saw him again, Con was hers.

Lilah's gift touched Con in a way he'd never felt. His chest flooded with warmth, and a host of emotions rose in him — desire, tenderness, a need to protect and shelter, all tangled together with an unaccustomed uncertainty, even trepidation.

"Lilah . . ." He curled his hand behind her neck and leaned closer. "Are you sure?" He wasn't entirely certain what he was asking, knowing only that he could not make a misstep. There was so little room for error with Lilah.

"I am." Lilah drove every thought out of his head by stretching up and nipping his lower lip.

Con groaned and kissed her, bearing her down to the floor, his mouth hard and hot on hers. His lips traveled down over her throat. Her bodice was the sort of modest dress she favored, with a high collar of lace. The faint scratch of the lace against his lips, her skin warm and soft beneath it, was intensely arousing. He lifted his head. "The door," he managed to croak. "It's open."

"Well, then . . ." Lilah's smile sent a shiver through him. She wriggled out from beneath him, rising to her feet and moving away.

She paused and looked back at him over her shoulder, her mouth curving up playfully. "I propose we go elsewhere."

Turning, Lilah sauntered out the door. Con stood for a moment, staring after her. Then, breaking from his paralysis, he grinned and started after her.

Lilah was standing in her open doorway when Con reached the top of the stairs, and he stopped just to look at her, to take in that smile, that hair, the long, slender figure in a prim dress that perversely increased his passion. Then in two long steps he was inside her room, closing the door behind him and twisting the key in the lock.

When he turned back around, Lilah was strolling away from him, reaching up to unpin her hair. Con leaned against the door to watch, hands thrust into his pockets as if to keep them from reaching out for her, his body outwardly relaxed and inwardly electric.

With every pin she tossed into the porcelain dish on her vanity, with every curl that slipped from its moorings and tumbled to her shoulder, the hunger in him swelled. Combing through her hair with her fingers, she looked back at him. "How are you at unfastening buttons?"

Con was across the room like a shot. "Taking things apart is one of my primary skills."

He felt her low laugh all through him. Con gathered the bright fall of Lilah's hair and moved it over her shoulder, letting it slide like silk through his palms. He undid her buttons slowly, letting his anticipation build.

The sides of her bodice sagged apart, and Con bent to place his lips gently on the delicate white skin revealed. He wanted to rush, to consume, to satisfy his need in a hard, bright burst of pleasure. Yet he held back, enticing them both with his slow caresses and the long, lazy journey of his lips.

"Lilah," he whispered, sliding his hands over her body to cup her breasts as his lips roamed up her throat to tease at the cord of her neck, to nip at her earlobe.

Lilah made a breathy noise of surrender, melting back against him, and that almost undid him. Con shoved down her chemise, and the pop of the ribbon tearing loose sent a stab of lust through him. In the mirror above the vanity table, he could see his hand sliding over Lilah, and that, too, was amazingly erotic.

With infinite care, he continued to undress her. His own clothes he whipped off with considerably more haste. Slowly, languorously, they made love. Hands and lips exploring, testing. Laughter muffled against skin. Bodies moving in wordless invitation. Every breath, every moan temptation and satisfaction. At last he slid inside her, finally joining in heat and hunger, in a blinding explosion of pleasure.

Afterward, as Con held her in his arms, spent and at peace, the familiar words from the wedding ceremony drifted through his mind. *With my body, I thee worship.* He had never realized before how very apt that phrase was. He could, he thought, continue worshipping Lilah this way forever.

If only things were different, he would. And suddenly he wished they were away from here, living in some secluded cottage by themselves, with time stretching out in front of them. Nowhere to be, nothing to do, no catastrophes to prevent, no kidnappers, no threats. Just long lazy days spent discovering each other, talking, laughing, making love.

He let out a sigh. Maybe someday. But now they would have to catch their moments of pleasure when they could. They had to find a hidden key. They had to locate a secret room. Come up with two other keys that were or were not stolen. Renew some mystical bond with an unknown, unseen, but fiercely powerful entity. Avert catastrophe.

All by Midsummer's Eve.

It was a good thing, Con thought, that he was an optimistic sort of man.

CHAPTER THIRTY-FOUR

Con stood, gazing down at the now-empty trunk and its contents spread out on the floor around it. Yesterday evening, they had gone back down to the smoking room and removed the last of the items from the chest, even checking beneath the lining. There had been no sign of a key, and finally, discouraged, they had gone to bed.

He had awakened this morning with renewed enthusiasm, but the contents of the trunk looked no more hopeful now. "The most promising thing we have is your ancestor's journal, but I've been able to make out only a few words of it."

"Why didn't my father tell me about any of this?" Lilah asked in exasperation.

"He might have thought that you would reject it out of hand," Con pointed out. "You held rather decided views on mysticism. Would you have accepted it if he had told you about the Sanctuary three years ago?"

"No," Lilah admitted. "Probably not."

"Still, it seems odd that he didn't leave you any warning, given the consequences of not 'renewing the bond' every three years."

"I would have thought he would leave the key with his attorney to give me after his death, along with some sort of explanation. But Mr. Cunningham gave me nothing like that."

"Perhaps he didn't want the attorney to know about the key," Con offered.

"He could have hidden the key, then, and left a letter telling me where it was. A sealed, private letter. Mr. Cunningham wouldn't have opened and read it, surely."

Con shrugged. "Not unless he was unscrupulous."

"I suppose Father could have hidden the key and left a letter for me somewhere in the house, telling me where it was — though that seems a trifle haphazard. But why hide both the key and the note telling me how to find it? Why didn't he leave the information in an obvious place?"

"Maybe he had some reason to hide it. He thought someone was after the key — the successor to his title, for instance, or Dearborn, who had taken Sabrina's key already. Sir Virgil feared that person might find it first. And it would do little good to hide the key but leave the message revealing its location where it could be easily found."

"That would make sense. Perhaps Roberts might know something about it."

"Who?"

"My father's valet. Cuddington told me yesterday that he retired and is living in a cottage on the estate." She added in a confiding manner, "I suspect Cuddington may have a personal interest in the man."

"Cuddington? You're joking."

"I'm not. She blushed when she talked about him."

"Do you think your father confided in him?"

"I doubt my father revealed secrets of the Brotherhood or their rituals, but Roberts was close to him. He'd been his valet for years. He might know where Father would have kept something important like that. Or if Father had spoken of leaving me a letter."

"A valet is privy to all sorts of information, more than most of their employers even realize. You're right. Let's go visit the man."

Roberts, it turned out, was unsurprised by their visit. He welcomed them at the front door with a smile and ushered them into the parlor, saying, "Bettina said that you might come."

"Bettina?"

"Miss Cuddington, I should say. I happened to see her last night as I was taking my evening constitutional. Wonderful woman, Miss Cuddington."

"There's no one like her," Con agreed.

Roberts insisted on making tea and bringing out biscuits for them, but once he had taken care of all the pleasantries, he went straight to the heart of the matter. "Miss Cuddington said you were interested in Sir Ambrose. I knew him of course. I came to the house as a footman when I was sixteen. Your father was but a young lad then. I often had the task of minding him." He smiled reminiscently. "But I doubt that is what you're interested in. What is it you'd like to know?"

"I wondered if my father might have left me something," Lilah said. "Not in his will, but perhaps a personal object."

"I'm not sure what you mean, miss."

"I thought you might know where he would have put something he wanted me to have."

Con added, "Or perhaps he wrote something down for Lilah."

"His notebook?" the valet asked. "He

burned that, I remember. He wasn't sleeping well there at the end. One night I brought him a cup of hot milk, hoping it would help him sleep, and he was standing at the fireplace, ripping pages from that little book and tossing them in the fire." Seeing Lilah's stricken expression, he added, "I'm sorry, miss. I should have realized that he was ill. But he'd been distressed for some months before that — he and Mr. Dearborn had had a disagreement, a falling-out of some sort, and I just thought his spirits were low because of that."

"A disagreement? About what?" Con asked. He felt as disappointed as Lilah looked. Why would Sir Virgil have burned that notebook? What had been in it?

"I really couldn't say, sir. But Mr. Dearborn looked like thunder when he left, and after that he never came to Barrow House." Roberts added, "Please don't fret about the notebook, Miss Lilah. I don't think there was much in it that he hadn't already put down in his letter to you."

"His letter? What letter?" Lilah stared.

Roberts frowned. "Why, the one he left for you with Mr. Cunningham."

"His attorney? He left a letter to me with his attorney?"

"Yes, miss."

"Are you certain that he gave this letter to Mr. Cunningham?" Con asked. This thing was becoming more of a tangle with everything they discovered, it seemed.

"Yes, of course, sir. I was there when Mr. Cunningham came to the house with the will for him to sign. I brought their tea. Sir Virgil gave him the letter then, and Mr. Cunningham put it in his portfolio."

"But . . . I didn't receive any letter from Mr. Cunningham," Lilah protested. "Only the will."

"It wouldn't have been at the time of his death, miss. I'm rather sure he told Mr. Cunningham the letter should go to you on your twenty-first birthday."

"That was last year."

"I'm sorry, miss," he said helplessly.

"It's not your fault," Lilah reassured him. "I just —" She turned to Con. "I don't know what happened. Mr. Cunningham never sent me a letter on my birthday or any other time."

"We'll have to have a visit with Mr. Cunningham," Con said grimly.

"Oh. Sir. Miss." Roberts looked apologetic. "Mr. Cunningham's no longer here. He retired last year to Bath."

"Of course he did." Con went on, "Do you know what was in the letter?"

The old man shook his head. "No. I think it must have been a very private matter. He told me nothing about it. Perhaps he had the feeling that he was going to die soon. Sir Virgil was always sensitive that way."

"Yes. Of course." Lilah forced a smile.

They stayed a few minutes longer, chatting with the man about more pleasant memories. But as soon as they were outside again, Lilah turned to Con. "Father *did* leave me a letter about the Sanctuary." Despite the disappointment, there was a note of satisfaction in her voice.

"It might have been a personal message of farewell, but my guess is he was worried about the Sanctuary," Con said. "He and Dearborn had an argument over something. After that he was distressed. Then he wrote you a letter to give to you on your twenty-first birthday. Which would have given you ample time before this pact with the Sanctuary would have needed renewal."

"But why didn't Mr. Cunningham give it to me?"

"I don't know. But we'll find out. His records must still be around somewhere. Maybe he had a partner who continued the business."

"I think his son was with him."

"Very well. As soon as we get home, we'll

go to the village and find him. Maybe he was just careless and forgot to do it in the bustle of his retiring, as Roberts said. It could still be sitting there in his files."

However, their plans were interrupted when they rode into the courtyard at Barrow House and saw an unfamiliar carriage. "Good Lord, another visitor?" Con said in disgust. "Who now?"

His question was answered when they entered the house and heard voices coming from down the hall — including one very familiar man's tone. "Alex!"

Con strode down the hallway, Lilah hurrying after him. They found Alex and Sabrina sitting in the drawing room, having tea with Aunt Vesta. Alex was already on his feet and crossing the room when Con stepped through the doorway.

"Con!" Alex laughed. "What the devil have you gotten into now?"

The two men laughed, clasping hands and clapping each other on the arm in masculine greeting, before abandoning dignity and hugging each other.

"Sabrina! Alex!" Lilah swept into the room after Con, holding out her arms to embrace her friend.

Laughing and chattering, the four of them exchanged excited greetings.

Aunt Vesta, with unaccustomed tact, took her farewell of the group and went upstairs, leaving the two couples alone.

"What are you doing here?" Con asked Alex. "You're supposed to be in America."

"We were," Alex replied. "But then, well . . ." He shrugged.

"You knew Con needed help?" Lilah suggested.

"Just a minute," Con protested. "I don't need help."

"I knew Con was . . . something. Not in danger, or I'd have cabled a warning. But something strong."

"Sit down and have another cup of tea, and I'll tell you all about it," Con said.

The telling of it lasted through several cups of tea and cakes, as well. When Con finished describing their most recent discoveries and fruitless searches, there was a long moment of silence. Then Alex said, "Honestly, Con, I cannot leave you alone for a moment, can I?"

Con laughed. "Oh, I can manage to get into scrapes with or without you. And I had Lilah here to tether me." He looked over at Lilah, and out of the corner of his eye, he could see his twin's suddenly sharpened gaze going from Con to Lilah and back.

But Alex said only, "So you have to find

this place by Midsummer Day? That's only a week away."

"Unfortunately, we're well aware of that. But now that you two are here, we can speed up the search."

"Then I guess you'd better show us this book." Alex set aside his cup and stood up.

Con led them to the Clock Room, taking the longer route so that Alex could see the rest of the old wing. His brother's reaction to the Great Hall was everything Con could have hoped for. If possible, Alex's eyes grew even brighter when they stepped out of the stairwell into the silent gallery.

"Wonderful Elizabethan glass." Alex stopped and peered through a window. "Is that a maze?"

"Yes, it's overgrown but a good pattern. I'll take you out there tomorrow. Then there are the dungeons."

"The dungeons?" Delight lit up Alex's face, mirroring Con's.

Sabrina, with a roll of her eyes to Lilah, linked her arm through her husband's and propelled him forward. "I always thought this gallery was so eerie." Sabrina gave a delicate shiver at the memory. When they stopped outside the tower room, she said, "But I don't remember this room."

"We never went in here," Lilah told her.

"I don't think my governess ever let us get this far."

Con opened the door and stepped aside, his eyes on his twin's face. Alex entered the room after Sabrina and stopped, staring all around him in amazement.

"Good Lord. Look at all those clocks." He frowned. "It's like that dream you —" He stopped, turning to Con in dawning realization.

"It's exactly like it," Con confirmed. "I recognized it the instant I walked in."

"Exactly like what?" Sabrina asked, puzzled. "What dream?"

"A nightmare Con kept having before our wedding." Alex glanced over at Con. "A room with curved walls — I should have thought of a tower."

"What a thing to dream about," Sabrina said. Her eyes turned to the steps across the room leading downward. "What's downstairs? More collections?"

"No, the rest is only stairs leading down to the outside door," Lilah answered. "There aren't entrances into the house on the other floors."

Con snorted. "There isn't even a *landing* at the next floor down, only the stairs going around and around. It's enough to make one dizzy."

"Like a lighthouse." Alex went down a few steps to look around, then trotted back up. "Lilah, your home is a treasure trove."

"A treasure trove of oddity," Lilah said wryly. "You may explore it all you wish." She glanced from him to Sabrina. "You are going to stay with us for a while, I hope."

"We're opening up Carmoor again," Sabrina replied. "Alex and I would like to try living here. I loved it when I was a child. We brought a few servants with us to get it in order, and we'll hire the rest of the staff here."

"That will take days. You must stay here with us in the meantime. We can all look for the Sanctuary. It will be great fun. Won't it, Con?"

"Of course." Con wondered if Lilah was aware of the natural way she had turned toward him, the inclusion of him in issuing the invitation. "That's settled. Let's look at the book."

He pulled the book from the cabinet and handed it to Alex and Sabrina. Sabrina shook her head in amazement. "This is so unbelievable. I hardly know what to make of it."

"You could find nothing about the location of the tunnel?" Alex asked. "How did Sir Ambrose find it?"

"By reading one of our ancestors' journal. Unfortunately, he didn't explain it further, and the journal is more or less illegible now."

"What are these designs on the cover?" Sabrina asked, tracing the symbols with her forefinger. "They're lovely."

"They're triskeles. Sir Ambrose had an obsession with threes. The spirals, we've read, mean eternity or perhaps an endless rebirth. It was an important symbol to him. One can find them as decorations all over."

"Yes, and I've examined every one of them," Con added. "I can't help but think they're involved somehow, given Sir Ambrose's affection for them. But I've pushed and prodded and twisted every blasted one I could find, and I haven't been able to find one that opens anything."

"Alex," Lilah said suddenly. "I just had a thought. Perhaps you could — I mean, do you *feel* anything from it?"

Alex shook his head, rubbing his hand over the leather front. "Excitement, anticipation, but that's recent, probably you and Con. I can tell it's been in Con's hands." He shrugged and handed the book to Sabrina. "I can try it with this old journal, but the older something is, the harder it is to read."

They were all quiet for a moment, contemplating their lack of discovery. Sabrina, once again gliding her fingertips across the gilt symbols, said, "You know . . . this is probably silly, but if you're looking for spirals, what about the one we're standing on?" She nodded toward the steps leading down into the circular staircase.

"My God," Con breathed. "Do you suppose? Hidden in plain sight."

Almost as one, they hurried to the staircase and started down the stairs. "The most likely place would be in the floor at the foot of the stairs, don't you think?" Con asked. "A trapdoor into either the tunnel itself or another staircase?"

Alex agreed, but still all of them scanned the walls of the tower as they descended. When they reached the bottom floor, they went over it even more thoroughly, but they found nothing.

Lilah sighed in frustration, wiping the dust from her hands. "This seems like such a perfect place."

"Let me check something." Alex ran back up the stairs. Lilah turned questioning eyes to Con, who only shrugged. It wasn't long until they heard the clatter of Alex's steps descending. "I think I may have it." He popped out the courtyard door, and in a moment came back in.

"Alex, what the devil are you doing?"

"I know the likeliest place for it." Alex's eyes were shining, his words rapid. "The door into the tower from the gallery is set in the corridor wall. But then you take a step or two into the room before the curved walls start. That space between the straight corridor and the round tower is a sort of very short hall or a very deep door frame. But here —" he gestured behind him "— the walls are perfectly round, no doorway. On the outside, you can see that the square space between the house and the tower is bricked in all the way up and down."

Con's eyes lit up. "Creating a perfect shaft in which to hide a closet. Or stairs."

He rushed to the wall where a door into the house should have been and skimmed his fingers over the rough stone. "There's a crack." He ran his fingers up the wall, following until it turned and started in a horizontal line. "It's a door."

"Now we just need to figure out how to open it." Two feet over, Alex was tracing the line downward on the opposite side. "I can barely get my fingernail into it."

Con ran his eyes over the wall, then thought to look up. Above him, attached to the bottom of the stairs, was a single narrow wooden slat. The sharp thrill of discovery ran through him. He tugged on one end, and it moved beneath his hand. He pulled harder, and a third of the bar slid up to stop at a forty-five-degree angle.

Grasping the other end of the bar, he pushed that portion of the slat upward until the two ends touched, forming a triangle with the stationary middle section below. There was a distinct thud, and a section of the wall eased open.

Alex gripped the edge and pulled. The small door was heavy but well balanced, and it swung out easily. All four of them crowded in, staring down at the small staircase twisting downward.

"The secret passage."

CHAPTER THIRTY-FIVE

Lilah stood, transfixed. Power flooded up, twining around and through her so that she almost vibrated with it. It tugged at her viscerally, and she moved toward the open door.

"We'll need a lantern for that," Alex said.

"Two," Con answered. He turned and saw Lilah, and his face whitened. "Lilah! Are you all right?" He hooked an arm around her waist, stopping her movement.

When Con's arm wrapped around Lilah, pulling her against his side, much of the massive rush of energy flowed out of her into Con. She could see by his raised eyebrows that he, too, felt the sweep of power.

"What is it?" Alex asked, watching them closely. "What's happening?"

"I'm not sure." Con's voice was a trifle breathless. "Lilah can sense it. She feels the force of whatever's down there." He gazed into her face. "Better?"

Lilah nodded. "Yes. At first it was almost unbearably strong, but you took away some of it." She offered a shaky smile. "I think I'll be able to control it now."

"I'll be right here with you." Con linked his hand with hers.

Lilah straightened her shoulders and turned to Sabrina. "Can you feel it?"

Sabrina nodded. "There's this little low . . ." She wriggled her fingers, searching for the right words. "Hum. Only it's inside me."

They looked toward Alex, who shrugged. "I don't feel a damn thing except confused."

"I think Lilah and Sabrina sense it because of their family bond with the Sanctuary," Con offered. "All I got from Lilah was a surge of strength and a sharper focus. She makes me better."

Alex laughed. "I'm sure that's true."

Con grimaced at him. "What I mean is, her ability heightens mine, but I don't feel the connection to the Source the way the ladies do." He looked back at Lilah. "Are you able to explore further?"

"Of course. Surely you don't think I'm going to stop at this point."

"No." Con grinned. He glanced over at Alex.

"I'll get the lanterns." Alex loped off across the courtyard.

The tumult inside Lilah had settled down — though she wasn't about to test it by letting go of Con's hand just yet. She turned toward Sabrina. "Are you all right?"

Sabrina nodded. "Yes. It was unsettling at first, but I'm growing accustomed to it now. What are we to do with this thing? I'm not in favor of donning robes and chanting incantations every few months."

"Nor am I. I also don't like the idea of living here with that pulling at me all the time. Yet if what Mr. Dearborn says is true, we must renew the bond to keep this power from ruining everything."

The door opened, and Alex entered, carrying two lanterns. "Your butler thought I was mad, wanting a lantern in the daylight — and two of them, at that."

Con shrugged. "He's already convinced of my insanity." They lit the lanterns and turned to the open entrance. Con started to step onto the first step, but Lilah put a restraining hand on his arm. "No. I should go first. I can scarcely believe I'm saying this, but the Sanctuary seems to recognize me."

Con frowned. "We don't know what's down there. What if the stairs collapse?"

"The same things apply to you."

"Lilah's right," Sabrina said. "She's the Holcutt, the owner of the land under which it sits. And, as the descendent of another of the Blessed, I should go after her."

The twins looked at one another, clearly uncomfortable with that idea, but as they scrambled to come up with a good argument, Lilah settled it by picking up the other lantern and starting down the stairs.

"Oh, the devil." Con leaned in and said, "Promise me you'll come back up if it looks risky."

"Of course. I always follow the rules, remember?" Lilah smiled up at his scowling face. She was beginning to understand why Con enjoyed teasing her.

She continued down the stairs. The wooden planks were sturdy beneath her feet, but she could see only a few steps ahead of her, even with the lantern, because of the tightly coiled nature of the stairs. It gave her the uneasy sensation that the stairs were endless and she was descending into the void.

With every step she took, the pull became stronger. The energy inside her had risen from a vibration to a throb. Without Con there to absorb some of the power, it was multiplying. She envisioned it sweeping through her, taking her over as it had long ago at the séance. Her hand trembled, making the light dance, and she thought for a cowardly moment about turning around and fleeing.

But the sound of Sabrina coming down right behind her steadied her. She had to go forward. This energy belonged to her, and she must deal with it. And suddenly Lilah understood how to control it.

It wasn't a battle. She must cease fighting it and make the power her own. Lilah consciously relaxed her will as she continued down the stairs. She imagined opening her mind, dropping all barriers. When she reached the bottom of the stairs, the full force of the Sanctuary's power rushed into her. For one terrifying moment, she thought she had been wrong, that she had lost herself. But stubbornly she held on, refusing to fight the power and instead accepting it.

The pressure eased, and suddenly the energy was flowing through her unimpeded, filling her head and singing through her veins, sweeping downward into the earth beneath her feet. A conduit, that was what Con had called her. The power moved through her, not consuming but strengthening. The pull that had been there was no longer a compulsion but an offer, beckoning her home.

Lilah turned as Sabrina joined her, and they stepped back to allow room for the men, clattering down the stairs at a more rapid pace. In the golden light of the lantern, Sabrina's face glowed. "Do you feel it?" Sabrina asked, taking Lilah's hand. "How it got stronger but somehow easier, as well?"

"Yes, exactly."

Sabrina's eyes widened. "Even more since I touched you. I can — oh, I can feel Alex so clearly — he can't decide whether to worry or be angry at me." She grinned and looked over as Alex emerged from the stairs.

"I wasn't worried," he told her, belying his words by pulling Sabrina to his side and kissing her forehead. "I knew you were fine because the whole way down, I could feel your amusement at thwarting me."

Con looked over at Lilah, raising his eyebrows in question, and she smiled and nodded in reply. Con edged his way around Alex and Sabrina and took her hand. He glanced at her in surprise, no doubt feeling the change in the energy. Con took the lantern from Lilah and held it up to shine down the tunnel. It illuminated only a few feet in front of them, leaving the rest in uncertain darkness. It was, however, enough light to see that the tunnel was both low ceilinged and narrow, necessitating, as the stairs had, going forward in single file. The two men had to duck their heads to keep from scraping the stones above them.

"I suppose you are still of the opinion you have to lead the way," Con said to Lilah, frowning.

"No." Lilah suppressed a grin at his startled expression. "I think we are . . . accepted. And I know you're dying to explore." From the look on Con's face, Lilah knew he would have kissed her if they had been alone.

They walked into the seeming void, the dark closing in after them. "I have no idea where we are or where we're headed. Are we under the house or outside?" Lilah asked.

"Under," Con said with assurance. "But we're walking toward the maze. I think that behind that wall —" he gestured to the right "— are the dungeons."

"A parallel tunnel?" Alex asked.

"More or less." Abruptly the tunnel widened, so that they were able to walk side by side and the men could stand upright. "This must be the newer tunnel. The extension built by Lilah's ancestor."

"We're very close." Lilah had felt the power increasing with every step they took. Now it filled the air, almost palpable in its intensity.

"We're beyond the house now," Con said, and a moment later, the edge of the lantern's light fell on a wooden door. Having read her grandfather's thoughts on the Sanctuary, Lilah had expected the door to be a grand thing — large, dark and heavy; she would not have been surprised to find it fitted with a handle of gold.

But there was nothing grand about the sturdy door — except for the large padlock securing it. Shaped like the familiar triskele, each spiral was a separate lock, centered by a keyhole. Con and Alex inspected it closely.

"I've never seen a triple lock." Con glanced at his brother, and Alex shook his head. "We can try to pick them. I wonder if they have to all be unlocked simultaneously."

"Or in a certain succession," Alex added. He glanced around the edges of the door. "Hinged on the inside, so no hope of taking off the hinges and removing the door."

"I'd guess it would take a battering ram to break through this thing." Con rapped the wood. He turned to Lilah. "Maybe you could put your hands on this and command it to open."

Lilah gave him a repressive look. "I don't have command of it." Still, she laid her hands against the door. "I feel remarkably foolish."

Energy surged beneath her hands, pushing against the door from the other side. Taking a deep breath, she concentrated on the power beyond the door, inviting it in. The power rushed into her, and she turned it back into the door, imagining the door crashing down. The door vibrated beneath her hands but didn't move.

Lilah dropped her hands and the energy ebbed. "If I have the ability, I've no idea how to use it." She did, however, feel more certain of her control.

There was a burst of noise at the other end of the tunnel, and they all swung around. A vague glow became a bobbing light, then a figure holding a lantern.

"Aunt Vesta!"

"There goes any hope of keeping this entrance a secret," Con murmured.

"I knew!" Aunt Vesta exclaimed as she drew nearer, her breath coming in pants. "As soon as I heard Ruggins talking about the lanterns, I knew you had found the way. Why didn't you tell me?"

"I'm sorry, Mrs. LeClaire," Con replied.

"But we didn't want to get your hopes up until we were certain."

Aunt Vesta, however, was paying no attention to his words. She scarcely even glanced at Sabrina and Alex. Her gaze was fixed on the door, her eyes shining. "Oh, yes. I can feel the power." Her voice was filled with wonder. "Can you feel it, Lilah?"

"Yes." Looking at her aunt, so eager and hopeful, Lilah felt a long-buried affection wind its way through her chest. Her aunt was selfish; she had abandoned her young niece without a thought to her welfare; but inside Lilah, beneath the hurt and resentment, there was still an ember of the love she had once felt for her capricious aunt. "Yes, I do feel it."

"I knew it. I knew it would answer to the Holcutt women." Vesta put her hands to the door. "Oh, yes, it's strong. I can feel it feeding me."

"Sabrina senses it, as well," Lilah offered.

"Really?" Vesta cast a speculative glance at Sabrina. "But not the men?"

"No," Con answered.

Lilah knew that was not entirely true, for she could feel the energy flowing through her into all the others, heightening each one's abilities. She suspected that Con was too kind to take away any of Aunt Vesta's elation at the return of her powers. Indeed, her aunt's expression was so rapturous it was vaguely unsettling.

Lilah could feel the energy flowing softly from herself into Vesta in the same manner, but she also sensed the tentacles from the other side of the door that led directly into her aunt and Sabrina. Those separate threads of energy were narrow and mild, her aunt's no greater than Sabrina's. Lilah feared Vesta would be greatly disappointed if her connection to the Sanctuary was not the deep link she desired.

Impulsively, she took a step closer to her aunt. Vesta beamed. "Ah, yes, it's growing greater." She turned to Lilah, holding out her hand. "Lilah, come here. You, too, Sabrina." She reached for the other girl, as well. "Let us see if our bond will affect it."

Too late, Lilah saw the danger of magnifying her aunt's power with her own. It might make Vesta joyous for the moment, but what about when she alone couldn't raise such power? Lilah hedged. "We don't know what might happen."

Con agreed, "You don't want to take a chance with such tremendous power."

"My niece is turning you cautious, dear boy." Vesta wagged her finger playfully at Con. "It won't harm me." Sabrina had taken Vesta's hand when she asked, and now Vesta reached out and grabbed Lilah's hand.

Immediately the energy swept through Lilah into the other two. Lilah was glad that she was not between the women, for she suspected that would have made the connection even greater.

Her aunt clenched Lilah's hand, her face glowing with excitement. "Yes, that increases it tenfold. This is wonderful. Lilah, take Sabrina's hand to complete the circle."

"No," Lilah said firmly. "That could prove explosive. We need to know more about this."

Vesta sighed. "You always were such a timid creature." Her aunt released Sabrina's hand, then nodded as if she had proved something. "That lowers it, but it's still strong."

Lilah jerked her hand from Vesta's and moved back. "This serves no purpose."

Vesta blinked in surprise. "It left so quickly."

Con stepped in. "It's no surprise that the link of two Holcutt women would be stronger, so the break stronger."

"Oh. I hadn't thought of it that way. No doubt you're right." Vesta's face brightened.

"Now, ladies, I think it's time we find a more comfortable location for this discussion. Mrs. LeClaire, if you will lead the way," Con said.

He took Lilah's aunt by the arm and steered her away, keeping up a steady stream of chatter and flirtation to deflect Aunt Vesta's thoughts. It was typical of Con, Lilah thought, her chest warming with gratitude. She realized, with some amazement, that the behavior she had once disdained in Con had become a quality she admired.

And one of the many reasons she had fallen in love with Con Moreland.

CHAPTER THIRTY-SIX

Something nagged Con out of his sleep. For a moment he lay there, enjoying the cozy feel of Lilah's body curled up against his side. Then he glanced around, and the faint light outlining the windows galvanized him into action. He had awakened late.

No one could enter Lilah's locked room, so there was no danger of anyone walking in on them, but the servants were up and about by dawn, and the longer he stayed, the more chance there was of being seen sneaking out of her room. He got out of bed and began to pull on his clothes. Lord, but he hated this. He wanted to sleep one night with Lilah and wake up to her in his arms, with no reason to leave her.

Con unlocked the door and opened it a crack. Finding the hall empty, he slipped out the door and into his own room. Alex was sitting in the chair by the window, waiting for him.

"Bloody hell." Con closed the door behind him. "You're up early."

"Mmm. As are you," Alex replied mildly. "Sabrina and I plan to ride over early to Carmoor, you remember."

The four of them had stayed up late the night before, discussing their problems, and had come to the decision that Sabrina and Alex would check on their estate the following day before returning to join Lilah and Con in their search for the key.

Alex went on. "One wonders, though, exactly what it is you're doing." He glanced pointedly at Con's undisturbed bed.

"You have a Reed face on, I see." Con turned away, needlessly straightening his toiletry set, then sighed and said, "Oh, the devil. Let's take a walk." It was Con's way to meet trouble head-on, and that didn't change, even when he faced the unusual prospect of being at odds with his twin.

Shrugging on his jacket, Con led Alex downstairs and out to the maze, where Con turned, crossing his arms over his chest, and said, "Very well. Out with it."

"You act as if I'm going to lecture you." When Con simply raised his eyebrows, Alex let out a low growl of aggravation. "What if someone had seen you? What if it had been a maid who came into your room instead of me?"

"I am normally not so careless."

"That's not the point. Blast it, Con, I thought you and Miss Holcutt couldn't be in the same room for five minutes without arguing."

"As it turns out, we can." Con turned and started down the leafy green aisle.

"What are you thinking?" Alex followed his twin. "Lilah is Sabrina's dearest friend. What is going to happen when this ends? If you break Lilah's heart, Sabrina will never forgive you. And then what am I to do?"

"I don't know why you assume it will end."

"What else would happen?"

"I intend to marry Lilah."

"What?" Alex came to a dead stop. "You're engaged?" The tightness in his face disappeared, and he began to grin. "Why the devil didn't you tell me?"

"I didn't say we were engaged. I said I intended to marry her. I still have to bring Lilah around to the idea."

"You're joking. She turned you down?" Alex looked even more astonished. "How did you botch that?"

"I didn't. Not yet anyway. I haven't asked her."

"Would you stop being so damned irritating and tell me what is going on?"

Con started forward again, not looking at Alex. "I'm scared."

This time he'd rendered his twin speechless. Finally, weakly, Alex said, "Good Lord. You really *are* in love with her."

"Either that, or I am seriously ill." Con turned to Alex, saying earnestly, "You promise you won't tell Sabrina any of this?"

"No! What do you take me for?"

"A married man."

"That doesn't change the fact that I'm your brother."

As if some dam had been breached, the words began to spill out of Con. "I know Lilah and I don't have the makings of some grand pair of lovers. We didn't fall in love at first sight. Instead she slapped me. I've had to fight her every inch of the way. We don't have that harmony of mind the other Morelands have with their spouses. We share no connection as you and Sabrina do. We're complete opposites. But . . . whenever she comes into the room, I feel as if the sun just broke through the clouds. I can't think about anything but her. All I want is to be with her. And if she turns me down, I don't know what I'll do."

"Why would she turn you down? You're

sleeping in her bed, aren't you? Surely she must care for you."

"Yes." Con looked down at the compass ring and rubbed his thumb over it. "I think she cares for me. But when I brought up marriage, she looked as if she was — well, I'm not sure what she felt, but I can tell you, it was *not* happy. She turned me down without even thinking about it. You see, Lilah doesn't do what she *wants*. She does what is *right*. And she doesn't think I'm at all right."

"Why? What's wrong with you?"

Con gave him a wry smile. "Would you like a list? I am impulsive and rash. I'm not serious. I have a reputation for being absurd. Off-kilter. I am, unfortunately, all the things she's spent the last ten years trying to get away from."

Alex furrowed his brow. "I don't understand."

"Her family is as daft as ours. Her father was obsessed with spiritualism and ghosts. Her grandfather made up this bizarre religion. And, well, you've met her aunt."

"Her grandfather wasn't entirely mad, was he? There is something down there. I felt the Sanctuary last night. I know you said it didn't affect us, but my ability was heightened — holding that lantern told me the gardener had been using it to go poaching. And when Mrs. LeClaire joined us there, I could feel the emotions coming off her in waves."

"Technically, it was Lilah giving you the power, not the Sanctuary. She somehow transmits psychic strength. Your ability is stronger around her. Had you taken her arm, you'd have felt it even more. She's connected to that place. It pours into her. I could feel it absolutely flooding her."

"And you were able to ease some of that, weren't you? Dilute it or consume part of it. How can you say you two don't have a special connection?"

"But that's just our abilities. As you know, she can give that to others, too."

"Not, I think, to the same extent."

"But, you see, she doesn't want to be like that. For years she made herself believe it didn't exist. It had to hit her in the face to make her acknowledge it. She's damnably stubborn."

"Says the man with a head like a rock."

Con ignored him. "She knows it now. Even accepts it. But she doesn't like it. You heard her last night, saying she couldn't believe she was talking about these matters as if they were real."

"I wasn't fond of getting smacked with a

vision whenever I touched something either, but one adjusts. She seems to have done so."

"Because she wants this matter resolved." Con shrugged. "And she's drawn to the adventure in the same way that she's drawn to me. But she doesn't want to be. It's not the life she's always dreamed of. When this is over, she'll return to the life she wants — the peace, the order and simplicity. I don't fit there."

"But she loves you. Sabrina told me last night Lilah was in love with you."

"She did?" Con glanced over, his heart suddenly lighter in his chest. "How did Sabrina know? Did Lilah tell her?"

"I don't think they talked about it. You know how women are. Sabrina just knew."

"I'm pathetic, aren't I? Sometimes I wish Lilah was pregnant because I know she'd marry me then. That's an awful way to think, isn't it? Wanting to force her into marriage. Mother would be appalled."

"You are no worse than every other man in love. I suspect at some point we've all wished to tie a woman to us any way possible." Alex clapped his brother on the shoulder. "You said you intended to marry her, and I've never known you not to get what you went after. How do you plan to win her over?"

"I have to prove that I can give her the life she's dreamed of. That I can be the kind of man she wants. I must be patient. Steady. Show her that I'm not rash, that I won't be running off to Cornwall or Scotland to follow an investigation. That I won't cause a scandal. Proving that takes time. I can't just say, 'I'm going to be different,' and expect her to believe me."

"You sound like a knight on a quest."

Con laughed. "Maybe I am. I have to slay a dragon. Only the dragon I need to slay is me."

"Con . . ." Alex frowned. "You shouldn't have to change yourself to win her love. If she truly loves you . . ."

"One *does* have to change. It's inevitable. Are you the same man you were before you met Sabrina? You needn't answer because I can assure you that you are not. You're stronger, more mature. You've accepted your ability, even come to value it. But you also have a new vulnerability — you have worry and fear for someone else, the desire to make Sabrina happy, the need to protect her. Love always changes a person. The only question is whether it's for good or ill."

His twin stared at him, stricken. "How can Lilah not realize that you already are serious and thoughtful? Con . . . talk to Lilah. Tell her all this. What you feel for her, what you think. Ask her to marry you. A traditional proposal might go a long way toward making her believe you know what's proper."

"I can't. Not yet." Con's chest tightened. "What if she says no? It would be over. We couldn't go on as if nothing had happened. I can't risk that. I have to wait until I'm sure."

"Since when have you ever been afraid of a risk? You're the boy who went after that thug with your cricket bat. I'm the one who lost my lunch when we found a dead body. You went for help. You're the lad who took on a dray driver even though he was twice your size and had a whip in his hand."

"He was beating his horse!" Fire flared in Con's eyes at the memory. "What else could I do? As I remember, you ran to join me. Anyway, that was different." Con sighed. "All I risked then was a beating. This is a different matter altogether. If I lose Lilah, I'll lose everything."

CHAPTER THIRTY-SEVEN

Lilah loitered in the entryway, waiting for Con. They had planned to go to the village to track down her father's lawyer, but after Alex and Sabrina left, Con had disappeared into the garden. After a moment, she wandered down the hall. Her aunt was in the sitting room, her hands in her lap, staring off into nothing. Her face was wan, and her eyes suspiciously puffy. Had she been crying?

Vesta looked up and smiled. "Hello, dear. Come and sit with me." She patted the sofa beside her. "I'm quite lazy this morning. I had trouble sleeping last night." As Lilah sat down, Vesta went on, "It's because the Sanctuary is calling to me. We must find that key. If we could release the Goddess . . ."

"Well, freeing it is what we *don't* want to do," Lilah pointed out.

"Yes, of course, dear. What I mean is bind-ing the Sanctuary to us." Vesta fell silent, absently running her finger over the arm of her chair. Not looking up, she said quietly, "The power went to you, didn't it? I felt it. It was much more powerful when you joined me."

"I'm not sure," Lilah demurred. She told herself it was silly to feel guilty for being the recipient of the Sanctuary's power. She would gladly have given it over to Aunt Vesta if she could. Still, she couldn't help but feel sorry for her aunt.

"I always believed it favored me. Fed me. I thought if I came back, my power would return." Vesta's face was sad, something Lilah had rarely seen on her aunt.

"Give it time, Aunt Vesta."

"That's sweet of you to say. You were always such a good little girl." Vesta straightened her shoulders and pushed a smile onto her face. "It was much stronger, wasn't it, when we were together?"

"Yes, it was."

"That's good. You're right, I should give it more time." Vesta's smile turned more natural. "Now, what are you and that young man of yours doing today? Are you any further along in finding the key?"

Lilah was glad to change the subject. She launched into a description of their visit yesterday to her father's valet, ending with his revelation that Sir Virgil had left her a letter with his lawyer.

"You think that Mr. Cunningham took the letter? Oh, my. He always seemed such a nice man."

"I suppose it could have been a mistake. Con and I are going to his office this morning. His son has carried on with the firm, hasn't he?"

"I believe so."

"It might be that it simply slipped Mr. Cunningham's mind. If not, Con plans to track him down in Bath and question him."

"But there's so little time . . ."

"I know. But surely Father must have told me the location of the key. He was more straightforward than my grandfather seems to have been."

"That's true. Virgil wouldn't have been cryptic with you." Aunt Vesta's expression grew hopeful. "Perhaps our luck has turned. That letter will be sitting in his files, gathering dust." She looked beyond Lilah. "Ah, there you are, dear boy. Lilah's been telling me about your adventures."

Lilah turned to see Con standing in the doorway. He made quick work of extricating them from Aunt Vesta's conversational clutches — Lilah wished she was as adept as he — and they walked out to the carriage waiting for them in the courtyard.

Con seemed rather more quiet than usual, even pensive. When they were settled in the carriage, she reached out to lay her hand on his arm.

"Is something wrong?"

He looked at her, startled, then smiled, whatever shadows there might have been in his eyes fleeing. "No." He laid his hand over hers. "I was just thinking — an odd occurrence, I know."

She made a face, but settled back, feeling reassured.

"I talked to the head gardener this morning," Con went on.

"The gardener? Whatever for? I hope you are not about to tell me that the garden has been left to run wild."

He laughed. "No. Unlike Sir Jasper, I have few opinions on gardens. I was talking to Harvey because I'd asked him to keep his ear to the ground for me. His sister is married to the baker, and his cousin runs the tap in the tavern, so he is privy to all the news."

"Con Moreland. How on earth do you know all this?"

He shrugged. "I chat with the servants. I like to know things."

"So you've developed a ring of spies?"

"I wouldn't say spies. It's more like informants. I learned it from Megan. Knowing people — and being trusted by them — is very important in reporting."

"Investigating, too, apparently."

"Besides, I'm universally curious."

"So what did your 'informants' tell you?"

"That Niles Dearborn was in the tavern."

"He's back?"

"It seems so. I'm not sure what he's doing. He was asking questions about you and me. According to Harvey, everyone was very tight-lipped."

"What do you think he wants?"

"I don't know. But I've set the gardeners and grooms on the alert for him. I wouldn't be surprised if he comes poking around the estate."

It occurred to Lilah that Con was carrying on her business for her. It had been most annoying when Sir Jasper did so; with Con, she didn't mind at all. In fact, strangely, it made her feel warm inside.

When they arrived in the village, they found that the law office had indeed remained in the hands of Mr. Cunningham's son, who bustled out to greet them, smiling broadly. His good cheer fell away, however, when Lilah asked him about the letter that had never been delivered to her.

In shocked tones, Cunningham assured them that his father would never have been derelict in his duty. To prove it, he had his clerk haul out the boxes of his father's old files and dig through them, finally coming up with a thick stack labeled "Holcutt."

"Yes, here it is." He pointed to a paper atop the file. It was a list of dates with notations beside each date. "You see? 'Aug. 17, 1891 Ltr., priv., Sir V. Holcutt, del. Aug. 17, D. Holcutt.' He entered his delivery of a private letter to D. Holcutt — that is you, miss — on that day last year. These are his initials, showing he had successfully completed the task." He gave them a triumphant smile. "Father was always very careful with his files. As am I."

Lilah thought that a task checked off on a piece of paper was scarcely evidence of the truth of the statement. As they returned home, she said flatly, "It's not true. He didn't send it to me, let alone deliver it. I wouldn't have forgotten."

"Of course not. Something happened. Mr. Cunningham Senior was not as careful as his son would like us to believe — or he wasn't as honest. Either the man read the letter himself or he gave it to someone other than you. Did you notice the entry in the ledger above yours?"

"No. What was it?"

"A meeting with Jasper Holcutt. Not only that, the date was the same as the supposed delivery to you."

They discussed the topic the rest of the way home, but Aunt Vesta greeted them with eager questions, so Con and Lilah had to sit down with her and go over it all again.

"Sir Jasper?" Aunt Vesta said doubtfully when they had finished. "He seems far too dull, doesn't he? It's more likely Niles is playing a deep game, trying to get our key by making us believe he lost his."

"It seems too coincidental that Cunningham met with Sir Jasper and delivered my letter on the same day," Lilah pointed out. "I never got it, but Sir Jasper started courting me a few months later."

"You think he paid Mr. Cunningham to give the letter to him instead?"

"I intend to find out," Con replied. "It's possible Sir Jasper might not have even had to pay him. Perhaps Sir Jasper offered to take the task off Cunningham's hands and give the letter to Lilah himself. It would have been unethical of course, but it wouldn't be the first time a lawyer handed over a woman's business affairs to her closest male relative."

"That's true. Mr. Cunningham was rather old-fashioned." Aunt Vesta shook her head in disapproval. She looked thoughtful. "And it would explain, I suppose, why Sir Jasper kept poking his nose in everywhere when he was here. He asked me a number of questions that I thought were quite rude, really."

"What sort of questions?" Con asked, his gaze sharpening on Vesta's face.

"Oh, I don't remember exactly . . . things about Papa's office. And the Clock Room of course. He was very interested in that. Why, once I walked out of my door and saw him standing in Virgil's bedchamber — can you imagine the gall of the man? As if he were measuring the master bedroom for his possessions. He was even making a list."

"A list?" Lilah asked, exchanging a glance with Con. "What sort of list?"

"He was writing things down?" Con added.

"Well . . ." Vesta said vaguely, turning her gaze upward, as if the answers were written on the ceiling. "I don't know that it was a list, really. It was just a piece of paper." She drew in a sharp breath and looked at Con. "Ohhh. You think it was the letter. He was using it to help him find the key!"

"I think it's worth a look."

Con stood up, holding out a hand to

Lilah, and they left the room. Aunt Vesta trailed after them as they went up the stairs and down the hallway to the bedroom where Sir Jasper had slept during his brief stay. Their steps grew faster by the moment, and Lilah's heart beat faster in anticipation.

"He wouldn't just leave it here," Lilah said, trying to temper her hopes.

Con opened the door and they surveyed the disappointingly tidy room. The linens had been removed; the dresser top stood empty; the floor had been swept. Lilah let out a sigh. If anything had been dropped here, it obviously had been picked up and thrown away.

Still, she began pulling out the drawers of the dresser and looking inside them. Con went to the wardrobe and opened the doors, moving next to the washstand and bed.

"Nothing," Lilah said in disgust. She turned away from the dresser to see Con lying on the floor, peering under the bed.

"Wait." Con's voice was muffled, his head partly under the bed. He backed out quickly, scrambling to his feet. There was a streak of dust down the side of his face. "The maids, it seems, are less meticulous where it's unseen." He climbed onto the bed, reaching his hand through the spindles of the headboard and groping down.

"There's something here. Ha!" He pulled his hand out and turned to Lilah, a triumphant grin spreading across his face.

He reached out to Lilah, offering a folded piece of paper.

It felt as if every drop of blood in Lilah's body had just drained down to her feet. "You found the letter."

CHAPTER THIRTY-EIGHT

Lilah stared at the notepaper as if Con were handing her a snake.

"Go on." Con waggled the note. When she still hesitated, he said, "Would you rather read it alone? I can leave."

In the doorway, Aunt Vesta let out a little squeak of dismay. The sound seemed to break Lilah's paralysis, and she shook her head, reaching out to take the letter from him.

"No, I'd rather you were here." She smiled. "Though that was a handsome offer, I must say, given your curiosity."

"Perhaps I've turned over a new leaf," he replied lightly. "I'm glad you want me to stay."

Lilah broke open the seal and began to read aloud.

"My dearest Lilah,

"I have never been the father I should
have. I've come to realize how much of
my life I wasted on things I couldn't
change instead of raising the wonderful
being the Lord entrusted to me. I can
only beg your pardon and pray that you
will read this letter with an open mind
and a forgiving heart."

Lilah's voice caught and she stopped,
pressing her lips together for a moment.

"Little as you wish to acknowledge it,
you hold great power within you.

"Many years ago, my father and his
friends discovered a tunnel beneath the
tower. It led them to an ancient cave of
wondrous beauty, steeped in magical
power. I do not know what force caused
this or why it was revealed to my father,
but he recognized it as a holy place.
They turned it to their own advantage,
receiving great blessings, and guarding it
with great secrecy.

"The cornerstone of the Brotherhood
is the eternal balance of the Three. The
Sanctuary requires three keys to open it,
and each of the Brothers holds one of
the keys. I pass my key on to you, rely-

ing on your character to use it wisely. I have left the key in your house, where only you would look."

" 'Left the key in your house'?" Lilah exclaimed, looking up from the letter in indignation. "That is all he tells me? He hid the key somewhere in the house?"

"Doesn't narrow it down much," Con admitted.

"It's useless." She waved the page. "If that isn't just like Father."

"You don't know what he means?" Vesta looked crestfallen and every bit her age. "I thought — I hoped —" Turning, she left the room.

Lilah gazed after her. "Poor Aunt Vesta. I can't help her."

"Perhaps Sir Virgil said something more about it." Con nodded toward the letter.

"Yes, you're right." Lilah took up her reading again.

"In each of the chosen Three, there must be a balance of good and bad. We were granted abilities in the areas most dear to us, but we were also given the counterparts of these qualities in equal magnitude.

"The Dearborns' gift of wealth is

countered by a rise in their greed. Hamilton's wisdom was balanced by the terrible headaches that plagued him all his life. My father could not be pulled from his dreams and visions. I clung so tightly to my connection to the afterlife that I lost the love of the one closest to me.

"With Hamilton's death, the sacred balance of the Three was destroyed. The abilities of those who remain have diminished. Niles has had the more visible decline in his talents, as he began to lose money at a rapid rate. But I, too, have begun to feel my connection to the Spirit fading, my ties to my beloved Eva and the Otherworld slipping away.

"Realizing the problem, I put away my key and refused to open the Sanctuary until such time as the Three can be restored."

"The argument between him and Dearborn that Roberts overheard," Con interjected.

"I imagine so." Lilah nodded and went on.

"Since that time, however, I have meditated much on balance. Nothing we do comes without consequence, and nothing is given to us without a sacrifice in return. I have realized that a sacrifice was required from the Brotherhood. Though I believe they did it unknowingly, they took from their own life forces in order to bring life to the Sanctuary.

"The three original Brothers all came to untimely ends. Hamilton also left this life too early. Tellingly, the excess of their gifts has caused the manner of their deaths. I have little doubt that Niles and I will meet the same fate. I do not fear this, for I am eager to rejoin my beloved, but I fear for you, Delilah, and for Sabrina and Peter, whose lives may be cut short.

"I realize now that the Sanctuary should never have been opened. I believe it should be closed forever. I intended to destroy the key, but I was too weak. I leave the decision of what to do with the Sanctuary in your capable hands. You are better suited than I to choose the right path. Pray forgive me for laying this final burden upon you.

"Yr. loving father"

Lilah set down the letter and looked at Con in dismay. "We were right. The Sanctuary has made all three families die young. Sabrina and I will —"

"No!" Con said fiercely. "You aren't going to die young. We don't know that it will affect you and Sabrina. The two of you have never been inside the Sanctuary. You've never taken any gift from it. Nor have either of you lived your whole lives here. Perhaps by stopping their visits, your father had already canceled the obligation."

"The power is still there. I feel its pull, its energy. I'm sure we need to do something more."

"Then we'll do it."

"How?"

"I don't know. But I am not going to let you die."

Alex's reaction when he and Sabrina returned from Carmoor was predictably much the same as Con's. He clenched his fists, glaring at his brother. "Sabrina is *not* going to die."

"Stop glowering, Alex. It's not Con's fault," Sabrina said pacifically. "As Con said, Lilah and I haven't lived here for almost half our lives. It must take some kind of proximity, don't you think? If worse comes to worst, we just won't live at Carmoor."

"You're right of course. Sorry." Alex sighed and took a seat. "Does it strike anyone else as rather convenient that this thing dropped down like manna from heaven? After all the searches, suddenly it's just there, waiting for you."

"Yes, it looks suspicious. But Lilah says this is her father's handwriting."

"It is. And the wording and style are just like him. I think the letter must be real," Lilah added.

"But why would your cousin leave something this incriminating lying about his room? That's what puzzles me."

"Carelessness has tripped up many a criminal," Con said. "And the man did leave in a bit of a rush after Lilah turned him down. This might have fallen out of a pocket and gone unnoticed." Con shrugged. "Granted, it's surprising, and we're lucky. But it's even stranger that he would have left this here deliberately. As you said, it incriminates him."

"Perhaps it was supposed to," Lilah suggested.

"You mean, the real thief is trying to throw us off his trail?" Sabrina asked. "Make us suspect Sir Jasper?"

"Yes. It sounds like Dearborn." Alex set his jaw.

"I wouldn't think Dearborn would give us the very thing we're looking for just to implicate Jasper," Sabrina said.

"But it's not really what we're looking for, is it?" Alex pointed out. "This letter has told us things about the Brotherhood and about the thing we're searching for, but it isn't the least bit helpful for finding the key. He left it in the house? What help is that?"

"Maybe it's a code," Con suggested.

"And maybe my father believed I could read his thoughts," Lilah said tartly. "It's the sort of thing he would do. The point is, whether Sir Jasper accidentally left this or Dearborn put it there to implicate him, we still are no closer to our goal. All we learned, really, is this warning Father gave us about the ill effects of the 'blessing.' "

"Perhaps there's some sort of clue in that. What did he mean, 'the excess of their gifts caused the manner of their deaths'? Could that be a hint?"

"Unfortunately, that's the way my father wrote — everything was formal, philosophical. I think he meant that all the men died from some disease that's in their realm — my father was the spirit or heart, and he died of a heart attack."

"And mine had apoplexy," Sabrina added. "My grandfather died of a brain tumor.

They were the head."

"I don't know how Niles's father died."

"I do," Sabrina said. "I heard Mrs. Dearborn once say that gambling was the death of him. And Mr. Dearborn said, 'Just because Father died at the tables doesn't mean I will.'"

"They were killed by their gifts, basically," Lilah said. "That's why I think we must close the Sanctuary, shut it down, not just ignore it."

"We will. Perhaps if we did the opposite of their ceremony — do the same things except tell it to leave or go back or we return its gifts," Sabrina offered.

"First, we have to find the key," Alex said.

"And the other two," Lilah added.

"We'll get the other two," Con said grimly. "One way or another."

"Right now, all we can do is continue to search for the key," Alex said.

"At least now we know we're looking for a small hiding place rather than a secret door or staircase," Con pointed out.

Lilah groaned. "Unfortunately that only makes the task bigger."

Con smiled. "I've always liked a challenge."

The next morning the two couples split up,

with Con and Alex searching for the key in the original section and Lilah and Sabrina working on the most recent addition. The two women went first to the old chapel at the farthest end of the building. Sabrina looked around the large room and sighed. "It's a daunting prospect."

"I know," Lilah agreed. "I keep thinking I'm missing something, that there must have been a clue in Father's letter, but I've no idea what. Con spent all yesterday evening trying to find a code in it." She smiled fondly at the memory of him bent over the letter, scribbling things on a notepad, his hair sticking out in all directions from his tugging at it when he was deep in thought.

Glancing over at Sabrina, Lilah saw that the other woman was watching her with shrewd eyes. She had the sinking feeling she had just given herself away.

"I knew it!" Sabrina said. "There *is* something going on between the two of you."

"Don't be silly." Lilah turned away, aware that her voice was too high and breathless. "I can't imagine why you'd think that."

"Because I have eyes? The two of you haven't argued once since we got here."

"We've, um, learned to put aside our differences and work together."

"Mmm-hmm." Sabrina looked skeptical.

"I'd say you've done a lot more than 'work together.' Come, Lilah, tell me." She waggled her fingers. "Everything. What happened?"

Lilah struggled for a moment. Then she let out a groan and sank down onto one of the hard wooden pews. "Oh, Sabrina. I don't know what I'm going to do. I think . . . I'm afraid I've fallen in love with Con."

CHAPTER THIRTY-NINE

"I told Alex you loved him." Sabrina hugged her friend, then pulled back, looking at her critically. "This should make you happy, not sad."

"I am. I'm very happy. But . . . it's all terribly confusing. I feel so good when I'm with Con. He's been kind to Aunt Vesta, and you know what a trial she can be. I think he genuinely enjoys people, foibles and all. He teases everyone, but once I got used to it, I saw that he isn't unkind. And somehow I always wind up laughing."

"You sound smitten with him." Sabrina paused, then went on delicately, "Is it — do you think he doesn't return your affection? He seems very . . . attentive to you. He looks at you, well, the way Alex looks at me."

"He has feelings for me, I think. He's attracted to me."

"As you are to him."

"Yes. Oh, yes." Lilah was unable to look

Sabrina in the face as she rushed on. "I have — I fear I will shock you, but we have, um, shared intimacies." She blushed to the roots of her hair. "Please don't think too badly of me."

"It does shock me a little because I know how proper you have always been, but I don't think badly of you. It would be most hypocritical of me, given that Alex and I did, as well."

Lilah's eyes widened. "You mean you slept with Alex before you were married! Why didn't you tell me? I had no idea."

"Well, as I said, you're very proper, and I didn't want *you* to think badly of *me.*"

"Was I really such a prig as everyone thinks? I wouldn't have been disappointed in you. I was very attached to propriety, but I hope I wasn't judgmental. It was *I* who I felt must be careful of the rules. And now . . . well, obviously I have let go of even that. I've been absolutely brazen."

"So we are both wicked women." Sabrina laughed lightly. "But I'm still not sure why you are upset." She sucked in a breath. "Are you with child?"

"No. At least I don't think so." Lilah sighed. "I almost wish I were, for at least then I know that Con would marry me. The matter would be all settled, out of my hands."

"I see. You think Con doesn't love you. That he wouldn't marry you unless he had to."

Lilah nodded. "He's never said a word of love to me. I mean, he calls me 'Lilah, my love' sometimes, but that's just a manner of speaking. He tells me I'm beautiful and . . ." Her blush returned a little. "He makes me feel as if he loves me."

"But he doesn't say it," Sabrina finished for her. "I think it's hard for men to say such things, to be emotional."

Lilah cocked an eyebrow. "When has Con ever hesitated to say anything?"

Sabrina laughed. "That's true. But maybe it's different when he's in love."

"Perhaps." Lilah shrugged. "But if you could have seen his face when he said he would marry me . . . It was clear he would force himself to do the honorable thing, but it was equally obvious he didn't want to."

"When did he do this?"

"After the first time. He felt duty bound."

"That was some time ago."

"Not so long, really."

"Are you sure he still feels the same way?"

Lilah shrugged. "You and I both know I'm not the sort of woman he should marry. He has told me how little he values my qualities. Whatever he feels for me — lust or affection — he does so against his better judgment. He finds me rigid and priggish — I'm fond of rules. He is not. I'm skeptical, and he is open-minded. I doubt. He trusts. He's warm, demonstrative, affectionate. I am none of those things. I don't make friends easily. You are the only one I am truly close to."

"A husband and wife needn't be the same. Alex and I have differences."

"But not so wide, not so strong."

Sabrina looked thoughtful. "Very well. But have you ever thought that maybe what Con needs, what he wants, is not agreement but balance."

"Not 'balance' again." Lilah made a comical face. "Now you sound like my father."

"Con and Alex have been like this their whole lives." Sabrina held up two fingers, crossed. "They share a great deal, but there are ways in which they differ. Con is more impulsive, Alex more likely to give thought to something. Con is more emotional, Alex cooler. Maybe Con's nature *needs* someone who steadies him. He doesn't like to follow rules, but sometimes one has to."

"I might be useful to him in that way, but he wouldn't enjoy it."

"You don't know that."

"We would argue constantly."

"How many rows have you had with him since you got here?"

"I'm not sure — I can't really think of any." When Sabrina raised her eyebrows significantly, Lilah said, "But he wants me now. That colors it a great deal. What about later, once he's accustomed to me? When desire no longer drives him?"

"Are you sure that's going to happen? Lilah, I'm talking about more than being useful — it's a matter of fitting together well. Like puzzle pieces — they aren't the same, but they go together to make a complete whole." Sabrina sat back, studying Lilah. "Are you sure that it is *Con* who's reluctant to marry?"

Lilah looked over, startled. "What do you mean? I just told you I love him."

"Yet you bring up all these objections. Are you sure you aren't looking for obstacles?"

"Nonsense. Why would I do that?"

"I don't know. But you push aside every argument so quickly, deny any indication that he loves you. Maybe it's not confusion you feel, but fear."

"Fear of what? That I will love him too much? That I will become obsessed with him as my father was with my mother?"

Lilah jumped to her feet and began to walk aimlessly around the room, emotions churning inside her.

Sabrina followed her. "I was going to say, afraid of being hurt. But it seems telling, doesn't it, that your mind leaped to loving him too much?"

Lilah whirled. "Of course I'm afraid of being hurt. And of loving him too much. They go hand in hand. I never saw aught in my father's love but pain." Her voice choked.

"Lilah . . . it doesn't have to be that way."

"Perhaps that's true for others, but my family seems to be unwilling or unable to let go of what is dear to us. The center of Father's life was his love for Mother. Apparently the center of my grandfather's was his love for this mad religion. They were eaten up with their love."

"You aren't them."

"What if I am like them? Maybe I just haven't met my downfall until now. What if I fall so deeply in love with Con that I can never be happy without him? What will I do if he doesn't return my love? How will I bear it? I feel as if I'm standing on the edge of a precipice, and one misstep could send me tumbling down into my doom."

"What if you fall into happiness instead?

What if Con loves you in return?"

"I don't know if I can take that risk."

"Maybe you have to. You already love him. All you're doing is trying to avoid it. Ducking and dodging."

"So I should just stop and take the blow?" Lilah asked.

"If you wrap up all your feelings, if you buffer yourself from love, you're already dooming yourself to a life of emptiness."

Lilah sucked in her breath, her friend's words piercing her through.

"I'm sorry." Remorse flooded Sabrina's face. "I didn't mean — I shouldn't have said that."

"Not even if it's true?"

"I didn't think it through. I was . . . I was carried away by making my argument. Of course you'll be happy. Your future doesn't depend on Con."

"No. It depends on me. But I must have the courage to face it."

Sabrina and Lilah returned to their work but learned nothing of significance. When they met Con and Alex again, they found that the men had come up with nothing either — though from their disheveled and dusty appearance and cheerful smiles, they had apparently enjoyed their search more.

Since it was time for tea, Con and Alex went upstairs to clean up, and Lilah and Aunt Vesta settled down in the sitting room. Vesta looked almost as flushed and cheerful as the men.

"I'm glad it's just the three of us girls for the moment. I had an idea."

"What?" Lilah asked warily.

"I visited the Sanctuary again."

"What do you mean? We have no keys."

"Not *inside* it. I stood outside the door in the tunnel and communed with it. It's that strong, you know."

"You should not go down there by yourself, Aunt Vesta," Lilah told her, alarmed. "It's dangerous. What if the tunnel had collapsed? We would have had no idea where you were or what had happened."

"The Sanctuary would never hurt one of *us*. Anyway, the important thing is the Sanctuary gave me an idea."

Lilah suppressed a sigh. As soon as she felt the power flow between them last night, she had known that Aunt Vesta would be a problem.

Aunt Vesta prattled on, "The great Goddess watches over all of us of course, since our families pierced the veil to the Otherworld. She blessed the men, but just think . . . how much better would it be if it was a sister-hood! I have read that the triskele represents not only rebirth, but divine feminine power, as well. The Goddess would be happier if *we* conducted the ceremony of the gifts."

"We?" Lilah asked, though she was sure where her aunt was headed.

"The three of us of course. You, Sabrina and I."

"Aunt Vesta, no . . ."

"But it's supposed to be one from each of the three families," Sabrina pointed out. "It would still be out of balance."

"Would it? That was just Virgil's guess. What if the real reason was because the Goddess knew that there were women to do the ceremony now? Maybe she was tired of dealing with the men. That was why she was displeased." She gave a nod, as if she had proved her point. "Father believed the Sanctuary belonged to the Matres. You said that yourself, Lilah. Three women." She paused for emphasis. "The old woman." She laid a hand on her chest. "The married woman." She gestured at Sabrina. "And the maiden." She swept her hand toward Lilah. "It's perfect. You felt the power the three of us brought out of it last night." She sat back, beaming.

"It's pointless to talk about a ceremony,"

Lilah said. She didn't want to have this discussion with Vesta now. "We have yet to find the key, and we also have to obtain the other two."

"You'll find it," Vesta said complacently. "I'm sure of it. It's meant to be."

Fortunately they were saved from any further discussion by the entrance of the two men, followed shortly thereafter by the butler with the tea cart. But after tea, as soon as Aunt Vesta left the room for her afternoon nap, Lilah turned to Con and said, "What am I to do about Aunt Vesta? She's going to be terribly upset when we close the Sanctuary. *If* we can close it."

"If we can even open it," Sabrina added. "It's only four more days until Midsummer Day. We have to renew the Sanctuary before then. Whatever the ruination Mr. Dearborn thinks this thing will cause, I believe it. The energy I felt from it last night was enormous, and that was through a rock wall and a heavy door." She looked over at her friend. "I can't imagine how strong it would be if it was released."

"It would be folly to deny the power of the Sanctuary," Lilah agreed. "It could cause a massive amount of destruction. We cannot afford to wait and see what happens."

"Alex and I had planned to move into Carmoor tomorrow. But we can still come over here during the day to help look. Or perhaps we should stay longer. It would give us a little added time to look."

"I don't know that it would be enough," Alex said. "It could take weeks to find it, and even if we do, there's the problem of the other keys. I've been thinking that perhaps we should all move to Carmoor if we can't locate the keys before Midsummer Day. At least we'd be at some distance."

"But we don't know what it's going to do. The consequences could be a great deal more than just leveling Barrow House." Lilah asked, "What if it's some sort of illness or evil that infects people? We can't just let the world be exposed to it."

"I've been thinking, too." Con spoke up. "There are other ways to open a door. Dynamite, for instance."

"Dynamite!" Lilah exclaimed. "You're going to blow it up? That's your solution? You'll bring the house down around our ears."

"Not necessarily. Con's idea just might work." Alex's eyes started to gleam. "Blasts can be controlled. That's rock beneath this house. If you had an expert, he could place it so that most of the damage would be to the door. Some of the wall around the door might crumble, but I don't think it would harm Barrow House."

"Besides —" Con took up the argument "— the Sanctuary isn't below the house. The tunnel starts there, but I'm sure that the Sanctuary itself lies between the maze and the house. It's open ground above it. Even if it caved in, it would only damage the lawn, not the house."

"But what about this renewal we need to do?"

"If only the door is blown, you'll be able to go in and perform whatever ceremony you need. I can't help but wonder if your aunt is right and three women would be better, but if you'd rather go the route of descendants of the original men, we'll get Peter. If his father is lurking around here, you know that Peter is, too."

"But even if the house doesn't collapse, it could cave in the Sanctuary," Lilah pointed out.

Con shrugged. "Hopefully, if it's destroyed, that would end the whole thing. The force would be buried where it couldn't get out. This is just a last-gasp effort anyway. We'll still look for the key. As Sabrina said, they can continue to come over and help us look."

"I'll track down Dearborn and Peter," Alex offered. "Twist their arms to make them agree to the ceremony and bring out the other two keys. If nothing else, we know money will work on Niles Dearborn."

"What if it *is* Sir Jasper who has the keys?" Sabrina asked. "He's in London. Or maybe even Yorkshire."

"Then we'll have to rely on Con's method."

"So . . ." Con got up and paced about. "Here's my plan — Alex and Sabrina will go to Carmoor tomorrow as planned and prepare to take in three houseguests. Alex will also hunt down Niles Dearborn and Peter. Lilah and I will go to Wells and get dynamite, as well as an expert to set it off. We'll continue searching for the key in the meantime, but if we can't find it, come Midsummer's Eve, we're going to blow the door in."

CHAPTER FORTY

Con's plan had not accounted for Lilah awakening the next morning with a pounding headache and a sore throat. The thought of going to Wells — indeed, of doing anything but spending the day in bed — did not appeal to her.

When she told Con, he said easily, "We'll stay, then." He sat down beside her, laying his hand on her forehead.

"No, that's good of you to offer. But you should go to Wells without me. We don't have time to waste. It's only three days now."

Con frowned. "I don't like the idea of leaving you here alone. Alex and Sabrina had already left when Cuddington told us you were ill, but I could send someone to fetch Sabrina back."

"No. Let her enjoy setting up in her own home," Lilah said. "And I'm not alone. Aunt Vesta is here." Con's lifted brow at that statement made her chuckle despite the way she felt. "Really, Cuddington will see to it that I'm all right. She's bringing me some warm lemon and honey for my throat, and the cook is busy making up some noxious potion for my fever. I'll just sleep. I'll probably be feeling much better by the time you return."

She did, in fact, spend the morning in bed after Con left, and when she awoke that afternoon, Lilah was feeling enough better that she dressed and went downstairs, thinking that she could at least be useful by searching for the key.

The house seemed very empty without Con. What would she do when he left? Lilah pushed that thought aside and sat down in the library. She should make up a list, she thought, of places her father might think she would look for a key.

Unfortunately, Aunt Vesta decided to keep her company. Her chatter was not conducive to thought, and after a time Lilah gave up on the list. Perhaps she had come downstairs too soon. She thought of going back to her room, but it seemed too much effort, so she sat down in one of the comfortable wing-back chairs, leaning her head back and closing her eyes. Where would her father have hidden the key? What place did he think was special to her?

Aunt Vesta, of course, was quite capable of carrying on a conversation by herself. She ranged from her favorite cures for a sore throat to the wonders of the waters at Wiesbaden to Vesta's own apparently dire case of fever when she was seven. "Father rode into Wells to fetch a better doctor, he was so worried — and he was not the sort of man to fret over every little case of sniffles or cut finger. Not like Virgil. Do you remember how frantic he was whenever you were ill?"

Lilah murmured noncommittally. Was her aunt right? Had her father worried over her every illness? Had those last years of living apart from him colored her memories?

"I remember when I had the measles," Lilah said. "He gave me the dollhouse." She smiled faintly. "It was supposed to be for my birthday, but he gave it to me early because I was bored with staying in bed."

"Virgil was never good at keeping secrets."

She had loved that dollhouse. It had been such a pretty, normal house, tidy and square in the Georgian style. Nothing at all like her own crazy, sprawling . . .

Lilah's eyes flew open. "My dollhouse!" She jumped to her feet, startling her aunt.

"Lilah, dearest, whatever —"

But Lilah was already gone, running down

the hall and up the stairs. She was charged with energy now, the lassitude of illness fleeing in the face of her excitement. How could she not have seen it? Her father's letter *had* held a clue only Lilah would know. He hadn't said *Barrow House* or *my house* or *our house.* His note had read "*your* house."

She hurried to the playroom in her bedroom, shoved aside the chair in front of it and flung open the door. The late-afternoon sun shone in through the dormer window, casting a grid of light across the floor. In the hushed stillness, dolls gazed vacantly forward. Games and toys lined the shelves below them.

Lilah went to the small table that held a graceful white dollhouse, its bow-windowed front facing forward. The rear wall of the dollhouse was open, revealing the rooms, each decorated with miniature furniture and peopled with the tiny dolls of a family and servants.

Lilah went down on her knees beside the table. She heard her aunt come in, but she paid no attention to Vesta hovering behind her. The three enclosed sides showed the facade of a foundation at the base of the house, closely flanked by a low ornamental hedge. But along the open back side, there was a space between the table and house.

Lilah slid her hand under the house, and her fingertips touched smooth velvet. Her heart pounded as she removed a velvet pouch and reached inside to pull out a large gold key. Parallel wavy lines were etched into the head of the key, centered by a dark blue sapphire.

Lilah held it higher, studying it. If only Con had been here; he would be so upset to have missed this. The triumph of her discovery was suddenly dampened. She wished she could share it with Con. She shouldn't have rushed in. She should have waited for him to return.

"You found it," Aunt Vesta breathed.

"Yes." She cast a glance up at her aunt. Vesta's eyes were bright, her smile gleeful. Lilah looked back down at the key in her palm. "Now we just need the other two."

"Isn't it fortunate, then, that I have them?" Vesta said.

Pain slammed into the back of Lilah's head, and she went tumbling into darkness.

Con rode toward Barrow House. It was almost dusk, as it had been the first time he saw the place, but now the house looked not so much odd as dearly familiar. His heart warmed inside him. The last few miles had seemed to take forever, so eager was he to get home.

He had found the explosive and a man experienced in using it. The fellow would be coming down tomorrow with his dynamite to inspect the door in the tunnel, so his trip had been a success. But he had wished the whole time that Lilah was with him. He was eager to share his good news with her, but even more than that, Con wanted to see Lilah.

Oddly, no groom came running to take his horse. Stranger still, no footman opened the front door, and when Con walked inside, the entryway was empty, the house was eerily silent. A frisson of alarm snaked up Con's back.

"Lilah?" He strode down the hallway, his steps quickening at the continued hush. "Lilah, where are you? Ruggins? Mrs. Le-Claire?"

"Con!" As he reached the foot of the staircase, Vesta came running down it, her face panicked. "I didn't expect you so soon!"

"Where is everyone? Is Lilah all right?" He had visions of Lilah's illness turning into pneumonia in the hours he'd been away. "What's happened?"

"She's gone," Vesta said wildly, wringing her hands. "I sent the servants out looking for her. Come, you must help me." She latched onto his arm and pulled him toward the back door.

"What? Gone where?" Con went with her, his alarm burgeoning. "What do you mean? She was sick in bed."

"That's why I'm so worried! We must find her. I fear she's gone down to the Levels."

"The Levels! That's mad. Why would she go there?"

"That's just it. She's crazed — with fever."

"Fever? She's sicker? I shouldn't have left. What happened?"

"I'm not sure. I fear she has something far worse than the sniffles. Wait! Where are you going?" Vesta's voice rose in agitation as Con pulled his arm from her grasp and started down a different garden path. "We must find her."

"I need a light. It'll be dark soon." He yanked open the small gardener's shed and pulled out a lantern, sticking a box of matches in his pocket, as well.

Vesta, who had been shifting impatiently from one foot to the other, took his arm in an iron grip and propelled him through the garden. Along the way, she described in dramatic detail her niece's fever spiking and Vesta's own efforts to bring it down.

"Did you send for the doctor?" Con asked.

"That's when she disappeared! I left the room to send a footman for the doctor, and when I came back, she wasn't there. It was only a few minutes!"

"Damn it. I should have been here. Why the devil did I go to Wells?"

"It wasn't your fault, dear boy. How could you have known? And I was there to tend to her."

Con had his own opinions about the efficacy of Vesta's care, but he kept them to himself. "But why would Lilah go to the Levels? Are you sure?"

"She was talking about them earlier. In her fever. She was . . . She was raving about going to see her nurse."

"Her nurse?"

"Yes, that's when I realized she was out of her head. The woman died two years ago. Lilah was adamant about seeing her, and of course I told her Nanny was dead, but Lilah insisted she was not. I think she must have gone to find her." Vesta clung to his arm as they scrambled down the path from the tor to the flatland below.

Vesta continued to describe her efforts to find Lilah, sending all the servants out to look for Lilah while she combed the house herself. Con did his best to ignore her, searching the landscape in front of him for the faint shimmer in the air that would indicate Lilah's path. How could he not see it? Her passage had been so clear the other time. Perhaps it was the distraction of Vesta's constant conversation. Worse, Vesta was slowing him down.

"Did you send word to Alex?" Con cut into her stream of talk.

"No. I sent some of the servants toward Carmoor. They'll find her if she went that way. But she's on the Levels. I can feel it."

"You should go back," Con told her. "Send a message to Alex."

"No, dear boy, I must *help* you. You don't know the area. The rhynes and embankments — it's all so much the same. It's easy to get lost. And when the evening fog sets in . . ."

"I'll be fine. I have the lantern." Con stopped and untwined her arm from his. "I need you to go back to the house. Someone should be there in case Lilah returns. Go," he told her firmly. "It's almost dark, and the fog is starting to creep in."

"If you're sure . . ."

Con turned and strode away before she could pursue the subject. But still he could not make out Lilah's trail. The numerous short canals made it harder to keep on a course, cutting him off and forcing him to backtrack or wind around between them.

Dark fell quickly, and wisps of fog came slithering in, obscuring the landscape. He stopped to light the lantern. The more he walked, the more doubt gnawed at him. Had she really come this way? Perhaps the fog covered up the glimmer.

Something rustled behind him, and he whirled, peering into the dark. "Lilah? Hello? Lilah? Can you hear me?"

There was nothing but silence. He started on. The fog was growing thicker, covering the ground so that it seemed he was walking through snow. It would be easy to stumble into a rhyne. He could hear one now, but he was unsure of its location. His steps slowed.

Out of the corner of his eye, he caught a flash of motion, and he began to turn. A dark figure ran at him, swinging a thick branch. He froze in astonishment. "Vesta!"

The branch slammed into his temple, and he staggered backward, stunned. She swung again, knocking him into the water.

CHAPTER FORTY-ONE

Lilah's head ached. She was lost in a dull haze somewhere between sleep and consciousness, unable to open her eyes. She reached up to touch her head, and strangely her arms seemed stuck together.

"There, there." Something wet and cool touched her forehead, then her cheek. "Time to wake up now."

"Aunt Vesta," she mumbled.

Memories trickled back in through haze. *Aunt Vesta. The key.* Her eyes flew open.

"There you are," Aunt Vesta said and patted her cheek. "I feared I had struck you too hard. And I wasn't sure about that dose of laudanum. I had to put you to sleep so I could prepare, but I thought I might have given you too much. You know I would never want to hurt you."

Laudanum. More vague memories came to Lilah — someone holding her nose and pouring liquid into her mouth. The bitter taste was still on her tongue. Lilah raised her head, and the world tilted. She lay back down. Her hands, she realized, were tied. "Why?" The word came out in no more than a whisper.

"It isn't as if I wanted to," her aunt answered plaintively. "But I can't let you close the Sanctuary. You must see that. It isn't as if I was going to take all the energy. I was willing to share it with you. I even offered for the three of us to share it — Sabrina added a bit to the power, and she was always such a biddable girl. It would have worked out well. But you were so unreasonable." She scowled. "I don't know why you've always had to be so stubborn."

Lilah's head whirled. Where was Con? Wells. Yes, he'd gone to Wells. "Why — you didn't have to give me laudanum."

"But I did, child. I had to do everything on the spur of the moment. I couldn't really plan because I had no idea when you would find the key. I was beginning to think you never would. I finally had to leave that silly letter for you to find — thank goodness you figured it out."

"The letter — what? It was you?" Astonishment, mingled with anger, brought Lilah more fully awake. "*You* stole my letter?"

"It wasn't stealing, dear. The man gave it

to me. Really, I think it was very sloppy of him, handing it over to me just because I was your aunt. And telling me to give it to you — as if it were my job. It was his responsibility, but that's just like a man. Even my brother, who was really a very nice man, took advantage of me. You can see that, can't you? He shoved all the responsibility of raising you onto me so he could sit around mooning over his dead wife. It wasn't fair at all."

"But why didn't you just give me the letter?"

"I couldn't turn it over to you! You wouldn't have believed it for a second. I knew what must be in the letter. I'd been searching and searching for a year for that blasted key and couldn't find it. So I opened it — very carefully, you see, so I could give it to you if it wasn't instructions about the Sanctuary. But all those terrible things Virgil said! I knew they weren't true. Virgil was always the most pessimistic man. And he didn't even say where he had put the key. It was the most nonsensical letter. But thank goodness I didn't throw it away."

"You left it so we'd suspect Jasper."

"As if that stupid man would know what to do with the key." Vesta snorted. "But when you told me you suspected him, it was perfect. I'd been trying to think of a way to show it to you. I realized that you might know what Virgil was talking about. Of course, I couldn't just hand it over. You would have been so irritated that I'd opened it. But then — there it was, the perfect opportunity. Things so often work out that way." She smiled in a self-satisfied way. "Just as it did today. It was fate working, you getting sick, that nice young boy out of the house . . ."

"Con . . ." Lilah whispered. "When Con gets back —"

"He won't. That was too bad, too," her aunt said regretfully. "I didn't want to hurt him. Such a charming young man — and one who understands the occult world. I thought I could get it all done before he got here, and nothing would have to happen to him. But he returned too early."

"You hurt Con?" Fury surged in Lilah, and she shoved herself up on her hands, struggling to rise. Her feet were bound as well, making it difficult to stand. It didn't help that her head was spinning. She breathed shallowly, fighting her nausea.

"I fear he got a trifle lost." Vesta smiled to herself as she squatted down to untie Lilah's ankles.

Con was never lost. Lilah's fear receded a

little. Whatever her aunt had done, Con would find his way back. He would find her. She needed to buy him time; that was all. Lilah raised her hands to her face. She didn't have to pretend. "I feel sick."

"Just breathe. It will pass. I *did* give you too much." Vesta's lips twitched in irritation. "It's so hard to judge these things. Ah, well, I'm sure you'll still be able to get downstairs."

"I don't want to go downstairs."

"You don't have a choice. Now, come along, Dilly." Aunt Vesta put both hands under Lilah's arm and pulled. Lilah made no effort to help her. "Stop that! Stand up!" She dropped Lilah's arm and pulled a gun from her pocket. "Get up. I don't want to shoot you here, but I will if I have to."

Lilah's stomach lurched. "You would shoot me? With no more thought than that?"

"I don't *want* to. But this is too important. The Sanctuary needs you."

"Needs me? Don't you hear how in —" Lilah stopped. Perhaps it was not a good idea to tell her aunt she sounded insane when Vesta was holding a gun on her.

"Now get up." Vesta waggled the gun at her.

Lilah staggered to her feet with an assisting pull from her aunt. She slumped against the wall, wishing that she didn't feel as groggy and unsteady as she looked. "I don't understand."

"You never did." Vesta sighed and pulled her through her bedroom toward the hall. "I tried. You cannot say I didn't try. You refused to see the Otherworld even when it was right there in front of your eyes. And now — now that you can see it —" she shook Lilah hard, making pain radiate through her head "— you want to destroy it!"

"I don't — it's dangerish." No, that wasn't the right word, was it? If only she could think more clearly.

"It's not dangerous," Vesta said impatiently. "Not to me. Not to us. The Goddess will welcome us."

"Auntie, you can't." Lilah reverted to her childhood name for Vesta.

"Don't tell me I can't!" Vesta jerked her forward, and Lilah stumbled into the hall. " 'You can't, Vesta, you're only a girl.' 'You wouldn't understand, Vesta.' " Her tone changed from bitter mimicry to anger. "*I* don't understand, Niles? You're the fool. It was obvious when Hamilton died that I should take his place. None of *them* had the talent I had. I told them, but of course they refused to let me. Even my own brother. I knew better than to even mention it to Niles after Virgil passed. He would never let me join. I knew that I would have to do it all myself. Isn't that always the way?"

"No, it will kill you. Father said . . ." Lilah's voice trailed off. Her legs felt like noodles, and the world swam around her. She grabbed at the banister at the top of the stairs, clinging.

"No!" Vesta dragged her down the steps, Lilah holding on to the railing as best she could to keep from tumbling to the bottom. "Virgil was wrong. She won't hurt me. It belongs to me. We are one. They just didn't know — they were men. But the power called to me. I finally understood that it was the source of my ability. If I came back, if I entered the Sanctuary, the Goddess would heal me. She'd restore my power. It had to be me alone. I just had to get all the keys."

"So you stole them from Niles?"

"Only one was Niles's. The other was Sabrina's, which *he* had stolen. And I didn't steal it. My goodness, I wouldn't know how. But I've met some skillful people over the years." She frowned. "Though it was most foolish of Sid to tell them to grab you when you were with the Morelands."

"And you —" Lilah's brain was operating

at a crawl. "*You* were the one who tried to kidnap me?" Tears sprang into her eyes. Even now the betrayal stung.

"I didn't *want* to. They weren't to hurt you. I told them straight-out that they could not harm you. I wouldn't have had to do it at all if you would have accepted my invitations. I wrote time and again, asking you to visit me. But you refused to come. You avoided me — after all this time, after all I've done for you, you snubbed me."

"All you did for me! You used me. You used me, then you left me." Lilah wrenched out of Vesta's grasp. Off balance, she staggered and fell, tumbling down the last few steps and landing hard, the breath knocked out from her.

Vesta yanked Lilah to her feet. Overbalanced, they reeled against the wall, and Lilah's head rapped painfully on the corner of a picture. Dizzy and gasping for air, Lilah put up no fight as her aunt wrapped her arm around her and hauled Lilah down the corridor.

"You ungrateful wretch." Vesta fumed. "I showed you the power. I let you in, let you absorb it. And you took it from me! All those years I was gone, my talent draining away from me, you were here, pulling it into you. Making it yours."

"I never — never —" Where was everyone? Why had no one come, with all the clatter they'd been making? They had reached the front entry and Lilah realized that in another moment they would be out in the courtyard, where no one could hear her. Dragging in a desperate breath, she screamed.

"Hush!" Vesta jerked her out the door. "Stop it. There's no one to hear you. I've sent them all away. I'm not the silly, fluttery fool you think. My plan worked. Those fools botched the job, but my plan worked anyway. It brought you back here. I was so surprised when I saw you, I nearly fainted. I thought they had you, and then there you were on the doorstep. What a stroke of luck, I thought, but then I realized it wasn't luck. My plan had worked, just in a different way than I envisioned. Everything had happened as it should. As the Goddess wanted."

Vesta propelled Lilah across the courtyard. Lilah hurt all over — her battered head, the ankle she'd sprained when she fell down the stairs, the rope digging into her wrists. Worse, her brain felt swaddled in cotton batting. She knew she must do something, but she had trouble even taking in what was happening, let alone thinking of a way out.

They were headed for the tunnel. Vesta

thrust her through the tower door. She dug the barrel of the gun in harder. "Pick up a lantern and light it."

Several lanterns sat on the floor where Con and Alex had left them, along with matches. Lilah's movements were slow and clumsy; she felt so benumbed it took little pretense to move at a snail's pace. At Vesta's direction, she opened the door concealed in the wall, and they started down the stairs, Lilah carrying the lantern before her.

She could use the lantern, she thought. No chance of it here in the tight confines of the staircase, but when they reached the tunnel, she could whirl around and swing the lantern at Vesta. Would she be able to do so before her aunt squeezed the trigger? It seemed unlikely. A day ago she would have said her aunt wouldn't shoot her if it came down to that. Now, with Vesta in the fevered grip of her delusions, Lilah wasn't so sure.

"What *is* your plan?" she asked her aunt as they stepped into the tunnel.

"What you are too scared to do. I'm setting the Goddess free." To Lilah's surprise, Vesta released her arm and grabbed the lantern, taking a long step back. She held the gun pointed at Lilah's chest. "You cannot escape. I'm standing between you and the only way out. I won't hesitate to shoot you, and at this distance I can't miss. Go forward. Now!"

"But why?" Lilah did as she was told, starting down the tunnel at a slow pace. Where was Con? How long would it take him to find her? She wished she could sense him the way Sabrina could Alex. "You have all the keys now. You don't need me."

"Ah, but I do. It takes more than unlocking the door. She punished me for leaving her. She gave what was mine to you. I knew it as soon as you took my hand, and I felt her power."

"You can have it back! Believe me, I don't want it. Take it."

"I intend to, you ungrateful girl. You cannot throw away the gift the Goddess has given you. But I can seize it. I was in despair when you said you would close the Sanctuary — do you think I didn't hear the four of you plotting against me? But then I saw the Way. I found the Sacred Path, as every supplicant to the Otherworld must."

They reached the heavy door to the Sanctuary. Lilah could feel the power humming from beyond it — oozing around the door, vibrating in the stone. The hairs on the nape of her neck rose; her fingertips tingled; the soles of her feet were rooted to the floor.

Lilah suddenly ached to feel that power, to open the door and let it wash over her. To have it.

A yearning for freedom whispered through her veins, hungry and insistent. Lilah braced her hands against the stone beside the door, pushing back against the urge. She would not do this. She would not.

Vaguely she noted her aunt set the lantern down and reach into her pocket. Lilah couldn't move. She watched as Vesta, her face alight, fingers trembling with excitement, drew the keys from her pocket. One by one she thrust each key into its slot. Then she turned them, the yellow citrine sun first, then the sapphire sea and lastly the obsidian. Reverently chanting the creed of the Brotherhood beneath her breath, Vesta turned the keys in order, each tumbler falling with a click that echoed in the stone chamber.

There was a clatter behind her. *Con!* Lilah's heart leaped, and she started to turn. Vesta rotated the final key, and with a snap the door unlatched. The hinges shrieked. Vesta shoved Lilah through the doorway into the dark.

"Con! Con!" his brother's voice was loud. Insistent.

Con turned over, trying to escape Alex's voice. *Let me sleep.* Suddenly, water was in his mouth, up his nose.

"Con, get up. Get out."

Con thrashed around, pulling himself from the deep black cave of unconsciousness. *The wedding. He was late. How could he have —*

"Alex?" He opened his eyes. The world was white and soft around him, and he was being swept along, pulled down. Once again water swamped him.

He came up, coughing and spluttering, struggling against the inexorable tug of the water. He was soaked, the weight of the water in his clothes and boots pulling him down. Con realized he was about to drown.

Instinctively he struck out to the side, floundering, tumbling, not fighting the current but cutting across it as it carried him along. He'd heard that somewhere. Undertow. But this couldn't be the ocean, could it? Where the devil was he?

The water beneath him was dark, and the air above him white. *Lilah!* The thought of her speared through his head. He could see the dark earth of the bank now, and he swam toward it in a more coordinated way. He grabbed at the bank, scrabbling for purchase, clawing upward.

He was out. Con collapsed against the dirt, coughing, as the water lapped around his boots.

"Alex?" He'd heard his brother; he knew he had. Con crawled the rest of the way out and stood up shakily. The whiteness all around him was fog. It was night; it must be dark, but all he could see around him was mist, dense and white.

Dizzy, he sat down with a thump, sweeping his hands across his wet face and back through his hair, squeezing away the water. He winced as his fingertips touched the side of his head. He felt it gingerly. He'd been hit on the head.

Lilah. He was looking for Lilah. He remembered now — he had been walking beside the water, calling her name. He'd heard a noise and started to turn. He'd seen . . . something. Then his head had exploded, and the next thing he knew he was being swept down the rhyne.

Alex's voice had been in his head. He had no doubt that Alex knew Con was in trouble; just as certainly, Alex would start searching for him. But Con couldn't wait. Lilah was in danger. The face he had glimpsed before his head exploded was Aunt Vesta's.

Of course. Why the devil had he never

once thought of her? This woman who had known about the Brotherhood, who had grown up with the men, whose father had started the whole bloody thing. It was so obvious now. Vesta had long felt the power of the force beneath the tor. She had realized she had no power away from Barrow House, and she had returned, wanting to find the Source, to rekindle her abilities.

But he hadn't suspected her. Even when he'd been unable to "see" Lilah's path, it hadn't occurred to him that Aunt Vesta had purposely led him astray. He had fallen like a dolt for her silly, fluttery act, dismissed her as a gullible, foolish old lady.

There was no time to sit around, castigating himself. He didn't know what Vesta intended to do to Lilah, but it couldn't be good. He had to get back to her. Whatever Vesta intended, it would be at Barrow House; otherwise, Vesta wouldn't have needed to lure him away.

Con yanked off his boots and dumped out the water before putting them back on, then stripped off his sodden jacket and dropped it on the ground. Standing up, he turned full circle. All around him was featureless fog. There were no landmarks; he was in a place he'd never been before; and he could see no farther than his outstretched hand.

Con touched the ring Lilah had given him. For once in his life, he actually needed a compass. How bitterly ironic was it that this compass, the one he was never without now, didn't work? He could rely on nothing but his ability.

Con set out, moving at a brisk walk. He ached to run, but he held himself back. Haste could prove disastrous. It would be easy to fall into one of the many waterways, not to mention the fact that there were still remnants of the former bog in spots. He wished he had taken the time to explore the area and set the layout of it in his mind. He wished he had the lantern he'd dropped when Vesta bashed him on the head.

But he couldn't let regrets cloud his thoughts. With his actual vision negligible, he must focus on the map in his mind, the subtle tug in his chest. Even in the fog, he could tell north from south and east from west, and he was certain in which direction the house lay. However, a straight line to the house made no allowance for rhynes or bits of bog.

He had no idea of this rhyne's length or how far he had floated down it before he climbed out. Nor did he know where he had fallen into it. Before landing in the water, he had twisted his way through the small canals like an obstacle course. How would he know where to turn? Con wished that he could "see" the trail of his own passage lingering in the air, but apparently that was not part of his talent.

He kept on, his senses alert. The ground was muddy beneath his feet, and he didn't notice that the mud was becoming softer, more giving, until he stepped down and water rushed into his boot. He had stumbled upon one of the pieces of marshy land. Panic swarmed into his chest, and he had to fight back the primitive fear.

He pulled out his foot, though he left the boot behind, and took a step backward. He was able to feel for the top of the boot and pull it, too, out of the muck. Emptying it of water, he stared into the fog and thought. He would have to retrace his steps, though everything in him urged him forward, his instinct telling him that the way to the house lay straight before him.

But he couldn't be rash; Lilah's life depended on it. As he started to turn around and go back, he saw a shimmer of light on the ground less than a yard from where he had stepped into the bog. He froze. Faint but visible through the fog, stretched a light — no, not exactly a light, but a line the color of moonlight, leading across the ground.

"The Fae Path," he breathed, hardly daring to believe it. The legendary safe passage through the bog. No wonder it had also been known as the Silver Way, for that pale, luminous color.

He mustn't be rash. But he must have faith, as well. Con started out along the path. His foot sank into the mud, but only a little. It varied in depth, but beneath the muck was always solid footing. He had heard of ancient tracks, narrow paths made of split logs laid in V-shaped braces, but how had it survived this long in the watery land?

The path disappeared, but the ground was now firm beneath his feet. He could no longer hear the water, and he felt a faint rise in the land. His steps grew ever faster, eating up the ground, following the arrow spearing through him, drawing him on. The fog grew wispier.

And there it was. The tor loomed up above the fog, a blacker mass against the dark sky. Con broke into a run. His legs churned, and his breath rasped in and out as he pelted up the slope, but it seemed as if nothing moved, as if his goal would never be reached.

Then he was atop the tor. He saw Barrow House ahead. He ran, heedless of the dark, of stumbling, aware of nothing but the thought of Lilah, the certainty of danger that vibrated throughout his being.

It was easier along the garden paths and into the house. He didn't bother going to Lilah's room. He could see the hum in the air that told of her passage out the front door. He knew — had known from the beginning — where they had gone.

He tore across the courtyard. He and Alex had set four lanterns in the base of the tower, and he prayed that no one had moved them. Lilah had passed this way; the glimmer in the air was thick, jumbled with the presence of another.

The lanterns were still at the foot of the stairs, though now there were only three. He lit one with shaking fingers. The doorway to the hidden staircase stood ajar. He raced down the stairs. The lantern flickered with his movement, and he had to slow his pace to keep the flame alive, even though his heart was pounding and his stomach churning with the need to hurry.

He saw a glow ahead, and hope surged in him. He heard the clink of metal on metal, then clicks, and finally he saw Lilah and Vesta, illuminated by the lantern on the ground. Vesta was at the door, turning the keys in the lock, one by one. Beside her, Lilah's bound hands were flat against the stone wall. She stood unnaturally still, staring straight ahead.

The door opened with a screech. Con raced forward, and Lilah whirled around. Vesta shoved Lilah into the black void beyond the door, whisking up the lantern, and jumped in after her. Con had a glimpse of Vesta's wild-eyed face as she threw herself against the door.

Con dropped his own lantern and lunged the last few feet. The door snapped shut an instant before he slammed into it. "No!" He pounded uselessly at the thick wood. "No! Come back. Lilah!"

He was locked out. Vesta had taken the keys with her. Lilah was gone.

CHAPTER FORTY-TWO

Lilah screamed and jumped to her feet, throwing herself at Vesta. Vesta swung the lantern in a wide arc, forcing Lilah back. Vesta pointed the gun at her, motioning her forward. "Go. Go."

Lilah stepped back. "Let me go. Please, Aunt Vesta. You have the keys. You're in the Sanctuary. You have what you want. You're welcome to it. Just let me go."

"No. Walk on."

"Why? Why won't you let me go?"

"Because you're part of it. Can't you feel it? The Goddess calls you. She wants you. Turn around and walk. We're not there yet."

Lilah was viscerally aware that they had not yet reached the heart of the power. She turned. They were in a narrow cave that opened into another, and it was there that the energy thrummed. The truth was, Lilah wanted to go there.

"Con . . ." She wanted even more to

return to Con.

"He's a resourceful young man," Vesta said. "I underestimated him. But he's too late. He can't help you now." She jabbed the gun at Lilah, her hand trembling so much Lilah feared she might accidentally pull the trigger. "Forward. Go on!"

Lilah moved slowly toward the opening. Con *would* come. She had no idea how, but she knew Con. He would find a way. She must keep her aunt occupied — and wait for a careless move, a moment of inattention, just in case Con didn't make it in time. Lilah stepped warily through the open doorway. Energy surged in her, so strong and fast it made her dizzy. The very air crackled with it.

Lilah stared around her, too astonished to speak or even move. The room — cave? — was almost perfectly round, with two more gaps in the walls leading into what appeared to be other anterooms. Once again, the number three. A short square cabinet stood against one wall. On top of it were a few ancient artifacts, as well as a bejeweled knife that looked wickedly sharp.

Near the cabinet stood a large oval-shaped stone, hollowed out over the centuries into a shape like a great bowl. In it lay much more modern objects — bracelets, necklaces, tiepins, small books, carved figures of ivory and jade, all sorts of trinkets, piled high above the surface. Sacrifices from the Brotherhood.

It was not these things, though, that entranced her. It was the walls. They were decorated all over with seashells. Though Barrow House lay thirty miles from the sea, there were small shells by the score, of all sorts of shapes and sizes. They stretched around the room in rows, the pattern broken in three places by a spiral design.

The shells glistened in the dim glow of the lantern, appearing almost wet. Lilah looked up. Even the ceiling was embellished with shells, forming a spiral over the exact center of the cave. Below that spiral, the focal point of the room, was a long low slab of rock rising up from stone floor almost as if it had grown out of the rock.

"The altar." Lilah could scarcely breathe. She knew this place even though she'd never seen it, knew it because it lived in her, reverberated in her. She took a step forward, hardly noticing as her aunt came up beside her.

"Yes, the altar." Vesta's voice was filled with awe. "This is where we must make our sacrifice."

Her aunt moved to the other side of the

altar. This was her chance. Lilah knew she should run back to the door, but she was frozen to the spot and could only watch as Vesta dropped to her knees before the altar.

Vesta braced her hands on the stone slab. Her face glowed, the light of the lantern on the floor beside her casting eerie shadows over her. She chanted the words of the creed Sir Ambrose had written, changing them by ending, "My Lady. My Queen. Come to me."

The power punched into Lilah, sweeping through her in a storm and racing back to the altar. It pulled her forward, and she took an unwilling step toward the altar, struggling to gain command of the primitive force filling her.

Vesta gazed at her with wild eyes. "You see? You see how it must be?"

"Aunt Vesta, you must not do this." Lilah moved toward her.

Vesta jumped up, grabbing her gun again. "No. Stop right there."

"Can't you see? We're trapped in here. The minute you walk out, Con will be waiting."

Vesta smiled slyly. "It won't matter. By then I will have so much power he won't be able to touch me."

"I won't help you," Lilah told her flatly.

Vesta seemed unperturbed by her statement, sidling over to the small cabinet as she kept her gun aimed at Lilah. "The power will be mine, not yours." Her eyes flashed. "At first I was furious. I thought the Goddess had betrayed me, that she'd taken back all my power. Then I realized what I must do. How I must get it back. The Goddess requires a sacrifice." She reached out for the knife.

In that moment, Lilah understood exactly what her aunt intended to do. Lilah leaped at Vesta, heedless of the gun. She slammed into Vesta, and the pistol clattered to the floor, but Vesta slashed at her. The knife sliced across Lilah's arm, opening a long cut, and blood welled out.

Lilah grabbed Vesta's wrist with both her hands. Lilah had the advantage of youth and height over her aunt, but Vesta was imbued with an all-encompassing rage, and Lilah was hampered by the fact that her hands were bound. Vesta kicked and scratched and hit at Lilah with her free hand. They crashed into the stone bowl, sending jewelry and figurines tumbling, and reeled away, grappling in fierce silence.

Lilah took a step back and her heel hit the lantern Vesta had set on the floor, knocking it over. The lantern rolled across the floor into a stone wall. The flame sputtered and went out, leaving them in utter blackness. Lilah, off balance, stumbled and came up hard against the stone altar. Vesta's weight bore her over, and Lilah fell back onto the altar.

Con beat at the door, shouting Lilah's name, teetering on the brink of despair.

No. He wouldn't accept that she was gone. He couldn't. Con stepped back, pushing his hands into his hair. *Think.* Lilah was alive. He had no idea what Vesta intended to do to her, but she was alive. And he was going to find her.

He turned back and realized that everything around him was pitch-black. His lantern had gone out when he'd dropped it. It didn't matter. The tunnel led straight to the staircase. He groped around until he came to the rock wall, then started forward, fingers trailing along the wall. As he trotted along the tunnel, he considered his options.

The dynamite was coming tomorrow, so he couldn't yet blow up the door. Why the devil couldn't that old man have had the foresight to build a second entrance? After all, the tunnel could have caved in and —

Con stopped short. Wait. What if Ambrose *had* built a second entrance? In his ramblings about the Goddess, he had said he communed with her on a daily basis. Maybe he went in person; maybe he wanted to meditate in the Sanctuary alone. The thing lay right there, only yards from him. Why not build an entrance just for himself?

The maze. It would be in the maze. Ambrose visited the maze frequently; Vesta had said he liked to sit there and meditate. And the maze was equally close to the Sanctuary. Con took the staircase at a run. The likeliest spot for an entrance would be in the center of the maze. Somehow that sundial must move. He'd looked it over, but he must not have been careful enough. He had been too certain the Sanctuary was beneath the house.

Con grabbed another lantern at the top of the staircase, but didn't take the time to light it. He could see well enough out here. After the total darkness of the tunnel, the moonlight seemed bright. He ran across the lawn into the maze, making his way easily through the twists and turns until he reached the center. His stomach churned as he lit the lantern and began to search the base of the sundial, looking desperately for some line or knob, any oddity to indicate an opening. Nothing.

Con stood up and braced his hands on the sundial, fighting down panic and fury.

His eyes fell on his ring, and the world stopped for an instant. The ring. The frozen compass. His dream — the compass needles spinning uselessly as he fought not to fail.

Suddenly it all became clear to him. The frozen compass had been no accident, no flaw. The needle had been stopped deliberately, turned so that it pointed in only one direction — toward the edge of the maze lying closest to the Sanctuary. The cove where Lilah had been drawn in her sleep.

He spun and charged back through the maze to the dead end where he had found Lilah. He went to the ornamental bench. It had to be here. Three triskeles decorated the board of the back. He bent instinctively to examine the middle one. It did not budge to pushing or pulling. But, he discovered, there was a tiny slit in the very center.

His heart tripped in his chest. Con flipped up the top of the ring, exposing the miniature sundial beneath. The little triangular wedge popped up, and carefully he pushed it into the tiny slot. It fitted. He turned it.

With a groan, the bench slid back, revealing a deep dark hole. Attached to the side was a metal ladder. Picking up his lantern in one hand, Con swung over the side and started down into the pit.

■ ■ ■ ■

Lilah's head knocked against the stone, sending bright shards of pain through her. Dazed by the blow, she managed to hang on desperately to Vesta's wrist, keeping the knife at bay. Vesta's weight pinned her down. Vesta bore down, panting with the effort. "Your blood must feed the altar. The Goddess demands sacrifice."

Lilah's hands grew slick with the blood flowing down her arm from the cut. She slipped for an instant, then recaptured her hold and with a great heave, jerked Vesta's hand to the side. She heard the knife graze the stone, and Vesta's weight slid half off her. Lilah squirmed to get free, but then Vesta rolled back, pressing her into the stone.

Lilah's head throbbed, and Vesta's weight was pushing the air from her lungs. Above her, Vesta again began to pant the creed from her father's ceremony, adding her own words that called the Goddess. Beneath her back, the stone warmed. Power blasted into Lilah, filling every inch of her body.

With a loud cry, Lilah shoved her aunt up and over, forcing Vesta back onto the altar. She straddled Vesta, holding her aunt down, and slammed Vesta's hand against the altar. The knife fell from Vesta's grasp, clattering on the stone.

"No! No!" Vesta shrieked. "Come to me! Goddess, come!"

Lilah was filled with strength, pulsing with energy, her connection to the altar as solid as a steel chain. Yearning permeated her, keening and deep. She felt the ache, the thirst, the need for freedom. She understood.

"Go!" She cried, her voice ringing through the cave. "I sever the chains that bind thee here."

There was a scrabbling and scraping behind her, and light pierced the dark. "Lilah!"

Con! She let out a laughing sob. He *had* come. Of course he had found a way to her. She heard his footsteps rushing across the floor, and she called out, "No! Wait."

"What —" He stopped. She could hear his harsh, fast breaths behind her, but he didn't speak or touch her.

Con's lantern illuminated the altar beneath her. Vesta struggled wildly, but Lilah had no fear that she would escape, for the strength that held her there was not Lilah's.

"I release thee!" Lilah went on, the words flowing out of her without thought. "Thou art bound no more. Return now to thy home. Dwell in peace in the Otherworld, no more to be disturbed."

With a joyful leap, the power poured out of her, sinking into the altar, the floor, the walls of the cave.

"No. No." Aunt Vesta began to cry, her head shaking from side to side.

Lilah sagged, suddenly shaky and weak. "Con . . ." She turned, reaching out to him.

He pulled her from the altar and, grabbing the knife, sawed through the rope that bound Lilah's wrists. "Lilah, my God, you're bleeding. And your head!" He started to pull at his ascot.

"No, no, there's isn't time." Lilah grabbed his hand. "We must go."

"What? But —" He gazed around him in awe. "This place."

"We have to go," Lilah repeated, unable to explain but certain she was right. She pulled Vesta up. "Auntie, come. We must go."

A deep rumble started in the earth. The floor of the cave began to vibrate.

"This way," Con said, grabbing the lantern and starting toward one of the openings.

"No, no, leave me alone! I don't want to. You horrible, wicked child!" Vesta slapped at Lilah's arm.

With a curse, Con came back and grabbed Vesta's arm. "Shut up. You're coming with us, though God knows why she wants you."

He dragged Vesta through the opening, and Lilah followed. The rumbling grew louder. The ground shook beneath their feet. The room seemed to have no exit, but Con directed them around a jutting rock that hid a narrow gap. He handed the lantern to Lilah. "Go on, slide through."

She did as he said, slipping between the rocks into a long, narrow chamber. At the other end of the tunnel, there was a metal ladder mounted on the wall, and at the top of it, a very faint light. The exit. The rumbling was growing ever louder, the shaking stronger. Behind her Con pushed her aunt through the gap and ran to Lilah.

"Up! Up! It's caving in." Behind them they could hear rocks crashing. Con put his hands on Lilah's waist and boosted her up.

Lilah started climbing and glanced over at her aunt. Vesta was gone. "Aunt Vesta!"

She started back down, but Con shouted, "No! Up! Don't stop."

He whirled and started back, but the ground shook violently, knocking him to his knees. The other end of the room disappeared in a pile of rocks and dust.

"Con!" She couldn't see him. She began

to back up.

"Run, damn it, go!" Con burst out of the cloud of dust.

Lilah hiked up her skirt and hurried up the ladder. Con was right behind her, their steps ringing on the metal rungs. Behind them the earth thundered and stones crashed. Dust billowed up, filling the air. The ladder trembled beneath Lilah's hands, and her fingers slipped on one rung, but she held on tight with the other hand, steadying herself, and in an instant Con was close behind her, his arms around her on either side of the ladder. She began to climb again.

They reached the top and climbed out, crawling away to collapse on the path. Con wrapped himself around her, and she clung to him. The ground continued to vibrate beneath them, but gradually the rumbling quieted, then stopped. The earth stilled.

Lilah felt like crying and laughing and screaming, all at once, but was too exhausted to do any. It was enough right now to rest in Con's arms, listening to his still-ragged breathing, feeling his chest rise and fall against her. She looked up at the moon above them. How could it still be night? It felt as if days had passed.

They could hear voices calling and

through the branches of the hedge Lilah saw the bobbing lights of lanterns. Con rose to his feet and pulled Lilah up. They turned just as footsteps pounded into the maze and a man came running toward them.

"Con! Thank God."

"Hallo, Alex." Con took Lilah's hand, and they started toward his twin. "Lilah decided to close the Sanctuary."

CHAPTER FORTY-THREE

They walked out of the maze with Alex as Sabrina ran up to join them, throwing her arms around Lilah. Servants clustered around them, all staring at the jumble of dirt, rocks and grass that lay before them like a wide, shallow cup in the lawn. A buzz of voices filled the air, but Lilah and Con could only hold each other and stare.

After a time, they began to tell Alex and Sabrina what had happened, their tale breathless and disjointed. Sabrina and Alex, their eyes going wider with each detail, then related their own side of the story. They described how Alex had shot up out of his chair earlier that evening, certain that Con was dying. That terrible feeling had lessened, but, still sure something was wrong, he and Sabrina had ridden over from Carmoor, arriving in time to find the servants milling about in distress, unable to find Con, Lilah or Vesta.

It was then that the great rumbling had started beneath the ground, rattling even the dishes in their cabinets in the house, and everyone had run out to find that part of the lawn was now sunken and the ground broken. Alex, certain of his brother's location, hadn't bothered with the cave-in, but had run straight for the maze, Sabrina following not far behind.

"What will we say?" Sabrina whispered, turning to gaze at the broken ground.

"She's right. There are bound to be questions," Alex agreed.

Lilah was still too shaken to think and even Con had trouble coming up with any coherent idea, so it was left to the other two to create a story of a midnight exploration in the underground tunnels that had ended in a tragic cave-in. However implausible it sounded, it was more believable than the truth, and the evidence of the collapsed ground was indisputable.

In the miraculous way of small villages, it didn't take long for word to spread. It seemed as if half the town was there in a flash. The doctor arrived first in his buggy and began to tend to Lilah's cuts and bruises. The village constable came next, followed by the magistrate, his hair still standing on end from yanking off his nightcap. Lilah was glad that their sympathy kept them from questioning her but made them turn instead to Con, who was always more accomplished at making nonsense sound like truth.

As they interrogated them, a rider came tearing up the lane, another horse some distance back, seemingly chasing him. Everyone turned to stare, mouths agape, as Niles Dearborn slid down from the horse and tore across the lawn, shrieking.

His speech was almost unintelligible in his rage, his words liberally sprinkled with curses, but his intent was clear as he ran at Lilah, shaking his fist. Con quickly stepped in front of Lilah, extending his hands to stop the man.

"Damn you!" Niles roared, starting around Con to reach Lilah. "You interfering, sanctimonious b—"

Con shut him up with a right hook that sent the man staggering backward. Niles sat down on the ground with a thump, but scrambled back up, paying no attention to the blood trickling down from his nose. "You ruined everything! It's gone! It's all gone."

He lunged forward again, but Alex had come up behind him and grabbed him, holding him back. The constable, staring at the scene agape, finally recovered his wits enough to take Dearborn's arm. Dearborn twisted, raving wildly, spittle flying.

"Take this madman to jail," the magistrate snapped, and two other men came up to help the constable drag him away.

The rider of the second horse had arrived and now ran toward them. "Father!" Peter Dearborn stopped beside the constable, panting for breath. "Please, no, he — he doesn't know what he's doing. He's gone mad. Please don't lock him up. I'll take him away. I swear. Please let him go."

Niles had now dissolved into tears, mumbling and cursing as he cried. The constable hesitated, turning to look questioningly at Alex and Con.

"The devil I will," Con began. "He belongs in jail. Many times over." Lilah reached out and touched his arm.

"No, Con, please . . . let it end."

Con grimaced and muttered a curse. "Oh, very well. Take him." He scowled at Peter. "This is only because it would upset Lilah. But you better lock him up, however you can, or the next time he'll end up in prison. I swear it."

"I will. I promise. Come, Father." Peter led his father away, still muttering and weeping.

After that, the magistrate could think of no more questions, and the four of them returned to the house. The servants had laid a midnight repast of cold meats and cheeses on the dining table, and after Lilah and Con went upstairs to wash up and change their clothes, they joined Alex and Sabrina at the table. As they ate, Con and Lilah went over what had happened in fuller, more coherent detail.

"I still cannot believe Aunt Vesta tried to kill you!" Sabrina said when they had finished. "She was always peculiar but harmless."

"She was desperate after she learned we planned to shut the whole thing down. She convinced herself that she if she sacrificed me, she would gain the Goddess's favor and be given all my power. I think over the years, feeling her powers diminish, she grew . . . obsessed with getting them back, until it reached the point that nothing else mattered. Not even her own life," Lilah finished sadly.

"I'm sorry." Con squeezed Lilah's hand. He hadn't let go of her since they'd escaped, holding her hand even during the magistrate's and doctor's visits. "I shouldn't have released her arm. I never guessed she would run back in like that."

"Don't blame yourself. There was nothing you could have done. She wanted to stay there. She wanted to be with her 'Goddess.' Now she is. Forever. Maybe she's happier."

"How did you know what to do?" Sabrina asked. "What the Sanctuary really wanted? Or how to return it to the Otherworld?"

"I can't explain it. I just felt it deep inside. It wasn't even a conscious thought. I knew in my bones, it seemed, that it wanted its freedom, but I realized that we were wrong in thinking it would run wild and destroy everything. It just wanted to go back where it belonged."

"I think that when your grandfathers found the place and did their ceremony with blood, even though it was a lark to them, it actually called the entity and anchored it to that room," Alex said. "They imprisoned it, though I don't think that was their intention. They believed they were honoring something and being given blessings in return."

"It's no wonder the gifts came with bad consequences," Sabrina commented. "Do you think it's really gone? The curse, too?"

"I no longer feel the energy beneath the ground," Lilah said. "Or inside me. Do you?"

"No."

Lilah smiled. "I think we're safe from it."

"At least there's that." Sabrina yawned, delicately covering it. "I'm sorry. I'm afraid it's catching up with me."

"You should spend the night here," Lilah urged. "There's no need to go back home."

"Thank you." Sabrina nodded. "It'll take care of the chaperonage problem, too."

"The chaperonage problem?" Con echoed, suddenly wary.

Sabrina nodded. "Yes. I mean, now that Lilah's aunt's not here. Of course, now Con can stay with us, so that would make it respectable."

Con stiffened. "Sabrina," Alex said in a careful tone. "That can wait until tomorrow."

Sabrina glanced at the others and began to blush. "Oh. Yes." She jumped up from the table. "Well, then . . ."

"We'll just be off to bed." Alex joined her.

Quickly Sabrina bent and kissed Lilah's cheek, bidding her good-night. Lilah rose, too, but Con reached out. "Lilah. Wait. Please, stay. I need to talk to you."

Lilah turned. She had turned to ice when Sabrina had pointed out that it would be scandalous for Con to stay here with her. It was over. Con would leave now. That was what he wanted to say to her. Somehow, she must gather her courage and accept it. She wouldn't break down.

"About what Sabrina said," Con began slowly.

Lilah sank onto her chair, her legs too shaky to hold her up.

"I suppose she's right," Con went on, not looking at her. "It would be more respectable if I stayed there. Would you rather . . ."

"If that is what you wish," Lilah said through bloodless lips.

"It's not what I wish," he shot back. "I don't wish it at all." He drew a breath. "But I don't want to do anything that might harm your reputation. I know how much it means to you to remain above scandal. I don't . . . Oh, the devil."

Con scowled and jammed his hands into his pockets. He began to pace about the room, his long legs eating up the space and making the room seem much smaller than it was. Lilah knew she should probably ease Con's way and give him an open path to leave, but she couldn't find it in her to be that gracious or selfless. If Con wanted to leave, let him thrash about for the words to say it.

"Blast it!" He whirled and came back to her. "I didn't mean to do this."

"No. Of course not. I don't blame you, Con." There. She could manage to be a little selfless. "I knew this day would come."

"You did?" He looked surprised. "You think I'm rash." He scowled. "I'm not rash. I make judgments quickly. That doesn't mean they're wrong."

"Con, please, just say it. Get it over with."

"You're right. I will." He went down on one knee beside her chair, startling her. He took her hand, gazing intently into her eyes. "I wanted to show you. I was going to let you realize that I had changed. But I can't wait that long. I can't bear it."

"Changed? Bear what? What are you talking about?" Lilah was utterly at sea now.

"I can't bear the thought of losing you. I don't want to be away from you, even for a day. I cannot wait to ask you. Please say you'll marry me."

Lilah's jaw dropped. This was so far removed from anything she had thought he was about to say that she could hardly take it in. "You what?"

"You don't have to make a decision right now. We can wait. I'll . . . I'll move over to Carmoor if you'd rather. But tell me you'll think about it. Tell me you'll give me a chance to prove it to you."

"Prove what? Con, I don't understand."

"Prove that I can be . . . well, normal, I suppose. I won't hurt your reputation. I won't cause any scandal. I've been thinking. I've decided to give up the agency."

"What?" Lilah stared.

"I'll hand it over to Tom. He does a great deal of the work anyway. We'll get a house in London, if you like, and, um, I'll go to parties and . . . all that."

"Are you serious?" Lilah reached out, cupping his face with her hands. "You want to marry me?"

"Yes." He sighed. "Lilah, I'm not joking. I promise you. I'm not teasing. I'm quite capable of being serious. And steady."

"You would really do that for me?" Tears clogged her throat. "Why?"

"*Why?*" Now it was Con who stared. "Because I love you, that's why. I want to spend my life with you."

"Oh, Con!" Lilah leaned forward and kissed him gently. "I wouldn't ask you to change." She kissed him again. "I don't want you to change. I love you exactly as you are."

"You do?"

"Yes. I never disliked you. Indeed, I think it frightened me that I liked you so much. Against all logic, all expectations, you were the man I wanted. I tried to dislike you. I wanted to. But I could never succeed. I think . . . Maybe I was searching for a man to suit another woman, a woman I tried very hard to be. But that's not the woman I am, and for me, you are the right man."

Con wrapped his hand around the nape of her neck and kissed her more thoroughly. Leaning his forehead against her, he whispered, "I was so scared. When Vesta slammed that door shut, I thought I had lost you forever. I knew if I didn't have you, I had nothing." He kissed her again, then sat back on his heel. "Then you'll marry me?"

Lilah smiled into his eyes, her thumb softly tracing his cheekbone. "I should say no. I fear madness must run in my family."

"Then you'll fit right in. Welcome to the Mad Morelands."

"There's just one condition," Lilah told him.

"What is that?" He stood up, pulling her up with him.

"You should keep your agency. Make Tom your partner if you like. But I'd never ask you to give up your investigations."

"I'm not sure I want them anymore," Con admitted. "They would take me away from you."

"Ah, but I intend to go with you."

Con laughed. "In that case, I shall most certainly keep it."

"Then, yes, I will marry you."

Con pulled her to him for another kiss. "Soon, yes? I can get a special license. I know that's a bit scandalous, but I don't want to wait."

"Neither do I. Get the special license, and till then . . ." She looped her arms around his neck. "I find I no longer care about scandal. I want you to stay here with me."

"Always. My beautiful Delilah." He bent to kiss her.

Lilah made no protest. On Con's lips, she realized, her name was beautiful.

EPILOGUE

Con stood quietly with Alex at the vestry door and looked out across the church. His family was all there, taking up several pews. His mother, regal as always, kept a monitory eye on Brigid and Athena. That impish pair, bracketed between the duchess and their mother, were for the moment frighteningly angelic. His father sat on the other side of the duchess, his hand linked with hers, his head lifted in seeming contemplation of the unidentifiable saint's statue at the front of the church. Con suspected that the duke's mind was actually somewhere in Greece.

Uncle Bellard, on the other hand, was fully alert, looking all around the blocky and exceptionally plain church, which he had extolled yesterday as one of the rare untouched examples of pre-Norman religious architecture. His diminutive uncle had been happily occupied the past few days visiting ancient British sites in the area and going through the Barrow House library. He had started the painstaking restoration of the journal they had found in Sir Ambrose's trunk. Con had the suspicion he might take up residence with them.

Con's siblings had come in force to celebrate his nuptials, filling up Barrow House with laughter, talk and children. It would be no surprise if they had several nieces and nephews begging to stay with them, as well. Barrow House was a perfect spot for playing hide-and-seek or acting out days of yore — and only two of them had gotten lost in the maze.

Con glanced over at his twin beside him. Alex grinned. "Seems like we were doing this only yesterday."

"I could hardly let you get ahead of me."

As in everything, Con was racing into marriage. It was Lilah's choice as well, and she had decreed the small wedding be in the quiet country church. Con turned his gaze to the other side of the narrow church, where Mrs. Summersley sat. Kyria's twins and Olivia's oldest daughter had decided to keep her company for reasons known only to them. Lilah's aunt cast a wary eye at them now and again. Con was glad that love had won out over propriety in her aunt and uncle. Lilah needed what little family she had. Despite everything that had happened, she had mourned Aunt Vesta.

In front of Alex and Con, the priest, pale with excitement and trepidation in the face of so many important visitors, poked the altar boy in the back, and they began their procession to the altar. Alex turned to Con. "Ready?"

"Of course." Excitement blossomed in Con's chest as it did on the verge of a discovery.

"You aren't the slightest bit nervous, are you?" Alex said with some envy.

"No. I'm about to start the best part of my life. I'm eager."

Alex chuckled. "That's you in a nutshell."

The two of them started forward, keeping pace in the way they always had. Con thought about his brother's wedding less than two months ago, the loneliness that had pierced him at losing Alex. Con had learned these last few weeks that he would never lose his twin; Alex's marriage hadn't changed their bond any more than Con's would. He had also found a bond equally enduring, a chain of shining links connecting him forever more to the woman he loved.

Standing beside Alex, Con watched Sabrina come down the aisle to face them, her face alight with happiness. But Con's eyes went past her to the open door, where Lilah stood beside her uncle. The morning light glinted on her red-blond hair. The color of sunset, Con thought, as he had the first time he saw her. It was, he realized, the color of the dawn, as well.

He was going to spend the rest of his life with this woman. He would have the delight of discovering her every day, of learning each twist and turn of her mind and heart. She would be with him always; she would bear his children; she would be the rock that anchored his very soul. Doubtless she would also bedevil and frustrate him and turn him inside out in that way that only she could. He couldn't wait.

Lilah started down the aisle on her uncle's arm, her eyes going to Con's. He smiled as he stood beside his brother, watching his new life come toward him.

ABOUT THE AUTHOR

Candace Camp is a *New York Times* best-selling author of over sixty novels of contemporary and historical romance. She grew up in Texas in a newspaper family, which explains her love of writing, but she earned a law degree and practiced law before making the decision to write full-time. She has received several writing awards, including the RT Book Reviews Lifetime Achievement Award for Western Romances. Visit her at www.candace-camp.com.